BALANCE
OF
POWER

BALANCE OF POWER

THE CHOZIEN PATH SERIES

KYRSTAL B. CLARK

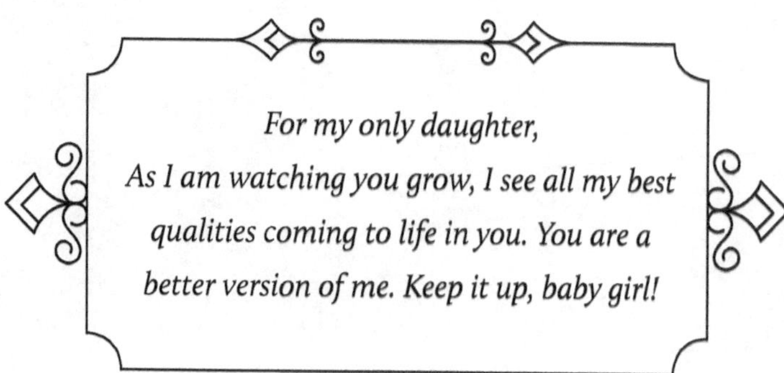

ISBN: 979-8-9889102-0-6 (Paperback)
979-8-9889102-1-3 (Hardcover)

Any references to historical events, real people, or real places are used fictitiously. Names, characters, and places are products of the author's imagination.

Cover Artwork & Design by Jeff Brown Graphics.
Interior design by Travis Hasenour/To the Moon and Back Design.

Krystal B. Clark
13165 W. Lake Houston Pkwy
#215
Houston, TX, 77044

THE
MAREAN
DIMENSION
THE
TERRITORIES
OF THE
TWELVE
ORDERS
151 AB - 278 AB
THE BROKEN STRAIT
Crystal/Onyx
Border
DUN
ONYX
GOLD
CRYSTAL
RAIN
TRACE
JUNE
HAWK
GLEN
HUIN
RHYNE
JADE
AZURITE
CARNELIAN
MOUNT
HOLLOW
ZIN
GARDIEN
HOLD
SPIRIT
HOLD
CANDOR
AMYTHEST
BLOODSTONE
AMBER
HEMATITE
RHODONITE
TIGER EYE
THE BARRENS
N
W E
S

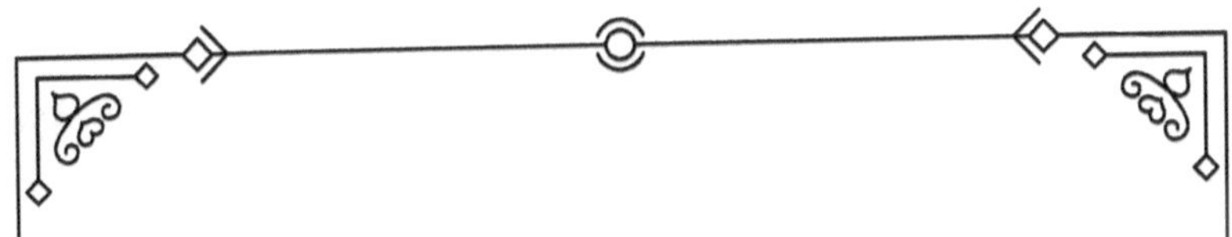

INTRODUCTION

As a chronicler, I have the honor to tell you of our people, our existence, and the world we live in. But first you must know how we came to be.

There was a time, many centuries ago, when our world thrived. Tables were covered with a variety of food in abundant proportions. Husbands and wives embraced and enjoyed the sweet joy of each other's presence. Children laughed and played daily without a hint of tomorrow. The poor received charity, remedies healed the sick, and great inventions fueled the economy, easing access to food, travel, and living quarters. Indeed, our forebears enjoyed a glorious time when we were at our best.

Those days are but a mere dream now ... for those who do still dream.

Our ancestors' appetite for excess grew beyond its limits, causing devastating battles with horrific weapons that resulted in the mass destruction we know as the Breaking. Once we had two moons, but the catastrophic capacity of those weapons destroyed the smaller of the two, Illuminatus Minor. The remnants can still be seen in the night sky. Only Gloris Major remains.

The aftermath from that proved far too cataclysmic for the people to recover their previous greatness.

So the time of democracy and science has come and gone. Only rulers and the ruled now exist. Gone are the conventional institutes of higher learning and the incredible "machines" used to transport people over great distances in a matter of days or even within a day of changes of the sun's sky shadow. Historians tell us that immense water vessels once had the ability to dive deep into the Great Waters and explore their wondrous secrets; these, too, are no more. Gone also are the devices used to destroy Betrayers of the Peace; gone are the legendary heroes from the world before our own.

Religion is nonexistent in this time, but spirituality flourishes. Through fervent practice of introspection and humility, we began to access a gateway into our own being. It is as if you can reach inside yourself and watch the makings of life itself; it is quite exhilarating—so much so that we called this ability the Reach.

With the Reach, our service in the Great Spirit deepened, as did our ability to connect with the intangible elements of other living entities. What the people of the Old Nations shunned as taboo and crazed, we welcomed as the corporeal evidence of our belief.

This brought an end to religious organizations that preached the salvation of an esoteric deity by which they profited while the worshippers sought fulfillment without answer. Twelve sects replaced such religion. These communities became known as orders, each driven by its own guiding principle as an obligation to ensure the preservation of our established union, with the guiding principle known as the ducall.

The Jade Order—chose the preservation of peace as its ducall.

Maintaining peace is no easy task, as they remain in constant conflict with the other orders, tipping the balance of peace and unrest. Not every order holds the same belief as to the meaning of peace. Some consider fulfillment through achieving wisdom over all; others judge it by the amount of power and influence they can wield. They would not rest until equilibrium is achieved across all orders.

In most of the orders, we use our feet and animals for transport—and if we are fortunate, a cart of some sort constructed with natural or, if of the Azurite Order, fabricated materials.

We must rely on our own abilities and physical strength for our defense. If a being cannot find a talent that contributes to the order's continued existence, then his or her existence becomes a burden not ignored for long.

We've structured our economy on a bartering system. Each day, vendors and consumers engage in negotiations to trade for basic needs—meat, flour, eggs, soap, and the like—or items of luxury, such as baked sweets or fine-grain leather. The Jade Order's unique blends of flavors and spices and their highly sought-out medicinal plant, kassmint, serve as their prized currency with the other orders, and also within their own.

We have learned that every living entity possesses an *ame*—the essence of life. To be separated from your *ame* is to leave this world behind and be released into the next. I do not refer to the Old Nations' elusive Heaven and Hell. No, through the efforts of the scholarly Azurite Order and the reverent Crystal Order, a sort of dimensional plane has been revealed. I have heard the term "parallel universe," though that is the extent of my knowing, as I am no Azurite academic.

It is said that the *ames* of those who've passed have been *felt* in these other worlds, leading to the conclusion that we share this existence with many others. We do not know how many they number, but it is sure that a new *ame* begins within them there. It is everlasting life, I suppose.

The strongest spirit seekers are within the Crystal Order, although seekers across most of the orders highly debate this. Even still, the seekers of the Crystal were the first able to establish a link with the "others" in the discovered dimensional plane, albeit inconsistent and unstable. Once it was identified, they began attempting to commune with the others, and so they immediately recruited the historians of the Amber Order to assist with the translation.

Through their astute examination of the discourse, they were able to string together unusual words and discern not only the meaning of the words, but also that they made up a collective of foreign speech with various dialects. From these, we integrated the most alluring words into our own language, and we adopted into our everyday speech those concepts that held the most meaning, *ame* being one of many.

I have digressed.

The Great Spirit has entrusted one special *ame* to us all: It resides in a child. A child to be groomed in the fashion of his or her order. A child known as the Chozien and sent by the Great Spirit. This child has a heightened *ame* capable of molding and shifting the way of our world. A Chozien has always been born since the Breaking, but we were too ignorant in the beginning to seek him or her out, with the world too perilous for any of them to seek us.

Once our study of the spirit language achieved a degree of sophistication, we were able to receive the Great Spirit's counsel. This instruction calls to the spirit seekers of all orders, advising them that a new Chozien has been born, though his place of origin is always unknown. After one Chozien's *ame* has left this world, a new one is born and the cycle begins again, as does the quest to find him—known as the *Quête*.

The order that finds the Chozien can subsequently disrupt or soothe the world we live in. In *this* world, the Chozien cannot even conceive of such an incredible feat alone; therefore, it is the order's responsibility to train and educate the Chozien with the abilities and knowledge to survive and flourish within it.

The Onyx Order, in the eastern Upperlands, has always coveted the Chozien for themselves. They are a manipulative sort, preying on the disheartened, tempting them with promises of abundance and influence. They embrace domination, by which their strength is determined and their numbers multiply. Their order is a constant menace, yet their fear of being overtaken keeps them from maintaining a ruling grip over the other orders. As temporal as that flaw is, it does not overshadow their might. They are indeed a formidable rival.

This is our world today, where constant conflict exists among unity, self-preservation, and power. In this world, we have few great legends; thus we must make our own. The order that holds the Chozien can make or break the future. As such, the progress or peril of our days ahead rests upon the shoulders of the order that lays claim to the Chozien.

In this tale, the Great Spirit has called to all orders that a new Chozien has been born. The search has already begun. All have released their finest huntsmen and spirit seekers to find the child.

We can only hope that we are not too late.

CHAPTER
ONE

A lone man walks the outskirts of the land where the remnants of the Old World lie scattered about, deteriorating—not uncommon in these parts. The inhabitants here survive as scavengers. They feed off the scraps others leave behind and cherish the filth they sleep on. This place has neither ruler nor a people willing to be ruled. The sun shines brilliantly, but darkness has made a home here. Even so, the shadows provide some comfort. The stench of decaying flesh, bodily waste, and forgotten hope is enough to turn the greatest warrior's head in disgust.

It is a sad place; it is the Barrens. It received its name because of the infertile ground and lead-filled water. It is a wonder that there are inhabitants—castaways mostly, or those who see the rule of the orders unfit to live among. Infants do not live beyond their first few moons, given the lack of access to nutrition.

This man does not belong. He looks to be of good health and well nourished. His clothes cover his entire body, worn only from his travels. He wears a loose-fitting, brown leather shirt. His pants are of black leather, some type of animal hide—perhaps cow or goat, and pig for the softer bits, just loose enough for comfort and movement. He wears a loincloth at his waist, stopping mid-calf, and a cloak of the darkest green, with his hood pulled over his head to shield his eyes from the sun's rays. His wrists show differing decorative leather cuffs. On his left, a bracer covers his entire forearm, indicating he is a huntsman, and on his right, the cuff stops just before mid-forearm—common for a warrior.

His arms and hands are free and steady, hinting at his caution. The length of his stride says he is in a hurry. The way his head continuously moves suggests his alertness. His posture declares he is dangerous. This man searches for something. However, he does not inspect the ground, he does not stop to look into the burned buildings, and he does not even riffle through the piles of debris and trash that lie about in abundance. No, this man is not looking for *something* ... he is looking for *someone*.

A boy, a few months shy of two years, wanders in his forlorn surroundings. He is famished and awaits his parents' arrival with the day's collection of rotten scraps. He is disappointed because he cannot find the plaything from his past days. Out of boredom, he sets out to find a new one. During his search, he steps on something unfamiliar, hearing its quiet snap. He moves to look at it and finds the object interesting. The boy picks it up and after a simple inspection decides he likes it. Smiling now, the boy walks, waving the object in the air, his earlier distress forgotten.

From a distance, Branson scans the horizon of the Barrens.

Such a pitiful land. He lifts up one side of his lips in disgust.

Branson's eyes are drawn to a small, crumbling piece of a once-thriving structure. He notes a pulsating light, so bright it causes him to squint a bit. It beckons to him. He changes direction and quickens his pace. As he closes the distance, he notices the light not only flickers, but also moves. How can there be light in such a dark place? Is there a source of power that makes this light as bright as the sun? Who wields this light in the darkness?

Branson asks many questions to which he cannot find logical answers. He must trust the Great Spirit to lead him. Faith in the unseen has put him on the path to seek the Chozien, and he remains confident it will take him further.

As he gets closer, he realizes the source of the light is in the hands of a child. A male child, perhaps in his second birth year, holds a shard of glass. Under further investigation, and to Branson's relief, the boy suffers no cuts or abrasions from the jagged edges of the broken shard.

The boy sees Branson staring at him. He utters a small sound and offers to share his toy by raising it to the newcomer, boldly stretching his arm up, offering the shard to Branson. Even in this horrid place, the innocence of a selfless child endures.

Branson uses this opportunity to take the sharp fragment from the boy and then checks his hands and body for sores. Surprisingly, he discovers none, save for the feet, no doubt from months of walking on grime without sandals for protection.

Hearing movement a short distance away, Branson looks away from the boy. Astonishingly, another child—an infant and also a male—lies upon a bed of nested garbage, sucking on his filthy fingers; he can be no more than six moons. Branson goes and inspects the infant as well, finding the child to be warm to the touch, stinking of the soiled waste on his body, which is obvious from his naked state. Both children clearly suffer from malnourishment—severely underfed by the size of them, a clear sign of neglect. Branson shakes his head in disgust and begins to look around for those supposedly responsible for the children.

They are not difficult to locate. He spots them just a little ways off, rummaging through a broken and burned wagon. He calls for them in a hard voice.

The couple looks around suspiciously. Once they spot the owner of the voice, their eyes widen with alarm. Branson waves them over. They comply, but with slow, cautious steps.

Once they get close enough to hear Branson speak, he asks the man, "Did you father these children?"

With downcast eyes, the man speaks in a trembling voice, "Yes, sire."

The man looks at the woman, and she replies in the same fashion, "They are ours, sire."

Branson tosses them two sacks containing bread and dried meat, then a skin of water. "They are now mine."

Confused, the couple open the sacks and then shake the skin. Instantly, they clutch their payment and slink away to examine their undeserved treasure.

Turning, Branson looks at the worried boy, who now watches his only known family leave without looking back. The child gazes up at Branson while tears begin to well up in his small eyes. Branson smiles and squats down, pushing back his hood to reveal his features to the boy. Branson's hair seems to be growing backward, with wavy brown locks extending to just above mid-neck. His eyes are a darker shade of his hair and show youth but maturity. A few days' worth of unshaven facial hair covers his cheeks, chin, and upper lip.

Branson extends his hand. Despite Branson's overpowering presence and the long, pinkish laceration extending from his eyebrow to the cheek on the right side of his face, the gesture offers solace that the child happily accepts.

Next, Branson walks to where the infant lies. He takes out another skin and lightly rinses the baby with water, freeing him of some of his waste. Afterward, Branson wraps his cloak around the child and cradles him in the crook of his arm. He then picks the boy up and starts toward his camp. He must hurry if he hopes to be back before the sun sleeps and still keep the children—and his head.

As Branson walks, he thinks: *What a small price to pay for two innocent children destined to be great men.* His search for the Chozien is over, and he can feel a new world beginning.

The spirit seeker Uric begins setting up the night's camp in the Barrens. The spot is small but spacious enough for two men and secluded from possible thieves by a forest of trees and brush.

No water exists in this area, and Uric would not touch it even if it did. The corruption in these waters is more than he can cleanse on his own. Three horses graze nearby, tied to stakes driven into the ground. The grass is tough and so thin that the ground appears to swallow the bit of greenery left. The forest lies on the outskirts of the broken city just beyond the horizon—a safe enough distance from the inhabitants and their polluted *ames.* Of course, none really drift far from outside the city, unless something has caught their selfish interest.

The Jade Order chose a team of seven huntsmen and six seekers for the Quête to find the Chozien. Before they set off, the elected kinsmen gathered at the Jade spirit hold to have their *ames* ceremoniously intertwined by the spirit keeper, enabling the seekers in each party to discern the *ames* of the others.

The team then separated into six bands: Three of one huntsman and a seeker went west, and another two of the same headed east, with all five bands dispersed to various regions. The final band consisted of two huntsmen and one seeker, sent to the region known as the Barrens—a miles-long desolate stretch of land that lies to the south.

Of the entire team's seven huntsmen, two *ames* have been released, and one of the six seekers, according to Uric.

The dwellers in the Barrens are called the Lost. It is too dangerous a place for children to exist, primarily because the Lost's *ames* are weak and dwindling. A child cannot survive with so little spirit, if one is even created. The Lost have no order, their minds have become twisted from their constant desperation, and it seems their greed is stronger than that of even the Onyx. But nevertheless, it has been thirteen moons since Uric, Yuen, and Branson headed here to find the Chozien.

Uric stands a head taller than Branson. He keeps his head and face clean-shaven, as do most of the seekers, with the Jade Order's spiritual tattoos covering his head, extending into his face. Whereas Branson is a big man with a muscular build and broad shoulders, Uric has a medium build with a lean frame. His eyes are the color of stormy clouds, and his skin is copper-toned. He wears a loose, sleeveless vest, soft leather pants, and a loincloth, all dark green with silver lining. His boots are made of thick, coarse material used for traveling. His wrists bear thin silver cuffs with rounded jade stones at each end, all standard seeker attire.

Yuen's *ame* returned to the Great Spirit nearly a month ago. None can be trusted in the Barrens, and it is best to sleep with both eyes open. Yuen made that mistake and did not survive; now he was counted as a lost huntsman.

Uric feels an unexpected slight shiver up his spine—a different kind of shiver, though: warm and innocent. It is not one of a man or woman, but oddly enough of a ... child. Uric, being a seeker, should have felt the spirit of any child long ago. A child's essence is strong and reaches farther than any others. This one feels different from all the other children. It is complete ... wondrous ... even weighted?

It cannot be, Uric muses. *The Chozien, here?*

He finishes digging the fire hole the depth of a man's forearm as the sun begins to wane, pausing in place when he hears the chirping of a familiar bird. Uric recognizes the sound as the signal for Branson's approach and replies with a slightly higher pitch, assuring that it is safe for the huntsman to enter the camp. Soon after, Branson slowly and carefully stoops through the foliage into the small camp.

Uric suddenly inhales deeply and blinks several times before releasing his breath.

"Good. I thought you were going to lose your *ame* from suffocation. Pick up your jaw and help me, seeker," Branson says smartly.

"You have found the Chozien! There are two? We cannot take but one," Uric says as Branson hands him the infant.

"We cannot? I do not know which one is the Chozien." Branson places the boy on the ground and turns to remove his satchel, revealing twin blades held by their scabbards at his back and a hunting knife at his waist.

"It is the young boy," Uric says. "His birth matches the time of the new life cycle. I have also felt his spirit. Those who search will know soon that he has been found."

Uric refers to the Calming of the Chozien's *ame*, which is sensed by seekers of all orders to signify that the Chozien has been claimed.

"Why is it, then, that you did not feel his spirit sooner?" Branson asks.

"I did. Just before you arrived. It is … weak. But we will mend it in time."

"No one has ever known a child to survive past two moons in the Barrens. Yet, here are two. They must both be the Chozien."

Uric is silent for a moment and then, while rubbing his chin thoughtfully, says, "Perhaps a bond has been created between the two; that would explain the spirit's heaviness."

After looking over the boy, Uric realizes that the children need some food and to be cleaned, by his obvious aversion to the smell from his upturned nose. He starts a small fire and sets to heating some water in a pot the size of a green melon, which had been packed on Yuen's horse. Meanwhile, Branson retrieves a small bar of white soap from his satchel, two small towels, and some fragrant oils. Once the water just barely begins to steam and feels slightly warm to the touch, Uric removes the pot from the fire, and both men begin the paternal task of bathing the children.

First, they shed the boy of all his rags. They soap and scrub him from the roots of his hair to the soles of his feet. The boy seems frightened of the black pot as he hesitates a moment before Branson hoists it and empties it over him, rinsing all the excess dirt and suds away. Branson notes the boy's features as he dries him: tightly curled, dark-brown hair, skin reminiscent of honey while slightly darkened by the sun's rays, and gray eyes with specks of green. Uric rubs oils into the child's skin, covering his entire body except the areas around open sores.

Branson retrieves child-sized undergarments colored a shade of light green from his pack, as well as three soft, thick pieces of cloth varying in lengths and cuts. Each piece is as green as the grass and bordered with a silver strip, which shines like the steel of the finest sword. He dresses the boy in the undergarments, then wraps one piece of the fine cloth around the boy's waist, where it falls long to the boy's ankles as a loincloth, similar to Branson's and Uric's own. The next piece of cloth is larger, and Branson places it around the boy's shoulders for a cloak.

They give the boy water, bread, dried meat, and a trail bar made of oats, honey, and dried fruits to eat while the men busy themselves cleaning the infant. They treat the infant with the same cleansing routine. The babe resembles the boy in looks, except that the infant's hair is truly black and the curls are looser. While Uric struggles to design some kind of baby napkin out of an extra towel, Branson turns his attention back to the boy, smears aloe vera ointment over his sores, then wraps his feet in strips cut out of one of Yuen's undergarments and finally fits him with sandals. Uric wraps the baby in cloth and feeds him water and tiny pieces of bread made soggy by water. Once the baby is asleep, Uric places him on a blanket previously laid out on the ground as Branson cleans his cloak.

By the time they finally sit to enjoy a meal of coarse, tasteless bread and seasoned dried meat, the boy has devoured not only his earlier portion, but also an additional serving he sought, which Uric graciously gave him.

His belly full, the boy crawls onto the blanket next to his sleeping brother and covers them both with Branson's cloak. Branson places another blanket on the resting duo and motions to Uric for silence so as to not disturb the sleeping children.

In hushed tones, they discuss future preparations for traveling with a small boy and an infant.

Branson starts, "If we hurry, we can arrive within one moon before the White Rain season."

Uric has a look of shock before he replies, "That will take us four moons. No, we need a wagon. With the speed of the wagon, we will return two moons before the white rain. They are children and cannot ride a horse for long hours. Yuen's food is not enough to feed the boy, you, and me. The infant needs milk and softer food."

Branson nods. "A clan from the Hematite Order lies just east. We can replenish our supplies there and trade for what we need." As an after-thought, he adds, "I do not trust their order, so we will need to make our stay a short one."

"Neither do I trust them. Their seekers will know the Chozien has been found, but they will not know by whom. I can see that your stamina is drained. You need sleep—a contributing factor to motivate continuance in living. *Ames* are brighter with it. This is one thing you can control. I will take the dark watch; I need you at your best."

Uric arms himself with his weaponry of two throwing knives and a champion blade, then disappears into the shadowy forest. He finds a tree positioned close enough to the camp but allowing him a view from all sides, protecting him from the vision of any bandits. He settles into a comfortable nook and watches.

Back at the camp, Branson places himself at the foot of the sleep-ing children. He has been more vigilant since Yuen's demise, the tender wound on his right cheek standing as a reminder from fending off the raiders. He falls asleep with one of his twin blades in hand. He is not known for his carelessness.

Soon enough, Uric shakes Branson awake. "It is time to prepare to leave. Pack the horses while I gather the children."

Branson blinks the sleep away while standing up. It is a little past the time of the light watch, given the dark gray of the sky and the fading stars. Uric must have let him sleep longer. He makes a mental note to return the favor.

Branson goes a short distance and relieves himself. He removes some trail bars and water for breakfast from the extra satchel, then walks a perimeter around the camp. Returning to the campsite, he sets to saddling the horses and packing the pot and dried linens on the extra horse, then smothers the fire hole.

By this time, Uric has the children ready for travel. "We must hurry to the Hematite clan for fresh supplies and food."

Uric makes a sling out of his cloak to carry the baby while he rides, wrapping it over both shoulders and crisscross in front. Branson ties the ends at Uric's back. Uric then fastens the reins of the third horse to the back of his horse's saddle, finally hoisting himself into the saddle. Then Branson hands the baby up to Uric, who places him safely into the sling.

Branson smirks, noticing the sling and its sturdiness. "So it seems you are good for something, seeker."

Uric laughs. "Come. Let us begin our return home."

CHAPTER
TWO

Branson lifts himself and the boy onto his horse. With one hand holding the boy and the other on the reins, he leads the way. After just two sun sky shadows, Uric calls for them to stop; the baby needs changing.

Their progress is slow throughout the morning, stopping for the children frequently. The boy's legs have yet to get used to riding in a saddle for long periods. With the sun sitting high and the full heat of its booming rays beating on them, they decide this time to make it a break for the horses as well. Branson hands the boy a couple of trail bars and begins to feed the horses before finally resting and eating.

The boy calls out, "Da!"

Branson and Uric both look at the boy, then at each other. The boy must have been referring to Branson since he's still holding out the trail bar, directing it toward him.

"No. No 'Da,'" Branson says to the boy, emphatically shaking his head and finger as he walks to the boy and receives the piece of food he is offering.

Branson looks toward Uric and sees a mischievous grin on his face. "Don't," Branson warns.

Uric holds his hands up. "I haven't said a word."

The boy is obviously growing a fast attachment to Branson, which wouldn't be advantageous to him. Their dewan—the leader of their order—might choose to name Branson as gardien—the boy's foster parent—but Branson does not consider himself a father figure, nor does he have a desire to be a father.

The four endure the crowded conditions of riding two to a horse for nearly the time of a quarter moon. As the sun begins to set one day, they reach the borders of the nearest Hematite clan. They decide to stay in full view of the scouts staggered across the forested region and continue riding until they reach the clan hold.

They appear to be tired and sore strangers as they plod up to the massive entry door to the hold of this Hematite clan; it stands close to the height of four horses, wide enough to fit through five horses abreast.

"Speak your place," an aloof voice calls from a small side door located to the left of the wooden entry. It is customary when in the territory of a different order: You are to state the names of the traveling party along with your order and reason for the request.

Branson answers in a loud voice, "Branson Kuo-Lin and Uric Kale of the Jade Order ask for hospitality for ourselves and a small boy and babe for only one night."

"Granted."

Sounds of unlatching follow, then the gates creak open and the travelers make their way inside. They dismount and lead the horses and children inside the order's hold, which can hold nearly five thousand kinsmen, but is too small to be the order's spirit hold. The Hematite garb is a bright gray, accented by black threading. The paths show the hold's guards walking and chatting with their kinsmen. Lanterns light the streets. The buildings and houses line the byways as patrons and homeowners begin their nightly routines.

The doorman directs them to the hold's stable, where they can board their animals. The stableman charges per day for lodging and more if they want him to feed and care for the horses. Branson haggles with the man and drops a small sack in the stableman's hand—filled with spices, a popular blend in the Jade Order, but rare and expensive in other territories. Branson leaves strict instructions for their horses' care and feed.

They then begin their search for an inexpensive inn with the accommodations of a bath and warm food. The people do not acknowledge their presence; if anything, they make a wide arc around them in avoidance. The guards eye the four openly and suspiciously—no surprise ... and no secret to anyone. The Hematite clan is known for its security and isolation. Their order has a high level of civil unity and stays neutral if at all possible. They tend to take sides when it will be most beneficial for themselves. Branson and company were probably allowed entry because of their brief stay. This order is a secretive lot, their motives unknown.

"The spirit here is abnormally warm. It makes me uneasy," Uric whispers to Branson.

The Hematites' *ames* are always cold or lukewarm, and so the abnormality of their "warmth" gives Uric an ominous feeling to the point of interrupting his concentration.

"We will leave the moment we wake and tend to the supplies," Branson replies, hopefully relieving some of his companion's uneasiness.

Finally, without the assistance of a Hematite kinsman, they arrive at a small inn, the Iron Rod. They walk inside and notice it to be as small as it looked outside. A small counter for the bar on the right, a cook pit to the very far left, and four spaciously placed tables for four to provide privacy complete the interior. Two doors at the back wall: assuming the one with the swinging door is where the kitchen lies, with the other for lodging. They see only two kinsmen in the place, other than the owner behind the bar and one serving girl stirring something in a heavy and deep pot over the cook pit.

They recognize the aroma of beef stew and warm bread. After surveying the room, they walk to the owner.

Branson speaks first: "Good eve to you. Are you the owner?"

The owner replies in an emotionless voice, "I am."

Branson cuts straight to the point with, "Do you have rooms to rent?"

"I do," the man answers curtly.

"Good. One room with two beds, meals for my party for tonight and the morning, as well as a bath?" Branson asks.

The owner looks up and, still monotone, says, "Of course."

Branson and the owner haggle back and forth for a few minutes discussing the value of the spices. They decide on two slightly larger sacks than the one given to the stableman.

The waitress directs them to their rooms through the second door. She offers to watch the children while the men carry the tub into the room. The tub is of medium size and oval-shaped.

Once the men finish, she says, "You will heat your own water in the kitchen. I will bring your meals here and food for the babe."

"You are kind, Mistress," Uric responds, nodding.

Branson goes to work hauling the ten gallon buckets of water for their baths while Uric tends to the children. It takes some time, but eventually everyone is clean and fed. Branson makes his choice to lie in the bed with the baby, while Uric and the boy take the other. They all fall asleep as soon as their heads touch the pillows.

Branson wakes to the sound of movement. He slides his hand beneath his pillow where his blade is hidden.

"Do not be alarmed, huntsman. It is I—Uric."

Branson makes a silent expletive; Uric should not have seen him reach for his weapon. Huntsmen are known for their silent and concealed movements. It is a slight against Branson for Uric to see his actions, as seekers receive the least amount of combat training. Branson rises, stretching his well-muscled arms, hearing the bones release their tension.

"I see you slept well," Uric says, smiling, pointing at his shirt.

Branson already knows what Uric means. When he had stretched, he felt the dampness on his shirt. Uric is right. He did sleep well—so well that he did not notice when the child relieved himself on him.

Branson cleans his shirt, dons another, and does the same with the baby. Uric has finished his breakfast already and now prepares to get the supplies they need for the remainder of the journey.

"I will have the waitress send your food in," Uric says from the doorway. "I should not be long."

Branson nods and turns his attention to some horseplay with the boy.

Odd for him, Uric thinks as he closes the door behind him. He notifies the waitress about the meals for the rest of his traveling party and settles their tab for their stay before he leaves. A dark-gray sky greets him as he steps outside. He and Branson already discussed a few places they had seen on their way to the inn the night before that would be suitable to purchase food and a wagon.

Equipped with five more small sacks of their order's spices, he heads in the direction of the food markets. Uric trades two sacks for five bundles of vegetables, two sacks of bread, one set of clothing for the infant, and a small basket for a temporary bassinet. Milk would spoil on the road, so water will have to do. He uses the last three sacks to trade for a small but sturdy wagon, which the owner has his son bring to the stable and hitch up to two of their horses.

By this time, the sun has risen to a height where Uric must shield his eyes from its light. As he walks back to the inn, carrying their supplies on his back, he scans the interactions of the Hematite patrons. He senses something strange about their spirits—they are just *too warm*. He concentrates on his training. He repeats the oddities to himself again: a warm spirit with cold behavior. The guards' eyes follow him, and when he meets their gaze, they nod. And the way the wagon owner entrusted his son with a man of another order? *This is not their way,* Uric thinks. *Something stirs here.*

He reaches the inn and sees three guards having a late breakfast. Uric maneuvers between the tables and heads to the room. He knocks three times, pauses, and then knocks once more. Branson opens the door, holding the boy, hair tousled and laughing.

Uric hurries in, his eyes fixed, his mouth in a taut line.

Branson notices and puts the boy down. "What's wrong?"

Uric tells Branson of the questionable actions the clan exhibited. "There are three guards here at the inn too, breaking their fast," he finishes.

As if that last sentence ignites a flame in the dark, they both look at each other and whisper, "They know."

Uric says, "The animals are ready, and the wagon is hitched at the stable."

Branson nods once, pleased at the seeker's proactiveness.

They pack all their belongings immediately and settle the children. They dress and adjust their weapons for easy access. They make a plan so as to not seem suspicious or in a rush to leave. They will have to make their way to the road if they are to stand a chance against any attackers, believing that the Hematites' sole mission is to take the children. It would be near impossible to protect the children while defending themselves from multiple opponents in open ground.

Branson carries the infant in his arms and the supplies on his back. Uric carries the boy in his arms, with their satchels on his shoulders. They make their way through the front of the inn. The room falls silent. Branson uses the infant to disguise his surveying of the entire room. He readjusts and recovers the blanket to insinuate the idea that he is making the babe comfortable. Uric takes to a lazy walk to seem tired and unconcerned with his surroundings. They nod to the owner and head straight out the front door.

It feels as if many sun sky shadows pass by the time they reach the stables. Uric proves right: Two of the horses have been saddled and the wagon is hitched to them, with Branson's own horse still unencumbered. Branson and Uric put the supplies and satchels in the wagon. Uric sits the boy down in the wagon bed and gives him a piece of wood carved in the shape of a wolf. The boy eagerly takes the toy and turns his attention to playing with it, Uric already forgotten.

Branson unties the harness and lays it over the basket previously filled with hay, then sets the baby on top. Uric takes the reins for the wagon, and Branson mounts his horse before leading the way out of the hold. It is early enough for the gates to be opened. The doorman gives the order to the gatekeepers. Using four draft horses, two on each gate, the handlers command the horses to move by tugging on their reins, gently but firmly. The heavy wooden barricades creak slightly and then inch open. Branson nudges his horse to a walk so as to not cause alarm.

The doorman calls, "Safe journey!"

The farewell is just as good as an admission itself. Branson nods at him. They travel in silence for some time until they are well on the open road.

Branson slows his horse to walk beside the wagon. "It was a mistake to risk lodging there."

"It had to be done. Did you notice they did not close the gate behind us?" Uric asked.

"Yes. They will send scouts first. I do not know for how long."

"Why would the Hematite attack outside the protection of its hold?"

Branson shrugs. "We continue until dark."

By the time Branson calls a halt for the day, he has spotted four scouts. The Hematite are clumsy and terrible at concealing themselves. Because of their neutrality, the Hematite do not think there is any reason to properly train their militia. The scouts do not pose any threat; however, they will gather information about their camp. Again, it is unusual for them to be so organized.

Branson and Uric make camp. They continue to act as if oblivious to the threat on their solitude. While Uric begins cooking a pot of stewed vegetables, Branson settles the children down and attends to the horses.

Shortly after, Branson excuses himself ... seemingly to relieve himself. He goes to the edge of their small camp just through the trees beyond eyesight, though within earshot, where he sits down, crossing his legs. He raises his hood over his head and rests his hands, fingers intertwined, palms up, and forearms over his thighs. Closing his eyes, he focuses his thoughts on nothing but himself. He hears only his controlled breathing. He frees his mind until only he exists.

The soft wind that teases among the young limbs of sky-seeking trees with the densely forested shrubbery now aborts its play. The delicate movement above the calm comfort of shade-bearing clouds becomes frozen in shadow. The security from Branson's self-awareness in the surety of practiced strength and memorized surroundings escapes him while his body goes motionless, immovable, as if molded of stone. He equates this state of mind akin to a lucid dream.

His mind is new, infantile, experiencing sensations and images as if for the first time—his vision now one of extrasensory perception, seeing with his mind's sight beyond the physical world's constraints. His first emotion is fear, as he frantically searches for the familiar. He remains determined, yet recognizes he is powerless in this timeless void. He cannot use the world around him as in his training because this place is not alive ... though neither is it dead. It exists outside reality ... perhaps where things are created, shaped, transformed. Unknowingly, curiosity replaces fear. He continues his quest, though with more intent. If this place has no life, then he will explore its purpose.

He recalls a memory from his huntsman training. An eager boy of nine or ten years sits aside from the other trainees, visibly frustrated. He jumps with surprise as a hand relaxes on his shoulder. He recognizes the man as one of the huntsmen, though not a devenir—the title of a trainer. After the man inquires about the boy's thoughts, the boy says he struggles with tracking. He either loses his prey or ends up getting lost himself. To the boy's irritation, the huntsman laughs.

The huntsman apologizes for his ill-mannered silliness and explains, "It is a game. The beast wants to outsmart you. It must if it is to live, no? The beast will lure you to where it wants you to be. It will create a false trail that seems true but will confuse and delay you to your destination. All creatures are this way, even you." He points to the boy for emphasis. With a more serious tone, he taps the boy's head and adds, "You must *always* rely on your senses for what is truly there. Never your heart. Nothing and no one can hide forever."

Taking in the logic from the recollection, Branson employs the huntsman's counsel. First, he focuses his vision; there is nothing but the stillness, though it is not truly … dark. Then he listens. He hears his own ragged breathing. Taking notice of its pace, he centers his thoughts briefly, bringing his heart rate down to an equilibrium, the tempo equivalent to the hum of a soothing lullaby.

He feels nothing … not even the tough smoothness of the garments he wears or the coarse calluses awarded to his leather-hardened palms and fingers. Absent of all that is familiar to him, he finds comfort in an immovable awareness. He has reached the state between the present and timelessness. At this moment, a sensation of calm and joy washes over him as he realizes he has entered the presence of the Great Spirit.

A spark of light flickers in the seeming distance. In the instant the light appears, it flashes brightly as if the light races toward him. If he could have recoiled from the fear of impact, he would have. Another one follows, and then another. The flashes become so close in interval that he *feels* himself closing his eyes to shield them from the brightness. The bursts of light cease, though he does not allow himself to resume his gaze immediately … hesitating.

Just as he relaxes, scenes and symbols materialize. Two hawks fly and one is captured by dark netting, interrupting its flight. Another flash of light and the scene changes. A gloved hand conceals a black knife in a green garment. A flash again. Sounds of fighting. Women and children screaming, so much blood, so thick that he smells it. A flash. He feels … rage and pain, then he sees a simple cage … and then suddenly, a burst to his chest. It is so intense he believes he is being knocked backward. Finally, it fades to dark.

Branson blinks his eyes open, inhales and exhales rapidly, seemingly from holding his breath. He is left with a feeling of loss and failure.

He realizes his fists are clenched tightly. He loosens them gingerly, revealing small red indentations where his fingernails meet his palms. He pushes back his hood. A warm, light wind breezes across his face, and he feels the dampness. He reaches up and touches his cheek, shocked to find a trail of tears.

The smell of Uric's stew brings to attention his rumbling stomach. Branson stands and blinks a couple more times for focus and wipes away the tears before walking back to the camp.

"You look like you have run the hills. Are you well?" Uric asks, observing Branson's pale appearance.

"Yes," Branson replies absently.

Uric hands Branson a bowl of his stew and some bread. He is skeptical but decides against further questions.

"How long was I away?" Branson asks.

Uric shrugs. "Just a few moments."

Branson shows his surprise by the slight rise in his eyebrows. He was sure at least the time of one sun sky shadow had passed. Reminded of his appetite by the growling in his stomach, he takes his initial slurp of the warm, seasoned stew, grunting acknowledgment to the cook at its preparation. He continues his meal, though not without distraction, as he ponders over his visions and concludes that it best to discuss with Uric.

Branson looks at the sleeping baby and half-asleep boy lying nearby on a thick blanket, then he whispers, "It was different than usual; typically, I have visions of things in the past. This time, I saw two hawks flying and one was captured in a dark net, a black knife in our robes, and a cage. Sounds of many dying. I ... felt it."

"I have heard of something like this before. Our teachers call it Foresight," Uric says.

Unknowing of the gift of Foresight, Branson shrugs.

"Death," Uric says. "It sounds like the Onyx Order is involved." He rips a piece of bread from the whole.

"I have never had visions like this. I could smell the blood. The future will be challenging and heartbreaking, Uric."

Uric responds calmly, "Evil surrounds us now. This is always true." He changes the topic to the immediate matter: "We should have a plan for the attack. It shall be upon us soon."

Branson repositions himself as if he'll somehow discover a more comfortable spot on the hard, cold ground where they sit. "You are right, seeker. We shall return to our dewan with the children."

Soon Branson's thoughts keep interrupting his sleep. He's never felt loss or failure with such intensity as a huntsman before. The feeling was so strong he doubts he will ever forget it. His visions now draw his attention to the children. He moves closer to sleep next to them. Surprisingly, his sleep goes uninterrupted until Uric wakes him for the light watch.

The four travel through one whole moon. The scouts reduce their numbers moon phase by moon phase. Over the course of the last four days, Branson and Uric have been sharpening their weapons and riding very cautiously. They feel sure the day of the attack will soon be upon them. Branson thinks he will not be able to use his longbow; he expects he will be fighting many in close combat.

Uric keeps his eyes on the woods. Nature is unusually silent for this time of day.

Atop his horse, Branson suddenly raises his hand, signaling for Uric to stop the wagon. Movement in the trees ahead captures his eye. Focusing on the direct spot of the motion, he can see a figure behind the cover of branches and leaves. Too close to the road. He moves his hand to grasp the dagger at his waist. Uric unsheathes his blade slightly from its scabbard. Branson nudges his horse to a slow walk. Uric follows.

The boy and infant sleep in the wagon, but the infant unexpectedly utters a soft whine, beginning to escalate in volume. Uric quickly turns to silence him. In that moment of distraction, gray-clad warriors spring forth from the foliage. Branson kills two in the throat with a pair of his daggers, yelling to Uric to guard the children.

Uric dodges backward, evading a menacing swipe of a warrior's sword. He catches the attacker with a forearm to the nose, breaking it instantly, the victim recoiling from the injury. Uric jumps from the wagon, his sword out as his feet meet the ground. He fends off two warriors in a series of trained defenses.

Branson uses his battle-trained horse to separate the warriors from the wagon. He kicks at one and then jumps down from his mount. Close combat is a huntsman's specialty. With both of his short swords in hand, he fights with a series of feints and slashes. His training in stealth and agility ensures he will make quick work of two warriors by deeply slashing the throat of one and burying half of his blade in the belly of the other, leaving it embedded so the man will die slowly and painfully. Branson then works on a third, calculating his attacks. He notices that this one has a broken nose.

Uric continues to avoid hacks and slashes from his pair of assailants. It is apparent that the two are having trouble fighting the same target. Uric decides to disable the better fighter of the two. As a seeker, Uric can channel the essence of nature to come to his aid, a rare skill. He does so by concentrating on separating his body from his mind. Then he calls for the spirit of the land, a hard task to complete while in fierce combat. Thick roots spring up from the ground next to one of the warrior's feet. They entwine themselves around the ankle up to mid-calf, locking in place, disabling movement. It catches the warrior off guard and leaves Uric fighting just one. He deflects a striking lunge and sidesteps, kicking the warrior fully in the side, sending him flying back, probably cracking a rib or two.

Temporarily distracted, the bound warrior jerks violently at the roots with his leg. Remembering his sword, he hacks away at the roots hindering him. Upon finishing, he searches for his opponent. Too late, though, as Uric stands before him, sword raised. Uric brings the sword down in a slash, connecting at the top of the man's shoulder, continuing through the flesh and bone of his neck, nearly decapitating him. The man slumps and falls dead.

Uric turns to finish the other and dodges just in time to only sustain a slash to the upper arm, but loses his footing. Uric swings wildly while trying to get to his feet and catches the warrior in the wrist of his sword arm. Unfortunately, it is with the flat of Uric's blade, so the strike doesn't maim but temporarily stings, enough though that the sword falls from the warrior's hand.

Instinctively, the warrior charges at Uric, who's still unbalanced, and slams him into the side of the wagon, leaving Uric breathless. Uric uses the hilt of his sword to strike the warrior between the shoulder blades. The warrior grunts and loosens his grip. Uric starts to strike him again, but the warrior lunges upward, catching Uric under the chin with the top of his head. Uric falls to the ground, blinking to keep his consciousness. The warrior hurries to pick up his dead accomplice's sword and positions for the death stroke.

Meanwhile, Branson disarms his third opponent and speedily cuts the warrior's lower arm by the wrist, then uses a flurry of fist and leg assaults to knock the warrior out cold. He hears movement and a childlike cry from the wagon. He alters his hold on the weapon and turns, raising it for a fatal throw, pausing his release in midair when he sees one warrior roughly dragging the screaming boy from the wagon by way of a dark net that subdues his movements, with another warrior in the wagon and reaching for the infant. Yet another warrior stands on the opposite side of the wagon, raising a sword in both hands, clearly meant for a death strike on ... Uric.

Branson has to make a decision: He can't lose the Chozien, but if they stand any chance of making it home, he can't do it alone. He throws his sword; it hits the chest of the warrior standing over Uric, knocking him backward. Then Branson leaps in to break the warrior's neck as he's leaning down to steal the baby.

Uric and Branson can hear the boy's frightened screams as the thief disappears into the forest with him.

Branson scans the surrounding battlefield before yelling, "Uric, are you alright?"

Uric rises, using the wagon for support. He rubs his chin and wipes blood from his mouth, then replies groggily, "Yeah."

"You can thank me later. Over here—I have one alive." Branson jerks his blade from the body of a Hematite warrior.

The warrior, barely able to retain his *ame*, utters a loud gasp.

Uric picks up his sword and walks to Branson's side of the wagon. Upon advancement, Uric sees the boy had disappeared from the wagon. "Where is the boy?" he exclaims.

"I sacrificed his rescue so you could keep your *ame*, seeker."

Uric's eyes widen with embarrassment and anger at the obvious insinuation of him being at fault for the boy's capture. Before Uric can respond to the obvious admonishment, he sees the unconscious warrior.

"Wake him," Uric says in a low voice, seething with anger.

Branson kicks the man awake. The man shakes his head and then realizes his present situation. He tries to sit up, but Branson puts a boot to his chest, setting him on his back.

"Why does the Hematite Order betray the *Quête* Treaty?" Branson asks.

The man upturns his mouth in disgust. "You ask because you are curious, or because you no longer have the boy and infant?"

"One seems to be in the company of your order," Branson answers unemotionally.

The captive responds again with a disgusted appearance first, then sneers. "Then it is too late. Enjoy your days, for death is approaching. The adopted son of our dewan has returned."

Branson grounds the heel of his boot into the man's chest, causing him an enormous amount of pain. The man takes hold of Branson's leg, trying to release the pressure while uttering empty threats.

"Answer my question, Hematite."

Breathing raggedly, the man says, "You disgrace me with that name. You have my answer. I will speak no more."

Branson yields a confused but thoughtful look, then turns his head toward Uric, who nods. Uric raises his sword and plunges it into the man's chest. The man opens his mouth and eyes wide before all life drains away and his *ame* leaves his body.

Uric pulls his sword free and wipes the blade clean on the warrior's garments, then declares, "He was not of the Hematite Order."

"No. The others were easily slain. This one would not have spoken anything useful, as is the way of the Onyx. He was a neophyte, and as such, nothing beyond the mission was disclosed. The Hematites are slow and weak-minded and would have broken at the first incentive of pain."

Branson rips open the warrior's vest and sees his proof. Five claw-like scars begin at the right of the man's abdomen to curve around the right side, ending at the beginning of his back. The mark of the lion, symboliz-ing power—the spirit animal and mark of an Onyx Order warrior.

"Come," Branson says. "Let us not waste more time."

Uric sheaths his sword before removing the dead warrior's body from the wagon bed. As he lifts it, he feels his wound burn with pain. His next duty must be to himself.

Branson walks around the litter of bodies, searching each one. They traveled very light. Only their weapons are present. Branson knows they must have a camp nearby for them to travel with nothing on them to eat or drink for any long period, so that is where the child would be taken. They could risk rescuing the boy, but it would certainly cost them their lives. With Uric's arm wounded, they would not stand a chance against more.

Branson collects his weapons from the corpses. He tears open each warrior's vest and notes that the one who had been standing above Uric shares the same marks as the Onyx warrior. Hurrying back to the wagon, he sees Uric hastily bandaging his arm with a torn strip of cloth from his shirt.

"I will clean that once we stop for the night," Branson says.

Uric nods, wincing as he pulls the bandage tight. Branson loads the wagon with the supplies that had been thrown out in the warriors' attempt to steal the children. Uric checks the infant, who seems to be complacent. Satisfied the child is well, he picks up the reins, awaiting Branson's lead.

Branson says, "There must be a camp near. These warriors had no food, nor horses to bring them here. We will travel until we cannot and make a great distance between them and us."

Branson mounts and begins at a trot fast enough to get them out of distance from another ambush, but not too strenuous for the baby.

The four, now a trio.

THREE

Night comes soon. They've covered a fair bit of ground already. Branson does not want to stop yet, but it would be troublesome traveling in the dark for very long. The baby needs to be fed, and Uric seems faint and looks pale.

Branson first helps Uric to the ground, where he rests his back against a log, apparently exhausted. Branson hands the baby to Uric, then prepares to feed and change him. After setting a small fire and warming some water, Branson bathes the child and puts fresh linens on him. He gives the child the wooden toy his brother dropped until he is ready to feed him. He heats more water to boiling. Then he gives Uric a drink of water from a waterskin and gently removes the torn cloth, now red from the blood, noting that the wound badly needs cleaning and will require stitches.

Uric sees the damage and winces. "Do you know how to stitch?" he asks, his eyes showing hope.

Branson nods, and Uric exhales, thanking the Great Spirit. Branson's father taught him suturing skills in case a severe wound ever required stitches and a healer was not within distance to attend. However, Branson's knowledge does not extend past that and bandaging.

Under Uric's specific direction, Branson fills a bowl with hot water and soaks a towel in it. He retrieves a stitch kit from Uric's satchel. He wrings out the towel and lays it carefully over the gash. Uric clenches his teeth more from the heat than the pain. Branson repeats the towel-laying three times, each time wiping around the wound, cleaning it thoroughly. He sanitizes the needle by heating it in the fire, then waits for Uric to signal he is ready. Uric nods his head and closes his eyes. Branson pierces the skin, beginning to mend the gash.

Uric does not move the entire time. He seems almost asleep but aware. Interesting, these seekers. Branson cuts a clean strip from a shirt and properly bandages the arm.

Branson cleans his hands and prepares a stew for their meal by mixing together a small amount of dried herbs and potatoes, then adding it to the pot of vegetables and water. He sets a small bowl of it to the side to cool while he dishes out meals for Uric and himself.

Uric eats his as if he hasn't eaten all day. He actually has a second bowl. It is a good sign to see that he still has an appetite; otherwise, it might mean fever and infection had already started to set in the wound.

Branson rushes through his meal so he can feed the child before he begins to whine. The silence brings comfort and awareness. He cradles the baby in his arm while slowly spoon-feeding him a slightly different stew; this with mashed potatoes and vegetables. The child smiles at him and reaches up to play with the spoon.

"He fits you," Uric observes.

Branson looks his way, confused. "What? Who?"

Uric laughs. "You are smiling. Haven't you noticed?"

Realizing, indeed, he was smiling, Branson quickly erases it from his face and shrugs. "This is very new to me."

"Do you have any family?" Uric asks, seeing this as an opportunity to learn more about the huntsman.

"Some. My father was a warrior and died in a battle against the Bloodstone Order when I was fourteen. My mother left to help take care of her sick sister in the Glen Clan once I was named huntsman. I have no siblings. Some cousins, but we are not close." He finishes feeding the baby and starts the burping phase from Uric's instructions.

"Any friends?"

"Yes. They are mostly huntsmen. I find little time to interact with others outside my service," Branson responds with his attention mainly on the babe.

"What could possibly take up so much of a huntsman's time?"

Branson looks sternly at Uric and retorts, "Huntsmen provide the food that sits at your table. It is our kills that are distributed throughout the clans. It is a great responsibility to provide for our people and we gladly accept it. It may take an entire day to kill even three beasts. Not to mention skinning and butchering the meat. It is many birth years before one is named huntsman because of this."

Huntsmen kill and apportion the meat for their entire order. Most are generally quiet and distant because their service requires they spend an enormous amount of time training and hunting. Patience and silence are taught to the point that it becomes part of their personality. It is very uncommon for a young huntsman to actively socialize with others outside the service, primarily because they spend the majority of their time with each other. Older huntsmen normally take up the duty of skinning and butchering the kills. Given the arduous responsibility, huntsmen typically find their mates later in life when time is most likely to be available.

Uric realizes his mistake. With a smile, he says, "My apologies, I meant no disrespect. I blame my ignorance of the other services. I offer my friendship, if you will have it."

Branson replies, "I accept. Now tell me what it is you seekers do?"

Uric shows outward shock at the huntsman's interest in his service. He explains enthusiastically, "Our service involves quite a bit of discipline and practice to be named spirit seeker. We use and keep the essence of life-giving energies. Some, not all. The skill varies from seeker to seeker. It is what enables us to be great healers. We can see and feel others' spirits. It aids in the agricultural life, in healing, and in reading people.

"We seekers are quite a gregarious sort, mainly because we interact with so many people because of our healing abilities. Our training provides our people with a clean living but also aids in military and political strategy, since we are able to detect untruths and intent—we 'see' beyond words. We tend to marry young, always drawn completely to our mate's *ame*."

Branson furrows his brow and asks, "Only one *ame*?"

Uric pauses, considering his next words, then clarifies, "It is possible your *ame* can call to more than one concurrently or after one dies." Uric finishes with a big smile and a protruding chest, exhibiting his pride in his service.

Branson isn't so easily impressed. "What do you mean by 'clean living'?"

"We maintain the forest and cleanse the water of our streams. The beasts you hunt must dwell somewhere. You must quench your thirst, as well as your appetite. Because of our Reach, we are the best advisors for the dewan and our clan leaders. Not to mention, our wives are known as the best midwives in all the orders."

Branson nods impassively. The baby has fallen asleep, but Branson still holds him, rocking him in his arms. "I recall you mentioning a wife and children. I have none, but you do. How do you find the time to tend to them?"

Uric laughs. "You sound as if you are referring to horses."

Branson narrows his eyes.

Uric continues as though he does not see Branson's expression, "My service does not require me to be away from my home for an entire day. I am with them after the sun wakes, as well as before it sleeps. Sometimes, I even have the entire day."

Branson looks at the baby thoughtfully and asks, "How were you able to find your wife?"

Uric smiles and looks at the thin silver ring adorning one of his soiled fingers. "Leesha. It was as if our *ames* spoke to each other first. I initially noticed her with her friends while they were bringing food to our sire's kitchen. I heard her laugh and looked toward the sound. It was her. She saw me and smiled. It was the most beautiful sight my eyes had ever seen. I courted her, and a year later she was my wife."

"And your children?"

"Two boys and a girl. My eldest son is now five, then my girl at three, and finally a baby boy some moons older than the baby you hold. She was with child when I left…. It was difficult to leave." He looks solemn for a moment. Then, shaking off the memory, he continues, "It is incredible what children can do to one's *ame*. They are a part of me as much as I am a part of them. I miss them very much."

He says this as he sees the vitality of Branson's spirit glowing … pulsing, rather.

"Do you think any man can be a father?" Branson asks.

"Yes, even the greatest evil can hold love for his offspring. To reproduce and protect what is created is the nature of the spirit."

Branson just nods, looking at the baby.

Seeing that Branson has completed his inquiry, Uric begins his: "You do not have a woman?"

Branson looks up, and after a moment of thought, he answers with a smile, then says, "Not one of any interest, but many of pleasure."

Both men laugh before Branson adds, "My social time is limited, so it is difficult to find a woman before another man sets his claim. I never cared to have a wife, though, just the companionship of a woman. But now I think that maybe I have changed since the beginning of this quest."

Branson moves to lay the baby down for the night, fussing over him for a while. He returns to quiet the fire a little.

Uric starts again, "It is odd. I have never spoken with a huntsman in so much detail or for this long before. Then I am joined with two on the highest, most valued of all quests. It is only now that we have a full conversation concerning something other than the Chozien."

Branson stretches. "Interesting indeed."

After an instant of consideration, Uric says gladly, "Then it is certain. We must have the Chozien."

Branson smiles. "I am pleased to share this honor with you, seeker." He stands and gathers his weapons to begin what remains of the dark watch. "You should rest. It will be a long day tomorrow."

Uric agrees, but before he can lie down completely, Branson adds, "The net that took the boy today was the same as in my vision."

It is the first time that Uric has ever been left speechless.

During his watch, Branson thinks about how he can get the boy back. He considers many well-planned strategies, but none will suffice. It hurts him that he has lost the boy. Once he figured that the boy was gone, though, he directed his attention to the Hematite/Onyx attack.

They didn't use any aerial attacks from arrows or projectiles, which suggested a hurried attack. With their numbers now so severely depleted, they wouldn't be tracking them any farther to steal the other Chozien. The Onyx were clever, so they wouldn't let their greed to have both Chozien interfere with their goal for power and influence—and thus would be satisfied with the one they had.

It seemed like he and Uric faced more attackers than there actually were because of the warriors' success in the first wave of attacks. The other warriors were probably from the Hematite Order, and they most likely ran into the fight, but at the sight of their fellow kinsmen being cut down, they decided otherwise, proving their cowardice by running away.

Branson remembered the words of the captured Onyx warrior: "Enjoy your days, for death is approaching." Stealing the Chozien after one had been claimed broke the rules of the *Quête*. Not even the wretched Bloodstone had ever attempted such a thing. Such an act could loosen the laws by which the orders were governed.

The Onyx Order is up to something, Branson muses.

He decides to also take Uric's watch, allowing him additional rest to recover from his wounds.

The time of a few sky shadows later, Branson readies the horses and loads the wagon before he wakes Uric. While stretching and flexing his arm, Uric winces slightly at its tenderness. While he prepares himself, Branson tends to the baby. He loses himself in playful laughter so much that Uric has to call to him that he is ready and they should get a move on. Branson picks the baby up and brings him to the wagon, placing him in the basket, wishing he had more time to spend with him.

They travel for some time before Branson admits fatigue and requests that he stretch out in the wagon bed and sleep. Uric agrees, of course, and takes the lead for most of the day.

Sleep in the back of a wagon proves unsettling. The ride is bumpy from the uneven trail, jostling at every protrusion and dip. However, Branson feels so exhausted that he sleeps right through it, but awakes at every stop to change Uric's bandage and the baby's napkin.

After one moon, and with the sun just dawning over the tops of the tall trees, the men see the beginnings of the Jade Order's territory. The air has already begun to cool, signaling the coming season of Falling Leaves. They welcome the weather, when the heat from the sun's rays will be abated by the crisp, cool, refreshing breeze. Falling Leaves is the most famed of all seasons because the weather works well in conjunction with the people while in the fields, crafting various items, or training.

Uric sees the aura of his home, brightened by the brilliance of his people's spirits. His body eases from any tension due to the warm, joyful feeling from their energies, reminding him of the comfort he's headed to.

Branson beams with pride and stops the wagon to lift the baby from the basket and carry him. He wants to share this blissful experience with the Chozien. He regrets that he cannot share the moment with the boy as well.

It will be a day and a half until they reach the first clan holding and then another a quarter moon before they reach the dewan's house in the Jade's spirit hold, where their journey began and where it would end, presenting the infant Chozien to their leader.

They tell their great news to every kinsmen they pass. Even knowing it goes against seeker training to alter the course of nature, Uric uses his Reach to bloom some dormant trees.

Once they finally reach their spirit hold, lires—official couriers of every hold—will be sent to all clans with invitations to attend the Beni, the Jade Order's customary jubilee in honor of their claim to the Chozien. There have been five Chozien since the last time the Jade Order last held this festival. The clans will then prepare to leave their holds and gather there, where they will celebrate the presence of the newest Chozien for three days.

FOUR

Agreat crowd has gathered, and an enormous cheer goes up as the trio enters through the gate into the courtyard inside the spirit hold.

Branson raises the baby high for a moment, and the cheer increases in volume. The baby smiles when he brings him down and cradles him in his arms. Many people reach up to touch the baby, but Branson shields him protectively. Before the people's excitement becomes uncontrollable, they hurry their horses along to the dewan's greeting hall. The guards speak to the people about the upcoming celebration and advise them that their time would be better spent in preparation.

Upon reaching the house, they see that the dewan stands out in front of his home at the top of the ten steps leading into his hall.

He calls out to them, "Stay where you are. It would be an honor to come before the Chozien."

To outsiders, this dewan could be considered young, based on his appearance. He is approaching four and a half decades, tall and straight with a full head of brown hair, not a strand of gray, sporting a small beard on his chin. His face holds not one wrinkle except for the tiny ones by his eyes when he smiles. His build shows strength and well-being. His walk radiates authority and wisdom. He wears a dark-green, sleeveless robe outlined in light green and silver, with soft, dark-green pants underneath. The robe is made of fine cotton and falls to his knees. The sides are secured with a roped belt made of black leather. Thick silver armbands adorn his upper arms, one on each. There is a silver hoop earring in the left ear, and around his neck hangs the medallion of the Jade Order, depicting a hawk and a bear with the sun in the background.

He stands before the men and baby and greets them, "Namaste."

The men bow their heads and respond in unison, "Namaste, Dewan Gaylen."

Gaylen reaches for the infant, picking him up and asking, "Is this the Chozien, then?"

Branson answers, "It is, Dewan."

Gaylen looks out the corner of his eyes at Branson. "Do not insult me, huntsman. This *infant* does not match the age of the Calling."

Uric answers, "We should call a meeting with the clan leaders to discuss this matter. There were two Chozien: a boy matching the Calling and this infant. The Great Spirit would not allow us to find them until the child was born and able."

Still not placated, the dewan asks, "Where is the boy, then? Bring him to me."

The men lower their eyes, and Branson says, "He was stolen by warriors of the Hematite and Onyx Orders."

Shock, rage, and curiosity fuel Gaylen's outburst: "What's this? Stealing the Chozien!"

Before the men can supply their speculations, he hands the baby back to Branson and calls for his most senior-ranked warrior in the order, elected with the rank of general: "Haru! Haru!"

Haru rushes up from his position at the bottom of the stairs. "Yes, Dewan."

"Send our fastest riders to all clan leaders requesting their immediate attendance. Be discreet, though. I will also send a second message inviting the clans here for the Beni celebration. We will carry on as if nothing has happened."

"It will be done," Haru says, then runs off, calling for his men to gather the lires.

Gaylen then calls for another—the nursemaid to his own children: "Suriah, you will care for the infant until the Appointing."

Suriah walks to Branson and holds her hands out, waiting for him to give her the baby.

Branson looks at him once more, smiles, and gives him a soft squeeze, promising his return. He hands the baby to her.

Suriah smiles and nods her understanding to take care of the child.

The men are treated as honored guests and given rooms in the guest wing of the dewan's home. Clan leaders are the only known people to have had the privilege to stay there. The men will reside there for the length of the celebration, and then they will return to their own clans.

Branson and Uric are placed in adjacent rooms. Their satchels and supplies are brought to them and their horses tended to. Their remaining food is fed to the dogs.

The dewan's home is organized in a way that allows for an easy flow of many people. The greeting hall is first and used for entertaining guests and always for dining. It is a vast space with one long dining table having twenty chairs per side, as well as a green runner with decorative silver and golden hawks down the middle. The walls have portraits of the great bear—the Jade Order's selected protector and guide—alongside other wild beasts. There are also hanging quilted pictures in the Jade Order colors, softening the stone walls, compliments of the dewan's wife, Dewana Zahrine. Two closed doors lead to the parlor, and a wide-open doorway leads to the kitchen. A fireplace deep enough to hold four, six-foot burning logs is at the far wall, unused during this season.

Many stewards and maids bustle about, already organizing, cleaning, and preparing for the coming celebration. The news has spread through the household.

A stone staircase fixed to the wall is located to the right of the main entrance. This leads to the upper level and bedrooms belonging to the dewan and his wife, their children, and guests. The rooms for Branson and Uric seem to be designed identically, both of them spacious, with soft, thick furs covering the stone floor. The beds are long and wide enough to fit tall, heavy men, also covered with furs and positioned on the right wall. Against the opposite wall is a dresser made of cedar, judging by the soft scent of the wood. Two cushioned chairs sit by one barred window on the left; a small table stands between the chairs, a candle-lamp on it. No adornments hang on the walls.

The windows have shutters to close and lock against heavy rain or wind. However, as it is the day, it is bright and warm where the light touches. Heavy curtains are there to draw over the windows to dim the room. Candle-lamps sitting on the dresser and small table will provide a soft glow later, transforming the room into a meditative haven.

These rooms would be called plain by eyes used to grandeur, but to the two men, they are magnificent.

Bathing tubs are brought to the men for baths to calm the senses and relieve muscles. The water is fragrant with the oils of rose, fig, and ginger. Female attendants, skilled in the art of hospitality and holistic relaxation, stand by, waiting.

Uric does not feel comfortable with a woman washing him other than his wife, so he excuses his attendant, expressing his deepest apologies.

Branson, on the other hand, strips himself and eases into his hot bath. He lies back and closes his eyes while the woman wets his hair and slowly runs her fingers through it. She massages his scalp, neck, shoulders, arms, and legs. She bathes him thoroughly, making sure every part of his body is clean. She washes away all the dirt and grime from his travels and smooths all tensed and cramped muscles from camping, fighting, and riding horseback.

As she tells him she is finished, she holds up a long towel, waiting for him to step out of the tub. He rises and pours a bucket of lukewarm water over his head, the liquid feeling cool to him. While she dries him, he takes note of her; she is a very thorough attendant, removing every drop of water from his skin. She ruffles his hair playfully, and they share a brief laugh. He stretches out on the bed, where she massages his back. She kneads his body, using firm pressure with her elbows, untangling any knots before they set in. Just before Branson feels himself falling into a comfortable sleep, she removes her weight from him and tells him to stand so that she can rub a forestry-aromatic balm on him. He does as she requests. She fills her palm with the oil and gently rubs her hands together. Branson can smell the scent released from the oil by the warmth her skin generates: frankincense.

She begins at the nape of his neck, rubbing the oil until it has blended with his skin before she moves down his back and repeats her attentions, first over his shoulders, then down his arms. She does so in similar fashion down his chest. Next, she lays a soft linen blanket across his lap. Branson holds his breath while she spreads the oil over his hips, thighs, and calves, praying his body does not betray his thoughts. Too late. She does not seem to take offense or notice at all. He wonders with a smirk if he should be offended by her reaction or not.

She sits cross-legged, comfortably, at the base of his feet, tilting her head to the side. *What is she thinking about?* he muses. Then he groans as she kneads her thumbs in the various parts of his right foot. He never realized the amount of tension his little toe could release or how much stress he could carry in his heel and sole—or how great it feels to have his ankle rotated until now.

A clipping of the toenails completes his partial grooming. She fits him with a sleeveless white undershirt and dark-green pants. She wraps soft linen around his waist, the fabric falling to the ankles in the standard Jade Order colors, and then she places a matching vest over him—cut in a "V" shape where the head and chest are. Finally, she finishes the ensemble by clasping a belt of roped black leather around his waist and fitting him with sandals.

Branson takes in her beauty while she dresses him. Her hair is dark brown and thick, twisted in small braids that run behind her head and extend to the middle of her back. Soft and small curly wisps at her hairline give her a youthful presence. Her face is focused with smoothly arched eyebrows and full lips. Her body is petite but firm, her skin chestnut-colored, and she wears a light-green, sleeveless dress made of thin material, possibly silk. Indeed, she is more than beautiful.

She finally speaks again: "You will wear this until your clothes are freshly washed and mended." Her voice is quiet and kind.

He smiles and tilts his head slightly to the left unknowingly.

She looks him over once. She tousles his hair, then arranges it neatly.

"This will have to do for now. I will send someone to trim your hair." She turns to exit the room.

Branson is intrigued at her disregard to his obvious interest. He stops her with a bold question to an attendant from a guest of the dewan's: "May I know your name?"

She stops and looks over her shoulder. "Ahni."

"Ahni. It is a beautiful name, fitting its owner."

She smiles and replies, "You are kind." She exits, leaving him with her image.

Branson waits a few moments before he leaves his room and knocks on Uric's door. Uric opens the door dressed in the same attire right down to the sandals. They both look each other over and chuckle at their matching clothing.

Uric is the first to speak through his amusement: "I was beginning to think you had fallen asleep."

"My attendant made for great company," he replies with a smile.

Uric raises his eyebrows, saying, "Ah, yes. I sent mine away. My spirit is not at ease with the attendants."

"Well, my friend, if your stomach is as empty as mine, we should hunt for a healthy meal to appease our appetites."

Uric agrees and the men journey to the kitchen, where they are met with the dewana, Zahrine, organizing the menu for the clan leaders' arrival and stay, as well as the celebration.

Bowing their heads and lowering their eyes, the pair formally greet her with, "Namaste, Dewana Zahrine."

She accepts and responds, "Namaste, Branson and Uric. So you are the Bringers of the Chozien?"

They smile that their dewana has greeted them by name—another honor.

"Yes, Dewana," they reply in unison.

She is a pleasant woman—short, coming up to Branson's chest, and lively. Her hair is a silky almond color, a bit darker than her skin, tied up in a bun with two small strands in the front curling past her shoulders, hinting at its length. Her eyes are hazel and she has a respectful manner when speaking, confirming her status and kinsmen's loyalty. She wears a silver necklace accenting her clothing.

Her dress looks like one full piece of cloth, or else made well to appear as such. The stitching is such that the dress fits her shape, which is a slight bosom and sound. A scooping neckline stops above her breasts, with sheer sleeves featuring a fashionable cut made inside the arm to reveal some skin. The dress is a shade lighter than the average male's dark green, with silver lining fitting her body decently.

She returns their smiles and opens conversation informally: "There is no need for such formality in the kitchen. You boys must be hungry. I have had an extensive spread arranged for the two Bringers of the Chozien. Sit at the table and I will call for my husband to join you."

They reply, "Yes, Dewana."

The men walk to the long dining table and sit, awaiting their dewan's arrival. Just a few moments later, Gaylen enters and the men stand.

"Please sit and let us enjoy this meal my wife has prepared."

He claps his hands twice and servants flow in from the kitchen, carrying big platters of succulent meats, warm herbed bread, spiced vegetables, and sweet-smelling pastries. They place an empty plate in front of each man and a cup for drink. The dewana pours a dry red wine in each of the men's cups and places a filled pitcher of it on the table. Before she leaves to finish her preparations, she kisses her husband lightly on the lips and brushes her fingertips against his cheek. He smiles after her.

The men close their eyes and thank the Great Spirit for the plentiful hunting and for the nourishment of their bodies. Once finished, they begin filling their plates by tearing pieces off the various meats, picking at vegetables, and ripping at portions of the different breads. The men sup in silence until their eating slows enough for them to converse.

After swallowing a juicy piece of rabbit, the dewan asks, "Where did you find them?" He licks his fingers to not let any part of the rabbit's life go to waste.

Uric points to Branson, and so Branson answers around chewing some vegetables, "In the Barrens."

Amazed, the dewan inquires, "A child does not live past a full year there. How were you able to find two?"

After swallowing, Branson again answers, "It was a light in the darkness. The boy held it and I followed it." And then with disgust, he says, "Their parents are worthless and did not argue once I gave them a day's worth of food and water."

Gaylen nods. "The Barrens—Wait, were there not three of you in your band?"

Head bowed, tone somber for the fallen huntsman, Branson replies, "You speak of Yuen. He was killed on watch during the night by some of the wandering Lost."

Uric adds, "We heard the struggle. We killed the bandits, but it was too late to save him. We did not count on there being so many so far from the city."

Gaylen asks, "How many?"

"Eight. Yuen had killed three by the time we engaged in the fight," Uric answers.

Gaylen offers, "I will notify his clan and we shall celebrate his sacrifice. He died bravely defending his order." He steeples his fingers in front of him, then muses aloud, "An attack after our order has successfully located the Chozien, the Hematite ally with the Onyx, and now the Lost are bold enough to drift past their borders." He shakes his head. He fists his hands and puts them under his chin as he continues, "Something is ... strange. You two will attend the meeting with the clan leaders. This is not to be discussed openly. Our people must not be distressed in these upcoming festive days."

He waits for their nod before he finishes, "You are guests in my home. Feel free to join your service here for training or contribution, although it is not necessary. Enjoy."

Gaylen stands, as do Branson and Uric, and then the dewan picks out two pastries and takes his leave.

Branson and Uric finish their cups of wine, a fine burgundy as fragrant as it is light. Perfect for a midday meal, surprising them, as they are used to the hard, gut-rotting swill at the taverns. They consume a few more pastries, then depart. Licking their fingers and trying to suppress their belches with little effect, the men take the opportunity to explore the grounds of the spirit hold. They have never come here out of leisure or visitation, only for celebrations when providing their services— Branson hunting food for the feast and Uric either cleansing water, rooting the fruit trees, or in the company of his family. It is an exciting allowance to participate in the celebration, especially one such as this.

They spend the rest of the day walking the hold. It is exceptionally well built and covers many acres of land. The taverns vary in size, some even being two stories. It seems appropriate, being that this hold has the most outsiders from visiting orders, as do all spirit holds. They see an enormous amount of bustling about: traders bargaining or loudly advertising their crafts and how unique they are, blacksmiths working in their open smithies with their apprentices at hand and creating all sorts of weapons from different metals, seamstresses mending clothes or taking measurements, entertainers juggling, playing tricks, or acting, laundresses scrubbing laboriously at clothing, dyers with their rolled-up sleeves and ladles stirring fabric in huge round vats of colored water, and the many voices of men, women, and children laughing and enjoying each other's company. The aromas of the Jade Order's renowned spices from cooked meats, vegetables, and stews—and the fresh bread just out the oven—all remind Uric of his home with his family.

They pass by the warriors' enormous bunkhouses and their gigantic training yard. Some warriors are training horses, others work on sword techniques, still more spar, and many pull wagons, lift boulders, or engage in other strength exercises. Branson and Uric know from their own clans that warriors practice endurance fiercely by running hills and long distances with weighted packs on their backs, with bunkhouses serving as the residence of unmarried warriors.

Farther still—far off from the rest of the hold—they come upon the tannery, where hides are being hung and tanned. It is an incredibly different place from the tannery in Branson's own clan hold, this one being divided into sections, with many of the elder huntsmen working tirelessly. A high stone wall encloses the tannery on three sides.

Branson introduces himself and asks where he will be able to find the chief huntsman. They welcome him warmly and direct him to the training field and house where novices study. Branson thanks the men and leaves with the intention of visiting the training field the next day.

Uric doesn't fancy the smell by his upturned nose and the distance he puts between him and the tannery. Laughing, Branson hurries his visit so that Uric will not lose his meal. Toward the end of their private tour of the hold, they come upon the spirit house.

Spirit seekers mill about, laughing and socializing. Uric greets his fellow seekers with embraces. All have shaved, tattooed heads, in addition to tattoos on their necks, with most extending onto their faces. Uric introduces Branson as his friend and shakes many welcoming hands. He also asks after the spirit keeper, Keno—the champion seeker appointed by the dewan—and is informed that he has taken the novices and many of the others to the surrounding forest for training. Uric is astonished that there are more seekers than he sees now.

Unmarried seekers occupy the spirit house. Young novices live in their homes with their parents until they are named.

On their way back to the dewan's home, they see that four plots of ground, each measuring of nearly a thousand kinsmen, have been cleared and servants are setting up the outdoor cooking apparatuses and tables. Because of the number of people about to visit, huge amounts of food will have to be prepared. The meat will be cooked on thick, sizable spits fit to hold considerable weight over open fire pits. This task will take the entire day and be served in the evening. Only the dewan, General Haru, clan leaders, and their wives and children will have seats at the tables.

The sun just begins to sleep when the men return to the dewan's house. When they walk into the greeting hall, they see Gaylen, Zahrine, and their four children having their supper. The conversation stops, and they all look toward the men as they enter.

Gaylen waves them over. "Come and join us."

The men walk to the table and apologize for their tardiness.

His wife waves off the apology. "Nonsense. You two must have wanted to see the hold and visit your service. Please sit and eat. Children, make room for them."

The children opposite their mother move down two chairs, providing spaces for the pair by their father at the head of the table. Branson and Uric sit, and two servants provide them with plates and cups. They fill their plates again with similar food from midday, with the exception of the pastries so as not to tempt the children.

Gaylen introduces his children: "These are my sons, Warwick and Nolen, and my daughters, Koren and Leaha."

The children nod and smile as their names are called.

Gaylen then nods to Uric and Branson. "Children, these men are Branson and Uric, who brought the Chozien to us."

The men nod in greeting.

Warwick is the eldest at eighteen; he has his father's brown hair, but thicker and cut close to his head. He has a short beard on his chin and a physically fit body. Next is the young lady, Koren, at sixteen. She has her mother's face and her father's hair, braided in one braid tossed over one shoulder. The boy, Nolen, at nine, and the girl, Leaha, at seven, have their mother's eyes and much of both their parents in them.

Warwick asks, "My father says you found the Chozien in the Barrens. Is this true?"

Branson confirms, "It is."

"What are the Barrens like?" Warwick asks.

Branson shrugs and replies, "A pitiful place, not worth looking at or living in."

"Many sad spirits there," Uric adds.

Eyes bright, Nolen smiles and chimes in, "Did you have to fight anyone?"

Gaylen laughs at his son's eagerness while his mother shushes him, making him apologize.

"My son has an interest in the warrior class, which he began only last year." Gaylen winks at him. "He began his training at a late age at my wife's insistence."

She returns, "I was hoping he would change his mind."

"Ah, Mistress, if I may?" Branson requests.

At her nod, he says, "It is very noble of your son to want to protect his hold. It is a sign of a great *ame* and honorable courage. My father was a warrior once."

Nolen perks up and exclaims, "Really?"

Branson points to his wrist bands as he replies, "Yes. These were once his. You will receive the same in time."

Nolen nearly falls out of his chair in excitement before his mother can calm him. A few questions and laughs later, the children retire to their bedrooms and the men to Gaylen's parlor room. The room is spacious, with twelve thickly cushioned chairs of dark green. Shelves and tables line the walls. Two quilted hangings—one of a bear and another of a hawk—are all the decorations Gaylen allows from his wife in this room. The men sit and begin to talk casually. A servant enters with a tray of small glasses partially filled with a sharp, light-brown libation for each man.

Gaylen takes a short swallow. "I sent my fastest riders to all nine clans today. However, the clan leaders of the farthest distance have left since you entered the border and word traveled. I expect them to all be in attendance within three days. I will have my general, Haru, and spirit keeper, Keno, here. My chief huntsman will be away hunting, but you will brief him on the discussion," he instructs Branson.

He continues explaining where the clan leaders will sit and where they will stand. Gaylen also explains the two men's involvement throughout the entire ceremony.

"You will both stand behind Haru at the end of each day of the Beni for the Chozien's Presenting, Appointing, and Naming ceremonies. Step forward when I introduce you and then back away behind the general afterward. The two of you will eat with me and the clan leaders at one table.

Uric, your wife will eat at the table with the other siras. I sent for your family at your arrival. I have made arrangements for them to stay where the clan leader's families are, at the largest and finest of all my inns."

Uric nods his appreciation.

Gaylen leans back in his chair and inhales audibly. "Now … tell me of these strange events."

Uric begins, "Strange, indeed. Branson found the Chozien in the Barrens. But it was two, not one. We searched for many days and found nothing until Branson sought out a shining light. It was not until then that I felt their spirits. They are indeed the Chozien."

At Gaylen's nod, Uric continues, "We lacked the supplies needed for an infant, so we decided to stock for those at a Hematite clan. We considered it to be safe since they have declared neutrality. I noticed, though, that their spirits seemed unusually warm and they were pleasant in an offhand kind of way. Guards were posted at the inn we stayed in. Even more suspicious …" Uric looks to Branson for him to finish the recounting.

Reluctantly, Branson picks up the discussion: "Sentries followed and watched our camp for a quarter moon. They staged an attack from the trees, many warriors in Hematite clothing."

Gaylen narrows his eyes and tilts his head, noticing the hint.

Branson says, "The boy was stolen while we fought. We killed all the warriors, save one. We questioned him. He mentioned something briefly about the adopted son of his dewan returning, but that was all. We released his *ame,* and underneath his clothing, we found the marks of an Onyx warrior. There was one more like him. It confirms that the Hematite and Onyx have an alliance."

The two men sit in restless silence, not able to read their dewan's face. He sits motionless, unmoved.

Gaylen strokes his chin before responding, "You will tell this to the clan leaders only when we meet and not before. I will think about this more. You may go and rest now; the day has been long."

Draining the last of their drink, Branson and Uric stand and bow their heads saying, "Good eve, Dewan."

Before the men leave, Gaylen says, "You did well. One is always better than none at all."

"Yes, Dewan," Uric says.

Branson grunts.

After the men leave, Gaylen takes another gulp from his cup. He exhales sadly as he leans back in his chair. He rakes his hand through his hair. He shakes his head and says to himself, "A great war is coming."

FIVE

Branson is eager to return to his room. He cannot seem to erase the image of the beautiful Ahni from his throughs. He replays her voice in his mind, saying her name to himself, "Ahni."

As he enters his room, an attendant is waiting for him, dressed in the same material but a different style—not Ahni, though.

Disappointed, he says, "You did not attend me earlier today."

She shakes her head and confirms, "No."

"Why is Ahni not here?"

"You want her here as well?" she asks, confused.

"No."

By her immediately lowering her eyes, he realizes that his tone might have been inadvertently harsh.

"Am I not pleasing?" she asks.

He exhales deeply before explaining, "My apologies. I do not mean to appear dissatisfied. It would seem I have an attraction to Ahni."

She lifts her head with a single raised eyebrow. "Oh, you are the one she spoke of." Deflating his immediate excitement, she educates him on the law: "It is forbidden for attendants to ... involve ... themselves with the dewan's guests. The punishment is banishment from his service ... for both."

He now understands Ahni's sometimes aloof behavior with him earlier and her evasion of him now. To displease the dewan resulting in banishment would require the offender to relocate to a new clan and, in some cases, a new order. Rumors of the eviction would spread like fire on hay throughout the entire hold, making it impossible to find a service willing to hire her. No one would employ a kinsman who had so displeased the dewan.

"Will you give her a message for me?" he asks.

She nods.

"Say this: Branson Kuo-Lin desires her affection and will wait until he is no longer the dewan's guest to seek her out."

The attendant nods. "I will give it to her." She steps aside and motions for him to come farther into the room so that she can prepare him for the evening. "Please?"

He shakes his head. "Just the message."

"It will be done," she replies, closing the door behind her.

It is a long night for Branson. His eyes refuse to close the majority of the night. Every time he shuts them, he sees Ahni. When he does drift off to slumber at times, disappointment in not seeing her interrupts his sleep and confuses him. He feels like a silly boy with youthful infatuation. Her voice rings in his ears, and her smile makes his heart race. This different and new feeling makes every position in the bed seem uncomfortable. He tosses and turns throughout the night until the graying of the sky.

Waking to hard knocks at his door, Branson drags himself out of the bed and trudges to the door, pulling it open.

Uric stands smiling in the doorway, wearing his usual garb. Responding to Branson's disheveled appearance, he says, "Slept well, did you?"

"What is it, seeker?" Branson asks groggily.

"It is time to train. Get dressed."

"Wait," is all the answer Uric gets before Branson shuts the door.

After a few long moments, Branson opens the door fully clad in his own huntsman clothing, their clothes having been returned to them the evening before. The men walk down the stairs into the greeting hall, where the table has food for breaking their fast. The dishes range from fresh fruits to thick, creamy oatmeal. Seeing that some of the dishes have been picked over already, they deem it appropriate to eat.

Everything is prepared to perfection: the eggs are soft and fluffy, the muffins are full of a variety of berries and nuts, and the sliced meats are succulent, with a hint of honey. The men eat their fill, gulp down the rest of their freshly squeezed juice from grapefruits and oranges, then make their way to their respective services. They separate, Branson to the huntsmen field and Uric to the spirit house.

Branson hopes that some hard training will ease his mind of the beautiful Ahni. He locates the chief huntsman, an older man with gray streaking his hair. The man introduces himself as Len. He seems delighted that Branson is interested in training with them. He shows Branson to the training yard, where several others are practicing close combat with and without weapons, training with alternative weaponry, and performing routine exercises. Being the ever-eager student, Branson delves into combat training.

He spars with three other huntsmen, each taking turns defending against three opponents. The men have been huntsmen for some birth years more than he, and Branson knows that the training here is more strenuous than at any of the Jade's clans. The men move continuously with feints and lunges, planning their attacks.

One of the shorter huntsmen teaches Branson leg assaults from the ground. The man moves on the earth as if he floats right above it. His agility amazes Branson, and he immediately latches on to the man for more ground training. He uses his hands and arms as leverage while swinging his legs, catching Branson in the midsection or taking him down at the knees or ankles.

A taller man demonstrates speed with swift hand blows. If the man lands a blow, Branson is immediately hit in three different places repeatedly, making him wince and protect the area, leaving another open for a strike.

The third uses verbal taunts as a distraction. He mocks Branson for his fighting abilities and says he only succeeded in finding the Chozien because a seeker was watching his back. His barbs provoke Branson, clouding his judgment and his peripheral vision of the other two opponents, who promptly, and with apparent amusement, pummel him as his reward for his appeal to the distraction.

Branson trains with them until it is time to eat the midday meal. It is a small one consisting of fruits, meat slices, bread, and water. The men advise Branson on different techniques he should learn and practice. They tell him the benefits of having such skills: defense against a loose beast from boars to deer, and overcoming multiple opponents without relying on a weapon. Branson is thoroughly interested, and after the meal, he asks if the men can train him more. They happily agree.

Later, Branson limps back to his room, rubbing his side. He makes a mental note to remember not to be so enthusiastic tomorrow. He aches so much that he excuses himself from dinner and asks for his meal to be sent to his room. He ends up sending another attendant away and soaking for some time in a tub of steaming water. He closes his eyes, thinking of a better way to rid his thoughts of the woman.

Finally, he cleans himself and rinses with a bucket of cool water over his head. He sits to eat his now cold dinner. Strangely, although he is accustomed to eating alone, this routine feels incomplete, and his solitude renders him ... lonely. While he eats, servants come and lug the tub away. Behind them enters the same attendant from the night before.

She smiles, then says, "She, too, will wait."

With that said, she hurries out.

Branson smiles. Still, his sleep is restless, with anticipation replaced by the idea of nervous chivalry.

The next morning, Uric is the first to rise again; only, this time Branson uses less force when slamming the door after Uric awakens him.

Uric seems to be in high spirits this morning. This amuses Branson. It is difficult for him to imagine Uric any more jovial than he sees him every day.

Soon enough, Uric reveals the reason for his extremely cheerful mood: "My family has arrived. I'll be visiting with them today. Would it be too much to ask for you to meet them?"

With surprise, Branson replies, "Me? Well, of course ... I would be honored, seeker."

Uric chuckles. "You are beyond my understanding, huntsman."

The men share grins all the way to the dining table. When they enter the greeting hall, five of the nine clan leaders are breaking their fast and enjoying the presence of each other's company. The sires present are Harwen of the Huin Clan, Remy of the Zin Clan, Connor of the Rhyne Clan, Clayton of the June Clan, and Marquis of the Glen Clan. All of them wear the medallion afforded to their title, depicting the sun and a bear. Two of the leaders are those of Branson and Uric's clans.

The gathering turns toward the men, and without delay, they begin congratulating the men with slaps on their backs. Harwen, Uric's clan leader, is a burly baritone yet, interestingly enough, mild-mannered. He exudes refinement and civility that his short frame and broad shoulders contradict.

He seems genuine with his compliments: "The Huin Clan is proud to have such a seeker."

Uric clasps forearms with his sire with pride. "I am honored to represent the Huin Clan."

Remy, Branson's sire, squeezes his shoulder. "It is good for the Jade Order what you have done."

Branson shows the same respect to his sire in clasping forearms. "The Zin Clan has prepared me well."

Remy is slightly shorter than Branson, although Branson always feels as though he has to raise his head when speaking with him. Remy's build is similar to Uric's—slim but muscular. His hair falls loosely just past his shoulders, and a trimmed goatee adds to his quiet manner. His voice is deep but formal. Branson's persona clearly mirrors that of his sire.

This display reveals some insight of Remy as a clan leader. For Branson to replicate his character to match his sire so much that it is easily observed, suggests that Remy is an active participant in his clan's society. He is visible and approachable, and it's also possible he trains with others in their services. Unique, as most sires tend to shy away from the populace as if they have somehow ascended to a greater height and the merest socialization with the public would somehow lasso their ankle, dragging them from their self-proclaimed pedestal.

The clan leaders ask many times the reason for their requested expedient attendance. Remembering the dewan's order, the two men decline to answer. Feeling the heat of the intense curiosity and not wanting to break under the pressure, the pair quickly excuse themselves to avoid any further questions.

Branson accompanies Uric to the inn where his family is staying. The dewan has been good on his word for lodging Uric's family. The inn is quite grand. There are high ceilings with chandeliers that extend six arms, each with a miniature plate holding candles the color of the tusks of the mammoth elephants, with these lit on overcast days and during the evenings. The place carries the scent of fragrant flowers and mild spices of cinnamon from the kitchen. The floors are beautifully polished stone. The counter at the bar looks sleek and clean, with the barkeep behind it serving drinks and carrying on casual conversation with some patrons. The dining area holds twenty tables, with ample room between them. The fireplace appears to be just the size to warm the inn during the cold seasons but not too great to overpower the room. A swinging door by the bar obviously leads to the kitchen, as waitresses flow in and out with trays of food for guests at the tables, seemingly the sire's families, as Branson notices spouses and children in majority.

Another doorway farther from the bar leads to the guest quarters. Branson and Uric go through this entrance to reveal stairs on the far right wall to a second floor of rooms. The first floor has a small lobby area, and doors line the walls that continue on behind the corners into a hall. Another high ceiling with an identical chandelier hangs in the center of the ceiling over the lobby. These candles are lit, illuminating the entrance.

Normally, those already staying at the inn who are not in the immediate sires' families would be moved to the second floor. However, Uric's family members are considered honored guests and hold the same, if only temporary, status as a sire's.

Since Uric's family is one of the first to arrive, they have been given a room on the first floor. This might annoy, perhaps even infuriate some of the siras, since one of the later arrivals will have to be placed on the second floor, an inconvenience shared by many. As Uric is not a sire, his family's presence among them will certainly cause purposeful isolation.

But a room on the first floor will trigger pretentious protests from the other "misplaced" patrons—protests that will be ignored by the owner.

Uric walks forward, turning the corner and down the hall. The halls have individual candles on the walls to light the path, but these are not lit. Light from the tall, barred window at the end of the hall and the chandelier proves sufficient. Uric stops at a door on the left and knocks.

A tall woman opens the door. She has reddish brown hair pulled back into one braided bun, and her eyes are a soft brown, with high cheekbones accenting her slow smile. Her skin is tanned by the sun's rays, and her posture suggests her weariness from traveling with two young children and an infant. A simple necklace of smoothed jade jewels circles her strong neck, as if fixed to it as a source for its own beauty, drawing the spirit of its owner to soften its raw state of crystalline stone, as though it still possesses its natural rigidity before it was taken from the land.

The woman's eyes begin to glisten, and she smiles, unable to speak.

"Leesha," Uric whispers before he captures his wife in a warm, affectionate embrace. He releases her, saying, "I have missed you."

"And I, you," she replies, touching the side of his face, tears now trickling down her cheeks.

Before Uric can say anything else, two children run to him, clutching each leg and exclaiming, "Da! Da!"

He laughs and scoops both of them up, giving them a tight squeeze.

"I have missed my little ones. Did you mind your mother?" he says, smiling wide.

The girl answers first, "Yes, Da."

The little boy looks to his mother first, then pokes his bottom lip out and answers quietly, "I tried really hard."

Uric looks to his wife for help.

She crosses her arms. "Davin has been fighting."

Uric says, "It is too soon for you to be training, but I don't see any harm in practicing."

"Uric!" his wife exclaims with her hands on her hips.

Uric laughs, and Branson smiles a little.

Remembering Branson, Uric steps farther into the room. "Come, my friend, and meet my life."

Branson joins Uric in the room and closes the door.

Uric begins the introductions: "Branson, this is my wife, Leesha; my son, Davin; my daughter, Kari, and—"

Uric stops speaking and puts his children down. He walks over to the crib near the bed and lifts up a sleeping baby.

He returns and finishes, "And this is little Romin." He kisses the infant on his forehead before placing him back in the crib.

It turns out that the children are just as friendly as their father. Davin walks up to Branson and waves his hand in greeting. Kari smiles up at him but stays close to her parents.

"Have you all eaten?" Uric asks.

"No, the children woke up a moment ago. I just finished feeding Romin."

"I will have food brought to the room. We can all eat here," Uric says.

Branson and Uric walk to the dining room, and Uric has meals prepared and sent to the room.

They clasp forearms and plan to meet for dinner at the dewan's home. He leaves Uric to enjoy his family and heads toward the huntsmen's field. Today, he plans to take it easy and train with his swords. Instead of using his true blades, he trades them in for wooden ones.

All huntsmen use the same weapons: twin short swords—longer than the common dagger and shorter than an ordinary sword, designed specifically for close combat. Because of the stealth and quick reflexes gained from training, the weapons complement their attacks. The weapons are Branson's favorite, and he trains frequently with them.

Branson begins with a few practice exercises, from lunging to jumping to sidestepping attacks. He partners with a huntsman close to his height and build. They square up to each other and begin to circle, moving closer every so often. The man suddenly lowers his guard a little and strides toward Branson, who shifts his feet, preparing for a sidestepping combination, gripping the hilt of one practice sword to be ready to hit him hard at the back of the head.

He waits for the man to close the gap between them before sidestepping. In a fluid motion, the man raises one sword for a downward slash. Branson moves to block the slash while shifting to sidestep just as the man stops his strike in midair. Too late, though; he is already in motion, and Branson eyes him for a strike of his own. But the man crosses his practice swords in front of him, locking Branson's lead blade between them. Branson finds himself immediately off balance from having his planned attack interrupted. He hurries to readjust his stance, but before his foot can touch the ground, the man puts a full boot in his stomach, knocking him backward.

The man speaks in an emotionless voice: "If you are going to base your attacks on defense, then do not show what your next move will be. Attacks are not planned; they are reflexes. Your stance and foot shift told me you were preparing to sidestep—a common defensive assault. Remember, your posture and hilt grips speak to your opponent."

Branson nods and stands ready. This time, the man tests Branson's swordplay, quite impressive and quick. Branson showcases his different hilt-gripping techniques and evasive defense. Still, it seems too easy for his sparring partner to defend himself. Branson tries to focus on his own attack and force the man on the defense. The huntsman finally puts an end to the scene by swinging his forearm and stopping just before he hits Branson's nose. Branson closes his eyes briefly, his pride bruised, and moves to stand ready again.

The man instructs, "A huntsman's best weapon is himself. Do not rely solely on your blades. You had multiple opportunities to hit me, but you avoided them because neither of your weapons were in position for a strike. You will tire yourself before your opponent."

Indeed, the huntsman is correct. Even in his battle with the Hematite warriors, Branson waited until he had overwhelmed his opponents before striking a blow. Still, even with his own lack of polished skills, any huntsman is likely to defeat a warrior. A warrior is trained for strength and killing, whereas a huntsman is trained for agility and defense. In nearly all cases, the most agile of the opponents end up the victor.

Branson pauses for several embarrassing breaks to catch his breath before continuing the training. He spends some time looking on as other huntsmen practice. He notes the way they make every attack or defense fluid from one move to the next. In a clench, when both opponents have each other's arms locked, they use their knees to overpower the other. Branson flinches inwardly as he sees a knee connect with the gut or the inner thigh or even high enough to strike the head. Each blow feels as if it is a breath stolen when the body is in mid-inhale or mid-exhale. It is astonishing how much he still has to learn. This realization reminds him of his feeling when he was just beginning his training during his ninth birth year.

The devenir—or trainer—signals him to join with him to continue. He trains all day, until the devenir calls an end.

Branson makes his way back to Gaylen's home as the sky dims to a dull gray. He passes by the tannery and, interest piqued, stops to speak with the tanners. He asks one of the tanners to explain the process for tanning hides. The man agrees, glad to see a younger huntsman interested in tanning.

The tanner takes Branson through the complex, meticulous process. All the animals are bled of all blood, the organs removed, and skin separated from the flesh by the huntsman before it reaches the tannery.

The skins are then submerged in water that contains handfuls of wood ashes. Not just any wood ashes, minds the tanner. The tanner describes the trees to be used for soaking the skin: those having leaves the width of a man's hand or greater, losing them during the season of Falling Leaves, and going barren during the season of the White Rain. However, when the ashes are not available, urine is used in its place and rubbed into the hide to loosen the hair for easy removal.

Branson widens his eyes at the thought.

The tanner chuckles. "Ah, lad, it is not so bad."

The soaking can last for anywhere between one to three days. Then the hide is pulled out of the water and placed over a tilted log. Branson watches as a huntswoman demonstrates the scraping process. She pins the hide and uses a dull knife to remove the animal's hair from the skin. The hair seems to fall away with little added pressure. The hide is turned over and the scraping continues, this time removing any remaining fleshy membrane. After completing this step, the hides are wrung out by twisting them between two wooden poles.

If that isn't enough, the tanner takes Branson deeper into the tannery and shows him how the hides are cured. One barrel is filled with well-mixed animal brains and water, and the other holds urine and water. The tanner explains that each barrel gives the hide different colors. The first is pale, and the other looks nearly white. The odor is a putrid smell of decaying flesh and human waste that the rest of the hold shies away from.

The hides are submerged and wrung out repeatedly until the tanner is satisfied with the pliability of the hide and the effectiveness of the curing. Next, the hide is stretched in all directions until it dries, and the stiff edges are cut away and discarded.

Finally, he shows Branson the smoking process which seals in the cure, waterproofing it. Tripods of damp, rotten sticks are built over a cluster of smoke-filled pits, with the hides lain over the tripods. Once the hide reaches a nice color, it is turned over. After this, the hide is ready to be traded or made into clothing, shoes, waterskins, etc.

The tanner shows him some examples of finished hides, some with the beast's hair still on them—these are referred to as furs. He remarks that those go for a much higher trade because of the care taken to pre-serve the hair. He notes that tougher skins are more durable and softer skins are less durable but very expensive, often owned by dewans and clan leaders. They are a luxury to have but are quickly traded for other necessary items when the need arises.

Branson leaves the tannery with an even higher appreciation for huntsmen and a greater pride for being one. On his trek to Gaylen's home, he lets his thoughts wander. They drift to the beautiful Ahni. He remembers her soft skin behind the aggressive massage that eased the tension from his muscles, how her dress flowed about her form, envy-ing the material itself for its freedom to touch and caress her body. He imagines sharing kisses in the moonlight and warm embraces in the cool comfort of the seasons. His mind drifts so far as to affect his vision.

He blinks his eyes and scolds himself for letting his emotions cloud his sight. He opens them, and yet there she is, still before him—in reality, smiling.

She stands at a trader's cart, smelling various oils. He feels his heart begin to race as his feet take him in her direction. Nervousness begins to give way to a sense of possession as he nears her. She hears his approach and looks curiously toward him. Her cheeks flare pink, and she lowers her eyes.

He smiles to soften his haggard appearance and says, "I didn't know the sun shines so brightly in the evening."

Her color deepens. "You are quite ... determined, aren't you? Are you enjoying your stay here?" She looks to the trader and confirms which oil she wants, and he seals it for her.

"Yes," Branson replies. "I am learning some new—" He pauses to flex his side, grimacing at its tenderness, then continues, "—learning some new training in my service. It is a beautiful hold and truly unfortunate that you cannot join me for an evening walk."

She clears her throat and glances around. She trades the man a small bag of mixed vegetables for the oil.

Branson notices her worry and bids her farewell. "I do not want to inconvenience your service to the dewan. Sleep well, Ahni."

"You as well."

He starts to leave, but she stops him with a hand on his arm. He turns his head and looks at her expectantly.

"Thank you," she whispers.

He tilts her chin up with a finger until she looks at him. "I am not so unsightly to look upon, am I?"

She smiles and answers, "Quite the opposite."

Ahni leaves him standing there, watching her walk to the back of

Gaylen's home to the servant's entrance. It strikes him that he is in front of the dewan's hall. He straightens his back as he walks in and sees the sires and the dewan laughing heartily over a table of food. Branson walks to the table and apologizes for his late attendance and worn appearance.

"It is all right. Wash, and then come eat with us," Gaylen replies, laughing.

Branson does so and returns with a noticeably empty stomach. He fills his plate and eats while half-heartedly listening to the men laugh and joke of old times. The sires will meet tomorrow, and he will be expected to recount the events that led to the boy's kidnapping. He thinks of the baby, wondering if Gaylen might let him see him. It has only been two days, but it feels like two moons. For some reason, Branson does not want the child to forget him.

"Did you hear me?" says Clayton, sire of the June Clan, interrupting Branson's quiet seclusion.

"No, Sire. What were you saying?"

Clayton claps Branson on the back, smiles, and repeats himself, "She is a beautiful woman you have set your interest in."

Confused, Branson asks, "What woman?"

"The one you were speaking with only a moment ago. I was returning from visiting my wife when I spotted you."

Branson's heart leaps. How could he have been so careless? Being an attendant, Ahni would undoubtedly be in service to any of the sires during their stay. The thought does not sit well with Branson in the least. Branson is not sure of Clayton's comment or the direction he means to head. A guest would feel dishonored to be attended by a taken woman. It was foolish of him to speak publicly with her. She knew it also, yet she still risked the chance of exposure.

His mind hastens for a reply. "No, Sire. I met her in passing. Quite a rude one, she is. But you do speak the truth: She is beautiful."

Clayton laughs. "Ah well, lad, your luck with the women will soon change."

He dearly hopes so.

CHAPTER
SIX

Dinner ends early for Branson. While the men retire for drinks, Branson leaves the group more out of discomfort than tiredness. He settles in the bed and lies there, resting his arms behind his head. A part of him feels incomplete—an unusual feeling for him. His birth years of intense training have taught him to rely upon himself for survival, embedding the trait of independence deep within him. He shifts positions in the bed to rid himself of this unease. But the feeling remains ... a small, absent presence at his side. He feels alone.

Branson thinks of the child and wonders if the maid feeds him often or holds him while he sleeps. It is amazing how fast the child fattened up while with Branson and Uric—from the constant care he received, or a response to the tiny amount of attention? He wants the child to find happiness outside of his fate as the Chozien. To be the Chozien has a way of riding down personal contentment. The child has a duty to this world, and it will be a heavy burden to carry alone.

The child has changed him, he knows. Branson considers the idea that stirs in his mind and heart, pondering the outcome of it before he acts. Being here at the spirit hold, he has already acquired many new aspects of his service. Branson always thought that being a huntsman represented one of great courage and exceptional talent. He has prided himself on his personal gains and has not seen beyond the horizon of his own achievements. Now he knows that it means more. The people depend on his service; if he fails, food will be scarce and the days would soon grow long. The people's well-being has always reflected his success, and they have had happier days because of it. If he hadn't been of the best huntsman from his clan and found the child, he would not have seen his life in a brighter light. He considers himself indebted to the child and the baby deserving of more than an offhand caretaker.

The next morning, Branson wakes early, but gets no answer when he knocks at Uric's door. A bit surprised, Branson heads off to quiet his stomach and sees Uric just as the seeker is entering the greeting hall from the opposite side.

Branson takes note of Uric's pleased persona, knowing he cannot let Uric get by without a jab: "I see you did not return last night. You look like you've seen the Great Spirit itself." Branson chuckles.

Uric shares the humor. "Glad to see you have lightened up since the *Quête*. A smile does make your face much more pleasant, though."

Both laugh at the friendly banter and continue toward the table for the morning meal. They see that two more sires have arrived—Graham of the Hawk Clan and Isaac of the Trace Clan. Both leaders give hearty congratulations to the men, then turn attention back to their meal and conversation, ignoring the two newcomers entirely. Branson and Uric begin to eat just as Gaylen walks in. All the men stand out of respect and custom.

"Good news," Gaylen says. "Tuan and Sim will arrive by midday.

Immediately after their arrival, we will meet to discuss what has brought all of you here ahead of your kinsmen. For now, enjoy yourselves; it is a great time to be merry."

As soon as Gaylen finishes, the sires vie for his attention and surround him.

Observing the sires with the dewan, Uric comments, "Quite a sight. Similar to the scene of a mother bird dangling a worm over her babies."

They share a quiet chuckle.

More seriously, Uric says, "Beware, my friend. There is much we do not know of these links in the chain. Best we watch our step and not tangle ourselves in the weeds."

Branson nods. "It is odd, this competition for a place in the dewan's favor."

They finish their meal and slip out unnoticed. Uric heads to the inn to see his family, promising to return before midday. Branson stands alone at the top of the steps to Gaylen's home. He sees the clans arriving at the main gate and settling themselves in for the Beni. The streets thicken as visitors grow in volume. Some servants erect giant tents, providing shade from the sun. Others dig additional fire pits for the bigger animals—deer, moose, and cows—to feed the entire hold.

A sudden swell of guilt rushes through Branson. If he had trained properly, the boy would be here along with the infant. His heart heavy, Branson considers himself not fit to even be sent on the *Quête,* nor is he worthy of such a grand title as Bonne Ame—a Bringer of the Chozien.

"Why the long face, my boy?"

Branson jumps from his own thoughts to find Gaylen standing next to him. "Dewan ... I did not expect you to leave the sires."

Gaylen looks down, shaking his head. "It is amazing how they do not see the translucence of their actions or the falseness in their words. I have chosen these men to guard the Jade Order's borders and the spirit hold. I wonder if they guard the borders as fiercely as they seek my confidence." He looks out over the hold. "Status changes people, but it does not move mountains. Only the purest in faith can do that. A dewan is seen as the leader of his people and their beliefs. I am not above the people, but of the people. The sires do not understand that. They see power and respect in their positions. The dewan dedicates his life to the survival of his order. A selfish and foolish *ame* cannot protect his people. They always consider themselves first."

Branson nods. "I understand."

Gaylen's words explain his position and responsibility. He is the youngest man to ever serve as dewan. He gained the title twenty-five years ago at the youthful age of twenty after his father died in a battle with the Bloodstone—a tragedy shared by both Gaylen and Branson: losing their fathers in battles against the Bloodstone. Being the eldest son of his fallen father, though, did not guarantee Gaylen's ascension to dewan. Five others from the surrounding clans challenged him for the title. Two happened to be the sires Graham and Connor; the others were a seeker from the hold and two warriors—one from the June Clan and the other from the Huin Clan.

All six contenders had to execute a series of strenuous trials demonstrating physical strength, endurance, and energy of the mind, body, and spirit. Finally, the survivors then had to face off in combat. The two warriors died during the mental trial, and the seeker suffered horrible wounds in the endurance competition. The last three men—Gaylen, Connor, and Graham—would pull straws for who would fight first, with the two shortest straws of the three fighting that evening, and the winner facing off against the other man the next day.

Death is not uncommon in these combats, men choosing to die

rather than swallow defeat. The clan, though, sees honor in accepting defeat; it is a man's pride that prevents him from doing so.

Gaylen and Connor drew the short straws. The combat ended with Gaylen being the victor by submission. It was not so easy; Gaylen suffered bruised ribs that slowed his reaction time and lowered his guard on his left. Gaylen lay that night bandaged and nursed by seekers, recovering for his bout the next day.

Graham was and is still known as an arrogant man. He boasted the entire day of how he would "give this boy a beating and send him back to his mother, rubbing his backside." He said that Gaylen would not even show up, but to his chagrin, Gaylen did.

The men fought long and hard. Gaylen's wound still felt tender, and he protected his left side more, leaving his right open. Graham threw out slanderous insults, advising him to give up and walk away. Keeping his assault strong, Graham grew in confidence with each hammering blow that brought Gaylen closer to his knees. Finally, he knocked Gaylen to the ground. Gaylen struggled to his knees, panting as Graham advanced. Graham asked him for submission. But with his head wearily bowed, Gaylen shook his decline. Graham closed the distance between them, raising his arm to prepare to drop a hammering elbow to Gaylen's exposed neck, effectively breaking it.

Suddenly, Gaylen leaped forward, hitting Graham's knee, dislocating it. Graham fell, yelling from both pain and anger, clutching his knee. Gaylen mounted him and struck him with numerous blows until he felt the man's nose break, and then Graham's blood spattered Gaylen's own face. Gaylen pulled Graham up to a sitting position and knelt behind him. He wrapped his arms around his head, prepared to break his neck.

He asked in a loud but fatigued voice, "Do you submit?"

Graham reached up and tapped Gaylen's forearm, signaling his submission. Both men spent at least a moon recuperating. Graham pledged his protection to Gaylen, as did all the sires, but the battle created a rift between them that exists still today.

Branson was just an innocent toddler that day, but his father told him of the contest many times. His father held high respect for Gaylen, and Branson is beginning to see why.

Gaylen continues, "So what is it that has you troubled?"

Branson confides, "I was thinking that I was not worthy to be sent on the *Quête*."

"Why? You have brought us the Chozien."

"No, I lost the boy. We only have one. Here, you have the greatest huntsmen I have ever known. They should have been sent, not me."

"It will have to suffice. It is our way, Branson. The best out of all the clans, save the spirit hold, were chosen. The spirit hold must be kept strong; it is the heart of the order. There is value in you, lad. The Great Spirit has deemed it so. You judge with your sight rather than with your *ame*. You were not sent because of your abilities but because of that."

Branson has a slight look of confusion on his face.

Gaylen laughs. "You are still young and there is much to learn."

Brow furrowed, Branson nods.

Before Gaylen can add anything else, Branson asks, "Dewan, would it be possible for me to see the child?"

Gaylen smiles. "Of course. I will have one of the servants take you to the nursery."

Branson thanks him and feels a combination of anticipation and nervousness. A servant—probably from the kitchen, given the apron she has on—takes him up the stairs and to the opposite side of the hall. They stop at the last door, and she knocks. Suriah opens the door and invites Branson in, offering a warm smile to him. The room is big and bright from the sunlight streaming in through the four windows. The curtains—a light shade of green—are pulled to the side. He sees rugs lying across the floor and a medium-sized bed, most likely for Suriah, with a small crib is set up by the bed. The child lies on his back on a soft sheepskin rug in the center of the room.

Suriah closes the door and asks, "You have come to visit the child?"

Branson nods. "Yes."

"It is good you have come to see him. He was a bit fussy at first, but he is beginning to warm up to me," she says while picking the child up and handing him over.

Branson takes him and smiles in delight.

The child laughs and reaches for Branson's face.

"I think he misses you … and you, him," she says, giving a small smile.

Branson turns to her. "Thank you, Suriah."

She smiles, accepting the appreciation. "Well, I will leave you two. It's time I enjoy some fresh air."

She exits, closing the door quietly behind her.

Branson lets the child poke playfully at his face and gently bites the baby's chubby fingers with his lips. They busy themselves with missed opportunities and moments. He sets the baby on the rug on all fours and helps him to crawl. He teases him with his toys and even makes faces that gets him to laugh all the harder even though he intended to frighten him. Time hurries by, and the baby begins to yawn and gets restless.

He cradles the baby in his arms and rocks him while he walks around the room. He holds the child close, smelling his natural infant scent along with hints of soft lavender essence, no doubt to help him sleep peacefully. He touches the child's arm and remembers how soft the skin felt. Reactively, the child grasps his forefinger and smiles, his eyelids drooping. He falls asleep soon after, yet Branson cannot bring himself to put him down. A soft knock at the door and Suriah enters the room. Branson motions for quiet and she nods.

She whispers, "The dewan summons you for the meeting; he is waiting for you in his parlor. You remember where it is?"

"I do." He places the baby in her waiting arms and whispers, "We had quite the time. I will see him again tomorrow if that is fine with you?" He looks to her for confirmation.

"Oh yes, I would love the time off."

Branson looks one last time at the child before he takes his leave.

Suriah's hushed voice stops him at the door: "The child will be lucky to have you as his donateur."

"It would be an honor," he whispers and closes the door.

On the way down to Gaylen's parlor, he thinks of Suriah's last words to him. Being the child's donateur would not satisfy him. The child should have more than a dedicated champion. And Branson himself should have more. The child deserves a father.

He makes his way to the parlor, where the leaders have just started gathering. He sees Uric there already, and relief shows on the seeker's face as Branson enters. They clasp forearms and discuss who will say what and when. Branson notes the different arrangement of the chairs: three chairs in the back of the room, five on one side, and four on the other, leaving the front area mostly open, with only two chairs there. Branson and Uric figure these to be their places. The men seat themselves, with Haru, Gaylen, and Keno occupying the three chairs.

Gaylen speaks first, bringing the room to complete silence: "Namaste, Sires. Welcome again to the Jade Order's spirit hold. Begin acknowledging your presence."

The clan leaders each stand, stating their name and clan. First is Clayton, who loves the drink and laughs the loudest at his own jokes.

Connor rises next, a loyal and humble leader. Then Harwen and Remy, both seeking promotion by showering gifts and bragging of their clans' achievements. Afterward stands Marquis, always the first to agree to a war. Next, Graham and Isaac, who resemble two serpents, for all their whispering and isolation. Lastly, Tuan of the Dun Clan and Sim of the Rain Clan—twin brothers and extraordinary strategists.

After the introductions, Gaylen declares, "We meet today to celebrate the Chozien. You see here the Bringers of the Chozien: Branson of the Zin Clan and Uric of the Huin Clan."

Upon mention of their clans, Remy and Harwen raise their chins proudly.

Gaylen continues, "It is also unfortunate that dire circumstances are upon us. What these two are about to tell you must be kept secret." He nods to Branson and Uric.

Uric stands and tells them of the two Chozien and explains how they had no choice but to stop to replenish their rations. He explains the Hematite's abnormal spirits, as well as the uncertainties. He finishes, and Branson stands for his turn. He describes the way the Hematite sent scouts first and prepared for their attack. He tells of their fight and how the boy was stolen from them. He discloses their interrogation of the warrior before his execution. Branson finishes by saying that some of the warriors were indeed Onyx.

Expletives are thrown out, along with angry grumbles.

Gaylen silences them. "We cannot let our anger blind us. What do you say of the Hematite spirits, Keno?"

"Young Uric speaks true. Hematite spirits are cold—or lukewarm at best. Cold spirits speak of fear and uncertainty. They must be benefiting from this alliance with the Onyx to feel secure enough that it warms their spirits. It is not a good sign." Keno finishes by shaking his head.

"And you, Haru, what of the battle?" Gaylen asks the general.

"They should have brought the warrior back alive. We have ways of questioning the Onyx. Although, Branson might be right: it is unlikely he would have told us anything. We must find out why the Hematite broke their neutrality."

Gaylen looks to the leaders for them to provide their input.

Marquis spits out, "The Hematite are cowards! The Onyx show great disrespect to the Jade stealing what is rightfully ours. It is but an invitation to war, and we should prepare for it."

Sim speaks up: "Nothing will happen for years until the boy is old enough to fight."

Marquis counters, "Only their numbers bring advantage to the Onyx. It would be foolish to wait for them to attack first. Let us reduce their size and their confidence by half."

Tuan shakes his head. He says honestly what the others are thinking: "We cannot fight this war alone, and no other order will agree to an outright slaughter by the word of an untitled huntsman and seeker— Bringers of the Chozien or not."

Branson and Uric nod in agreement.

Remy speaks next: "Sim and Tuan are right. Also, we have one of the Chozien. Do not let us forget that."

Graham and Isaac speak to each other first before giving their thoughts.

Graham says, "I agree with Marquis. Though we should not be hasty, we should prepare for war and the protection of the order."

Isaac nods. "Yes. War is coming and we cannot stop this. We should send for alliances."

Clayton laughs. "We are not fools. We should not seek to prevent this war. Focus more on convincing the other orders of this treachery first."

"This will be the greatest war since the Partition," Marquis says excitedly, referring to the war that broke the Old World.

Rolling his eyes at Marquis's comment, Harwen states, "All war is great to you, Marquis. It is surprising you even follow the ducall of the Jade Order."

Marquis retorts, "I am loyal to the Jade Order! I fight only when peace is the outcome. I am not as cowardly as you, Harwen."

The room erupts with thunder, and gray clouds threaten to shower the sires with a pounding rain of disarray and glory-seeking. Lightning streaks the room with insults callously thrown at a recipient's character and service, immediately changing the tide of the challenge facing them. Gaylen, Haru, and Keno remain silent, seemingly unmoved at the storm gathering before them.

Branson takes the nonchalance at this kind of display being a common occurrence. Disgusted, he thinks, *This is the anticipation I have been waiting for?*

Finally, Gaylen stands and shouts, "Are these the sires of the Jade Order? You quarrel like children. This is not our first war. We did not meet to discuss a war. We met to discuss the motives behind the betrayal."

The men become silent. At this moment, Branson remembers his visions. He cannot believe he has forgotten such a powerful Foresight. Immediately, he asks for permission to speak.

"You are free to speak here, Branson. What is it?" Gaylen asks impatiently.

Branson reddens slightly from embarrassment of not knowing the proper decorum in such isolated deliberations. He clears his throat. "My apologies. It is my mistake that I have omitted another detail. It was during a time of great confusion that I asked the Great Spirit for counsel. It is what we huntsmen call Seclude."

Arms cross and heads tilt in curiosity for him to continue.

"I had a vision ... many, actually. Two hawks fly and one is caught by a dark net; a gloved hand conceals a black-bladed dagger in robes of the Jade; the sounds of fighting and dying; and finally a cage." He pauses a moment before adding, "This same dark net was used to steal the boy."

Deep thought is shown on every face. No one moves. No one speaks.

Connor had been mostly quiet and calm throughout the earlier chaos, but he now breaks the silence: "Foresight. It is a very rare attribute—the ability to receive the future. Your visions tell of a traitor within us."

All the men share appalled and disgruntled mumbles at the mere thought of betraying their order.

Connor continues, "Be still. This deceiver most likely has not turned yet. The dagger confesses their employment by the Onyx. And the Onyx are not yet finished with their thievery by the image of the cage."

Remy asks, "If we already know the future, how do we survive it?"

Connor answers, "The future is not yet here. It can be altered."

The men nod in agreement, albeit not totally believing it.

Branson says, "Why is it we prepare to celebrate instead of riding out and retrieving the other boy?"

Sim gives Branson a look of confusion. "We cannot leave our borders unguarded for so long. The Onyx borders lies at least three moons from here. The boy would be well within their spirit hold before we even reach the Azurite Order. There is no getting into their spirit hold, not by force, nor by battling the Hematite and Onyx Orders alone. The boy is gone; he is with the Onyx. It is best we not dwell on matters of impossibility."

Branson nods his head in defeat, embarrassed to have suggested such a ludicrous solution. Still, the explanation angers him. The thought of not going after the boy stirs a sickly bile within him. It does not seem right to let a child go. To him, it is a loss greater than someone unknown.

"We must set in place eyes and ears in all holds," Tuan suggests.

Gaylen stands again. "The separation of the two Chozien brings balance to the orders again. But the insatiable greed of the Onyx will strive to tilt the scales in their favor. We will not be safe in the times to come when we cannot trust our own kinsmen. Today we make a vow of silence, an oath to root out treachery, and a promise to protect our way. This is what makes us whole and unites us."

It is agreed upon. The men will meticulously select their informants. They have to be trustworthy, have a deep loyalty to the order, and remain selfless, because the information that will enter their ears and pass between their lips will be critical to the survival of the order. Their location will have to be both advantageous and commonly frequented, without being conspicuous. Each clan will choose their agents, who will remain anonymous to the others.

Gaylen instructs everyone to keep a festive composure and not to let on that anything is amiss. The meeting adjourns, and the men file out with less enthusiasm than upon their arrival.

Connor pulls Branson to the side and speaks low and brief: "With visions, you must pay attention to the details. The surroundings, the jewelry, the attire all speak in volumes. Do you remember any details of this hand that clutched the dagger or what the cage is made of?"

Branson thinks back, trying to picture each vision. It was his first experience with such visions, and the intensity caught him off guard. He shakes his head. "No, Sire. All I remember is the sequence in which they came."

Connor leaves Branson with a warning: "Remember the details. This is vital. The Onyx do not just want the Chozien; they plan to control the Jade Order, if not destroy it altogether."

And then he is gone.

The shock of the responsibility for the safety and protection of so many shakes Branson. His heart starts to race, and the room suddenly seems too small. He feels hot, as if he has been working in the kitchen—no, the tannery! His throat goes dry. Only a moment later, he hurries past the sires with excused apologies and out the door into the open.

He fills his lungs, breathing deeply. He feels his chest expand, imagining his lungs like a waterskin being filled to capacity. He wipes his forehead, feeling the sweat there, and even though the day is warm, his body temperature cools. He takes a moment to sit down on the top step. Already he begins to feel better.

Uric joins him not too long after. "You seemed rather rushed to be out of there."

"Well, aren't you the clever one?"

Uric chuckles and then says sincerely, "It is good to help. But it is not to worry."

Branson stands and looks at the smiling faces of his fellow kinsmen. "This world can be so cruel at times. And yet we still find joy to celebrate."

Uric offers some consolation: "Ah, if our focus is to grieve what is lost or burrow ourselves in fear ... we will miss the paradise of love, the thrill of success, and the pleasure of today. Do not lose sight of what is in your hand for what might be."

Branson sighs. "Yes, this is true. It is just that this knowledge has a way of building this ... weakness in me."

Uric nods at finding some justification. "You bear the weight of a father with the loss of his child. I do not wish that upon any father or mother." Uric waits a moment, finding the right words, and then he says confidently, "We are stronger than we give ourselves credit for."

The men enjoy each other's company for a while longer before

Uric departs to be with his family again, leaving Branson to envy their companionship.

Branson just steps off the last of the stairs when he hears a familiar laugh. He smiles and follows the melodious sound around the left side of the house. He turns the corner and sees Ahni and some friends attempting to fold soft linens and laughing at how the breeze catches hold of them, hindering their chore. He hides in the shadows so as not to interrupt their amusement.

It is the perfect sight: the image of pure, innocent bliss. She is definitely worth waiting for. As he sits and watches the women enjoying themselves, he begins to understand the reasoning behind the dewan's demand on confidentiality:

She is beautiful, is she not? Before, the secrets stood so far from me—no, the lie of what is to come. It seems so … unfair to deprive the people of this knowledge and their choices. But now … it's clear to me in the likeness of the purest glass made by the vain Rhodonite Order. The magnitude of this truth would betray our leaders' oath of protection. It would terrify her, weakening her ame. If I can prevent this fear from robbing her of this fanciful joy, then so be it. She makes sense to me even if decisions to protect her do not. I see now. I do not want Ahni to carry the worry of tomorrow and the next day. I will bear that burden alone … for her.

He slips away silently without disturbing their fun. It seems that the worst of times brings out the best in him.

SEVEN

The day continues in a bustle of excitement. More and more kinsmen pour into the courtyard. Vendors thrill at the opportunity to increase the people's stores, which will be used later for significant trade. The streets are loud with men already drunk and women dancing to the music of the drums and flutes.

The mood seems to be contagious, for Branson drifts into the jubilee of people and soon finds he, too, is laughing and dancing. Some of the people recognize Branson as one of the Bringers of the Chozien and offer him oils, soft furs, ripe fruits that ooze juices down their consumer's chin, or warm, nutty sweet breads. He declines almost all the offers, thanking the giver profusely, although he cannot resist the tantalizing smell of the bread. He tries a piece and tastes the cinnamon and honey. The airy texture increases his appetite, wishing for the airy pockets to be filled with more spiced delight.

Soon the sun sets and his stomach aches for food. He makes his way back to Gaylen's house and enters surprisingly cheerful. Unfortunately, the arrogant atmosphere of the sires dampens the evening meal. It is good that Uric came for the meal, which the men endure purposefully out of respect for the dewan and from the Jade custom that during gatherings the order's leaders and protectors dine together. This is meant to bring harmony and solace among them all. Branson doesn't see the effectiveness and could do well with eating in his room.

All the men retire early in the evening, just after the dark hour, to rest for the first day of the Beni celebration.

The celebration is called the Beni, meaning the "Blessed" in thanks to the Great Spirit for blessing the Jade Order with the Chozien and the opportunity to bring peace to the orders. The Beni lasts three days, with each day devoted to the Chozien and signifying three important components of their life. The first day—the Presenting—is filled with celebration simply for the Chozien's presence within the order. His very existence will keep hope and faith thriving.

The second day—the Appointing—announces the Chozien's gardien, his caregiver. This day captures the essence of the Chozien's need for the order as much as the order's need for him. It signifies his joining of the order and the union of all kinsmen.

On the final day—the Naming—the Chozien is publicly recognized by name. This day is the most significant because it pertains to the Chozien's devotion and dedication to the order. He will then be considered unique in his own being and *ame*.

Branson and Uric will receive new clothing to be worn for ceremonial occasions exclusively. Tailors fit them with newly tanned and dyed-black pants, soft to the touch and hugging their thighs; Branson assumes that they are made of sheep's hide. A smooth, silky white shirt extends just over the thighs, seeming to float over the torso. Thick dark-green material is used to make their calf-length loin cloths, with a companion sash intricately woven and bordered by light-green and silver colors. Completing the ensemble are medallions with a sun and hawk imprinted on the metal, to be worn about their neck. Uric's wife and children also receive fine garments and jewelry.

The men remove the formal clothing after the fitting and again dress in their own. Their attire now includes a new item to be worn at all times: the medallion, representing their new place in the hierarchy, equal to the sires. Only the dewans and sires have the honor to wear jewelry symbolizing their order and title. Only rarely does someone not in those positions wear this medallion. The sires engaged in much debate over the dewan's decision for the sudden promotion. Nevertheless, he insisted they have the noble recognition, considering their inclusion in the clandestine meetings, where their involvement and knowledge was deemed valued. Gaylen thinks it best that they hold the title lest they arouse suspicion within the clans.

Each medallion has a separate meaning. For the sires, the sun is a universal icon for nourishment and growth, and the bear for strength and protection. Branson and Uric's display the sun and the hawk in representation of devotion to the Chozien—or a valiant act resulting in the preservation of the order. The dewan's medallion has the sun, bear, and hawk—symbolizing his duty as the unifying spirit for all clans and the mere existence of the order. There is only one medallion of this kind, with it passed on from one dewan to the next, receiving a periodic polish to give the precious titanium a bright gleam.

Titanium is the strongest and the most expensive of all the metals used in metalwork. It is so expensive and rare that the "desert walkers" are the only people known to have it. They live either underground in the hills or the mountainous regions far from the orders. Some have been said to be seen in the deserts, hence their name, although no one would ever venture there unless by banishment or aimless drifting.

Owning a sword forged by a desert walker serves as the sign of an excellent swordsman. Desert walkers remain selfish when it comes to parting with their craft, as that is where their value lies. Blacksmiths and swordsmiths can only dream of becoming an apprentice to a desert walker. The strongest weapons are made with a combination of metals and materials beyond any relican's exploration and thought—with "relican" being the name the desert walkers gave to the people of the orders. Desert walkers see the world as a new beginning, a way to create a new history free from the impurities of the knowledge in the past. In the desert walkers' cultural beliefs, a relican clings to the old ways to carry on ancient practices. They teach that those who seek the past are doomed to repeat it.

In the days before the Partition War, this way of thought also existed, but only by people in small numbers, by those who dared to come forward. As the war grew closer and greater, so did the greed and desertion. The desert walkers gathered together and migrated away from the warmongers. The desert walkers became rooted to their new land, finding much to be treasured. While digging through rocks and dirt, they came upon many precious stones. They traded these stones to the relicans during the time of the Restoration and the creation of the orders. Soon the desert walkers found that their mining produced not just raw gems, but metals too.

They began to mold and craft these materials into beautiful ornaments, solid walls, and sharp weapons. They quickly grew in population in these regions, driving out any existing inhabitants to maintain a monopoly on this wealth and want. They fast evolved into a wealthy and formidable people.

Their life span extends well past that of a relican due to the strong *ame* from the land they care for, so much so that they no longer consider themselves human, but a separate race: the attetne. They fear traveling too far from their homes for long periods of time because they believe they will "lose" birth years during the separation from their land.

Attetnes build their cities underground to aid in their mining and collection of precious stones and metals. They guard their cities carefully and adequately from outsiders. The closest attetne folk reside in Mount Hollow, a half-moon's journey west of the Jade Order's spirit hold and within the Bloodstone Order's territory. If attetnes are seen above ground, they tend to shy away from interaction, unless of course they come to know that a trade is the reason. One shouldn't expect harm from them, nor do they expect aid. There are many stories of past encounters with attetnes, none of which involve much violence.

The greeting hall is loud with sires and siras, sharing humorous stories and conversing cheerfully. Branson and Uric, joined by Uric's wife, enter the room, and as if their medallions are beacons of light, most of the sires flock to them and begin to introduce them to the siras. Branson sees Graham and Isaac give a wide-eyed look at the medallions and then begin speaking to one another again, their wives matching their husband's personalities, snickering behind them.

A woman introduced as Clayton's wife notices Branson's harsh look at the secretive pairs and offers some consolation: "Do not worry yourself, young huntsman. Those two have a long jealous streak. Truth, they've always been that way even after Graham lost to the dewan."

Branson smiles hesitantly and points to himself, asking, "Jealous of me? Why would that be? I am a huntsman barely two decades and five."

She smiles, shakes her head, and lowers her voice some: "Oh yes. To them, though, you are another obstacle to their advancement. Best you keep a close vigil on your own clan's sire as well." Then, tapping the medallion, she whispers, "He is the most likely to find faults with you to encourage the dewan to rescind your ... rise in position. He will not like the idea of one of his *young* huntsmen being considered his equal."

She leaves, finding her husband and entwining her arm around his. She immediately involves herself in the active conversation as if she did not just finish speaking about suspicion, deceit, and the like. Branson takes her words sincerely and quickly discovers that the sires are not the only ones he should be keeping a "close vigil" on, watching the siras cautiously. Suddenly, the weight of the medallion around his neck feels heavier than before he walked into the room.

They endure the morning meal and casually take part in the slightly pompous socialization. Finally, the dewan and dewana enter, and a cheer is raised. The couple smiles, and they are immediately surrounded by everyone. Wives begin catching up on the latest gossip, intermingled with boasting of their clan's newest developments, while the men boast how much drink each can hold before passing out or taking sick. Branson and Uric can hear the crowd gathering out front of the dewan's home and know that at any moment Haru will walk in announcing that the people are ready for the dewan to initiate the start of the Beni.

Just as Branson starts to make a wager on his drinking consumption, Haru walks in with a smile and announces, "The Jade Order awaits you, Dewan."

The men gulp down the liquid in their cups, take the last few bites of appetizers, and kiss their wives before filing out to stand in front of the house. When Branson steps out, he has to cover his eyes for a moment from the bright sunlight. He looks over the crowd of people standing anxiously below, glee on their faces.

The dewan's home stands ten steps above the ground, with the terrace spacious enough to hold all the sires and siras, if the siras were to be included in the ceremony. Branson and Uric take their place by Haru as instructed, with the sires on the opposite side, shifting often to ensure that each one of them can be seen. Gaylen appears on the terrace last of all.

As he walks out, the people shout cheerfully, calling out phrases like "Long live the Jade Order!" or "Beni, Dewan Gaylen!" Others just applaud happily.

Gaylen raises his hand in the air for quiet. "It has been a long time since the Jade Order has claimed the Chozien. It is good that we gather here to rejoice. We celebrate the blessings of the Great Spirit. We celebrate births and marriages. We celebrate peace. Today we will celebrate the Beni!"

The people cheer again, louder this time. Drums begin to beat and singing erupts. Men, women, and children dance together in merriment. The dewan and his council smile, wave hands, and cry out encouragement, but their spirits betray their actions. They feel sad and confused. They look on at their kinsmen's joy with doubtful eyes and guilty consciences. The leaders rush back inside before the seekers who have gathered sense the dullness of their *ame*.

Everyone stands quiet inside the grand room.

Uric tries to brighten the mood: "How about a drink to start the day off right?"

Clayton is the first to respond by slapping Uric on the back and saying, "That's the spirit, lad. It is not often I hear a seeker suggest a drink. I'll have to take the offer."

It is true. Seekers normally drink water or fruit juices so as not to dampen the strength of their Reach or disrupt the concentration required for their service, but sometimes a seeker will join in the revelry with liquor or wine.

The servants have cleared away all the food and are no doubt preparing dishes for the feast. The spouses have departed and are most likely enjoying the festivities. Servants soon return, bringing goblets and decanters filled with wine; if a goblet is held, it keeps getting filled. The mood lightens, and the sires begin to saunter back outside and mingle with their kinsmen.

A group of huntsmen intercept Branson when he goes outside, and he recognizes them as his training partners. They whisk him away to introduce him to the rest of the huntsmen, who turn out to be holding a jamboree of the nine clans, including his own. His fellow huntsmen welcome him proudly, even if drunkenly. As midday approaches, Branson begins to feel the effects of his own indulgence. He refuses more offers of the abundant, robust alcohol.

He participates in many entertaining contests that turn out to be quite competitive. One particular contest involves a man throwing a heavy stone as far as he can. The man is allowed a running start, provided he does not cross a line drawn in the ground. Branson has never attempted the game but has seen it played many times. He watches a few men take their turns heaving the massive rock into the air.

Branson decides to give it a try and steps forward. A seven-foot, maybe two-hundred-fifty pound warrior looks at him sarcastically and drops the heavy stone into Branson's waiting hands. Branson grunts under the weight of it; it is much heavier than it appears. He positions the stone as best he can to throw. Finally, he gathers his strength, runs, and heaves away. Laughter erupts; his stone is marked well behind everyone else's. The rude warrior who handed Branson the stone laughs uncontrollably. Red-faced, Branson steps back to allow the next warrior his turn.

He and Uric also compete in various weapons-throwing contests. Some are the twin blades of a huntsman, along with the bow and arrow, battle-axe, spear, and sword. In these contests, the participant stands behind yet another line, but this time without a running start. The participant must aim at the target and come as close to the heart, head, or gut as possible, although he has to name his intended target beforehand. As usual, the target consists of a wooden frame and a hay-filled makeshift body several feet away. As the contestants hit their target, servants move the target farther away. Contestants are eliminated as their strength or eyesight weaken.

Uric does very well at close range with the twin blades and sword. Because his skill with the spear, battle-axe, and bow is limited, he does not participate in those competitions. However, Branson excels in all the weapons. He wins the bow and arrow event. Even after all the competitors are eliminated, he continues to hit the mark at greater distances. He earns quite a bit of praise for his exceptional skill with the bow and an equal amount of spite for beating all the other huntsmen. With the spear, though, his aim lessens as the distance grows. He fares well with the other weapons, but the same result comes about, the greater distance leading to loss of accuracy.

Given the number of contests and competitors, the day passes quickly. The sound of a horn announces the Beni's Presenting ceremony. People begin to crowd in front of the steps of the dewan's home again. Parents lift small children up onto their shoulders, and older adolescents climb the sides of buildings to sit on roofs for a better view.

Branson and Uric are ushered up the steps to the terrace, where they stand behind Haru as instructed. Once the crowd settles, drums pound to a beat, and guards garbed in ceremonial garments march out in two single-file lines, one on either side of the steps, extending from the top of the stairs to two people on ground level. Each guard steps in unison with the other. As the last guard comes to a stop at the top step, all turn inward.

Next, Gaylen walks out and speaks in a booming voice: "The Great Spirit sends blessings of glory, faith, and hope. We stand here today by the peace we have always worked for. We must keep the peace and its meaning."

He turns his head toward the door, and Suriah emerges with the baby in her arms. People crowd over each other to see closely, and collective whispering begins. The baby wears white undergarments, wrapped in the same cloth Branson saw him in earlier. Suriah hands the infant to Gaylen and steps away.

The dewan speaks again: "The presence of the Chozien in the Jade Order represents the Great Spirit's approval for peace. Peace will reign once again. The child born with the strength to shape our world!"

He raises the baby up high. Cheering erupts. Women openly weep with a sudden wave of loving emotion and devotion. Branson fills with pride similar to that of a father for his son, and he looks on with great pleasure and an up-thrust chin. Uric gives him a congratulatory pat on the back.

Gaylen brings the child back down to his chest for fear he might upset him, and Suriah is instantly by his side to take the baby back inside. Gaylen holds both his hands in the air, signaling silence. After a few moments, there is calm again.

Gaylen moves on with the program: "Three kinsmen are responsible for the Chozien's presence: Branson and Yuen of the Zin Clan, and Uric of the Huin Clan. From this day forth, they will be known as 'Bonne Ames.'"

Branson and Uric step forward, and the crowd cheers again. The men step back in their initial place as instructed.

"Yuen will be deeply missed, yet greatly honored," Gaylen says.

The crowd roars again, giving praise to Branson, Uric, and the deceased Yuen. Two short blows from the loud horn announce the food is ready. The entire order begins to move toward the cooking grounds. As Branson and Uric approach their table, they notice even more roasting pits than they had seen earlier—all of them surrounded with people cutting at the aromatic meat, with juices falling from tender flesh slow-roasted the entire day, teasing taste buds and appetites. Huge mounds of bread loaves are ripped apart piece by piece, spicy vegetables cooked to perfection are forked up in great amounts, and dark-red wine is poured into cups.

Branson and Uric seat themselves at the dewan's table, featuring a spread that includes meat of every sort of beast Branson believes he has hunted—even more. The men fill their plates, and as they eat, servants bring them platters of the spicy vegetables and warm soft bread, offering them to each sire.

Every man, woman, and child eats to near bursting.

CHAPTER
EIGHT

The kinsmen begin to disperse by the time the moon and lanterns are the only sources of light. Drunken friends carry each other to safe havens to retire, and servants bustle about, cleaning the remnants of the day's celebration and preparing for the next. Branson thinks the night is coming to a close until all the sires and siras stand, gathered together and speaking excitedly.

Confused, Branson asks Uric, "What is going on?"

Uric shakes his head and shrugs.

Clayton sees confusion on their faces and drunkenly drapes an arm around each one. He laughs, then slurs, "A special celebration is in place for the two Bonne Ames. The dewan will have his best dancers perform the *Victoire* and, as requested of the siras, the *Rêve D'Amour*."

Branson's eyes widen while Uric smiles with excitement and immediately shares this with his wife.

Noticing Branson's discomfort, Clayton tries to console him, albeit clumsily: "No worries for you. I'm sure many would join you. All you have to do is ask."

Clayton's guffaw is as annoying as it is useless. His wife jabs an elbow in her mate's belly at the insensitivity of his advice. She sends her husband off while she attempts to fix his bungling.

She intertwines her arm in Branson's and walks with him, tapping his arm in a motherly way. "You know I was a huntswoman before I became a sira." She chuckles at Branson's surprise before she continues, "I remember when I was young. Clayton was patient when he courted me. Quite determined for a cocky warrior. But his ... jovial nature was contagious. Still is when I am a bit testy at times."

Branson grunts at the sira's sentimental recollection.

She explains further, "He is a part of me that I needed. There is a harmony between us that I have only seen in nature. The *Rêve D'Amour* is a dance to represent the passion between spirit partners. You do not want just anyone to share it with you."

Branson and the sira rejoin the others, where she finds her husband. Branson has not seen either of the performances, having never earned the right for this event. The entire gathering walks to a far side of the hold, where a brilliant bonfire glows with light. Fortunately, the beginning of the White Rain season has cooled the night air or the heat from the fire would overwhelm them. Also present are the musicians with their instruments—drums and flutes—and several dancers wearing hooded robes sit off to the side.

The dancers number around sixteen; Branson counted but doesn't trust his numbers because of the wine.

Branson watches the sires and siras prepare for the performance. He sees genuine affection between a few of them. Uric and Leesha look completely overjoyed and gush over each other; Clayton, Connor, and their respective siras clasp each in a warm embrace as they settle on a fur on the ground. In contrast, Graham's and Isaac's relationship with each of their siras seems to be more out of respect for their titles, as their interactions appear more mechanical and rehearsed than natural. Even more distant are Harwen and Remy; it looks like they're strained, or a void exists between them. They each exhibit annoyance, as if they would rather experience this honor with another person. Tuan and Sim and their siras are a mystery to him yet.

Branson stands alone. He once welcomed such isolation, but now he feels some envy for those with companions. He knows that it is not a good thing to envy the life of another. Yet, as he sees the high-ranking kinsmen joined with their partners, his *ame* cries for a happiness conceived from the love of another. He thinks of Ahni often, but he wants more of her. He wants to know her dreams and her fears. He wonders what makes her laugh and what makes her cry. He wants to feel her heartbeat as he lies comfortably on her chest and she strokes his hair. This is what his heart calls out for. It is she he wants here with him.

Finally, the assembled council sits in a semicircle around the bonfire.

Gaylen begins his introduction: "Our most valued and loyal kinsmen, tonight our dreams are made a reality. Tonight we honor brave men for their courage and devotion to the Jade Order. Branson Kuo-Lin and Uric Kale have been given great value in the eyes of the Great Spirit. It is only right that we respect them properly, fitting of Bonne Ames. We will dance in the memory of Yuen and for our future victory. We will dance the *Victoire!*"

He exclaims the last with his fists in the air, and drums begin to pound.

Three men and five women jump to their feet from the group of dancers, removing their robes in the process. The dancers are clothed in shades of green, black, and brown ceremonial attire. The women wear sleeveless tops, seemingly only covering their breasts, and skirts that come to mid-thigh, allowing ease for leaps and lifts in the dance. The men go shirtless, with their loincloths stopping just above the knees, swirling through the night air as they perform a series of skilled turns. Decorated bands adorn arms, wrists, and ankles. Portions of their hair are dyed green, and some used a gelled cream to stiffen it to short spikes. The dancers have painted their faces to accentuate the victory theme, detailing eyes and sharp cheekbones with variations of green, white, and black.

The *Victoire* is danced with much power and speed. The dancers emphasize the movements with high jumps, turns, and various gravity-defying suspensions. This is a fierce dance, and the only expressions from the dancers are smirks, sneers, and the flashing of their teeth. The *Victoire* symbolizes victory, the fearlessness of the order, and the veracity of the Jade's beliefs. It energizes the spirit, making the sky bright with its fervor. Hearts beat faster, blood flows fluidly, bringing the body alive in ways none could have imagined.

Branson watches in awe and fascination as a male dancer picks up a female dancer and tosses her high into the air, where she does a series of twists. At the peak of her aerial move, the dancers shout in unison, and she lands on her feet—a feat done only by an experienced dancer. The dance stirs excitement among the spectators, and the bobbing of heads and stomping of feet soon turn into leaps and shouts of their own. One of the drummers utters a loud, high-pitched shout that is unexpectedly melodious, and the beat moves faster. All around him, Branson sees the sires picking their wives up, with their arms outstretched, eyes closed, and heads back, spinning with them. Uric and Leesha move rhythmically with the beat, swinging their heads, stomping the ground, and shouting joyously. Before Branson knows it, a female dancer catches him and molds her body to his. At first, he follows her steps, and then he picks up the speed of the drum. Soon enough, he spins her and leaps rhythmically. He feels as if he is inhaling the essence of life this very moment.

Nearing the end of the dance, with the beat racing, the people can barely keep up, and the entire gathering shouts, mimicking the vocals of the dancers. Then the drums come to an abrupt stop. Everyone stops, breathing heavily, laughing, and smiling. Men wipe sweat from their brows, and women's eyes glisten with moisture from the pure joy they feel.

Branson shakes his head, laughing while hugging his dance partner. True, it was emotional for some, but unforgettable by all.

The men and women finally come down from the elation and return to their original spots on the ground circling the bonfire. Branson notes the wisdom of the dewan to start with the *Victoire*, as it has eased the previous tension he'd noticed between some of the sires and siras.

Each sira now sits wrapped in her husband's arms and snuggled close. Servants bring blankets to the couples for warmth from the chill. The audience applauds the dancers as they bow and back away to the side, where they cover themselves in the warmth of their robes and seat themselves as before.

Gaylen, holding his wife, says loudly, "Now, at the siras' request, the *Rêve D'Amour!*"

The audience gives an equally emphatic verbal cheer.

A soft, low tune from the panpipe begins, and new dancers slowly stand and remove their robes—again three men and five women. First, the women move in a line, stepping lightly and looking straight ahead. They wear paint on various parts of their body, along with sleeved midriff tops and long, flowing skirts made of thin green material. A small silver band is worn about their heads, with a small green jewel centered on their forehead.

Branson furrows his brow slightly, thinking that his eyes are playing tricks on him. He catches a glimpse of a female dancer who looks very similar to Ahni. Then the pipe changes tunes and is joined by another. The men join the women. They wear pants made of the same silky material, along with decorative armbands. The women move their hips in a sensually erotic motion while the men tenderly caress their bodies. The women perform a turn, switching partners, and then move affectionately with their new dancer.

There she is again. Branson stiffens and widens his eyes with surprise, then quickly relaxes before giving himself away. He tilts his head to the side, reveling in the sight of her awesome beauty. He notices how well she moves, stretching out her arms as she rolls her hips, her eyes closing and mouth slightly opening with a hint of a smile. He smiles briefly, and then she is in the arms of another male dancer. He narrows his eyes, feeling a possessiveness about the secret claim they have made to each other. She and the man are totally engulfed in each other, her eyes never leaving his and his never straying from hers. It is indeed a dance for lovers. Branson feels his teeth grinding and his fists clenching as the man brushes her cheek softly and she turns into his touch, begging for more. He dips her and slowly brings her back to him. Meanwhile, Branson wonders why she has not yet moved to another as do the others. When he does not think they could get any closer, she grips the man's hair, pulling his face close to hers. He picks her up high and slowly slides her down his body all the way to the ground.

Finally, Branson finds that he can release his clenched hands as the man leaves her ... until she looks back to her partner and the music speeds up. She stands, and the man turns back to her. They both run to each other, and just as the flutes stop, they stop, standing in the presence of the other, more passion. The music starts again. She looks away from him, and he brings her back to him. A small smile from both of them and they dance seductively, almost as if no one is there but them.

Branson looks away, not wanting to see any more of the dance. He has a sense of … betrayal. He does not understand why. Then the images of the dance come, reminding him of scenes he wants to forget. Ahni in the arms of another, her sharing that happy, innocent smile of hers with someone other than him. It angers him. No, she belongs to him.

He stops and mentally asks himself, *What am I thinking?*

The applause brings him from his thoughts. He sees that the dancers are bowed, and as they raise their heads to stand, her eyes find his. She stares, frozen. His expression speaks to her in great volumes. As the rest of the dancers rise, she is slow to join them, lowering her eyes in embarrassment. They return to their places and put the robes back on. Branson searches for Uric and sees that he is looking at him in a suspicious manner. The kinsmen stand and gather together to say their goodnights. Branson's farewells are empty; clearly, his mind is elsewhere.

Uric catches Branson's arm and pulls him off to the side, away from lingering ears. He asks in a sharp whisper, "What is it you think you are doing?"

Caught off guard by the question, Branson asks, "What are you rambling about, seeker?"

Uric squeezes his arm. "Your face betrays you. Who was that?"

Branson answers truthfully, "If you are referring to the woman, I have not touched her."

Uric fires back, "Then why does your face resemble that of my son's when his mother has scolded him?"

Branson straightens with a look of bewilderment. He shakes his head. "You are mistaken—"

Uric cuts him off: "Your spirit is duller. You are not happy. When you lie, it is a symbol of distrust. I am your friend; it is not necessary."

Branson exhales heavily. Uric is right. It was foolish of him to lie to his friend—and a seeker at that. He looks around first and then quietly explains, "Her name is Ahni. My head is constantly filled with images of her ever since our first meeting. She was my attendant until I declared my intentions for wanting her—and her, the same. We have also promised not to see each other until I am no longer the dewan's guest. But after tonight, I do not wish to wait."

Uric smiles. "What happened tonight?"

Branson replies smartly, "You know very well what I am speaking of. She should not be in the company of another man ... in *that* dance."

Uric chuckles. "You are jealous, my friend. But more precisely, you have fallen for her."

Branson shrugs. "Perhaps. I have considered that as the cause. It is not so bad, this feeling. There are doubts in me."

Uric shakes his head at his friend's reference to love as trial and error. "Branson, you do not choose to love any more than you choose to be born. It is the Great Spirit's decision. You could not have seen this, even in a vision." Then his tone turns stern: "But she is wise to remove herself from you. Do not be foolish. You must be careful. Do you know her fate if you two are found out?"

Branson holds his hands up. "Found out? We have done nothing."

Uric presses: "Her fate?"

Branson nods. "Exile from service."

Before parting, Uric makes one more comment, "Truly, she must love you to risk all that she is and her life."

Uric leaves with his wife leaning sleepily into him. Branson walks to Gaylen's home alone, thinking of Uric's last words the entire way. He considers how much he loves his service and how much he practices to perfect it. Then he thinks of loving someone more than his service; his dedication to being a huntsman goes unquestioned. It comforts him to know that Ahni seems willing to give up all she has for him. From all he has heard and see, that kind of love happens once in a life cycle; he cannot let her go. His love for Ahni will match hers.

As he nears Gaylen's house, he makes sure there is distance between him and the sires. He looks around in the still bustling nightlife, and after he is sure no one will see him, he diverts his route and hurries toward the servants' quarter. On his approach, he spots lovers enjoying late night trysts, emphasizing his envy.

Branson steps lightly, being careful not to alert the guards or roaming kinsmen. The servants' quarter has quite a few large houses directly behind the kitchen, and he guesses each can hold twenty servants. He isn't surprised that so many servants busy themselves racing about, what with all the festivities and the high-ranking guests of the dewan. He sees servants washing soiled linens, carrying buckets of water to be heated for the sires' baths no doubt, preparing fruits and vegetables for breaking fast, and still more milling in and out of the servants' houses.

Branson walks to the nearest house, and servants pass by him as if he is invisible. He has to stop one carrying folded linens to inquire if he knows Ahni. The servant does and tells him she is bathing. Branson follows the servant's directions into a lightly wooded area. He follows a small light and positions himself behind a tree. Peering around the tree into the lantern's light, he inhales sharply at the sight. There Ahni stands, bathing herself. Her nudity excites him. She bends to soak a cloth in a bucket of warm water and resumes washing the paint from her body. Branson adjusts his position to see more of her, and he steps on a small twig, cracking it soundly. He hurries to hide, berating himself for being so clumsy.

She calls out, "I'll be done in a moment, Dahlia."

He breathes an air of relief from not frightening her, as well as his concealment remaining intact. He closes his eyes and smiles. *Damn, she's beautiful.* He hears her pouring water out of the bucket, and before he knows what he is doing, he walks out from the camouflage of the tree. Still bent down, she looks up, smiling. Then, recognizing her visitor as Branson, she bites her lower lip and stands.

Shaking his head, he asks, "Are you not the least bit shy?"

She replies with a shrug. "My service requires me not to be."

He continues toward her and notices chill bumps on her skin, picks up the towel she brought with her, and wraps her in it, keeping his arms around her. She leans into him, welcoming the heat and his touch. She lays her head against his chest. He smiles and squeezes her before letting her go.

Her eyes dart around, and she whispers, "What are you doing here? You risk much by coming here."

"Do not worry, I am alone. I wanted to see you."

She looks somewhat relieved, but then her relief disappears, replaced with shame when he gives her a stern look.

He says, "I do not dream of you and another man dancing the *Rêve D'Amour*."

She looks away before defending herself: "Is that what you came for? I do what the dewan asks me to do. As do you. It was my hope that you would not be present. After all," she says, looking up at him into his eyes, "it is performed before spirit mates. Did you have yours with you?"

He opens his mouth, then closes it, knowing well that they are at a standstill. She shows a small smile before turning to prepare herself for attendance in the dewan's house. He watches as she dries herself and lets the damp towel fall to the ground. She takes out a small bottle and pours a small amount of the thick oil into her palm. She rubs her hands together, releasing the aroma of fresh ginger and orange, ideal for awakening the senses. Indeed, he is very aware. She felt wonderful in his arms, and now he feels compelled to touch her again.

He walks to her and opens her hands to rub his over hers to transfer some of the oil. He starts at the base of her neck and massages the oil into her soft skin. She closes her eyes and tilts her head to the right just a little to allow him more access to the tensed area. He smiles from her approval and consent. He continues this treatment all the way to her toes, retrieving more oil as necessary. Once he finishes, he stands up and sees that she still has her eyes closed. He cups the side of her face and affectionately strokes her cheek with his thumb until she opens her eyes—and he sees they are filled with desire and longing. His heart seems to fill with more appreciation and fondness.

He whispers, "You *were* beautiful tonight. You should teach me this dance."

She smiles shyly.

Suddenly, their hearts skip a beat as the sound of someone advancing comes from the trees. They both look around for a place for Branson to hide. It is too late; the bushes begin to move to reveal the intruder.

"Ahni, it is almost dawn. You are indulging yourself too much. We should make ready—"

The woman pauses as she emerges from the foliage and sees that Ahni is not alone. "Oh. I am sor—You should have told—It's time, Ahni."

The woman rushes away, embarrassed. Branson exhales before looking back at Ahni and discovers she is trying to cover her laugh and failing. He lets out a chuckle, and a rush of laughter flows from them both. After they get control of themselves, she begins to clothe herself in a similar fashion from their first encounter.

"What is so funny?" Branson asks.

"The look on your face deserves some reward alone. I must admit my expression felt quite similar. I am sorry, but I must agree with Dahlia. It is getting close to the morning hour. I should hurry."

Branson loses his good humor. The thought of her washing and dressing one of the sires—or any man, for that matter—does not sit well with him.

He is just about to tell her that when she speaks first: "I do enjoy seeing you, but you should be more cautious in the future."

Branson decides that he should not belabor the purpose for his unplanned appearance. He takes a shaky breath and begins, "It will be my pleasure. However, that is not the only reason I came to you, Ahni."

At the sound of her name, she stops dressing and looks at him skeptically.

Once he notices that he has her attention, he continues, "Ah. Well, you see, I can't stop thinking about you, nor do I want to. I want to be able to talk to you, to see you, and to touch you often. This courage to risk everything you have for me has not gone ... unnoticed. I have never known anyone like you. This is not the life I would have chosen, but I welcome it proudly. I want to—"

He stops. Apparently, something has upset her. She frowns and turns away from him sharply.

"What is the matter?"

She finishes dressing in a fury and answers, "You huntsmen are all alike. Your devotion to your service blinds you to the world around you. You think that I risk everything for you, when I risk everything for *us*.

Do not think because you are a Bonne Ame, I will jump at your declarations of desire. Change is inevitable, Branson. It is not welcomed; it is accepted."

Eager to rectify his statements, he grasps her by the arms, her back to him, and tries again: "I speak from the heart, woman. I misspoke earlier. Truth is ... I do not know what to say or how to say this. All I know is that my life has been empty without you in it. I came here to tell—no, to ask you ... to join your spirit with mine. Tonight."

When she does not say anything, he turns her to face him. He sees tears streaming down her face, and his heart sinks as she slowly shakes her head. Hurt is the first emotion he experiences. He lets her go, pushing away slightly. He tries to turn and leave, but she grabs hold of his arm to stop him.

"Do not be angry, Branson. I cannot marry you because you are still the dewan's guest."

Desperation replaces hurt. "I cannot go another night with you touching another."

"You must, if we are to marry. The dewan will not release me of my service until the end of the Beni." Nodding at his medallion, she informs him, "Besides, it is not common that a man of such status marries a dewan's servant."

"It is not uncommon either. The dewan will release you once I speak with him."

She smiles. "Your persistence is admirable. But even you, the Bringer of the Chozien, cannot sway custom. It would shame the dewan to release an attendant during a guest's stay. It shows off the servant's disobedience and a weak dewan. He would not like being known as either."

"He will after I speak with him."

Becoming concerned, she widens her eyes. "Do *not* ask him. I will be exiled and gone before you are aware of it—and dead before you can find me."

Confidently, he replies, "Do not worry. No one will harm you."

Dahlia calls for Ahni, interrupting the discourse.

Ahni gathers her bath items and hurries away. Before she disappears into the trees, she says: "Do not say anything, Branson. Please." Then she is gone.

He lets her go. He cannot understand why she does not trust him to speak to the dewan. After a few seconds pass, he starts on his way back to Gaylen's house. The servants are in full work mode when Branson emerges from the trees. As he walks through the bustle, the servants—being well trained in the decorum of hierarchical structure—see his medallion and scurry out of his path while pausing to respectfully offer their customary greeting. He barely hears the quiet greeting of "Namaste, Bonne Ame" from two passing servants.

Not yet accustomed to this, Branson lowers his head in embarrassment and quickens his pace, yet trying to nod at each servant.

He enters the house, seeing that the outside furor does not disturb the calm inside. All the lights are extinguished, save for a few in the halls to aid those servants attending the sires. He frowns at this, for he knows Ahni could be in one of the rooms. As he closes the distance to his room, he feels the events of the day settle in. The entire day has drained him with all the excitement. Only one thought passes through his mind before he falls asleep: *Two more days*.

C H A P T E R

NINE

He wakes the next morning feeling renewed, and he immediately realizes that he has overslept. He quickly dresses and hurries out of his room. Today is the Appointing ceremony, with the announcing of the Chozien's gardien; he must speak with Gaylen before he makes the decision. Rushing out of his room, he runs into a male servant who vehemently apologizes for his rudeness.

Branson interrupts him, "Quickly, man, has the gardien been appointed?"

The servant shakes his head and replies, "No, Bonne Ame. The sires are meeting now to make the decision."

Branson closes his eyes briefly, thanking the Great Spirit. He turns and rushes toward the stairs while the servant yells to him that the council is in the parlor. He gets to the door and takes a couple of deep breaths to slow his breathing before knocking on the door.

A command answers, "Enter."

Branson slowly opens the door to see the faces of the sires and ranked councilmembers looking back at him. Graham and Isaac both have matching smirks, which worsen his shameful tardiness.

To his chagrin, Isaac cannot resist stating the obvious: "It seems our Bonne Ame has not been informed of the proper procedures for governing."

And from Graham: "Mayhap it is too much for the lad to consider others before himself."

Graham is rewarded by the group with audible chuckles.

Gaylen says, "That is enough!"

The men are silenced and receive a disapproving glare from Gaylen. Not only were their statements an insult to Branson but also a blow to Gaylen's judgment.

"It is not for you to discipline a Bonne Ame, but for me. Perhaps it is too much to ask for my sires to lead by example?"

The two men scowl sideways at Branson a moment before turning their attention back to the dewan.

And to Branson, Gaylen scolds, "It seems the previous day's events must have overwhelmed you. As you can see, we are not too forgiving. Learn to pace yourself to keep up with your recent commanding rank." Without offering a moment for explanation, Gaylen continues, "Before I make the final decision, announce each candidate again and why the choice is a good one."

The process for appointing a gardien begins with announcing the kinsmen who have made offers for consideration as the Chozien's gardien, his caretaker. Once it became known that the Jade Order had found the Chozien, kinsmen immediately rushed to volunteer as gardien. Only a sire or dewan can nominate someone for gardien.

Warriors are typically rejected since their life cycle tends to be shorter due to the uncertainty of their service. Along with their willingness, the representative must provide very useful advantages and purposeful abilities as to why they would be the better choice. After all the candidates have been nominated, the dewan and sires meet to critique each one, and then they eliminate the choices in turn by vote. This process continues until the dewan feels satisfied and ready to make a decision. Apparently, this has already taken place, and Gaylen is offering Branson the chance to hear the choices.

Marquis speaks first: "My brother, Micah. He is a powerful warrior who has proven his skill exceptional, all the way through his promotion to high warrior of the Glen Clan warriors. He offers his care and personal training of a strong and loyal Chozien."

Harwen is next: "Rahim, a great seeker through his many years of service. The Huin Clan is known for our indulgence in the spirit. We have gained much from Rahim's teaching of healing crop cultivation, and cleansing waters. He offers assurance of a peaceful and attentive Chozien."

Uric nods. "It is true. Rahim serves well. He has my approval as well."

Connor suggests another warrior. Tuan and Sim speak for their cousin, a huntswoman, with a family that would enhance the Chozien's strategic and political maturity. Some sires do not speak, as their candidates have already been eliminated.

Branson waits in nervous anticipation for his chance to offer a candidate. He can see his chest beating as his heart pounds against it. He adjusts and readjusts in his seat to compensate for the building anticipation.

Finally, Gaylen speaks again, "Are there no more offers or objections?"

Gaylen scans the room, looking at each sire briefly. He pauses a moment on Branson, because of the huntsman's bowed head and the consternation on his face.

Just as Gaylen opens his mouth to announce the decision, Branson stands and says, "There is another."

Branson receives numerous exaggerated exhales and annoying murmurs as a result.

"What?" Gaylen responds. "And who is your candidate?"

Branson draws up, conjuring confidence. "None of the candidates will suffice for gardien."

This causes a commotion of more mumbling and angered glares directed at him—all except for Uric, who sits back in his chair with a knowing smile on his face, and Gaylen, with a look of curiosity.

Intrigued as to what the Bonne Ame has to say, Gaylen quiets the men and inquires of Branson, "Why is it you do not think these nominees will be good enough for gardien?"

Branson looks at every man in the eye as he speaks: "None of them know him. He should not be seen as the Chozien, but as a child. They will train an animal instead of raising a son. The gardien must love the child, and I know of one who does." He pauses briefly. "I love this child as if he were born of my own spirit, my blood. I offer myself as gardien."

Shock shows on every face; some jaws even slightly drop. No one expected this.

Graham laughs. "Ridiculous. You are but twenty-five years. You are a young huntsman, still studying his service. And if that is not enough, you have no partner to care for the child."

Branson nods, sharing Graham's assessment. Branson traces his mind for an answer until he settles on one. Truth—the truth is always known to set a spirit free. "Do not presume to judge me, Graham, as that right is reserved for someone far greater than you or I. That said, I was chosen by the Great Spirit to seek out the Chozien. I have brought him here. It is the child who speaks to me now. I need him as much as he needs me. It pains me at times when an entire day goes by and I do not see him. Is this not how you feel about your own child? I have found my place. The Chozien will be trained and knowledgeable in all components of the spirit so as not to be seen as weak or unworthy. I offer him the patience of the huntsman, the healing of the seeker, the strength of the warrior, and the love of a father."

As Branson spoke, he poured his heart into every word. He wants every man who has a child to feel the passion of raising his son into a man and the pain of failing to prepare him for the world. Again, the room sits in silence. Still, the faces carry the expression of shock, although satisfied. Branson scans the room in nervous anxiety. He waits for someone to decline his offer again.

After what takes a few moments but seemingly ages, Gaylen finally speaks, repeating the final question: "Are there no more offers or objections?"

When no one speaks and a few heads shake, the dewan looks over all who are present and declares, "I have made my decision. Branson Kuo-Lin of the Zin Clan will be appointed gardien."

Branson exhales, realizing that he was holding his breath. Applause rings throughout the room. All stand from their chairs, clapping and smiling for Branson, with the exception of Graham and Isaac. The kinsmen move to congratulate him with slaps on the back and forearm clasping.

Remy says, "We had you for donateur. You save us from another meeting for the Chozien's protector."

Because Branson does not have a family of his own, his attention will not be divided between his duty as gardien and husband. Therefore, a donateur—personal guard—will not be necessary unless by request or deemed necessary in the child's first years. Branson clenches his teeth, secretly hoping that his marital status will change shortly.

Then Sim says, "It is good to see so much passion in one so young."

Although Branson nods his head in gratitude and returns the strong grip of the forearm out of respect, he barely hears the kind appraisals from the sires. He stands speechless, smiling a little and crossing his arms. He does not come out of his daze until Uric appears with a hefty slap on the back.

"Well, my congratulations to you, friend. It seems you are now a father. You look ... shocked. Are you?"

Branson looks at him, still amazed. "I did not know how much I wanted the boy until I started to speak on my behalf. I'm going to be a father ..."

When Branson's words trail off, Uric puts his hand on his shoulder and nods. "You spoke quite well and true. I am proud to be a father myself, and your friend."

Gaylen claps his hands twice loudly, bringing the focus back to him. "We must prepare to announce the Appointing. We have lingered for far too long as the day grows late. I do not want a spirit hold full of impatient and angry kinsmen. It is time."

The sires begin to file out of the parlor when Gaylen says, "Branson, stay a moment. I must speak with you."

Graham and Isaac cut jealous eyes through Branson. He ignores them. He will not let bitterness sway his great accomplishment.

After all the men have left from the room and it is quiet, Gaylen offers a chair to Branson and they sit. Gaylen initiates the conversation: "The Chozien brings change to the world. Never have I seen a huntsman so eager to father a child not his own and from one so young. This is a very good sign. Your words hold true meaning, and any man with a child knows it. I am concerned that you have no woman to aid in the care of the child. Even with one child, it helps to have a partner. Our world is very demanding and does not leave moments for nurturing an infant and training in a service. You must choose a companion quickly—What is it?" Gaylen asks upon seeing Branson's shrewd smile.

"Yes, Dewan. There is a woman I want to ask for."

Gaylen exhales, smiling. "Good. Who is she so that we may make a quick ceremony?"

Branson hesitates for a moment and then inhales deeply. "Ahni. I have thought of nothing but her since I arrived. She is an attendant, and—"

Branson is cut off by Gaylen's swift explosion from his chair. He knows then that he has made a mistake and quickly tries to clarify his words: "Dewan, if you will allow me—"

"NO!"

"I know this is not acceptable, but—"

"Do you know what you ask of me, boy? You have violated our custom. If I were to allow you to marry this woman, I would lose the people. I will be shunned as weak and an unfit dewan. A weak dewan signifies a weak order. The Jade will become vulnerable where even the Chozien could not help us. No, you ask too much this time. The child you can have but the woman you cannot."

Branson opens his mouth to protest, but Gaylen narrows his eyes and speaks low: "Do not make me lose all respect for you."

Branson looks away, unable to meet his dewan's eyes. Already his heart mourns the loss of a wife.

Gaylen fumes with such anger that all he can say is, "Come," and walks to the door without waiting.

Head hung, Branson follows.

From the sound of it, the mood outside proves a complete contrast from that of the approaching two men. Laughing and abundant chatter explode as the door opens, revealing the dewan and Branson with expressions of displeasure. Gaylen wastes no time gathering everyone together to begin the Appointing. Haru announces that the people are present and ready. The procession begins as it did the day before.

Although Gaylen is furious with Branson, his words speak highly of the appointed gardien: "This day signifies leadership and loyalty. Today is the day one man, a great man, a bright spirit begins another journey to greatness. He gains the responsibility of shaping the Chozien into a leader and accepts it proudly. This man speaks from his heart. He says the gardien should care for the Chozien as if he is of his own blood. He says the gardien should train the Chozien in all services of the order and in all makings of life. So is the truth.

"My order, I give you on my living breath and my eternal *ame* that this gardien will raise the Chozien in the way of the Jade Order and bring us our long-awaited peace."

A murmur of awe and admiration spreads through the crowd. They have never heard the dewan speak so highly of someone as to have pledged not only his life but his *ame* on them. This vow is as truly bonding as it is precarious.

"I have appointed the huntsman Bonne Ame Branson Kuo-Lin as gardien."

A great cheer rises. Some come from Branson's Zin kinsmen. Others erupt from the joyous crowd, relieved that the gardien is worthy by his recent promotion and successful *Quête*. But most come from his service, the huntsmen, who cheer the loudest out of pride and gloating.

Branson is shocked by Gaylen's pledge and its hidden meaning: He knows well that if he pledges his life on Branson's success and abilities that Branson would not attempt to break custom again and risk endangering the order.

Branson temporarily forgets his earlier reprimand from his

unorthodox request, as well as the infamous pledge, and fully indulges in the moment. He walks to the front and takes position beside Gaylen, where he kneels. Gaylen places a hand on Branson's bowed head, and the crowd settles, allowing a brief silence for a private prayer by Gaylen to the Great Spirit, blessing Branson with strength and diligence that only nearby bystanders can hear.

After the prayer, Suriah brings the child out again and stands waiting. Meanwhile, Keno places a sharp blade with an ivory handle in Gaylen's waiting hand. Branson stands, presenting his outstretched left arm to his dewan. Two servants appear at his side, one holding a silver cup and another holding clean cloths.

Gaylen takes hold of Branson's left arm by the wrist and raises the knife high, saying, "By his blood, he vows to defend the Chozien with his own living breath."

Then Gaylen uses the knife to draw two horizontal lines across Branson's bicep with just enough pressure to pierce the skin, releasing bright red blood. Branson barely flinches from the initial sharp pain that quickly resides. The servant holds the silver cup under the wounds to collect the blood. After a moment, when enough blood has fallen into the cup, the other servant wipes Branson's arm free of most of the flowing blood with one cloth, then bandages the arm firmly with the other.

Suriah steps forth and holds the baby out to her dewan. With one finger, Gaylen dips his finger in the silver cup and places a print on the baby's forehead.

The baby starts to get restless, and Suriah tries to calm him, but he sees Branson and reaches for him. Branson looks to Gaylen for permission, and the dewan nods. Branson takes the infant from Suriah and feels a father's deep love for the first time. Happiness flows through him. He is sure the seekers can see the brilliance of his spirit.

He turns to the crowd, smiling and cradling the child with one arm. Then, raising the other, he shouts, "Peace in victory! Peace in victory!"

The crowd responds in like, shouting the Jade victory chant. The second day of the Beni begins. Branson holds the baby up, laughing while the baby happily plays with his face. Even in this joyous moment, he cannot forget the thought of Ahni. It hurts that she cannot join him—and will never do so.

He hands the baby over to Suriah, his reluctance at letting him go clear in his eyes. She tries to woo the child away from crying as he reaches back for his new father. Gaylen squeezes Branson's shoulder and tells him to enjoy himself. Branson nods gratefully and heads down the steps into a cluster of huntsmen, who eagerly await him. The huntsmen begin chanting his name while lifting him in the air. In his laughter, he remembers Uric and how he wants to celebrate this moment with him as well.

He looks to the top of the stairs for his friend, but the stoic faces of Gaylen and his general catch his eye. Gaylen turns and walks back inside while whispering to Haru. As they disappear into the house, Gaylen uses extreme hand gestures to emphasize his words. Branson does not understand the secrecy about something that obviously seems of grave significance at this time.

The constant noise and music bring his attention back to Uric. Branson waves, inviting Uric along as his fellow huntsmen carry him deeper into the throng of celebrating kinsmen. A cup of strong libation is shoved into his hands, and soon his frustrations are forgotten. All into the starlit night, Branson celebrates his fatherhood. He enjoys himself so much that he has to be carried back to his room, where he promptly falls asleep.

C H A P T E R

TEN

A sharp knock at the door awakens Branson. His head aching, he groggily walks to the door and opens it. Uric stands there, looking in somewhat the same condition.

"I did not want you to get another tongue-lashing, so I came to fetch you. Hurry, we must meet Gaylen for the Naming of your son."

Branson nods and closes the door to dress. For some reason, Uric's voice seems unusually loud today. Branson makes a mental note to let him know that he can hear perfectly well. No matter, Branson dresses quickly and joins Uric outside his door. The smell of food cooking fills the air, and Branson nearly gags.

"How is it that you are awake so early? If I remember, you drank just as much as I," Branson asks with a sickly look.

Uric yawns before replying, "You do not have the luxury of a wife to rouse you from a night of celebrating." He reaches inside his side satchel, retrieves a tiny bag, and gives it to Branson. "Mix two pinches of this powder in water and drink ... all of it. It will help ease the pounding in your head and settle your stomach. Be careful of the amount you use. Ground herbs are very strong."

Branson and Uric arrive at the parlor just as the sires are entering. It is apparent that they are just finishing their morning meal, as some are licking their fingers or taking the last bites of sweet buns. Branson has to close his eyes against the nauseating smell and sight of the food.

As everyone settles, Gaylen commences the meeting: "Sires, today we give the Chozien a name. This name will signify the Chozien for the man he is to become and encompass all that the Jade represents. Choose wisely."

Sim offers, "Name him Eron, for the peace the Great Spirit gives us."

"No—Damaris, for gentle and mild-tempered," counters his brother, Tuan.

Connor says in a matter-of-fact way, "Gentleness and peace are not in the life of the Chozien. He must be steady and focused. Etan would be fitting."

Graham laughs. "He will need to be clever and wise in the dealings with the Onyx from their trickery. Zeroun is best."

Isaac nods. "I second that name."

Branson inwardly rolls his eyes.

Uric nods his head slowly. "These are all exceptional qualities that he should possess. Let us not forget he is one of us and just as vulnerable. Call him Aitan for his power and strength. Anything else would dishonor his *ame* and his character."

After the names are offered, the room falls silent, in consideration. Gaylen stands to announce the decision. He nudges Branson, as he is still feeling the aftereffects of the night before. Branson straightens himself in his chair, trying to avoid suspicion but not succeeding.

The choice is made, and the name Aitan will be given to the Chozien. Even Graham and Isaac seem satisfied. Hearing his son's name for the first time, Branson hides his curiosity by applauding along with the other sires while making another mental note to inquire of Uric about its meaning again. The meeting adjourns, and the public announcement immediately follows.

During the proclamation of his son's name, Branson desperately tries to fight back his growing lightheadedness. As the third and last day of the Beni commences, Branson drags himself back into the house to get to his room. On the way, he stops a servant to request a cup of water be brought to his room. Branson can only hope Uric's remedy lives up to its promise. After mixing the suggested amount of the herbs and drinking the entire mixture, Branson lies down, waiting for the tonic to take effect, and soon falls asleep.

Repeated sharp knocks on his door jar Branson from his slumber. He rises slowly at first, but then upon realizing that his headache and queasiness have gone and left an empty stomach, he hurries to the door to see what the rush is about. He opens the door, and there stands the attendant who passed the message of his interest to Ahni.

Her eyes are wide with fear, and she keeps glancing around. Finally, she turns to him, and hisses, "What have you done?"

Surprised by her blunt accusation, he says, "I have no knowledge of what you are speaking about, woman."

"Your impatience! The guards have taken her. She will be banish—"

Branson cuts her off by roughly grabbing her shoulders and pulling her into the room. "What are you talking about? Who are you speaking of? Hurry, speak!"

With one eyebrow raised, she stares at him. "You *don't* know, do you? It is Ahni. I was with her when they came for her. They never said a word—just took her away. But I knew. That's why I came here. I will lose my friend because of you."

He releases her. He runs a hand through his hair. Shaking his head, he tries to make sense of everything. "I asked the dewan for her ... as my wife. I tried to explain.... I didn't know. "

The attendant looks at him wide-eyed. "You did *what*? You have all but condemned her yourself!"

Branson doesn't hear her. He tries to think of how he can save her. His heart feels like it will explode at any moment. He would die if she were to be banished. He continues to pace, scrounging his head for solutions. Then he stops. He grabs his hunting knife and slips it behind him at his waist.

He asks the servant, "Quick, where is she now?"

She looks sorrowfully downcast and points toward Gaylen's parlor. "She is being banished as we speak."

He never even sees the attendant collapse to the floor, crying. Branson runs to the nursery. He bursts into the room, startling Suriah. She is sitting on a fur rug in the middle of the floor with Aitan. He snatches up his son and begins to leave.

Suriah shouts, "Where are you going? You can't just take him—"

Branson whips around, coming close enough to touch the woman's nose with his own. He sneers, "Who are you to question me? I am Bonne Ame, and he is my son."

Suriah lowers her eyes and steps back.

Branson rushes out the door, headed to Gaylen's parlor. He notices some bed linen lying on the floor at the bottom of the stairs near the closed parlor door. At the door, he pauses a moment to look at his son, who smiles up at him. He remembers how empty he felt before Aitan came into his life and how proud he is to be a father. He asks the Great

Spirit for strength and courage, and later he will ask his son for forgiveness. He looks around to see if there are any eavesdroppers nearby, and then he hurries inside the parlor and shuts the door behind him.

Ahni awakens early on the third day of the Beni, and she cannot remember feeling this happy. It is uncommon these days to find love in its purest form. She smiles so much her face hurts. Even then, she doesn't stop. Her happiness seems to glow for the servants who have worked alongside her for years and never noticed her, but now they stop and stare as they begin their day of service.

Gaylen's servants feel great relief on this final day of the Beni. After today, the sires with their clan's kinsmen will be leaving, and the servants' days will go back to normal. Ahni stands around a vat of hot water the width of her outstretched arms, washing bedding with her closest friends, Dahlia and Reba. Her friends look at her suspiciously because of the ever-present smile and the dreamy look in her eyes.

Curious to figure out this mystery, Dahlia asks, "What is it that makes you so happy to wash filthy linens?"

Reba adds, "Yes. Do not be selfish. We want to smile as well."

Ahni blinks her eyes and grins bashfully. She responds, "Oh, I did not realize I was smiling. I was just thinking of the future."

Dahlia snorts. "Another decade of red hands." She lifts her hands from the hot water to add emphasis.

Ahni looks to see if any servants are close by before she speaks in hushed tones. "Branson wants to ask the dewan to release me and join our spirits."

The women cover their mouths with excitement. Dahlia and Reba tease Ahni with fantasies of marital bliss and lovers' quarrels, careful not to incite suspicion from their laughter. However great their joy is, it is short-lived.

The sky seems to grow dark and the air thick as two guards approach. They ask which of the women is called by the name of Ahni. No one speaks. They do not need to; their looks identify and convict her.

The guards grip each arm and take her, nearly dragging her since their pace is too quick for the small woman. Dahlia and Reba stare after the fleeing trio, disbelieving what they have just witnessed. Dahlia turns back to continue washing the linens, tears streaming down her rosy cheeks. Reba cannot accept the fate of her friend, nor can she understand why Dahlia has.

Reba lashes out at her, keeping her voice at a whisper, "How can you continue life knowing your friend will lose hers in a matter of days?"

Dahlia wipes her face before she responds, "Ahni knew the risk she took. It is her fate she has sealed. I grieve for her loss even now."

"Ahni does not need your grief. She would not go back to cleaning soiled linens so easily if it were you."

Dahlia snaps her head up to glare at Reba. "I would not give her the opportunity to make that choice." Then she adds, "What would you have me do? One life is gone; why lose another?"

Reba shakes her head. "You only live one life, Dahlia. It might as well be a just and true one. Show that you hold more value than washing the backs of others."

Dahlia plunges the linen back into the steaming water. "We are all significant to the preservation of the Jade Order. I do not judge my worth by my rank."

Reba turns away and says sadly, "Neither by friendship."

She leaves Dahlia scrubbing away at the linens.

Reba has no idea what lies at the conclusion of her actions or whether the Bonne Ame will remember her. She stops to gather some folded bedding. She enters the dewan's house through the kitchen. Reba is known for her role as an attendant, and her unnecessary presence in the dewan's house at this hour in the day could raise questions. She hopes the bedding will divert any attention directed at her that would impede her journey to her destination.

She keeps her eyes lowered, not wanting to provoke any suspicion. Her heart beats fiercely with anxiety, but the fear for her friend roars louder. She makes her way across the entrance hall and stops on her way up the stairs. She hears voices coming from the dewan's parlor and decides to inspect further. She tiptoes close to the door and leans the side of her face against it. She can't quite make out who is speaking … but the words are heartbreaking. She backs away slowly, shaking her head, her mouth agape. She lets the linens fall, and she covers her mouth from a gasp. She has no time to lose.

She runs up the stairs, finally coming to the door she once went through to pass along the very message that set this devastation in motion. She raps on the door hard. She waits. No answer. Panic rises. *He must be here!* She sends a prayer to the Great Spirit before striking the door again, harder. Finally, a tired Branson answers the door.

There is no use struggling; the guards have a lock on Ahni. Before they enter the courtyard, they stop and quietly offer her a chance at saving some of her pride.

The first one states the obvious: "It would be better for you to stop your squirming."

The second one's speech sounds curt, deliberate: "You save much face, walking through the door. Yes, better than dragging you."

She nods, thanking them for their harsh consideration. They continue the path to the front entrance of Gaylen's house. This course of action seems so familiar to her, being brought through the front entrance and escorted by guards.

Ahni wonders, *Where have I seen this before?*

Just as they turn the corner into the courtyard leading to the front steps, the memory comes to her, stopping her legs. The guards halt and look at her with raised eyebrows, and she hurries to pick up her feet. Escorting a servant through the front doors of the dewan's house is part of a punishment, shame by public exposure. She will be seen by all and marked as unfit and defiant.

She asks herself, *What have I done to displease the dewan so?*

Again, the answer comes to her. This time it does not stop her feet, but nearly stops her heart. She *told* him not to ask. He just would not listen. *Stubborn! To think huntsmen are known for their patience.* She holds back tears as the people turn to look at her. Her mother would always tell her to hold her head high, even if it was to her own death. For sure, this will lead to it.

Once they enter the entrance hall, the guards grab hold of Ahni's arms again. They come to stand in front of the door to Gaylen's parlor and knock. A reddened Haru opens the door. Once he sees it is Ahni, he narrows his eyes at her and steps aside to let them enter. The guards guide Ahni to the middle of the room and bow deeply before exiting. Haru closes the door behind them. She is left alone and defenseless.

Gaylen, followed by Haru, comes to stand before her. She keeps her eyes low. She notices a rough-looking gown made of coarse material lying on a chair at the side. They stand there in silence for a moment. That moment feels like forever to her.

Finally, the dewan speaks: "You know why you are here?"

Ahni nods. "Yes, Dewan."

He tilts her chin upward. Yet, she still will not look into his eyes. He suggests, "You may look at me."

She does so, slowly.

Gaylen remains quite calm and continues, "Why break custom for him?"

She looks away for a moment, then looks back at him and responds proudly, "I risk much for the one I love. Would you not have done the same for Mistress Zahrine?"

Haru breaks his mask into a halfway smile.

Gaylen cannot help himself by chuckling. "You are wise and quite brave, little one. I will ask you the same question again. This time, do not challenge me with your answer. Why break custom for him?"

Her eyes well with tears, but they do not fall. She takes on a faraway look and smiles when she answers, "He looks in my eyes when he speaks to me. He touches my spirit with his own. My dreams do not exist without him in them, and I do not see a future where he and I are apart. It is a bond that can only be created by the Great Spirit."

"Do you know the cost of your actions?"

She nods; this time, the tears fall.

Gaylen shakes his head. "Love can be cruel at times. We must take care of our fragile hearts. Time doesn't exist when we speak of our devotion to another. Tell me, can you count the number of life cycles you would live with this man?"

She replies, "No, Dewan. There is no number that would count as high."

He wipes her tears and says softly, "So then, what would have been one more day?"

Understanding, her mouth opens, but nothing comes out. She knows what will be next. She wants to throw herself at his feet and beg his forgiveness out of desperation. She cannot; he must not see her weak. Even now, she still holds his respect high.

Gaylen takes a step back, knowing she spoke true: he would break custom to be with his Zahrine. How could he punish a woman for loving so deeply? Still, it doesn't matter. It is heavy, this weight he bears. The orders ask much of their dewans. This is the path he chose freely. And so he must banish her, even as his heart goes out to her. Yet, he must maintain his name in order to protect the Jade Order. His duty and responsibility to his people strengthens him to complete the banishment.

Ahni stands motionless, waiting to become *banni*, the name given to those who have been banished. Haru goes to the chair with the dress, picks it up, and returns to stand beside Gaylen.

The dewan's voice sounds emotionless and cold as he sentences her, a stark contrast to his prior calm: "You have committed a grave breaking—a breaking punishable by banishment. A crime so great, it is only surpassed by treason penalized by death. I say before you that you have disgraced the Jade Order. You hold no honor. Your actions show no concern for the safety of the Jade. As such, the spirit hold will show no generosity for you this day forth."

He then begins the stripping. This act is done so that the offender can feel the true shame of their actions and know that they are no longer part of the clan. He will not strip Ahni of all her clothing, but enough to symbolize the separation from the spirit hold.

Gaylen first begins with the sleeve of one shoulder. Tearing the material from her arm almost effortlessly, and then the other, he says, "You disgrace the Jade. You are not fit to wear our colors."

Ahni hears the disappointment in his voice. As she sees each sleeve of her blouse float to the floor, she feels a piece of her fall with them. It is good; a part of her should stay. This was her home. She does not know of anything more, nor does she desire to. She knows how cruel the world can be, how it devours spirits and *ames* only to smile and thirst for more. And she is walking into it happily.

Once Gaylen finishes the stripping, Haru throws the coarse dress at her feet.

The dewan commands, "This will be your only possession when you leave. You are not to be seen within the spirit hold borders. You will not—"

Gaylen stops mid-sentence, interrupted by someone entering through his parlor door. All three turn to see who dares intrude in the dewan's private room without invite or permission.

Branson stands in front of the again closed door, cradling his son.

Everyone's reaction is unique to their interpretation of his intrusion. Gaylen narrows his eyes, grits his teeth, and takes in a breath of exasperation. Haru is more impulsive, already angered by the seeming threat Branson posed on the dewan and the Jade. He sees this interference as a sign of further insult. He reaches for his sword, ready to release Branson of his *ame*, but he stops when held back by a hand from Gaylen.

Ahni brightens for an instant and then dissipates to a face of worry.

Branson frowns at this; his presence should provide relief, not doubt.

Gaylen is fuming on the inside; however, his experience as a dewan aids with his calm appearance. In fact, he looks more irritated than angry. Still, he feels intrigued by Branson's appearance with Aitan and decides to inquire.

Gaylen crosses his arms casually and asks, "What is it now, Branson? Why do you bring Aitan?"

Branson finds himself a bit annoyed by Gaylen's lack of concern for the child. If Gaylen is willing to talk, though, then maybe Branson will not have to carry out his intentions.

Branson avoids the question involving the child and says, "Dewan, there is no need for this."

Gaylen mockingly lifts his eyebrows and looks to Haru and then back to Branson. "Oh, and why not?"

Branson grits his teeth from irritation at not being taken seriously. "I have not lain with her. We have committed no offense."

Gaylen takes a deep breath before speaking: "It is enough you have asked for this woman. It does not matter if you have taken her to your bed. I care not. It is the perception you have created. Rumors will spread like fire in the wind."

Branson offers another suggestion: "I will take her and we will leave."

Gaylen shakes his head. "It is too late for that. You cannot abandon your duty, your son, and your order."

Branson puts his head down, thinking quickly. The dewan is right: Branson cannot desert all that he knows, and especially his son. He cannot leave Ahni either.

Gaylen assumes Branson's silence as forfeit. His patience has worn thin; he motions Branson away. "You may go now. I will send for you to correct your offense ... again."

Branson shakes his head slowly. He positions Aitan upright with one arm, and with the other, he reaches behind him, clutching the knife but not yet pulling it from his belt.

Gaylen takes on a look of suspicion and states, "Do not be foolish."

Branson ignores the warning and instead answers a previous

question: "You asked why Aitan is here. Here is my answer." He slides the knife from his belt and places it to Aitan's throat, careful to position his thumb between the cold blade and the child's tender warm flesh. "If you send Ahni to her death, so you do with this child."

Again, Haru instinctively grabs for his sword, this time unsheathing it halfway. His stance, menacing, shows his readiness for an attack. Gaylen stands there, stunned into disbelief, his face filled with fury, having finally lost his patience. Meanwhile, Ahni falls to her knees, pleading for Branson to release the Chozien.

His eyes never leaving Branson, Gaylen says, "Silence, girl. You will bring others."

Ahni silences herself by covering her mouth, though her eyes show terror. Haru begins to creep sideways, as if circling his enemy. He stops when Branson narrows his eyes at him and brings the knife closer to Aitan's neck, drawing bright red blood. Ahni gasps, thinking the blood falls from the Chozien's neck.

Gaylen raises his hand to his general. "Be still, Haru." And then to Branson, he says, "You know what it is you do, boy?"

"You leave me no choice, Dewan. I give my life in service to you and the Jade. I do this not for what you can give me in return but for the love of my people."

Gaylen hisses, "What kind of love is this? This is treason."

Branson shakes his head. "This is more. I came to you in secret, for I knew what I asked could condemn me. Yet, even with this knowledge, I asked. I knew the risk, but I trusted *you*. All I ask is that you do the same of me."

Gaylen takes on a look of bewilderment and asks, "How have I broken your trust? You asked me for the release of a servant during the Beni. I refused and spared you a punishment fitting your offense."

"It is not enough to spare my life if Ahni is to lose hers. I beg for your forgiveness. I ask for Pitié."

Branson uses the word admitting to shame and a request for the dewan's mercy—a humbling statement usually used in dire circumstances, mainly before death. Throughout Gaylen and Branson's exchange, Haru notices Branson has lost his focus to the point that he has relaxed his hold on the knife. He inches closer to man and child, now standing at a rear diagonal to Branson's left.

Haru hears only silence, not even his own breath. He knows he has to be quick in dealing with a huntsman. He waits, keeping his eyes on the knife. He watches for the perfect moment. Soon Branson loosens his grip, and the knife drifts farther away from Aitan's throat. Haru jumps at this opportunity. He lunges at Branson, catching the wrist that holds the knife and wrapping his arm around Branson's neck, squeezing. Caught off guard, Branson struggles to hold both the child and the knife. His efforts are hopeless; Haru has an iron grip on his wrist.

Once Branson ceases his struggle, Gaylen advances. Haru tightens his grip on Branson's wrist, applying pressure that forces Branson to release the knife. Gaylen reaches them and tries to take Aitan. Branson sees this and immediately begins to fight back, however futile it may be. Haru does not wait until Branson tires himself again. He squeezes his forearm around Branson's neck, causing him to gasp for breath. Haru stops just before Branson loses consciousness, and Gaylen removes the child safely from Branson's hold.

With Aitan safely secured out of harm's way, Haru kicks Branson at the knees, and he falls forward. Haru hits him with a powerful elbow to the jaw and two jabs to the nose. Haru pulls back for another strike but stops when he sees that Branson is no longer defending himself. Instead of striking him again, he kicks Branson backward and places his boot on Branson's chest, pinning him to the floor. He waits for a command from Gaylen.

Ahni is racked with tears, her shoulders shaking and her hand covering her mouth to silence her weeping.

Gaylen handles the child gently and playfully bounces him up and down to calm him. Once Aitan settles, Gaylen keeps his eyes on the child as he asks Branson, "Why do you not fight back? Was it not your intent to force me to release Ahni?"

Branson responds tiredly, "It is not Haru who denies me the woman."

Gaylen raises his eyebrows at the audacity. "You wish to call me to combat? You huntsmen and your pride. Very confusing, wouldn't you say, Haru?"

Haru grunts, never taking his eyes away from his target.

Gaylen laughs. "Did you not ask for Pitié but a moment ago? Now you wish for combat. Do you expect me to take you seriously? Indeed, you have much to learn. Stand him, Haru."

Haru manhandles Branson to his feet. To Branson, it feels effortless.

Gaylen comes to stand in front of Branson. "Now look at the mess you have made. Surely you do not want to give up your son to another. Nor do you want to give up your woman."

Gaylen begins to pace back and forth, comforting Aitan all the while. His brow wrinkles, deep in thought. He taps his bottom lip. Finally, he nods. He looks to Ahni, who is still kneeling, and although her tears have not stopped, her sobbing has.

"Gather yourself, girl, and come stand here," Gaylen says as he motions to Branson's right side.

Ahni begins to collect her fallen sleeves, then remembers why they are there and leaves them behind. She comes to stand next to Branson, close to him but not touching—their skin but a whisper apart.

Gaylen stands in front of them. Looking disappointed, he states, "You will both be punished for your offenses."

Ahni hangs her head in despair, although she feels relieved that she will avoid banishment. Branson inhales deeply, tempering his compulsion to raise an argument.

Gaylen lifts one eyebrow, demanding obedience. "I will not have your impudence destroy the Jade. You will learn to respect and abide by the law. Not even I can commit this breaking." He pauses. "You ask for Pitié; you shall have it. You will bear the marks of your shame from today until the release of your *ame*. You above all should be more reluctant to risk the order on such selfish whims. I hope you defend our way as you have your woman."

Feeling his cheeks redden from shame, Branson gazes down at the floor as he replays his previous actions over the past days.

Gaylen looks at the child he holds. "It is true, this child brings much change. I hope it is for peace, but somehow I do not believe it will be without tragedy." He pauses. "I will allow the two of you to marry."

Ahni clasps Branson's hand in both of hers, shock overwhelming her. Branson stands motionless and wide-eyed, his voice caught in his throat.

"However, you will wait until the end of the Beni and fifteen days past. You will not seek another, nor speak the other's name. Your punishments will remain a mystery to all and each other, as will this ... amnesty. Understand?"

They both respond in unison, "Yes, Dewan."

Satisfied, Gaylen passes Aitan to Ahni. "Welcome your son—briefly."

Ahni holds him close, smiling reassurance. Aitan catches on and playfully grabs at her lengthy braids.

This heartwarming moment is short-lived, as Gaylen takes the child from her and hands him off to Haru, saying, "Have the Chozien taken to Suriah and Ahni returned to the servants' house where she resides."

Immediately, Ahni is reminded of her disobedience. Sadly, she gives Branson's hand one last squeeze. He smiles at her, then she leaves with Haru.

Branson's eyes follow her out the door and linger after it closes. Although his spirit feels stronger, he is filled with longing the moment her hand leaves his. Somehow, even with the fulfillment of his spirit present, it feels draining. Odd. He does not know how he will be punished; all he can think of is how he will show gratitude to the dewan for being merciful.

Gaylen, though, remains furious—with Branson and himself. The dewan knows he should have banished both for their breaking. Again, he risks his life for this huntsman. He chides himself for letting his personal feelings and experiences interfere with his decision. He has banished many before, and never has he rescinded his judgment. His anger with Branson stems from his defiance of the laws. Branson must accept his responsibility and deny temptations that threaten the livelihood of the Jade Order.

Gaylen studies Branson now as he looks at the vacant doorway—yet again distracted from his duty. Gaylen shakes his head, hoping against the obvious perils. He sees Branson's spirit is brighter and feels its warmth, yet even the intensity of the huntsman's spirit cannot sway his fury. As Haru steps back into the room, Gaylen eagerly searches for a release.

All who receive teaching in a service of the Jade surrender their energies to the dewan. Thus, Gaylen can draw on as many energies as he needs. It is meant for his survival: As long as the dewan lives, so does the order.

As Branson takes a deep breath and readies himself to express his deepest appreciation to Gaylen, he turns toward the dewan. In that moment, though, Gaylen channels between Branson and Haru's energies so as to not arouse suspicion. Those whom he draws spirit from can feel its draining.

Then the dewan strikes Branson in the chest with a blow that knocks him several strides back and to the floor, where he lies motionless and unconscious.

Gaylen straightens and folds his arms across his chest. He narrows his eyes at Branson's limp body and makes a promise to himself: *I will ensure he always remembers.*

CHAPTER
ELEVEN

A frightened boy sits alone in a corner. Streaks of dried tears stain his travel-weary and now chubby cheeks. Fear fills his heart because he does not know where his father is. He looks around. The boy sees that this place is as grand as it is spacious. He remembers a time in an open place and a lone bird landed on the ground—just pecking at any bit of edible grub, as they all did. But the lone bird caught the eye of the bigger birds with ugly bare heads. He likened their rush at it to rats scurrying away after their nest had been disturbed, which he also remembered. He cannot count but he remembers the big black birds' number blackening the ground. He imagines this grand space could hold many, many more even than the empty dirt that surrounded him back then.

The vastness begins to overwhelm him; never has he seen anything so great. He sees a man standing a little ways in front of him—a lean young man wearing black clothing, with a heavy black hide covering his shoulders. His expression is stoic and unchanging. He just stands there, watching. The boy shivers. He spots a cover, reaches for it, and pulls a smaller version of the man's cloak over him, immediately feeling its warmth.

The boy feels the floor begin to vibrate in short intervals. He widens his eyes and glances around even as he pulls the cloak under his chin and squeezes closer into the corner. A shadow appears on the floor in front of the young man. The boy fixes his wide eyes on the dark figure as it grows larger. Finally, two boots the size of a full grown man meet with the shadow.

A towering man, taller than the young one, comes into view. The boy runs his eyes up the length of the man, trying to match a face with the massive tower. This man has a full beard and thick, dark, straight hair. He approaches the silent, watching young man and speaks with him for a short time. When the tall one turns around to look at the boy, he is surprisingly smiling—a warm and inviting smile. He clasps his hands behind his back and walks to the boy. The man kneels in front of the boy and opens his arms, motioning for him to come closer.

The boy wrinkles his brow and tilts his head to the side curiously. This man reminds the boy of someone close to him. Someone he felt safe with, someone he misses very much. It feels good that he finds some familiarity and comfort in the shadow man. Still, the boy is scared, and he stays in the corner. The man utters a string of words the boy cannot quite understand, but then the man taps his own chest and says, "Da."

The boy knows this word: Father. This identity means much to the boy, for he has lost two fathers already. He will have a new father. He will not be alone. Tearfully, the boy stands, leaving the small cloak behind, and inches toward the man. The man takes him in his embrace, and the boy lays his head upon the man's shoulder, crying tears of abandonment and loss, but also tears of joy. Now this place does not feel strange to

him anymore. It feels like his home. This is where he belongs, finally. He will never leave here.

Alone with the boy in the corner, Makani stands with his arms folded, awaiting his father. The Chozien has finally arrived. Although Makani is pleased to see the boy unharmed, he feels confusion after being informed that there is another child. It angers him further that the Onyx warriors could not defeat a Jade huntsman and seeker. It is humiliating and an insult. It is good that those who failed lost their *ame*. Surely, if they had come back, death would have been their penance. Failure deserves no reward.

He looks now at the Chozien cowering in the corner. This is supposed to be his new brother. Such a weak one, he is. Makani hears his father's footsteps nearing. It will be intriguing what his father plans to do with the boy. Will he give him away like he did with their previous Chozien twelve births prior?

Makani was but a seed in his mother's womb when the Onyx found the last Chozien.

When Makani's training began, his father educated him in the ways of swaying weaker-minded orders. His father explained to him how he could see a growing torment between the nature of influence and the allure for bloodlust within the Chozien, and so he commanded the Chozien be taken to the Bloodstone Order and given to them as a gift. Of course, the Chozien became corrupted and maddened by those same conflicting identities. His father told him that such a creature could not be one of the Onyx. However, in giving a "gift" of the Chozien to the Bloodstone, he'd also created a formidable ally. Yes, his father is truly wise.

Dyconn—Makani's father and dewan of the Onyx—enters the hall. His presence dominates the entire room. Seeing his son's disconcertion, he asks, "What troubles you so, Makani?"

"He is such a weak youngling, Father. Is this what is to join our family?"

Dyconn shakes his head at his son's ignorance. "Ah, Makani. Do not be so quick to judge. He is just a wee thing. His eyes are big in this place. You do make matters worse when you isolate him. You were a child once too."

With a hand on Makani's shoulder, he smiles. "Be ever grateful. The Great Spirit shows much favor on the Onyx. The boy's spirit shines brighter than any I have ever seen. My only wish is that I could feel it as well."

And with that, Dyconn turns his attention to making the boy welcome. He is to be his son, after all. He walks to the boy, kneels, and offers his greeting as a father would a son. The boy looks on with a frightened curiosity but still does not come forth.

He tries cajoling him with comforting words: "It is all right. You are safe here. Come now, I will not harm you."

Dyconn makes a mental note to give Makani a tongue-lashing for keeping the boy alone for so long. He thinks back to when his children were little ones and remembers what their favorite word was. He is not sure how the boy will react or what kind of memories he has attached to this expression.

Dyconn sits back on his heels and taps his own chest, saying, "Da."

Upon hearing this, the boy nudges closer to him. He picks up the boy and embraces him tightly.

While the boy weeps softly, Dyconn tells him, "You are home now. I do admire your power, little one. Your spirit is still bright even during this painful time. The Great Spirit must have sent you with its strength. I shall name you ... Zeke."

It is a fitting name, for Zeke knows not his limits or the changes he will bring to the world and the Onyx.

As promised, fifteen days after the Beni, Branson and Ahni wed in an elaborate celebration. There is much excitement and joy. When the sun has gone to sleep and the moon lights the night sky, the newlywed couple bids good eve to the still-active celebrators. With Suriah graciously keeping Aitan to allow the couple several days to themselves, the two saddle horses, and Branson leads Ahni just over a day's distance from the spirit hold through the forest to a small, open plain. When they emerge from the trees, Ahni's jaw drops and her eyes widen. A temporary hut sits in the empty plain. Gaylen ordered it built for Branson and his wife until a more suitable home could be established.

Branson looks at Ahni to see her reaction. Her eyes glisten with fresh tears, and her lips curve into a small smile. His breath catches in his throat. How it thrills him that he will see this smile from her for the rest of their days together.

He grabs her reins and urges the horses into a gallop. They laugh cheerfully all the way to the small cottage. Branson jumps down and lifts Ahni off her horse, then promptly carries her into their makeshift home. He puts her down, lights a candle, and goes back out to bring in their satchels. After he brings in their packs, he tells her to have a look around while he goes to tend to the horses.

Ahni is stunned by the reality of everything. Just fifteen days ago, her life was about to end, and now she is a wife and mother. She scans the room in awe. The hut is simple and small, consisting of a table, bed, and fireplace, all strategically placed to create ample space for walking. Her heart beats fast with the excitement of having her own home. Never had she thought of this as a possibility. Of course, she has had many dreams, none of which she entertained fully. Branson has made her dreams a reality.

Another surprise catches her eye. On the table sit more packs. She opens them and finds articles of clothing. At second glance, she realizes they are her own belongings. The rest of the packs hold men's clothing; she assumes they belong to Branson. Ahni shakes her head in astonishment. Branson is wasting no time in caring for her. She smiles at his thoughtfulness and decides that she will treat him to a small surprise when he returns from tending the horses.

Outside, Branson works diligently, though quickly, so that he may return to his wife. His wife ... He chuckles to himself at the realization. He hopes that she will be happy with the tiny home for the time being. He has already made plans to build them a substantial home fit with all the accommodations for their growing family and the kinsmen that will surely come to be in his service. He laughs quietly again, shaking his head at the fanciful thoughts impeding him from settling the horses. Finally, he stacks the hay and goes to join Ahni.

When he walks inside, the room is dimly lit with fewer candles. His nostrils fill with the faint smell of lavender mingling with the scent of orange. Ahni stands by the bed in a sheer white material beginning just at the top of her breasts, split down each side from mid-thigh and stopping just above her knees, with no undergarments. He has no idea how the linen fit her without straps, nor does he care. Branson thinks she looks stunning.

Her brown skin shimmers through the material, and her hair hangs over one shoulder in a thick mass of small locks. He hurries to her and captures her in a full-mouthed kiss overflowing with passion. When the kiss finally ends, it leaves both of them breathless with desire. He runs his hands up her arms, feeling them shiver from his touch. Her skin is so soft, he worries he may cut her with his rough, callused hands.

She begins to remove his shirt and pants carefully, so as not to tear the tailored pair. She reaches for her oils, preparing to rub away any tension, with the intent to incite arousal.

Branson stops her with a light touch to her wrist. "I intend to finish what I started the night I came to you."

She lets him lead her to the bed. He turns her around, eager to remove the fine garment. He finds a tiny lace at the top in a loose knot. He gently pulls at it, and the entire piece floats to the floor. He lifts her and lays her down, turning her to lie on her stomach. He takes the oil and pours a good amount in one palm. After rubbing his hands together to generate heat, he releases the oil's essence. He begins to knead each and every muscle, working them into relaxation. Her continual moans encourage him to finish. He cannot wait any longer. He turns her to face him and cups her face.

"I love you, Ahni."

She reaches up and strokes his cheek tenderly. "And I, you—forever and always."

He brings his head down to kiss her softly on her forehead, each cheek, then her nose, and lastly her lips. They wrap their arms around each other in a lovers' embrace and pass the night in sweet bliss.

Later, in the middle of the night while Ahni lies sleeping across Branson's chest, he holds her tight. He caresses her back, goes down her arms, then up and to her back again. He cannot believe how soft her skin feels. He places his hand over hers, and without thinking, he pulls away suddenly. The hand he touched does not feel like Ahni's. It seems coarser than he remembers. He turns her hand over and sees slightly dried, cracked skin on her palm. Some areas show the marks of where blisters have healed, as well as marks from previous scratches and cuts. Branson wonders what she could have gone through for those fifteen days.

It is true attendants are not allowed to be married, and although widowed and separated women are rare, it is not uncommon for them to serve as attendants also. However, they could not have been contributing to any housework, as it would blemish their conditioned skin. Branson understands that the only way for her to attempt her service again would be if he were to lose his *ame,* for he knows he will never leave her. But with hands like this, she would never be able to return to the service of an attendant. Branson lies back, wishing he could have endured his punishment longer if it would have saved her from such cruel treatment; although, if his punishment had lasted any longer, it might have killed him. He tenses his back and flinches in memory. He will not ask Ahni of her punishment or what became of her hands, to avoid causing embarrassment. The dewan's command was that they would not speak of their punishments to anyone. He owes Gaylen that much and more.

The next day, Branson wastes no time. He asks Gaylen for some artisans skilled in masonry, architecture, and farming. Gaylen sends twenty kinsmen. It is all he can spare since he needs every hand working on reinforcing the spirit hold's walls, as well as sending aid to the clans' holds. Branson knows the significance of this and is happy that Gaylen can spare them.

Branson and the architect spend the entire day marking the grounds for a new home and planning the blueprint. The architect is very attentive to the design. She even includes setting up an area for a smaller house for servants, as she knows the need shall arise. Branson is impressed by its grandeur.

Ahni is aware that they will need to have another source for providing provisions aside from Branson's services. She works with the farmers to sow a garden that spans several plots, enough to supply their home with food and trading. In addition to planting vegetables, she plans to plant fruit and nut trees to make various oils for cooking, hygiene, and healing.

Sadly, the white rain will soon come as the weather grows colder every day and the ground hardens. Fortunately, Gaylen will be supplying their needs until she begins her planting. She has Branson saddle her horse—a wedding gift from Gaylen—and rides to the spirit hold accompanied by two warriors, a day's ride. The people all recognize her. Many congratulate her on her recent nuptials and surprisingly address her as "Sira Ahni." Her reaction to her new title is similar to Branson's: unease with the sudden rise in rank.

She uses some of her personal oils to trade for warm clothing for Aitan, needles and threading for sewing, and some material for making her own garments. Considering Branson's service as a huntsman, he does not engage in trading, as he has all he needs.

Ahni sits at an inn to appease her growling stomach. The owner will not take payment for her meal, insisting that the great honor of having the sira of a Bonne Ame dine at her inn is enough. Word will spread and customers will flock to her establishment; the innkeeper plans to capitalize on Ahni's patronage. Ahni does not know how to take what she has not worked for and tries her best to offer something in trade for the meal. Only when the owner explains that it would be an insult not to take something given freely does Ahni accept the generosity, although uncomfortably.

She eats her fill and prepares to return home. Before she starts on her way, she makes a detour to the servants' house where she lived. She eagerly seeks out her close friends Reba and Dahlia. Ahni knows quite well that the other servants will keep their eyes low and meekly move from her path as she walks by. She asks one servant she happens to be familiar with where Reba and Dahlia might be. The servant gives her an offhand response, saying that Reba is serving in the kitchen and Dahlia has gone off to fetch more water. One with many birth years of bearing the title of sira would have taken offense. Ahni, though, simply feels both concerned and puzzled by this callous treatment.

Now a bit worried, she strides into the kitchen, and when the first person there looks her way, Ahni asks after Reba. The servant points behind Ahni to the left. She turns and looks in the direction and hurries to cover her mouth before she bursts into laughter. Reba stands over a mound of dough, pounding at it with her fists. Coated in flour, Reba has a facial expression showing pure frustration.

Ahni composes herself and, with a smile, walks up next to her friend. "It looks like you are getting better."

Startled, Reba jumps from her intense concentration. Her response is wide-eyed and open-mouthed. "Ahni!"

The women give each other a tight squeeze and laugh at each other's silliness.

With a few giggles still escaping from her, Reba says, "It is so good to see you. What are you doing here?"

Smiling, Ahni responds, "I came to see you! I have missed you. I am afraid I will be gone before Dahlia returns. Would you tell her I came to see her?"

Reba snorts. "I do not speak with cowards."

Ahni is taken aback by this harsh reaction. "What is the matter? Has something happened?"

Reba opens her mouth to respond but thinks better of it with so many listening ears around. Instead, she makes light of the situation: "Ohhh, it is nothing. Tell me how excited you are."

Ahni's eyes brighten, and she entwines her arm with Reba's, walking with her toward the door. The head cook sees this, so Ahni looks at her and the cook nods scornfully, then calls for another servant to take over Reba's task.

As the two emerge from the kitchen into the noon air, Reba inhales deeply and exhales slowly before saying, "Thank you for bringing me out of there. I think the dough was getting the best of me."

Again, they share a few giggles. The women walk and talk of the previous days leading up to the wedding.

Ahni says, "I think I thank the Great Spirit every day for giving Branson to me. The love we share is rare as it is amazing. I can speak for days upon birth years about how happy I am. Sometimes I feel that I … do not belong. I am not sure how to be a wife, a mother, or a sira. It may be a bit much."

Reba stops and tells her softly, "There was a time when we knew not how to walk. With time, we learned. I do not remember this, but I am sure it was not easy. Do not be so hard on yourself. It will come." And then, with more firmness in her tone, she says, "We all deserve better lives. Some more than others and some less; nevertheless, we all deserve the best in life."

Ahni smiles and lays her head on her friend's shoulder. Just then, an idea comes to her. She lifts her head up. "Oh, Reba, I have the greatest idea. Just when I was thinking what I would do without you, I remembered something. Branson is building our home, and he mentioned something about adding a small servants' quarters. After today, I realize I am going to need more help, especially when Aitan comes. What do you think ... Well, I don't know. Or maybe not." Ahni pauses a moment to get her thoughts and courage together before she asks, "Would you like to join our little family? Of course, I will understand if you decide to stay here."

Reba quirks a smile at her for that little bit at the end, then exclaims, "Yes! I would love to serve you. I would be honored."

Ahni and Reba continue to chat, though briefly, since not even a sira can come between the dewan and his meal. She also knows well how strict each servants' house can be, so she reluctantly bids Reba goodbye, assuring her that she will call for her once the house is ready.

She rides to her home with a straighter back and a higher sense of confidence than what she rode in with.

L ate in the afternoon the following day, Ahni begins to prepare dinner. Fortunately, Branson went hunting earlier in the day, and on a butcher's hook in the kitchen hang a gutted and skinned rabbit, as well as two wild boars broken down into their primals, ready to be prepared and cooked. Ahni dices the boar meat into hearty chunks and throws them into an oversized cauldron along with chopped vegetables, spices, and water. As the cauldron begins to simmer, she blends some flour and water into a thick paste, then mixes it with a cupful of the stewed liquid until no lumps remain, finally adding it to the pot to thicken the soup.

After she has the rabbit roasting over the open flames in the fireplace, Ahni sets to making fresh bread. She begins by fermenting yeast— using dried fruits soaked in water and covered with cloth secured tightly with a string—and she'll continue to add more fruit and water over the next few days, at which time she will spread it thinly and wait for it to dry out. With the cool weather, that shouldn't take long. Once done, she will ground it into a powder, then store it in a corked jar.

Until then, she grinds some oats, adds maple syrup, a squeeze of lemon, and some mashed root vegetables. She rolls the mixture into a dough and bakes several bread loaves, as she knows there will be hearty appetites come sundown. She does this while keeping a close eye on the rabbit, making sure to turn it every once in a while and basting it with a ginger-maple glaze she prepared on the side.

She soon feels worn out, toiling over these home duties. She laughs to herself, concluding that the bakers and cooks must truly enjoy their daily jobs in the kitchen just as much as she enjoys aromatherapy. She dearly hopes more people flock to their home to offer service to the Bonne Ame like the warriors who accompanied her to the spirit hold. Her days in the kitchen are numbered, she thinks comically.

Branson and the masons come out of the forest with several wagons full of heavy stones the size of an ox's head just as the sun begins to fade. He made sure they gathered as many of the stones as possible so that he would not have to leave again for some time. He smells the meal cooking, and immediately his mouth begins to water. As if the scent of the roasting meat does not exist, the masons begin unloading the stones out of the wagon and laying them on the ground. Branson is astonished at the discipline they demonstrate. Gaylen certainly has a great skill for training his craftsmen.

Once all the stones have been removed from the wagon, Branson calls for them to supper before the light disappears entirely. They all start on their way to the cottage, but are stopped by the frowning architect. She points to a makeshift washing station. True, Branson's odor would not reward him with a warm greeting. He pulls off his shirt, hoping it carries the majority of the smell. He walks to a barrel full of water and splashes a considerable amount over his face and torso. There is a bowl of extracted saps from plants with hibiscus. With it, a quick shampoo, scrub, and rinse are done by all.

Satisfied, Branson walks in and finds his beautiful wife stoking the fire. The others have gone on to a crudely built shelter that will suffice until their efforts complete the Bonne Ame hold. On the table, Ahni has a delicious-looking rabbit plated in the center, the juices running down its roasted skin. Beside it sits another plate of steaming vegetables, with a loaf of fresh bread next to them. He isn't surprised when his stomach growls with hunger.

Ahni already turned her gaze after feeling a waft of air from the door opening. She watches her ruggedly handsome husband eye the table laden with food. His shirtless chest and hair are damp with goosebumps from the chill. She smiles and happily walks to him, then scrunches her nose. Branson looks down, a little embarrassed. When he looks back at her, she is covering her laugh with her hand.

He smirks at her. "What is so funny?"

Ahni clears her throat before she answers, "You remind me of the prickly fruit found in the Barrens or the Attetne lands." She cannot contain her laughter at his wide-eyed astonishment. She continues, "Not to mention you could use some of my oils to freshen up from your *bath*."

He laughs with her and scoops her up in his arms. "Well, my wife, you should do me the honor."

They laugh as they eat and create memories of their beginnings to tell their children.

Five days later, Aitan arrives. He is warmly greeted and embraced by Branson and Ahni. They celebrate his homecoming quietly and intimately with much joy.

Five moons later, the construction of the new home is complete enough for the family to move in, with Branson pleased by the results thus far. The residence is made of stone, with a substantial kitchen separated from the rest of the house by a swinging door, similar to the fashion of an inn; a grand spacious bedroom befitting the sire and sira; and eight additional bedrooms—four on the first floor already complete and the remaining four upstairs still under construction. A dining area and great meeting hall for socializing complete this home fit for a sire—no, a Bonne Ame. Branson speculates the artisans are used to building considerably sized, extravagant houses such as this, though it is much more than he needed or could have imagined. The architect has really outdone herself.

Ahni asks for permission to have Reba be part of her household. Gaylen agrees and grants her request. Even though the servants' house still requires another moon of work until it will be finished, she calls for Reba to come to her new home. The friends reunite and rejoice together. Reba stays in one of the spare rooms until the builders complete the servants' house.

With more people flocking to his hold, Branson continues to grow it and also advance his training. Soon he is able to take extended trips to the spirit hold to train, with his home populated with kinsmen serving in necessary capacities. Branson always worries over his family's security during an extended time away from home. Ahni always assures him that she is in no danger and that Reba keeps her company well enough, while the various kinsmen protect them well. Still, her bravery does not bring him relief.

During training one day, his frequent inattention rewards him a painful blow to his ribs. He falls back, tripping over his sparring partner's extended foot. Branson picks himself up and readies for the next round, but his partner just stands there looking at him.

"You miss the time spent in the arms of your woman," he says to Branson, then smirks and snickers.

Branson charges at the man and ends up face down on the ground. Branson jumps up again and prepares for another attack.

The man holds up his hands for a halt. "This does not help you. Let us break a moment while you gather your bearings."

The man does not wait for Branson to accept, but walks to a barrel and splashes water over himself. Branson does not feel thirsty or winded, but his thoughts do experience that of the body.

From not far away a fellow huntsman leaves a group of onlookers and walks up to Branson, saying, "What is it that takes you so far from here?"

Having not even heard the man's approach, Branson manages to maintain his composure while recognizing the voice as Talon, one of the three huntsmen he first sparred with on his return to the spirit hold from the *Quête*.

Branson trusts Talon enough to confide in him: "I worry for my wife and son. It is not like a man to leave his woman vulnerable to all the dangers of this world."

Talon shakes his head ignorantly. He does not understand the concern of a wife just yet; however, he does see the risk with leaving the Chozien unprotected.

Talon responds with encouraging counsel: "This is quite a fix. Perhaps it is time for the Chozien to take a donateur." At Branson's defiant look, he adds, "Aitan is your son, but he is the Chozien first."

Branson shrugs, accepting the truth. He knows Talon is right. The two men continue to converse until Branson's partner returns, ready to finish the training. The day ends quickly for Branson, as his thoughts are completely occupied with choosing a donateur. As he gathers his things to return home, he sees Gaylen approaching, flanked by two guards. His focus is set on Branson, and he does not look too pleased, which adds to Branson's unease.

Branson does not keep him waiting. He approaches Gaylen and bows at the waist. "Namaste, Dewan."

Gaylen replies irritably, "This is not a formal meeting, Branson. Come. Let us talk."

The guards start to follow, but Gaylen holds up a hand. "Peace"—a command meaning there is no threat.

Immediately after they have gone out of earshot, Gaylen glares at Branson. "I am beginning to think myself a fool for saving your *ame*! There are responsibilities to being a Bonne Ame. There are responsibilities to being a husband and a father. It is the same for a dewan and a kinsman. Your position affords you certain luxuries; however, postponing decisions is not one of them."

Word of Branson delaying to take a donateur has clearly fallen on many ears, and apparently, it did not miss Gaylen's. He waits for Gaylen to finish his chastising in hopes of mending his reputation.

"It was not my intention to offend you publicly."

Gaylen states impatiently, "It is not your perspective that matters."

Branson nods. "True…. This is about the donateur or lack thereof?"

At Gaylen's irritated nod, Branson continues, "It is not so. I have spoken of it briefly with another; nothing more. I would have asked your consent if I were set on the idea."

Gaylen looks confused. "The idea? The only choice you have is who?"

Branson explains his feelings as a father and how he is fearful for his family. Branson expresses his insecurities on delaying the presence of a donateur, as it would overshadow his parental influence. He feels that a father should be the donateur. Gaylen points out that when involving the Chozien, this ideal is not possible. While it is admirable that Branson sees himself as the Chozien's father, Gaylen says that he must remember he is gardien first and foremost. The donateur is more than a protector. He defends the life of the Chozien with no regard to his own. The donateur is present at every moment in the boy's life. A father cannot be everywhere his son is, but a donateur must. There is no alternative.

Gaylen concludes the conversation with an encouraging tap on

Branson's shoulders. "Word will spread after I herald that we are in search of a donateur. You will have many candidates soon. Return home to your family. I expect your choice soon. Also, a sire belongs at his hold. Your training will continue there after you have made your choice. Many will come to serve a leader who's present. You will be reluctant to leave your hold once you begin to think as a sire."

Branson accepts Gaylen's advice and heads home somberly. He is not sure how he can find a suitable donateur with his standards being so high. Over the next few days, many men and women of all services come to Branson, offering their lives as donateur to the Chozien. Branson gracefully declines every offer that is given to him arrogantly. Such vanity cries for public recognition and personal gain—qualities unfit for a selfless donateur.

Branson seeks a donateur who's not looking to be sought after. After it becomes apparent that Branson finds it undesirable to propose oneself as the Chozien's champion, the dewan arranges for contests of stamina, as well as strength in wrestling. Still, Branson is not impressed.

After several mornings and nights without progress, Gaylen feels it time to intervene. He sends for Branson before he goes off to an early-morning hunt.

Branson is prompt to journey to the spirit hold and again appears before Gaylen. "You sent for me. I am here," he says as he bows.

"You need not bow, Branson. I believe we have gone beyond diplomacy. You know when formality is necessary."

"Yes, Dewan."

Gaylen smiles and shakes his head. "Gaylen." With an emphasized exhale, he continues, "Now, this choosing a donateur has taken much time, wouldn't you say?"

"It is difficult to find one who has the qualities I look for."

Gaylen lifts an eyebrow. "You know what you look for?"

Branson nods. "Endurance, strength, generosity, self-provider, knowledge—"

Gaylen cuts him off: "Let us decide on two of the most beneficial. It will take many moons to find one with all those characteristics, if they even exist."

"But we must not risk an unsuitable choice for such a position."

Gaylen replies, "You thought once that you were not even suitable to be sent on the *Quête*. Do not judge so harshly; there is a purpose for all."

"I let my emotions blind my judgment."

Seeking not to stray too far from the matter at hand, Gaylen says, "This waiting will question your ability to lead. Decisions are made in moments of distress and times of leniency. This falls in both categories. People will lose trust and interest."

Branson nods thoughtfully.

Gaylen delves deeper: "How have you been looking for donateurs?"

Branson shrugs his shoulders. "Listening to the proposals ... overlooking the contests, really."

Gaylen offers, "You should try watching when they do not know that you do. Observe them in their normal life behaviors."

Just then, Gaylen's youngest son, Nolen, runs in, smiling and eyes wide. "Da, you said you would take me riding today!"

Gaylen smiles back at his son. "I did, didn't I?"

Nolen nods several times.

"Well, come on, then." With Nolen pulling him away, Gaylen says over his shoulder to Branson, "Try talking to them. There's more to people than just their accomplishments."

THIRTEEN

Since he is back in the spirit hold, Branson decides to visit the practice fields. Gaylen has given him much to think about. He sees a crowd gathering, and seeking to be alone with his thoughts, he cuts a path behind a few inns. He continues in the direction toward the practice fields. Soon he hears the noise of running boots on the ground. He tries to follow the sound, and then the boots quicken and the number increases. Branson turns around and sees a troop of warriors running toward him with oversized packs on their backs.

Branson looks around and realizes he has wandered into the hills. He hurries out of their path. The man leading the troop glances at him long enough to meet Branson's eyes and then looks away. The man seemed to be annoyed that Branson stood in the way. Branson notices that the man does not breathe heavily, nor is he as big as the others. Yet, he carries the same weight and leads the troop. *He must be the devenir,* Branson surmises, his interest now piqued.

He follows the troop at a small distance all the way back to the training yard. He stands off to the side, blending into the surroundings. He spots the devenir removing his pack and emptying out the great stones that fill it. He takes a long drink of water and stands a moment while the others do the same and catch their breath. When the group gathers together, they split into several smaller sets of two or three people. They begin sparring with wooden swords. He sees the devenir train quite aggressively, almost to the point of overwhelming the others. The devenir dodges a swipe and raps an opponent smartly across the ribs. His foe winces and grabs his side while the devenir instructs him of his mistake. Branson watches as the man cycles through each warrior and alters his sword technique according to each warrior's weakness.

Branson continues to observe the devenir until the light begins to fade. Throughout the training, he learns more of the man's personality. His constant supervision of the troop and shifting of training intensity demonstrates an attentive attitude toward preparedness in all scenarios. Branson makes a mental note to speak with the high warriors. For now, he makes his way to an inn to end his evening.

Branson wakes the next day eager to investigate this intriguing warrior. Instead of sitting back and silently studying the warrior, though, Branson strides into the yard looking for a high warrior. He hears shouts from devenirs to their warriors to remain focused as heads turn in excitement as a Bonne Ame walks through the training yard during an ongoing search for the donateur—surely a much unexpected sight, albeit an exhilarating one. Branson notices a warrior who appears to be a devenir and approaches him. The warrior sees him and puffs up his chest.

Branson greets him, "Namaste."

The warrior returns in like, "Namaste, Bonne Ame."

Branson asks, "Where might I find the high warrior?"

The warrior is disappointed but answers, "High Warrior Conrad? He does not ..."

The warrior's words drift off. Disappointment changes to embarrassment. He points his wooden sword in the direction. "You can find him there, speaking with Mishi."

Branson nods his gratitude. The warrior nods stiffly and turns away. Branson shakes his head comically at the warrior's pride as he heads toward the high warrior.

Completely engaged in their discussion, neither the high warrior nor the warrior named Mishi turns to acknowledge Branson, with both of them bent over a small table and looking at some kind of map from what Branson can see. He clears his throat. The warriors look out the side of their eyes first, clearly annoyed.

Mishi starts, "We are not to be distur—Oh!" He stands upright and says, "Namaste, Bonne Ame."

At hearing the greeting, High Warrior Conrad looks up, surprised. He straightens, smiles, and offers his arm in reception. "Namaste, Bonne Ame."

Branson smiles and clasps forearms. "Namaste, High Warrior Conrad. Forgive me for intruding."

Conrad waves off the apology. "Nonsense. You are welcome here."

Branson, uncomfortable with casual conversation, skips to the point and asks, "If you have a moment, I would like to speak with you?"

Conrad nods and then looks at Mishi, "Study the map until I return."

Mishi returns to analyzing the map while Branson and the high warrior walk away. Branson does not want to let on his interest in a particular warrior, so he asks if Conrad would kindly show him the warrior training grounds. Conrad nods and launches into a grand sermon about the different training exercises and the significance of each one. Branson endures the high warrior's presentation while he looks for the devenir he saw the previous day.

Branson nearly tours the entire training yard without a sight of the one he wants. Just when he is about to thank Conrad for his gracious tour and create a tale to excuse himself, he sees the familiar swordplay out of the corner of his eye. Branson stops and looks at the group and recognizes some of the faces, but not the one he seeks.

Conrad notices where Branson's attention now lingers. "I see you have noticed one of our most highly trained troops."

Branson raises his eyebrows to add to his guise of curiosity, which spurs Conrad's next offer: "Let's take a look at their training exercises."

He leads Branson through the different training troops.

Coming to stop a safe distance where they will not disrupt the training, Branson launches into his observations: "This swordplay is unique from the other training troops."

Smiling, Conrad nods. "Yes. This troop trains by their weaknesses rather than their strengths. The other high warriors had a difficult time accepting this practice."

"Why?"

"They believe that warriors are not afforded the time to perfect weaponry skills. We must be ready at a moment's notice. Our bodies are to be ripened and prepared for the grueling service of warfare. They feel that if too much time is spent honing particular skills and the warrior dies, then it is wasteful and poor planning." Conrad shakes his head in disgust at that last statement, clearly in disagreement.

Being a huntsman, Branson does not understand warrior rationalization, so the explanation does not satisfy him. He nods anyway. "But I see this training is taking place. Why, if the idea has been rejected?"

Conrad smiles proudly again. "The creator of such training convinced us of the high survival and overpowering rate. He has been right thus far."

Branson looks around at the other troops training. The high warrior notices and answers his question before he can ask: "Only a small number of the warriors agree with this type of training, just enough for two devenirs and two troops." Conrad shrugs his shoulders. "The majority believe in the traditional training. In my opinion, both are exceptional."

Branson nods again. "Who are the devenirs?"

"This troop is led by Mishi, the one who you saw with me studying the map. His second watches over them in his absence." The high warrior points out one of the men to Branson—not the one he is looking for.

Branson prods, "And the other?"

Conrad waves his hand absently toward the hills. "Trenton. His troop is running the hills again."

Branson smiles and raises his eyebrows. "You do not agree with this?"

Conrad shrugs. "Trenton is the one who convinced us of the training. It is true that his troop has the most stamina; however, more time should be spent with swordplay and stratagem and not running long distances. How does one expect to lead if he has no plan of attack? No, Mishi will rise to high warrior."

"What is the usual time Trenton runs the hills?"

Conrad shakes his head, not too happy. "Very early morning and after the sun sits high. I do not understand it—almost as if he trains his troop to flee more than to fight."

"And which route does he take?"

Conrad points to the steepest hill. "He starts there. You should find a path."

Branson stands for a moment longer before he excuses himself to retire for the day. Conrad leaves, welcoming his return in the future. Branson decides to follow Trenton's troop on their early-morning run the next day. Trenton's strange training methods intrigue Branson enough to continue his investigation. He has an itch to scratch that there is more to this Trenton who runs half of the day and trains a quarter of it. Even a huntsman knows that a warrior must train with his sword more than half the day.

At the inn that night, Branson does not sleep well, anxious to break the mystery of this Trenton and his unique but familiar training. Upon awakening, Branson finds the sky a dark gray, with the spirit hold just beginning to bustle as kinsmen ready for trade. Branson packs himself a waterskin, trail bars, and dried meat. The weather has already begun to change: the air cooler, the nights longer. He wraps a cloak and ties it around his waist. He lightens his load by leaving his bow and one sword behind, then hurries to the location Conrad pointed out yesterday. The high warrior's words prove right: Branson does indeed find a path—many, actually. He conceals himself in the foliage closest to the divergent point so should the troop change direction, he will easily keep up. Then he waits.

As the sky begins to turn a light gray, he hears the pounding of boots on the hill. Branson stands, ready to trail. He does not wait long; he sees the troop, with Trenton leading. They move fast and turn slightly to the left, away from Branson. He waits for the last warrior to disappear into the trees and then emerges from his cover, dashing after them and keeping a fair distance between him and them.

Branson does not know how long he runs, but his breathing soon becomes heavy and his chest burns with each breath. He slows to a walk, trying to catch his breath. He hopes they will stop soon.

He comes upon an area where many of those heavy stones have been dispersed. He looks around; he cannot see how the troop could have come in this direction. Branson freezes suddenly. He runs to the nearest tree and leans behind it. He closes his eyes, focusing on controlling his breathing. Once his breathing slows enough, he listens.

Finally, he hears faint voices. He crouches low and moves stealthily toward them, his steps soundless. He finds open land and sees the warriors unloading the packs they carried on their backs. Unlike the heavy stones Branson saw the men carrying two days ago, these packs contain weighted practice swords, shields, claws, armguards, knee spikes, and many more weapons used by the other orders.

He sees a cluster of bushes closer to the troop. He lies on his stomach and crawls to them. He positions himself where he can view them without giving away his presence.

Branson hears Trenton announce that he plans to try each of his warriors on the fundamentals he has taught them, then he equips himself with armguards and a wooden sword while ordering his men to arm themselves with sword and shield, if they so choose.

Afterward, Trenton calls out in a loud voice, bringing each warrior to attention: "I will call each one of you to test your skill. First, I will test you against the Amethyst Order's armguard. Jari, you will be first."

The man called Jari comes forth with a sword and shield. He looks determined and moves lightly on his feet, circling his devenir. Trenton's movements appear more controlled, sending a message that he can calculate an attack before its execution.

Branson tilts his head to the side and eyes the pair.

Jari seems hesitant to make the first strike, so Trenton eases in, closing the distance between them. As Jari takes a step to retreat, Trenton feigns a sudden overhead strike, catching Jari mid-step. Before Jari can plant his foot, he swings his wooden sword awkwardly to block the feigned strike. Jari realizes his mistake and falls in the direction of his swing and rolls, coming up in a low crouch.

They begin exchanging blows, neither able to gain the advantage. Soon Trenton presses Jari, using his armguards to block Jari's counterstrikes. Trenton makes a strong block against a strike, swinging Jari's sword arm wide. Then, with his own blade, he makes a lunge strike close to Jari's side that his deflected arm left open. Jari knows he cannot bring his shield up to block the strike in time; instead, he dodges under the protection of his shield. Trenton expects this. He hits the shield with his free arm, effectively slowing the shield's recovery time, then sends a swipe to Jari's ribs. Jari shakes his head in disappointment, his pride hurt more than his ribs.

Trenton calls for another warrior to fight.

The training continues on through the sun's highest position. Branson sits patiently, changing positions occasionally to stretch dormant muscles. He finds himself impressed by the way Trenton can adjust his swordplay to the current weaponry he uses and also by the way his troop can effectively defend against his attacks. Trenton is also clearly skilled in the proper defense. Yet, something seems different with his movements. They feel increasingly familiar to Branson—the way the devenir anticipates attacks, his use of groundwork, and the speed of his own attacks ... all uncommon characteristics of a warrior. Branson forms a sound theory and then dismisses it, for the idea sounds completely ludicrous.

The time finally comes when the warriors begin to refill their packs and place them on their backs, all save Trenton.

"Run the same route; I will join you soon. Do not forget to fill your packs with the stones." Trenton commands his troop with an authority that leaves no room for question.

The warriors gather their packs and head in the direction of where Branson saw the stones scattered about in the first opening. Branson stays in his position, eager to see more of this mystery of a man. Trenton's next action confirms Branson's suspicions, bringing a smirk to his face.

Trenton kneels, a bit winded from the training. He stretches his arms and rolls his neck and shoulders. Branson recognizes this technique: the same one taught to him years ago when he began his training for huntsman—a practice that relaxes the body to calm the mind and spirit.

Soon Trenton's breathing becomes more controlled, and once recovered, he stands with his back to Branson. He speaks over his shoulder with a smile: "How long do you plan to lie there, Bonne Ame?"

CHAPTER
FOURTEEN

Branson chuckles. He rises from the cover of the bushes and walks into plain sight in the open field.

Trenton turns around to greet the Bonne Ame properly. He bows. "Namaste, Bonne Ame."

Branson replies with a smile in his voice: "Namaste."

Trenton smiles proudly. "You made little noise when you followed us. I did not hear you until your exhaustion got the better of you."

Branson rolls his eyes. "What do you know of focus, warrior?"

Trenton shrugs, not quite catching the purpose of the question. "Surely, you are not blind. You know of the exercises performed by your service to calm the body. Did I not do so here?"

Branson does not respond. He just stares at the warrior, prompting an answer.

Trenton chuckles, and then dismisses his own question. "It is no matter. I suppose you are here to speak to me about my training. What do you think of my troop?"

Branson shakes his head. "Your training is not what I noticed first.

It is your stamina. To be able to carry a heavy burden and still lead is an admirable trait to possess."

Trenton loses his smile and looks a little wary. He folds his arms and waits for Branson.

"I spoke with High Warrior Conrad. He speaks very highly of Mishi." Branson pauses a moment to see Trenton's reaction, but there is none. "Though Mishi is not whom I seek. Conrad also spoke of your … unusual training methods. I wanted to see more, so I followed you here."

Branson stops speaking, and Trenton continues to remain suspicious, expecting more.

Branson goes on, "Something about your training is different from the other warriors—"

"I train my troop to fight different orders."

Branson nods thoughtfully. "Yes, that is good. But … I have never seen warriors use the ground as much as yours do. Warriors normally avoid the ground—"

Trenton interrupts him again, defensively this time: "Warriors do not train only one way, like huntsmen."

Branson ignores the slight. He begins to pace as if he is speaking to himself: "Your agility is above a warrior's as well."

Trenton crosses his arms nervously. "I don't understand."

Branson stops, peers at him, and gives his judgment: "You were a huntsman once."

Trenton looks appalled and shakes his head. "That is impossible! You cannot change services. You would be branded a coward. No service would train you."

Branson shrugs. "It is rare, though it can happen. But you didn't need any training, did you? As a huntsman, you were trained to be patient and to watch. You examined the warriors and began to mimic them.

Your years of huntsman training did not leave you. You were singled out because of your unique combat techniques. You gained a higher position and became a devenir. Of course, you would have had to leave your previous order to achieve this since, as you say, no other service would train you. Am I close?" Branson raises his eyebrows with his question.

Trenton forces a laugh. "You think because you hide behind some bushes and watch me and my troop train that you know my past and present? That is nothing but a dreamer's fantasy. I am nothing more than one warrior out of many."

Branson opens his arms innocently. "Let us have a match. I won't hurt you, I promise."

Trenton smirks and nods.

The men prepare themselves to fight. Oddly, Trenton does not remove his sweat-soaked shirt. Branson sees this as a test. If Trenton speaks the truth and he has only ever been a warrior, then the match should be Branson's. Warriors are used to fighting among many with weapons and rely on their power to quickly defeat their opponent and move to the next. Huntsmen don't mind tight spaces and utilize more agility, relying on their patience to disarm or confuse their opponent. Huntsmen and warriors have argued for many years over which service is the stronger. Normally, in brawls, huntsmen win because of the warriors' lack of ability to fight without their weapons. However, in war combat, huntsmen would struggle severely because of their lack of stamina.

Branson chooses two weighted swords while Trenton bears the Jade Order's sword and shield. Branson gives a few practice swings and nods his readiness. Trenton returns the nod. They begin circling each other. Trenton looks comfortable with his choice of weapons. Branson, though, is dissatisfied with the swords; he constantly switches his grip, lifting them up and down slightly, becoming accustomed to their weight.

Trenton sees this and closes the distance. Branson makes the first strike. He attempts a swipe, but the weight of the sword slows him. Trenton blocks with the shield, and instead of counterattacking with his sword, he does so with his shield. Branson dodges the blow marginally. He silently thanks Talon for upgrading his reflexes.

Trenton takes advantage of Branson's retreat and advances on him with strong, chopping blows. Branson has to use both of his swords to block the heavy strikes. He cannot return a counterattack until he regains his footing. He waits for Trenton to deliver another downward swipe, which he sidesteps and then gives him a sound roundhouse to the head. Trenton stumbles to the side with the hit. Branson does not wait; he charges at Trenton, gathers his strength, and swings both swords down. Trenton is forced to kneel, but swings his shield up to smoothy block the attack, then counters with a lunge. Branson has to drop one of his swords to jump out of its path.

As Trenton attempts to stand, Branson swings his sword, hitting Trenton's blade and knocking it awkwardly toward his shield. Then he kicks at the back of Trenton's knee, making sure to place the blow where it only brings him back to his knees, not injuring him. Trenton falls but rolls forward, landing in a crouched position. Branson's eyes widen, and then he smiles.

Trenton ignores his expressions and finally stands.

The men trade blows again. Without the weight of the other sword, Branson is able to move faster, although he does miss the extra defense it provided. Branson waits for Trenton to make a slip, but Trenton does not want to risk closing the distance again. Trenton tightens his lips as he realizes his mistake, angered by his caution. He moves as if going in for another attack with his sword, but then, with unsuspected speed, he flings his shield at Branson's head. Surprised by the attack, Branson has to duck while using his sword to deflect the shield. But as soon as Trenton let go of the shield, he began rushing at Branson, allowing him to now slam a powerful fist to his face. Branson's head snaps back, stunned. Before he can set up for a proper defense, Trenton grips his wrist that holds the wooden sword. This grip is familiar to Branson; he uses his free hand to strike the wrist of Trenton's sword hand. Trenton's blade falls from the sting.

Branson continues to throw blows with his free hand to divert attention from the grip; Trenton easily fends these off. The grip tightens, and Trenton twists until Branson is forced to drop the sword. As soon as the sword drops, Trenton rams his shoulder into Branson's head. The attack knocks him to the ground. He shakes his head to clear the daze. He attempts to lift himself, but he finds Trenton's boot in his chest, knocking him back.

Trenton goes for his sword. Branson curls his lip, and with lightning speed, he spins on his back, sweeping Trenton's legs from under him. In the same motion, while Trenton is falling, Branson jumps up and lands a hook kick to Trenton's chest, which slams him to the ground with the additional momentum. The move finishes with Branson spinning in cartwheel fashion to his feet.

Trenton reaches for his sword. Too late, as Branson is there and kicks his arm away. He catches Trenton's arm in a submission hold between his legs and falls onto his back. When Trenton refuses to give up and begins struggling, Branson lifts his hips, putting pressure on the elbow. Trenton finally taps Branson's leg to signal his forfeit. Branson releases Trenton's arm, and they stand and dust themselves off.

Trenton speaks first: "I would have let my arm break if it meant life or death."

Branson nods. "Yes, but this was not so. You went for your sword once you assumed I was done. That was your mistake. Although you did surprise me with your shield, I didn't think you would separate from your shield without being forced to."

Trenton chuckles and rubs his elbow. "Yeah, I figured I wouldn't need it after I'd beaten you. That was a nice hold you had me in."

Branson smiles. "I am wondering … after you threw your shield, you went straight for my weapon instead of attacking me with your sword. Why is that?"

Trenton lifts his eyebrow and, after a moment, shrugs. "I thought you might have used it to attack. So I had to—"

"Disarm me."

Trenton is speechless. He looks away. He knows he has been found out. How could he have been so careless? Disarming your enemy is common in huntsmen combat. Warriors always go for the kill.

Branson says, "You needn't be ashamed. I knew before we fought, remember?"

Trenton continues to look away and asks somberly, "You will keep this to yourself?"

Branson replies, "That is not why I followed you here. But I am curious to know why you switched services."

Trenton looks at Branson, then past him, recalling a memory. He narrows his eyes. "I would rather protect my order than feed them. A warrior would never leave another behind."

"What do you mean by—?"

Trenton cuts him off: "Why is it you followed me here, Bonne Ame?"

Branson lifts his eyebrows briefly. "As I have said before, I noticed the difference in your training. It's more effective. I would feel very confident—You see, my son, Aitan, is in need of a donateur. And I—" Branson stops at Trenton's wide-eyed smile.

Trenton bows. "I am honored that you would deem one of my warriors worthy to serve the Chozien. May I suggest a likely candidate?"

Branson shakes his head. "No, I have already chosen. It is not one in your troop but you yourself."

Trenton looks both taken aback and confused—not the reaction that Branson expected.

Lowering his eyes, Trenton replies, "I am sorry, Bonne Ame, but I must decline."

Branson cannot believe what he is hearing. "What? You would refuse to serve as donateur to the Chozien? Why?"

Trenton looks at him with obvious concern. "It would expose me. This promotion would lead to questions, and they would delve into my past. You spoke the truth: I was not born in the Jade Order. This knowledge will cause a great uprising against me." Trenton shakes his head. "No, we cannot lose the support of our people now. Not with a war gathering."

Branson furrows his brow. "What war?"

Trenton looks at Branson as if he is jesting. "Every Chozien brings a war. Why should this one be any different? The Onyx will stop at nothing to kill him."

"Yes ... yes, of course. I understand. It is just that there are other ways for achieving peace that I do not think of war first." Branson can feel his muscles relaxing, knowing that the pact Gaylen and the sires made to keep the coming war from the people still remains safe.

Trenton seems to have taken Branson's reasoning by nodding his head.

Branson hurries to continue, "Do not think of yourself. I would not be asking if I were not in need. It has been difficult finding your talents and skills all in one."

"Who will train my troop when I am gone? Also, there are many others with greater experience who would be better than I. As well, I am young—only twenty birth years. Gaylen will not approve."

Branson's voice becomes demanding: "No. You are the one. Your age says much. If you are great now, you will only get better with time. As for your troop, you have trained them for this day. Should you go into battle and not survive, who would take your place then? You fear failure and your past. Yet, you are a warrior. Warriors are trained not to fear."

Trenton snaps back, "Do not use your petty ploys on me. You show your ignorance of the warrior. We train not to fear death ... *only* death. To be absent from all fear is not human."

"You are right. I should not have insulted your service. It is that I see you are bound for much more. Still, I respect your decision. Accept my apology and come to my home. I will have my wife create a feast in honor of our friendship."

Trenton accepts with gratitude. They agree to meet at the front gate before nightfall.

Before Trenton leaves, Branson stops him. "By the way, I am interested which of your warriors you would feel confident to take your place should you die in battle."

Trenton smiles. "The one I chose first—Jari. He is the most promising."

They go their separate ways. Branson sends a rider to tell Ahni that they will be having a guest for dinner and to prepare a celebratory meal. After his match with Trenton, Branson feels the need to train more; he could use the additional training to brush up on his technique. He hopes Gaylen is right that more kinsmen from all services and crafts alike will come to him. Before going to train more, Branson makes a stop to speak with Gaylen.

FIFTEEN

As planned, Trenton and Branson meet at the front gate just before nightfall. Branson notes that Trenton now wears clean traveling clothes, and his hair looks damp. Apparently, he took a wash shortly before meeting him. Branson is taken by surprise at the quality of Trenton's clothes, even for traveling. Normally, a warrior would never be seen dressed so … lavishly. His pants are dark brown, made of a tough leather; his boots black and appearing freshly dyed. He wears a long-sleeved, light-brown leather shirt and a green cloak with a hood. Branson also sees a small item wrapped in a blanket strapped to Trenton's saddle.

Branson asks, "What do you have there?"

Trenton brushes a hand over the pack and says simply, "A gift for Sira Ahni."

Branson nods. On the way, they make small chatter, mostly about combat and different techniques. Branson is careful not to mention anything about Trenton's past or previous order. They arrive at Branson's hold in the early evening through a partially built stone wall and ride up to the new home.

Trenton inhales deeply and licks his lips at the aroma wafting from the house. "With a meal like this every night, I wonder why you are not home more often."

Branson smirks. "Ahni does not enjoy the kitchen. It is our maid servant, Reba, who aids her with the meals."

Trenton squeezes a laugh out, and Branson joins in. Branson shows him to the stable, and they rub their horses down.

"This is quite an impressive home you've built," Trenton says.

Branson smiles. "Yes, it is. I thank the dewan for lending me the resources. The architect is quite ... thorough. As you can see, there are many more buildings coming along. But for now, we should wash before dinner. I do not want to keep my wife waiting."

They enter through the front door to joyous laughter from Ahni and Reba. Branson's heart warms at the sight of his beautiful wife feeding Aitan. She and Reba seem to be giggling over another one of their childhood stories.

Reba sees Branson first. She immediately sobers up and stands. "Good eve, Bonne Ame Branson," she says, and then, looking to Trenton, "and to you as well, Trenton. I suppose I should address you as—"

Branson interrupts her, "Yes yes, we are very happy to have Trenton join us tonight. I don't mean to be terribly rude, Reba, but I must stink of a hundred warriors. I do not wish to offend you any longer. Is there a bath ready?"

Trenton has an awkward smile on his face. He's not sure what the woman was talking about, but decides against asking for further clarification.

Reba replies, "Yes, a bath awaits you in your bedroom. I lit a small fire to take the chill out of the air and laid out your dinner attire."

Branson smiles. "Thank you, Reba. I think I may ask my wife and son to join me."

Ahni smiles up at her husband. "Of course we will, my love, in just a moment. I am almost done feeding Aitan."

Branson rubs his son's head.

Before disappearing to the master quarters, Branson comments, "Trenton, did you leave something on your saddle?"

Trenton widens his eyes before he excuses himself to retrieve the gift. "Uh, yes. My apologies. I'll be right back."

Branson waves off the apology. "Nonsense. Go and fetch it. When you return, Reba will give you a tour and then show you where to wash up."

Trenton looks at Reba and smiles kindly. Reba bows her head to hide her own smile. Trenton hurries out the door. Branson peeks outside for a moment, then turns back around to see Ahni and Reba eyeing him.

Ahni has a smirk as she asks, "What are you up to, Branson?"

"Do not mention donateur to him or anything concerning him serving the Chozien."

Reba furrows her brow while Ahni rolls her eyes.

Ahni picks up Aitan for his bath. "We shouldn't be long, Reba. I am sure you'll pass the time easily enough showing our 'guest' around. Oh, Reba! Are you feeling well? I bet it's the fire. It's too warm."

Reba gives an awkward smile and struggles between nods and shakes of her head. "Of course I am. I suppose I have not settled from our laughter." She waves them on, hurrying them along and warning them that the food will get cold.

Branson and Ahni enter their quarters to the warm smell of eucalyptus. Small swirls of steam rise from the deep, wide tub in the room. The fire is stoked to a high flame to fill the grand room with heat without engulfing it. Branson undresses and eases into the lukewarm water with a satisfying exhale. He lays his head back and closes his eyes. Meanwhile, Ahni uses the small washbasin to bathe Aitan. Ahni looks over her shoulder at her husband. She smiles at his fulfillment. She decides to wait a little more before she begins her investigation about his suspicious behavior.

After she finishes washing the boy, she clothes him and sets him down on the soft fur rug near the tub, along with some wooden toys. He's already learned to walk and has taken to the incredibly soft fur. She smiles as he picks at the wisps and playfully rubs his hands on it.

Turning her attention to Branson, she dips a cloth in the water and rings the water out over his chest. She says, "You must have traded your medallion for that rug your son adores."

Branson looks out the corner of his eye and says dryly, "I will take that as praise for my long hours in the tannery."

Ahni laughs while she wets his hair and rubs soaked yucca plant roots in the water until suds form. She adds rosemary oil and massages his scalp with the mixture. He sighs with pleasure.

Ahni figures she might catch him off guard and leans in to kiss his ear. She says softly, "Is there something you are not telling me, husband?"

Branson loses his smile and opens his eyes.

Ahni can feel him tense beneath her hands. She mocks him: "Rest, my love. You've been away from me and you've only just arrived."

Branson sits up and turns toward her. He already feels contrite with guilt for tricking her into believing a falsehood by sending the message asking her to prepare a celebratory meal this evening. With her taunting him, it only makes his shame greater. He takes the washcloth and busies himself with lathering the soap.

She sets her chin on top of her hand over the edge of the tub and gives him a direct look. In a firm voice, she says, "Branson."

Branson slumps his shoulders and looks at her, heaving a sigh. He shakes his head. "I am a terrible liar, aren't I?"

She smiles. "Only to me. I think Trenton and Reba haven't a clue."

Branson chuckles a little. He tries to divert by continuing to clean himself. Ahni clears her throat to let him know she still awaits an explanation.

He closes his eyes briefly, composing himself to confess his trickery. He begins, "I want to tell you first that this is the best warrior I have ever seen." At an impatient look from Ahni, he stumbles on, "Well, I offered him the job and title, and he refused. Just like that." He snaps his fingers for emphasis. "He fears his past and said that this rise in title would be too great and cause him unwanted interest. I tried to explain to him that his duty would surpass his worries. Nonetheless, he would not accept. I am sure that if he could just experience the blessing Aitan is to the Jade and our family, he would think otherwise. So ... I invited him to visit our home to celebrate a new friendship."

Ahni still looks confused. "Then why fool me into believing that he is the donateur?"

"So that it would not be obvious that I brought him here to trick him into withdrawing his refusal. I thought if you remained unaware, it would prove convincing."

Ahni stands up and looks down at their son and shakes her head, clearly unhappy with his approach.

Branson pleads, "It is the only way, Ahni."

Ahni gives him a stern look, then says, "We will find another. You cannot do this. Already you are teaching our son treachery. Deception and betrayal ... these are not the qualities to live by."

She turns to leave the room, but Branson stops her, "Enough!"

Ahni stops and turns around, an incredulous look upon her visage.

Standing, he says, "I have spoken. You will not break our confidence. It is not for malicious reasons that I choose to bait him here. I do this for Aitan. You would fault me for ensuring the safety of our son?"

Ahni counters, "It is not the result that I contend, but your methods. It seems so … dishonest. You are changing, Branson."

Branson looks at their son, then nods once and smiles. "Maybe, but we all do. Trust me, Ahni, the times to come will not be pleasant. That is why I will take the necessary precautions to protect our family."

Ahni finds herself irritated that his explanation sounds reasonable to her. She walks over the rug and scoops up Aitan. "Well, Trenton certainly is handsome."

Branson narrows his eyes at her. "I hadn't noticed, and neither should you, *wife*."

She smiles and walks close to him and whispers, "I hadn't—although Reba has."

On his way to the stable, Trenton is furious with himself. He blames his forgetfulness on his awestruck admiration. He is amazed at the amount of progress Branson has made since his rise in rank. When he walked through the door of Branson's home, he first noticed the high ceiling and how the space didn't feel airy or distant, but comfortable and intimate. He heard females laughing. It sounded content, blissful. Trenton kept his eyes averted out of respect for the sira. One of the female voices he heard sounded happy, with a respectful undertone of loyalty. He smiles. Loyalty is a quality held high in his eyes.

He'd expected warm and loving words from a wife to her husband, but instead they seemed formal and submissive. When she addressed

Trenton himself, he looked at her and was struck by her awesome beauty. Her curly hair looked not quite brown, nor quite red, but somewhat in between, and it floated just below her shoulders. He caught a glimpse of her eyes, but not long enough to identify the color. She spoke to Trenton, but Branson cut her short. Her words confused him. However, he understood Branson's next remarks. The woman standing before Trenton was not Branson's wife but one in his service. Trenton smiled openly then, and she lowered her eyes timidly. It seemed but a blink of an eye when he'd heard Branson calling his name. Something about a gift ... He recalls how embarrassed he felt.

Finally, he reaches his saddle and gingerly unties the bundle. In Trenton's previous order, it was customary to bear gifts to a sire's home. He hears footsteps behind him and turns toward them, expecting the Bonne Ame. He raises his eyebrows in surprise. Walking around the corner is the woman, Reba.

"I thought that we could start out here first."

He cannot think of what she is talking about. "Here?"

In an accommodating tone, she offers, "Or if you would prefer to start the tour somewhere else?"

He laughs a little. "Oh, yes! Forgive me. I am normally not this forgetful."

She smiles and looks at the bundle in his hand. "Have you gotten everything?"

He looks down at his hands. "Yes, thank you."

"Then shall we begin?"

"Of course."

Reba shows him the servants' house first. The servants are settling in for the night and move around them with the assumption she is welcoming yet another servant. She mentions that Branson just completed building it and is working on the furnishings. The house has five bed-rooms—only two have beds and one with additional furniture—and a small kitchen connected to the living area. The rooms are small, and even with its state of unfinish, the house is filled with servants, yet Reba's voice holds much appreciation and enthusiasm. She says that every turn of the moon brings more kinsmen to the service of the Bonne Ame. She anticipates that the servants' house will be expanded, if not another one built.

Trenton is amazed and cannot take his eyes from her. He notices small details: how she clutches her cloak tighter to keep out the cold, the small puffs of air in front of her lips as she speaks. And her skin—he wonders if it feels as soft as it appears. He can feel himself being drawn to reach out and graze her cheek, just to appease his curiosity. Reluctantly, he moves away slightly, hoping the nearness of their bodies is the cause of his fanciful thoughts. She sees the movement and assumes he is ready to move on and invites him to continue. She leads him deeper into the plain. He sees a structure, obviously under construction.

Reba explains, "It would be better to see in the sun. Sire Branson is building a—"

"Tannery. It is rare for a sire to build one of this scale. It is much work to skin a beast and tan its hide. I have seen the huntsmen at the spirit hold," he says at her confused look as to how a warrior would know about skinning and tanning a beast. "How does your sire plan to main-tain this service himself?"

She smiles. "Aren't you listening? Many come to my sire's hold. We already have huntsmen to support the labor."

He chuckles. "Yes, yes, of course."

"While Sire Branson spends extended time at the spirit hold now, he does not care for the time spent away from his family. He would not be able to train and educate Sire Aitan. With more kinsmen, he will be able to remain at home more and also make his hold less dependent on the dewan. This will provide us with clothing, food, and crafts for trade."

Trenton looks at her, and even in the waning light, he can see her eyes glistening and a small smile touching her lips.

Reba inhales and says, "It is good to feel secure and cared for by your sire. Most people go a lifetime without this feeling."

He remembers his own past and nods. He, too, knows the absence of security within one's own hold and even one's service.

Trenton clears his throat before asking, "How does he plan to keep the stench from reaching the house?"

"By positioning the tannery at the back of the hold, a great distance from the main, highly populated areas, as well as building a wall to block against windy days. He said that the smell will be unbearable only if this tannery is as massive as the spirit hold's. It is larger than the other clans, but still considerably smaller than the spirit hold."

He nods. She is correct. The tannery looks like it will be small enough not to create an overpowering odor. His admiration for Branson has increased at the sight of his progressive planning and concern for his servants, though he feels a little jealous of her loyalty. He can't imagine why. He watches as Reba shivers in her cloak. He scolds himself for leaving his traveling cloak with his gear.

Concerned for her, he waves toward the house. "We best hurry back before we are missed."

Worried that he is losing interest, she asks, "So soon? Don't you want to see the warriors' bunkhouses?"

He smiles. "It's getting late. If you have time to spare tomorrow, I would enjoy seeing the rest of the hold."

The walk back is quiet. The light from the moon shines on her, and he settles his mind. Definitely, the color of her hair is a deep red.

Seeking to tamp down the building awkwardness, he makes idle conversation: "How is it you came to serve Sire Branson and Sira Ahni?"

She catches a clutch of her curls caught in the night breeze and takes a pin from the inside pocket of her cloak and secures it behind her ear, saying, "Sira Ahni and I served as attendants for the dewan. Our mothers taught us the service, and we followed. We have been friends since childhood. After she was joined with Branson, she asked the dewan for me."

"Your mothers? Where are they now?"

Her voice saddens a bit: "Sira Ahni's mother died many birth years ago. I believe the chill from the white rain may have been too much for her. My mother cared for Ahni and me until she left to serve under the Rhyne Clan, instructing others in the service of attendant. That was three birth years ago. I have not seen her since."

He responds to her sadness, "Ah. But she is well and thinks of you often?"

She nods and smiles as they near the house.

Since servants know their sires best, he hurries to ask one more question before they go inside: "What do you know of Sire Branson?"

Reba looks up at him thoughtfully at first, then replies, "He has a strong spirit, stubborn. He analyzes everything, sometimes overly much. He means well, though. His loyalty is great, but I sense concern in him at times, which causes him to hesitate. I am sure he would give his living breath if it meant our survival."

They reach the house, but before Trenton can open the door, Reba touches his arm. He looks back, his brow furrowed.

She meets his eyes. "Sire Branson looks for the most loyal of servants.

His trust is not given easily. He must see something special in you. I believe I see it too."

Trenton is stuck in place and speechless. She opens the door and walks in. He changes his mind about her hair—more auburn … with soft brown eyes. He follows her in. She removes her cloak and shows him to the guest room where his packs and a warm bath await him.

He doesn't tarry. He disrobes and washes himself, then takes care in dressing for dinner with the Bonne Ame. His pants are a soft and supple light-gray, loose-fitting leather. Like his traveling boots, his extra pair are a deep black and look freshly dyed. He wears a long-sleeved white shirt of the similar characteristics of his pants in its airiness and comfort. He finishes his ensemble with a deep-green cloak and a shiny silver clasp.

He hears voices outside his room and rushes the final touches on his appearance. He enters the dining room to a casual and informal atmosphere. Branson and Ahni flirt while Aitan sleepily rests his head on Branson's shoulder. He sees two different types of roasted meat, warm bread, and vegetables prepared in a stew. As she readies the table, Reba points out a creamy herbed butter for spreading on the bread. He only sees a meal like this prepared for special occasions, amazed that it has been set out just for friendship.

Reba sets out the plates and arranges various food items on the table. He takes a platter from her, sets it on the table, and asks her to instruct him where to put the others. With the food laid out, everyone seats themselves at the table, except for Branson, who has gone off with Aitan. Branson joins them after he returns from their quarters empty-handed.

Branson jests, "Ahni doesn't like to leave Aitan unattended—a mother's worry. Reba offered to stay with him while we ate, but we wouldn't hear of her eating alone."

Ahni kicks Branson under the table, and he laughs. They begin to eat. Throughout the meal, they entertain Trenton with some comical stories of their cozy life. Trenton compliments Branson on the overall layout and construction accomplishments he has made so far. At the end of the meal, Reba clears the table, with Trenton jumping to aid her. They return carrying a warm pie filled with cinnamon-spiced seasonal apples. The aroma waters the men's mouths all over again. After licking their fingers and with their bellies pleasantly full, Branson and Trenton retire to the living area, thanking Reba for the wonderful spread.

Trenton turns back around, though, as he remembers his gift, surprising the others. "Sira Ahni, I'd like to thank you for preparing this wonderful meal. I have a gift for your hospitality."

He carefully unwraps the bundle, lifts out a small object, and places it into her hands.

Ahni's eyes widen at the sight of the gift. She turns it in her hands: a blossoming rose with incredible detail, made of clear glass. She has heard of glassmaking but has not seen any. It is surely from the Rhodonite Order, and the piece must be worth much for its rarity and beauty.

She accepts it. "It is beautiful, Trenton. Thank you. We should have prepared a larger feast. Indeed, you are a wonder."

He beams at the compliment. Branson and Trenton split from Ahni and Reba, each pair retreating to their solitude. The men settle in broad, deep-cushioned chairs that were a gift from a spirit hold's kinsman for his promotion.

"That was some gift. My wife will cherish it. Thank you."

Trenton nods. "A great woman of a great man deserves beautiful things."

Branson peers at Trenton. "Yes, but I would think you'd save such a gift for the woman of your own heart."

Trenton shrugs. "There are more. I will find another."

Branson smiles inwardly, knowing that glass objects are difficult to come by and priced high—too high for Trenton to appear indifferent. Trenton seems to be just as bad a liar as Branson.

Just then, Reba interrupts them: "Sire, your beds are turned down. Is there anything else you require?"

"Thank you, Reba. That is all. Good eve to you."

She bows her head and leaves.

Trenton waits a bit, then asks, "Does she have an admirer?"

Branson chuckles. "Would it matter?"

Trenton puts on a sly look. "No."

They both laugh.

Branson yawns and stretches. "Well, what do you think of my little hold?"

Trenton says genuinely, "You are all very happy."

Branson leans back in the chair. "Yes, we are. I want to give them so much. But I am only one man. I need more of my own kinsmen, but I have to offer them more than service. That is why I am building the tannery and why Ahni plans a great garden with the farmers. They will serve if I can give food and furs of value to them. So much to do."

Trenton puts his elbows on his knees and sets his chin on his fists, thinking. Finally, he settles on a decision: "I would like to take a closer look at your tannery. I may be able to assist you with its construction for just a day or two, but then I must return."

Branson reaches his arm out, and Trenton grasps his forearm. "Good. I assure you that I need it. You may want to return and retrieve a pair of work clothes; don't want to bruise those pretty garments."

Trenton looks down at himself. "I have some on my saddle."

Branson laughs and stands. "Well, friend, I think I have kept my wife waiting long enough. We will rise early, then, and speak of these ideas you have for the tannery."

Trenton points out, "I will have to tell my troop I will be absent from training."

Branson raises his hand. "Do not worry. I will take care of that."

They bid their good-nights, Trenton to the guest quarters and Branson to the master bedroom.

Branson closes the door behind him and grins. He shakes his head, saying, "Petty ploys."

CHAPTER
SIXTEEN

Early the next morning, Branson and Trenton mull over many possibilities for the tannery. Finally, they settle on a plan and go to work. The men toil all day and into dusk. The second day comes and goes the same. Trenton's two days change to four and then six, always claiming that he finds more repairs that should be fixed immediately. One time, he says he needs to go into the spirit hold to retrieve more supplies. He returns with more of his own belongings than supplies.

Almost a full moon later, Trenton still remains at Branson's hold. Construction progress has increased dramatically with his help. Even the warriors' bunkhouses are completed and undergo some improvements, and the training yard is roughly composed. There has been considerable expansion in the hold, and with Branson's constant presence, it is sure to continue at the accelerated pace.

Along the way, Branson not only informed Gaylen that he had chosen a donateur, but Gaylen also made preparations for Jari to replace Trenton in his troop. Now Gaylen has commanded that Trenton be formally named donateur. Of course, this presents a challenge: Trenton has still not accepted the offer.

Branson decides that he will take Trenton on a hunt. He asks Reba to prepare some rations for them to take. Branson packs the fare, his bow, and a spare bow on their horses and leads Trenton deep into the hunting grounds.

Trenton remarks on his timing: "Sire, is the day not late to be hunting?"

He shrugs. "It is. Perhaps the Great Spirit will reward us for our intentions."

It is likely they will not come home with a kill, but Branson is not here to hunt. Making it to a familiar post, Branson stops his horse, and they dismount and tie their horses. They take their bows and string them. Branson suggests they hunt in a pair, instead of separately. With the sun beginning its slow retreat from the sky and no sign of any beasts plump enough for a kill, the men return to their camp to eat. Reba has packed a generous section of dried meat, crusty bread, and trail bars.

Tearing off another strip from the dried meat slab, Branson says, "You have been a good friend these past weeks. My home grows greater every day. It seems as though you share the same vision as I."

Trenton takes a gulp of his water before saying, "It is much more than that. Such loyalty and greatness should be rewarded."

"Yes, but you do not think you are worthy of such a reward?"

Trenton looks at his bread when he says, "Perhaps."

Branson raises his sleeve over his left arm, revealing the two healed horizontal lines from the Appointing. He touches them. "I wear the mark of gardien to none other but the Chozien. You will not see this mark on many, if any at all. I see that I myself have been chosen as well—by the

Great Spirit to find the Chozien and by our dewan to raise him. I have sacrificed much to carry such a burden, but I have also gained what so many can only dream of."

"You are a great man with great value."

Branson shakes his head. "You are too hard on yourself. I do not wish to know your past, but I do know your future. Is it so much to depend on another again?"

Trenton sighs. "Yes, it is much to trust another." He pauses for a moment to think through his words. "It is not so bad, this life. Every day, I find more of myself than I have from the first time I arrived at the Jade. It is time I put to rest my bitterness from my past. If I may rescind my early refusal, it would be an honor to serve you as donateur to your son."

Branson gets up and retrieves another skin from his saddle. He returns and raises the skin to his mouth and lets the cool burgundy wine drain into his mouth.

Trenton laughs. "Expecting a celebration?"

Branson chuckles because he drinks more out of relief than good cheer. "Well, I was hoping that I would finally change your mind. Gaylen wants to formally announce you as donateur. I already told him you had accepted, you see."

Trenton takes a similar gulp of the wine. "I assumed as much when I went to the spirit hold and many offered me their congratulations. And when I went to speak with my troop, somehow they had already been informed of my 'promotion.'"

Branson laughs. "Good. Then it is agreed. You will be donateur to the Chozien."

Branson and Trenton ride back to his hold in high spirits. They announce Trenton's acceptance, and the kinsmen cheer and offer congratulations.

The ceremony is held but a half moon later. Trenton receives similar marks as Branson, though his are vertical instead of horizontal and placed on his left shoulder blade. He is not presented with a medallion. Many warriors of the clans come to rejoice once word arrives that the donateur comes out of their service. The celebration lasts deep into the night, only for the celebrants to return to their home clans the following day.

The moons seem to come and go with the wind. Branson stays true to his plan, adding to his hold a manservant who seems to think only he can maintain the upkeep of the house. He brings with him his rotund wife to cook and manage the kitchen, along with their son of seven birth years, who serves as a stable boy. Another kinsman follows, a quiet young huntsman, who is an avid hunter.

As expected, Trenton has insisted that he assist in accepting any new kinsmen entering the Bonne Ame's service. Reba continues to share the room with Aitan while the servants' house continues to fill and expand with others.

Ahni becomes pregnant and gives birth to a son, Malan, in Aitan's second year. Shortly after Malan's birth, Trenton asks Branson for permission to join his *ame* with Reba's. Branson happily consents, and interestingly enough, six moons after the marriage, Reba brings an infant son into their world. They name the child Simi. Ahni bears another baby girl, Kaede, five years later, and Reba another boy, Zahn. Reba's days are full, caring for all the children.

Branson begins Aitan's huntsman training at the young age of five. He takes Aitan into the forest in the early hours of the day, with Trenton following behind them. Branson decides to educate Aitan on the significance of being Chozien before he begins training him in the service of huntsman. After tying off the horse, he walks with his son.

"Aitan, it is time that you learn your place in life. While your studies with your seeker tutor are important since they contribute to your basic understanding of economics, arithmetic, and communication, there is more. You are a very special person. You are Chozien. Do you know what this is?"

Aitan shakes his head.

"The Great Spirit sends a powerful spirit to his people. This spirit is born into a child, and the child then becomes Chozien. You, as the Chozien, can bring great change to all people. But we must be careful, as the change can be good or it can be very bad. Do you understand?"

Aitan nods. "I do, Da. But what needs to change?"

Branson pats his son on his head. "You are still young and have not seen the world. Once you become a man, you will see that the world is in need of much change."

Branson stops and sits for a moment. Smiling, Aitan joins his father on the ground.

Holding out three fingers, Branson says, "There are three important duties you must do for your family first: Feed them, heal them, and protect them. Remember that."

He waits for Aitan to nod, then continues, "You will learn to do all of these things in each of your service trainings as huntsman, spirit seeker, and warrior. I will teach you the first of these. It is the service of the huntsman. A huntsman knows the way of the land and of the beasts that live within it. You must be silent and hidden. Look around. Do you see any beasts to hunt?"

Aitan looks all around and shakes his head.

"Because we are too loud. You must not be seen … and also see what is hidden. Where is your donateur?"

Aitan looks around with an excited smile on his face but cannot find Trenton. Finally, Trenton walks from the brush directly in front of Branson. Aitan's eyes widen.

Branson says, "You should know your surroundings. Never let anything catch you when you are not ready. Understand?"

Aitan nods and thus begins Aitan's training in the service of huntsmen. Branson also sends him to the spirit hold, where he learns about the different animals and their marks on the ground. Various devenirs teach Aitan how to track through the forest and rough terrain, build and care for a bow and arrows, and how to conceal himself; even his stealth and awareness increases.

In Branson's previous clan, combat training was delayed to the last phase, around thirteen birth years, because the clan kinsmen considered it a minimal aspect of the service. Branson, though, remembers his shame from his lack of defense skills when he first arrived at the spirit hold and trained with the other huntsmen. He does not want this for Aitan.

Branson knows that a Chozien should be properly trained to defend himself in all situations. In the spirit hold, Aitan will learn the huntsman combat early, with years of practice to hone the skill. Still, Aitan will not be named huntsman and receive his first pair of the Jade Order huntsman's short swords until he is in his fifteenth birth year.

By his ninth year, Aitan can come within a two-person arm span of a beast without being heard and strike the smallest of them from at least a hundred paces. Branson is amazed at the speed of Aitan's progression. He then further challenges Aitan by training him in the dark, where he only has his ears, nose, and body to rely on. This takes some time for him to learn, though with his great desire to please his father, he succeeds. Soon Aitan becomes proficient in gutting and skinning, so Branson ensures that he splits his training to serve as butcher for the spirit hold. Branson seeks to instill the sentiment of truly employing his skills for the good of the Jade Order beyond that of his representation.

As Aitan enters his tenth year, Branson and his hold celebrate, for Ahni bears another child—a girl, Nadie. Aitan was granted a brief recess from his huntsman training to return to Branson's hold and reunite with his gardien and meet his new sister. Amidst all the joy, though, Branson feels distracted, as it has been decided that Aitan must begin his training as a warrior. However, Aitan will at least have his brother there as well.

After repeatedly watching the warriors train, and in comparison to the mundane activity of a huntsman, eight-year-old Malan has chosen to follow the warrior service and will leave with Trenton and Aitan to the spirit hold for the annual commencement of the young Jade boys and girls into warrior training. The donateur's son, Simi, has a passion to be a seeker; his time for training, though, has not yet come.

Ahni is tearful at Malan's departure and packs each of them a small vial of her eucalyptus oil to remember her by. Branson does not want to leave Ahni while she is recovering from childbirth and will not join them. At the disheartened expressions from Aitan and Malan, he promises to visit soon.

When Trenton and the two boys arrive at the spirit hold's warrior bunkhouses, he takes them aside before giving them over to General Haru.

He advises, "You will learn to depend on yourself and each other here.

Neither of you will not receive special treatment, not as the Chozien nor as the son of a Bonne Ame. It will be hard, and others will avoid you. You must be strong. I am not allowed to interfere during your training. Look after each other."

The boys nod their heads, Aitan more anxiously than Malan.

Trenton points to Aitan's medallion, depicting a hawk with outstretched wings. It does not vary across orders, this emblem; every Chozien's medallion bears the same animal spirit engraving.

"This will not bring you many friends, and it will attract those who are false and bear no honor. You will know who they are."

With that, Trenton fades into the background while the boys run to join the others. He asks the Great Spirit to watch over the pair when he cannot.

Aitan and Malan become part of the gathering crowd of young boys and girls, all of them excited and talking. Aitan feels Malan squeeze close to his side. He tries to seek out familiar faces, but he finds none. The only contact he's had with others are the huntsman novices he's trained with, so it is no surprise that he does not recognize anyone else. He tries stretching up on his toes to see over the crowd. He catches a glimpse of a familiar face. Aitan moves through the throng for a closer look, but Malan squeezes so tightly to him that he trips over Aitan's foot. With a quick reaction, Aitan catches Malan by the shoulders before he hits the ground. Some of the other boys around them snicker.

Aitan sighs and then shakes his head at his younger brother. "Malan, you cannot live by my side forever. I will not leave you, I promise."

Aitan suddenly smiles when he hears his name being called out by a well-known voice. Aitan turns to see his best friend, Romin—the son of Uric, his father's best friend and the only other Bonne Ame in the Jade Order. He cannot believe it is him.

Aitan and Malan meet him.

"How is it you are here?" Aitan asks. "I thought your father said he refused to have you train as a warrior."

Romin scruffs Malan's hair. "He did. He kept telling me to be more like Davin so I could care for my own family one day. But I begged and begged him to let me train as a warrior with you. He even brought me here himself."

Romin is ten birth years, the same as Aitan. They have known each other for as long as they can remember. They've always been happy their fathers are friends, because they can visit each other often. Aitan has never seen Romin with hair; his father keeps it shaved like himself and his brother, Davin. Romin stands a head taller than Aitan and the majority of the other novices there.

The friends continue to catch up and laugh for just a moment longer before General Haru appears, along with his high warriors. They don't look friendly at all. Their faces hold no encouragement whatsoever.

Aitan hears other novices shushing throughout the crowd, and the general's booming voice squelches any remaining noise: "Quiet!"

Once all voices have gone quiet, he continues, "You will learn that when one of your superiors enters, you are to be silent. There are penalties for such disrespect."

The general scans the crowd, making sure to direct his attention to the offenders. The expression on most of the recruits' faces is wide-eyed shock.

"You are to address me as 'General,' or 'General Haru.' From now on, you will do as I say. Neither your fathers nor your mothers have any influence here. The only one greater than me is the dewan.

"You are here to train in the service of warrior. It is honorable that you have decided to protect your hold against the enemy, although some of you will not complete your training. Look to the person on either side of you. One or both of them will not be there when you are named warrior. The training will be difficult, you will feel pain, and you will want to go home. But each day is a new day, and you will continue on. Only the weak will leave." In a loud voice, he yells, "Are you weak?"

The recruits yell back in unison, "No!"

General Haru smiles. "Good, good. Since I am unable to teach all of you, my high warriors will do so in my stead—Laten, Conrad, Victor, and Randol."

Each warrior steps forward as his name is called.

"Remember, only the strong are named warrior." With that, the general takes his leave.

High Warrior Laten steps to the front and announces, "The names that I call will follow me to my bunkhouse."

Aitan holds his breath while the names are being called. He does not know why but he feels nervous about hearing his name. The high warrior goes through his list, not calling Aitan's name. Now High Warrior Conrad steps forward with his list. Malan's name is called. Malan hangs his head as he leaves with the others. He looks back, and Aitan waves encouragingly to him. Malan smiles, waves back, and hurries to catch up with the troop. High Warrior Victor follows. This time, Romin's name is called. The friends promise to find each other later before parting.

High Warrior Randol comes forth and calls to all those remaining, "Gather your belongings and follow me to your new home."

Aitan picks up his bedroll and the satchel containing his personal effects. The novices walk to the bunkhouse in silence. He looks back at the empty yard where so many recruits assembled together to enter into a new life. He leaves behind his mother, his father, and his sisters.

He leaves behind all that has brought him here to this day. Yet, he is not alone; he takes with him the memories of his family and his role as a Chozien.

CHAPTER
SEVENTEEN

After what seems an interminable amount of time, Aitan and the all other warrior novices arrive at the many bunkhouses meant for them. The walk seemed so far that if Aitan had not seen other novices practicing, he would have thought that they had gone beyond them. The four troops split into their designated houses.

High Warrior Randol leads his group into an expansive, airy bunkhouse full of beds divided by a center aisle. Aitan surmises that one side is already occupied by absent warriors, for he sees bedrolls, blankets, and personal belongings present, but the other side is empty. The high warrior walks far enough into the house to allow all the recruits to enter.

When he speaks, his voice is authoritative but welcoming: "This is where you will sleep. You are never to leave the training yard without permission in the form of an escort. If you are found without an escort, you will immediately be sent home. No exceptions."

He walks to the empty beds. The beds appear oddly built, with one bed above another, supported by thick posts and ladders next to each set of two beds.

"These are your beds. We call them 'bunks.' Place your bedroll on the frame here. If you do not have one, one will be given to you, provided you repay it in additional training aside from the others. Those on top can use the ladder to aid you to your bed." Then he points to the other side. "That is where the three-year novices reside. I will leave you to unpack and settle yourselves. When I return, every bed should have a novice to occupy it. If not, I will make sure that your training will not be easy for the first moon."

The high warrior exits, and chaos erupts soon after. The recruits all scramble to claim their beds. Some are eager to have the top bed, while others dive to cover the bottom. Aitan runs to the back and sets his bedroll on the bottom bunk and begins setting up his bed. Soon more boys come and stake their claims on the beds around him. He hears some of the younger boys sniffling; they haven't found a bed yet. He decides to assist them because he does not desire a whole moon's worth of difficult training. Others follow Aitan's lead as they, too, do not wish to endure hard training. One boy with red hair and freckles seems overwhelmed with the uproar. Aitan calms him, finds him a bed, and helps him unpack. Unfortunately, the boy did not bring a bedroll. Aitan shakes his head, imagining the extra training the boy will bear.

When the high warrior returns, the room quiets except for a few whispers and chuckles.

The high warrior's eyes widen. He clenches his hands into fists and explodes in a booming voice: "Silence! You are not to speak when a high-ranking warrior enters your presence. This is how you repay me? With brazen insolence? I will not tolerate this form of disrespect. Everyone! Outside, now!"

When he does not approve of the grumbling and lack of urgency in their pace, he shouts again, "Faster! Faster! You are too slow!"

After every recruit stands outside the bunkhouse, Randol begins his scolding: "After today, you will learn to never speak when a superior is in your presence. Warriors are known for their strict obedience and high respect. When you are speaking, you cannot hear my commands. Then I will have to repeat myself, and there will be times when I will not be able to. Do you understand?"

The recruits nod.

Randol shakes his head. "No. You speak your answer and address me as 'High Warrior.' Do you understand?"

All the boys proclaim, "Yes, High Warrior!"

Randol smiles and nods. "Good. As for your punishment, you will run. A warrior must have endurance. So you will run until your devenir gets tired."

Each recruit receives a small skin of water, being told to use it sparingly, for they will have nothing more until their next meal. Of course, the devenir offers to refill their skins with water from her own, but she will make sure that whoever needs more water on the run will pay for it with additional training after the evening meal.

And then it is off into the hills. No one is allowed to quit or walk, the devenir stopping only every so often to let everyone catch their breath and then they move on again. During the run, the devenir points out areas of the warrior training ground. When some of the novices start to remove their shirts, the devenir tells them to leave them on. She says that a warrior will go to battle with thicker clothing than what they have on and that they should get accustomed to training with it.

Aitan runs—more like stomps—among the other boys. He looks up to see the sun shining. He closes his eyes to shield them from the glare. He must have kept his eyes closed too long, as he soon stumbles into another boy in front of him, who then shoves him backward.

Aitan apologizes and continues on. He can feel his medallion thumping against his chest. It's so heavy. He feels that if he does not hold his head up, he will tilt right over from its weight. He looks around him and sees that several others look just as exhausted. But the devenir does not seem the least bit winded.

Aitan does not know how long the run will continue and prays it will not be much longer. Just as some seem fatigued to the point of falling over at any moment, others steadily lead the group. The sting of humiliation pierces Aitan. He remembers that, as the Chozien, he is to bring peace to all orders. Yet, here someone else leads him.

Finally, the devenir calls for the end of the run. The recruits all fall to the ground, panting and heaving for breath.

The devenir smiles. "Soon this will not tire you. It would be best that you remember your manners to your superiors. Now get up and follow me. It is time to eat, and you are welcome to have more than one helping. You may retire to your beds after."

The recruits stand sluggishly and wipe the sweat from their faces. Aitan notices the low position of the sun in the sky, amazed at how much of the day has passed. By the time they reach the meal hall, Aitan's breathing has returned to normal. He sees a line of recruits standing with a plate in hand, waiting to be served. Some of them make a start for the line, but others pull them back, pointing to the high warrior. They all look at Randol, waiting for him to release them to eat.

He smiles at their quick comprehension and motions his head toward the hall. "Well, what are you waiting on? You must be famished."

That is all the encouragement Aitan needs. He runs for the line. He forces his way through the throng of his fellow hungry novices. The line moves faster than he expected, though. The servers dish out the food at a rapid rate. When Aitan finds a free space, he drops down and exhales.

He finally takes a look at his plate. His eyes widen. As he sees the heaping mounds of meat, potatoes, and greens on his plate, he cannot imagine how any of them will find the room to eat the entire serving, let alone another one. Still, he feels his stomach growling and begins to devour his meal.

He notices with his first bite that the food tastes slightly bland, something the Jade Order is not known for. He only gives the thought a moment before he ignores the lack of flavor, and it's not long before Aitan finishes his meal, consuming all the food on the plate. He's surprised that he could eat so much. He feels a tap on his shoulder. He turns to see Romin standing there.

Romin waves a hand at Aitan's haggard appearance. "What have you all gone and gotten yourselves into?"

Aitan looks down at himself and then back to Romin. He whips around and takes a look at the many of the other novices around him. For the first time, he notices that only his group appears to have begun any training.

He turns back to Romin. "You haven't trained today?"

"What?" Romin says, smiling. "Of course not. We went to our bunks, then toured the rest of the grounds. Wasn't that what your troop did?"

Aitan grits his teeth. "Yes, but we *ran* right through it."

Aitan feels himself burning with anger. The other boys in his troop will find this out and blame the intensity of the training on him, figuring that High Warrior Randol will push their group harder because the Chozien is among their ranks. He does not think he is off to a good start.

Romin raises an eyebrow. "I don't understand. Why are your clothes dirty?"

Aitan just shakes his head. Romin decides to lighten Aitan's mood and suggests that he meet some of the recruits in his bunkhouse. Not really caring one way or the other, Aitan agrees.

When they approach a group of boisterous boys near the bunkhouses, Romin speaks in a loud voice to capture their attention: "Hey, meat pies! I'd like you to meet a good friend of mine. This is Aitan."

They seem a lively bunch. A few merely wave their salutations, while others introduce themselves by name.

One thin boy leans in close to Aitan's medallion. He smiles impishly before mocking him, "Hey, fellas, we have a real, live Chozien among us. If we stay close to him, he may share his secrets with us."

The group laughs. Romin loses his smile. Aitan does not understand the rib, but he does know the laughter. The anger within rises again, and he clenches his fists.

The others see his reaction, and their laughter grows louder.

Another boy feigns cowering back. "Shhh! Don't laugh. He'll call for his *donateur*."

They roar with laughter, some even falling to the floor, cackling until they cry.

Aitan now feels embarrassment creeping in alongside the anger. He grits his teeth, attempting to tamp down their laughter. Tight-lipped, he responds, "It is not he you should fear."

Again, the laughter persists, with more of the boys pretending fear.

Romin's back stiffens, and he regrets the attempt to brighten his best friend's spirits. He feels sorry for Aitan.

A voice from within the group joins in the teasing: "If we're nice, he'll show us how his mother feeds cherries to his father."

Aitan hears Romin's sudden intake of breath, and then Romin reaches out for Aitan's arm. But Aitan has had enough. The joke mocked not him this time, but his mother and her previous time as an attendant.

He and his mother have always been close, and she has shared with him much about her past and present to keep that bond.

Pulling his arm away from Romin, Aitan charges into the crowd and rams his shoulder into the first body he sees, hitting a boy in the chest and knocking him to the floor on his back. Aitan does not stop there. He pins the boy to the floor by employing a huntsman mount, where he straddles the boy's torso, but he only gets in two strikes before several of the other rude recruits wrestle him away. They begin to beat him. He defends as many of the jabs as he can while in a seated guard.

Everything stops at the sound of a loud voice: "What is this? Let me through!"

The recruits release Aitan and leave him there on the floor. He looks up and sees one of the high warriors standing above him.

"Stand, Novice."

Aitan picks himself up and wipes his nose.

"What troop do you belong to?"

Not even trying to hide the anger in his voice, Aitan answers, "High Warrior Randol."

"I will let him set your penance. Warriors do not fight their own."

After the high warrior leaves, the crowd disperses.

Romin puts his hand on Aitan's shoulder. "I'm sorry. I didn't know they would do that."

Aitan jerks away from him. "I don't need your pity—and I certainly don't need your friends." He turns and walks away.

Romin stands there, confused. He didn't intend to see his friend get embarrassed. He really did want Aitan to make some new friends. Speaking of friends, how could Aitan so easily turn on Romin after all these years?

Romin's confusion gives way to a surge of anger. He calls after Aitan,

"Hey, I tried to help you! You're spoiled, Aitan. And you know what else? You're right: You aren't in need of friends!"

Aitan does not turn around. He walks alone with his thoughts. He can feel his donateur near. He is grateful, at least, for him not interfering. He walks until he comes up to the vast training yard. He stands on the outside looking at the warriors practice. He hangs his head, discouraged. It had not been so difficult when he trained with the huntsmen. Those novices welcomed him as an equal. He still has many friends there.

He looks back to the practicing warriors. It amazes him how long they can practice without falling out from fatigue. He laughs when a warrior takes a blow from a practice sword after being too slow.

"It is not good to laugh at another's mistake."

Aitan jumps at the familiar voice. He does not turn as he replies, "I did not hear you, Trenton. Thank you for not helping me earlier."

He snorts. "I am not here to protect you from these childish brawls but from those who wish to take your *ame*."

Aitan drops his head again. "I shouldn't have lost my temper. Da always tells me it is better to ignore their senseless bickering; there are better ways to use your time and energy." He shakes his head at the thought of already disappointing his father.

Trenton reaches out and pats Aitan's shoulder. "Your father would be proud of how you handled yourself in that bunkhouse. Your skills have improved greatly since you were younger."

Aitan turns around, wide-eyed and smiling. "Really? I couldn't even tell—the whole thing happened so fast."

Trenton chuckles. "That is good. You do not want your battles to last too long, do you?"

Aitan shakes his head.

Still, Trenton feels that something disturbs his charge. "I would be doing your father a disservice if I did not ask what troubles you. It is only the first day and yet you are here alone. What is it?"

Aitan sighs a little. "Even if it is the first day, this is not what I expected. The high warrior says that we will run every day, but when do we fight? I do not understand this training."

Trenton smiles. "Ah, well, being a warrior is not always about fighting. Your body must be trained to stand up to the conditions of war."

When Aitan furrows his brow, Trenton goes into more detail: "When you are at war, sometimes you do not have the advantage of being at home. This means you will not eat as well as you do here, or at all. Then there are times when you will not be able to sleep because you need to be ready for an attack. These conditions can weaken the body, and you need your strength to fight your enemy. Do you understand?"

Aitan nods.

But Trenton pushes on: "There is something else?"

"The other novices do not like me much. They are not friendly like the huntsmen novices."

Trenton folds his arms and eyes Aitan. "If friends are what you are looking for, why are you here talking to me?"

Aitan opens his mouth to reply but then pauses in thought. He smiles, understanding Trenton's implication. He leaves his donateur and heads back to his bunkhouse, picking up the pace as he notices the receding sunlight.

When he arrives, he sees some of the boys already winding down for the night by their clean appearance. Others somehow still have energy, as small cliques have formed—perhaps friends—playing games or laughing. Aitan feels so tired that he decides he would rather wash up than join one of the jovial groups. He keeps his gaze straight ahead, but he sees the other novices looking at him and whispering. Aitan ignores them.

Just as he enters the bunkhouse, someone calls out, "Hey, you! Hey!"

Aitan turns tiredly toward the voice, knowing that he is the intended audience. Another novice runs toward him waving his hands.

The boy stops in front of him. "High Warrior Randol wishes to see you. He is out back of the bunkhouse with some of the other novices doing extra exercises."

Aitan sighs and makes an annoyed face but nods. "Thanks."

Before he can turn around, the boy stops him again. "We saw your fight with the other bunkhouse. Did you know the one you attacked was a three-year novice?"

Aitan shakes his head.

"It looks like we could learn a thing or two from you. You gave us a very high standing over the other new recruits ... and a sharp tongue-lashing from High Warrior Randol."

Aitan winces at the comment.

The boy chuckles a moment, then points to Aitan's medallion. "We thought you would be different—selfish, maybe. Maybe we were wrong."

The boy offers his hand. Aitan nods and grasps the boy's forearm, just as he has seen his father do many times before. He knows without the exact words that the boy is offering friendship with himself and the others. When the other recruits see this act of amity, they, too, come forward, laughing, slapping Aitan's back, and asking many questions. Aitan finally feels his anxiety ease.

Still, he can see in the faces in the throng of recruits surrounding him that some hold less friendship and more bitterness. Trenton was right: He will have to be mindful of who he trusts.

Just when Aitan begins to enjoy his newfound acceptance, the loud, disapproving, but recognizable voice of High Warrior Randol sounds out: "What's this? Didn't I say to send Aitan straight to me?"

All the boys jump into silence and turn to look at the high warrior. Some of them answer with the correct response: "Yes, High Warrior."

"Then why is he here and not where I told you to send him?"

The recruits do not speak but instead move aside to give the high warrior a direct path to Aitan.

Standing there, Aitan wants to explain that his delayed arrival is not out of disrespect and that the others should not be held accountable. But when Aitan opens his mouth to speak, the high warrior holds up his hand for silence.

"I am not interested in your excuses, Novice. This will be added to your penance from your tussle at dinner. Follow me."

Randol does not wait to see if Aitan intends to follow him. He just turns and heads toward the back of the bunkhouse. When Aitan exits, he sees more than he expects.

The high warrior catches Aitan's expression and chuckles. "More than what you anticipated? You should learn to hide your thoughts; don't want to give your opponent the advantage."

Aitan frowns and puffs his chest to show he isn't intimidated.

The high warrior hides his smile, not wanting to discourage the young novice. He clears his throat. "I am sure you have a good reason for your scuffle today. However, you should control your anger. It is reckless to be led by rage; it numbs the senses and causes poor choices. For that, you will be disciplined."

Aitan nods. He understands the high warrior's lesson—and more: he is being punished for his judgment rather than the silly brawl. The high warrior takes him to a trough of water. Aitan sees other recruits standing with their arms out in front of them, holding buckets. Their arms shake as they strain to keep the buckets up. Whenever a recruit's arm lowers, a devenir smacks him across the back with a thin, flat stick, and they immediately lift their arms back up. Aitan notices that some of them have their arms out at their sides in a T shape. It looks to be equally as difficult. Aitan's eyes widen when he notices the devenir pouring more water into one novice's buckets, with the recruit pressing his lips together at the increased effort.

Having buckets shoved against his chest brings Aitan's attention back to his own penance. He grips the handles on the buckets and listens to the high warrior's instructions: "You are to hold your arms out in front of you like so." Randol lifts Aitan's arms in front of him until they are parallel to the ground.

Aitan stretches his shoulders involuntarily.

"You must not let your arms fall past this point." Randol shows him with his hand about a finger's length below Aitan's raised arms. "If your arms do fall, you will receive a strike across your shoulders, as you have already seen."

Randol waits for Aitan's nod before he dips another bucket in the trough and pours a little water into each of Aitan's buckets. Aitan's arms clench from the immediate weight—amazed at how much it increases by the small amount of water.

Randol continues, "Do not focus on the pain in your shoulders or the tension in your arms or the water. Those are but distractions. Center yourself around the Great Spirit. Listen for your heartbeat. Feel for the wind. When you can accomplish this, the weight will lessen."

Soon enough, after several strikes and two more pours, Aitan still cannot control his thoughts or maintain a focus. Sweat mats down his hair and trickles down his face. He tries tilting his head to avoid the sweat from flowing into his eyes. *Perfect, another distraction!* He jumps as another strike lands across his shoulders.

"You are not focusing."

Aitan begins feeling annoyed with the devenir. He grinds his teeth, wondering why the devenir always stands behind him. He knows it is not the same one who comes to pour more water into his buckets, because their steps sound different, shorter. His anger further increases when he notices that other recruits have started disappearing. Soon it becomes apparent that he alone remains to pay his penance. Just as Aitan nears letting loose an angry outburst, he sees a towel thrown across his arms and a small piece of soap thrown at his feet.

Before he can ask, he hears High Warrior Randol's voice: "That is enough for tonight. Grab a bucket of water and wash, and then you may retire for the evening. I would hurry; it will be an early morning tomorrow."

Aitan answers respectfully in the affirmative, grabs the towel and soap, then dips a bucket in the trough for the water. He glances behind him to see if the devenir still stands there. To his chagrin, he and the high warrior are the only people behind the bunkhouse.

Randol notices Aitan's anger. He crosses his arms. "You should be too exhausted to feel anything else."

Aitan snaps back, "Why is it that I am the only novice still paying penance?" After Aitan sees the high warrior's raised eyebrow, he adds, "... High Warrior."

Randol replies, "You arrived late; it would not be fair if I were to shorten your penance."

"I could have come early tomorrow and kept the sleep I am missing tonight."

Randol laughs. "You do not choose when or how to serve your penance. You arrived late, so you must stay late."

Before Aitan can continue his complaint, Randol cuts him off in a stern voice: "There is no negotiation. If you were to ask such insolent questions in front of the other novices, you would have cost them all another moon of grueling training. And from now on, you are not to defy me in private. Do you understand?"

Aitan presses his lips together. "Yes, High Warrior."

"Good. It seems that your anger has gotten the best of you again. You were not even aware your devenir had turned in for the night, nor did you hear my approach." He shakes his head, frowning. "You will learn to control this temper of yours. You will return here at the end of each day until I decide you've had enough. Now go and clean yourself. Oh, and before I forget, we clean our own clothes. You may use the soap and wash pan when you return."

Aitan does not go far from the bunkhouse since the hour is late. He removes his clothes and washes away the sweat and dirt from his body. Satisfied that the filth from the day's arduous training is gone, he lifts the bucket over his head and lets the warm water run over his body, further relaxing his muscles. His medallion glistens in the moonlight. He dries off and wraps the towel around his waist before heading back to the bunkhouse.

Feeling the exhaustion set in, he tosses his clothes into the wash pan and pours a bucket of warm water over them. He uses a combination of soap and scrubbing to create a good lather. He finishes and wrings the clothes out, then finds where the others have lain or hung their garments out to dry. Finally, he tiptoes into the bunkhouse and climbs into his bed, where he promptly falls into a deep slumber.

CHAPTER
EIGHTEEN

As a yawn starts, a devenir quashes it before anyone can see him. The first day for new novices is always the longest for everyone.

The devenir listens as High Warrior Randol says: "It is clear we have the advantage for endurance with our novices, although their discipline lacks. Only our novices were disciplined to begin training on their first day. We will need to be tougher and stricter if they are to last and become three-year novices. I do believe our troop regained some footing after that short fray at dinner, don't you think?"

The devenirs share a chuckle.

Clearing his throat, Randol continues, "What do you say of our Chozien?"

One burly devenir says, "I think he is strong, but unlikely to endure the harsh environment of a warrior."

Many grunts of agreement follow.

Another warrior offers, "Yes, true, he does come from a somewhat pampered home. Yet, so do many others here. It would be unfair for us to judge him prematurely. From his bout today, he is far ahead of these novices in the combat realm."

More grunts of agreement.

Randol lets the devenirs continue to toss about their views on the Chozien until he begins to grow irritable. He silences them and shakes his head, then says: "Are you blind? Have you grown too proud of your position to remember you were once novices yourselves? This boy has all the characteristics of a great warrior. Yet, that is not his only service. He will still train as a novice huntsman until he receives his swords. And after he completes the Awakening to become a warrior, he will leave to begin his training as seeker. This *boy* will accomplish more in his young life than any of you have at this point. Let us not forget *we* are responsible for training the Chozien; we should be proud. We serve him.

"By the time he completes his training as a warrior, he will be called 'Sire.' Do not let these titles sway your loyalty. This is what keeps you from receiving the rank of first warrior." Randol looks at every devenir in his presence.

Some lower their eyes; others nod.

He continues, "There is more to this meeting. I fear for the Chozien's *ame.* I have overheard several disturbing conversations from others without their notice. Many grim secrets lurk about the Jade. These secrets surround the boy, and it concerns his living breath. I do not know much about the politics of our leaders, but I am keen about recognizing danger, and my spirit screams of it. You are my devenirs; I have watched each one of you grow into what you are now. I trust none more than you."

With some apprehension, the same burly devenir from earlier asks, "What is amiss, High Warrior?"

Randol lowers his voice even more, as if he fears to be heard: "I believe we prepare for war—a war greater than the last and the one before that."

The others look at each other, confused.

Another devenir speaks up: "You must be joking. We would have been informed of such a war. Why would they hide this?"

Nods and agreeing grunts follow the remarks.

Randol responds, "I have asked myself this same question many times. Yet, the answer still remains unknown to me. I assure you something is different about the life cycle of this Chozien. We high warriors have been ordered to increase the novices' training. The Awakening will be held after their second year as novices."

Randal hears a collective intake of breath and disapproving grumblings in reply. He silences them.

Another devenir states, "It takes at least four birth years before the novices are ready for the Awakening! If we test them so soon, we will likely be sending them to their deaths."

Yet another adds, "It is not right for a boy of twelve years or younger to hold the title of warrior."

Randol folds his arms and slits his eyes as he peers at his devenirs. "The answer is simple: If a novice survives the Awakening, then he or she surely deserves the title of warrior. As well, it will be your training that will see them through it. We do not send them to their deaths until we go to war."

Far from the Jade Order's spirit hold, the young Zeke beckons his sparring partner on. While his foe rises from the ground on fatigued limbs, Zeke charges forward, knocking his weary opposition down. He raises his practice sword for a finishing blow, but a shout stops him. He looks in the direction of the voice and sees his elder brother walking toward him. Makani shakes his head. Zeke knows well the lecture his brother will now give.

Makani speaks in a low but heated voice: "You do try my patience, little brother. It is not our way to kill before converting. If we do so, then who will serve the Onyx? How will we spread our ducall? Who would we rule?"

Zeke argues, "Our enemies will not spare our lives so eagerly. We will appear to be weak."

Makani laughs. "You have not seen a battle. You do not know how the other, weaker orders shake within the protection of their own ranks. The mere sight of our numbers cowers our enemies into surrender. To shatter the will of an entire legion of warriors is not a sign of weakness."

"Yes, but the more corpses we leave on the field, the more our power will be feared, as well as our numbers."

Makani sighs. "You are proud and reckless—as was I at your age. We do not need to be reminded of our power, nor do the other orders. It is not wise to slaughter our future kinsmen. You must see them as the enemy now but also have the discernment to see them as one of us."

Zeke nods. His brother has never before spoken of himself and Zeke as the same. Doing so has made Makani's explanation all the more meaningful. Zeke didn't feel as if Makani chastised him because of jealousy or the typical sibling rivalry, but rather that he wants to teach him to be an Onyx warrior.

Makani waves Zeke's weary partner away. "That is enough sparring for now. Come, brother, it has been some time since we whispered with the women."

Zeke drops his practice sword and smiles. The two brothers walk away from the practice field, laughing about their upcoming conquests.

It seems to Aitan that the sun burns brighter this day. Every novice is drenched with perspiration from their intense training, completely shocked by the inexplicable change in the pace of their training. It started one birth year and six moons ago. The devenirs began waking them at the darkest hour of the night and had them spar with as little visibility as possible. Some showed a firm grasp of the training, while others struggled. Their runs in the hills became longer, and the pace, faster. Their bodies ached from exhaustion and the constant strength exercises. Soon enough, the nights grew to be as long as the days.

The troop has been split into two squadrons to allow for more training and individual screening of each novice's flaws. While Aitan's squadron trains for combat, the other runs the hills. Aitan awaits his turn to spar as two novices battle it out with their practice swords while the others watch. He looks down and frowns at the weighted sword he holds. He still prefers the huntsman's twin blades. He requested the use of them but was refused because those blades are not the weapons of a Jade warrior. His agility aids him where his unease with the sword falls short. High Warrior Randol, though, has informed him that his agility will be of no use on the crowded battlefield and suggests he practice with the weapon more so than the others. Still, Aitan ranks among the top novices in his troop, finding some encouragement in that.

Aitan looks on as a shorter, redheaded novice sidesteps a swinging strike and kicks his foe in the gut, knocking the wind out of him. The novice finishes with a hard blow to the opponent's back, which sends him to the ground, coughing. Immediately, the redhead novice positions himself as if another opponent is near.

Finally, the devenir calls an end to the match and says, "Excellent work, Kel. You have not let the height of others intimidate you." And looking at the fallen novice, he adds, "You must learn to not be over-eager with your attacks, unless you are asking to be released from your *ame*."

The redhead called Kel helps his opponent up. Before Aitan steps up for his turn, he sees High Warrior Randol approaching, along with the rest of the devenirs and the other squadron.

"What's this?" Kel asks Aitan.

Aitan met Kel on their first day as first-year novices—Kel being a sobbing, frightened child of nine birth years at the time. They became fast friends once they realized their faces were the most common among the others serving penance. This surprised Aitan since he did not think Kel would last past the first moon. Aitan offered to instruct Kel on some of his huntsman fighting techniques, and once Kel noticed Aitan struggling with the sword, he practiced with him. Today, Aitan finds it hard to imagine that the teary-eyed, whimpering child was once Kel.

Aitan shrugs and replies, "I do not know. It may be another lesson. We get so many each day."

Once the high warrior reaches them, Aitan notices two of the devenirs carrying large bags.

Both troops join together, and the high warrior explains, "I come to relieve you of your training today."

Smiles and relief appear on nearly all the novices' faces.

"Only to continue your knowledge of war by making known the weapons of the other orders."

The smiles disappear but the relief still remains.

"Come now and sit. We have much to cover."

High Warrior Randol unsheathes his own sword and holds it up so everyone may see. "This type of sword will be your weapon, along with a shield. You will learn to use this sword against the weapons of any of the other orders."

He motions to one of the devenirs with a bag to reveal one of the weapons. Then the high warrior unsheathes a sword that Aitan thinks looks more like a large cleaver a huntsman would use for butchering meat.

Randol's face turns to disgust as he says, "The Hematite Order ... they use this weapon. It is called the panabas. At first, you may see a resemblance of it to the cleavers our butchers use on the animals. Make no mistake, this will cut you in two just as easily."

Aitan smiles at the comparison.

The next weapon is another sword, the blade shorter than that of the Jade and decorated lavishly with a gold hilt and markings along the blade.

"Do not be fooled by the adornments. The Rhodonite Order is known for their attention to detail, as well as their swordplay on the battlefield. This is called the spatha. It is good for cutting and thrusting. Its weight is less than half of our Jade sword, which lends itself to quite the swordsmanship." He demonstrates with smooth, quick lunges and slashes. "Their thrusts are fiercely accurate at piercing a man where even the greatest healer cannot mend. You cannot rely on your sword against the Rhodonite. Use your shield well."

The next weapons emit ahs and oohs from the novices, whom Randol silences with a chastising stare. The weapons do not look as decorative as the Rhodonites' gold hilt, but they are made entirely of gold.

Randol holds up the first one. It resembles a club that has been modified with flanges at the head. "This is the Gold Order's weapon, the mace. It inflicts a great amount of damage to the area it hits." He holds the other weapon up—a broadsword with a decorative hilt that covers the hand. "This is another weapon the Gold Order uses. Typically, the mace is used for short-range attacks and additional defense, while the sword affords its wielder the protection from a distance."

A novice asks, "Why is it that the Gold Order goes to war with weapons made of complete gold?"

With the mace in hand, Randol walks to him, holding up the weapon close. He points to an area on the weapon where some of the gold has flaked off, revealing gray steel underneath. "Here. You see, it is only on the surface. Gold is a fragile metal; it would fall to pieces in a battle. Perception is reality to the Gold."

With a nod to the devenirs, Randol moves on to the next weapon. The devenirs walk up, each holding a different pole. Randol takes the first one. It is very long and has a sharp spearhead on one end. "The next group of weapons all belong to the Crystal Order. This is called the javelin. The Crystal use javelins as their first line of attack by launching them into the air. However, if they miss their target, it can then be used against them."

He goes to the second pole—shorter than the javelin, but on one end, it carries a spear tip, an ax head, and, behind it, a hook. "This is a halberd. It is swung with speed and able to cut through bone in one blow. The hook is used to drag warriors from their horses. Cavalry would be at a disadvantage against them."

The third pole looks to Aitan like a combination of both the javelin and halberd, with the length of the halberd but the spearhead of the javelin. Toward the bottom of the spearhead, it has two metal wings.

"This is a boar spear. It is best for hunting, but it has its advantages on the battlefield. Once the warrior is pierced with the spear, these ..."

He points to the wings. "… stop the spear from going in too deep so that it can be removed quickly."

The weapon sparks Aitan's interest at the mention of hunting.

Reaching into the second bag for the next weapon, Randol looks at the next weapon respectfully. "This is known as a battle-ax." He has to hold the bulky weapon with two hands. "The Carnelian Order wields this mighty ax with great strength. Be wary of this one. It kills whatever it comes in contact with. Yes … a mighty weapon this one is."

He continues on, "The Amber Order uses this short spear, a short sword, and a shield, weapons ideal for warriors fighting on horseback or close combat.

"The Amethyst Order favors a sword with a wide, curved blade, accompanied with a cylindrical metal shield that slides over the arm—the armguard." High Warrior Randol calls the curved blade a scimitar. "Its primary use is for hacking and chopping."

Then he pulls out a long, wide sword, nearly the height of Aitan's petite mother—the great sword. "The Azurite Order uses this sword in envy of the Tiger Eye Order. The great sword is best against spears and heavier weapons. It proves to be quite cumbersome otherwise, but quite lethal in the hands of one who knows how to wield it."

He pulls out another sword, with this blade equal in length to the great sword, though without the Azurites' decorative hilt. "This is the weapon of the Tiger Eye Order, the mightiest of all the orders. Even with its bulk, their skill with the weapon is unmatched by any other order … and yet it is not their primary weapon. They prefer their compound bows, though are not afraid to demonstrate their strength with the sword."

Before the high warrior presents the next weapon, he says, "The last two orders' weapons I'll show you are the cruelest and most merciless. They hold no honor among the Jade."

He removes three pairs of small, odd-looking weapons from the bag. He assembles them on his body. He places spiked metal plates on each knee. He slides a rigid shield over each forearm and latches them into place so that they fit his arms. Finally, he fastens what looks like a bear claw to each of his hands.

Once is finished, he explains the weaponry: "These are the Bloodstone warriors' weapons. They favor close combat. If they pass your guard, you must make quick work of them. Do not linger; they are vicious opponents and have no mercy."

He points to his knees. "These are known as knee spikes. They turn an otherwise subtle body part into a mortal weapon."

Next, he points to his arms. "Armguards, similar to that of the Amethyst. The Bloodstone do not believe a shield is an effective weapon and therefore do not believe sacrificing a hand to hold one. The armguards act as shields; however, a powerful blow from a heavy weapon could shatter or even sever the arm beneath."

Lastly, he raises his hands, displaying the claws. "The Bloodstone prefer to resemble the beasts of the land. Their minds are maddened with this parallel comparison so much that they cannot separate themselves from the creatures they mimic. They are fearless warriors with an unquenchable thirst for blood. Do not find yourselves caught within these claws; the cost of such carelessness is your *ame*."

Aitan feels a shiver creeping up his spine, and he does not like it. He recognizes the feeling as fear. He looks at the other novices. Their faces and stiff movements tell him that they are experiencing the same reaction. Suddenly, his stomach begins to turn sour. A bad taste touches his tongue, and his mind fills with disgust. He is afraid he may vomit. Then the high warrior removes the wicked weaponry, throws it back into the bag, and the rancid taste leaves Aitan. He exhales an air of relief.

The high warrior reaches into the large bag for the last time. He pulls out a sword with a long blade and a long hilt; still shorter than the Tiger Eye's sword, but longer than the Jade's. The steel looks darker than the others, even the Bloodstone.

Aitan's back arches spontaneously. The "feeling" has returned, but this is different ... demanding. He feels an arrogance of power. The emotions seem senseless to him. He tries to shake his head to rid him of them, but they still remain.

The high warrior's voice brings his attention back to the weapon: "This sword belongs to the Onyx Order. They darken the blades to conceal them during the night. The long hilt is used for pummeling the opponent. Be mindful, as some have fashioned spikes on the end of the hilt. They also use a variety of hand-combat weapons: hand axes, war mallets, spiked flails, and sword-breaker daggers."

A novice asks, "Why do they use so many other weapons?"

"Excellent question. The sword hilt is so long that it prevents it from being worn on its wearer's side; thus, it is always kept on the saddle. They carry the other weapons with them. It is not like a warrior to be without a weapon. It also makes it difficult to identify them as an Onyx warrior, since the Tiger Eye carry their swords on their horses as well. Look for the hand weapons."

Aitan had no idea that warriors have to think or pay attention to so much detail. The variety of weapons and their ferocity has suddenly made the world very real and life very fragile. He wonders what battle is truly like. Until now, he has not thought how real and frightful being a warrior might be.

After the high warrior puts the dark sword back in the bag, the "feeling" leaves Aitan. He is glad because it was becoming ... seductive.

CHAPTER
NINETEEN

The novices practice-battle against the weapons of the other orders. The high warrior comes by frequently to give lessons on the other orders' strategies, strengths, and flaws, and their common alliances. Soon the novices receive their own horses, and the devenirs add equestrian training to their daily exercises. The novices train themselves and their horses to ride together for one moon.

The devenirs instruct the novices to train their horses by voice command, as well as by the application of pressure. Aitan thoroughly enjoys this. He much prefers the motion commands, so he works tirelessly at using his knees and foot taps to indicate whether to gallop, walk, or turn a certain direction. He even spends his rare spare time practicing and playing with his mount. It is no surprise that he and his horse become fast friends. Aitan remembers how well his father takes care of his own horse and what Branson has taught him. In the same fashion as his father, Aitan makes sure he takes the time to rub his horse down, clean him, and feed him every night.

After the novices achieve proficiency in riding, the devenirs move to training them for battle. This will take longer than the riding, and it requires more attention to the horse. The novices must train their horses not to panic when weapons are waved around them—jumping, charging, and maneuvering while the rider is in combat. Once the horse has been trained for combat, it will learn to bite and kick during battle. It will take an entire birth year to complete this equestrian training. While training their horses, the novices also practice cavalry defense.

It becomes apparent that as the day for the Awakening grows closer, they see less and less of the other troops. At times, they even eat their meals in the bunkhouse.

With one moon left before the Awakening, Randol calls the troop to assemble in the bunkhouse. Aitan thinks this an odd behavior for the high warrior, as he rarely speaks with them inside the bunkhouse. Aitan files in along with the other novices and waits for the high warrior to disclose what surely must be a carefully guarded secret.

The high warrior takes his typical stern stance. Arms folded and with a straight face, he announces, "It has been decided that you have all gone beyond the level of a three-year novice. In one moon's time, you will perform the Awakening."

The troop waits. Then the high warrior smiles, and the bunkhouse erupts with prideful applause and congratulatory slaps on the back. Aitan gives and receives his own praises. But he doesn't *feel* as deserving as he would expect. There it goes again—a feeling. This one makes him uneasy ... similar to when he is hunting and a beast feigns a lost *ame* or when one lurks among the shadows of the forest.

Yes, he knows this feeling: It's caution. He tries to think what brought it on. Something about the high warrior. Aitan looks at him for a revealing tell. He can't seem to take his eyes from the high warrior's face. What is different this time? *The smile.* It appears ... false. It has no feeling, no confidence. The high warrior does not believe what he speaks. No wonder Aitan cannot find the desire for celebration.

"You must complete all the trials before you can be named warrior. We will use this last moon to prepare you. Your families were sent for and have arrived. You will be given one day of rest. Preparation begins in four days. Do not keep me waiting."

The troop takes the last as a dismissal and begins to file back out of the bunkhouse, but they stop and turn when the high warrior calls to them: "Wait." He searches for something to say as if he spoke too soon. "You've all done well." He gives one good nod, and the troop continues to file out again.

This time, Aitan knows that the compliment was genuine.

He sees Trenton waiting outside. Aitan can see by his donateur's anxious disposition that he is eager for something.

Curious, Aitan runs to Trenton. "What is it?"

Trenton eyes him. "Isn't there something you should be proud of?"

Aitan thinks for a moment and then hunches his shoulders. "High Warrior Randol says we are ready for the Awakening."

Trenton smiles and claps Aitan on the back, making him stumble forward. Trenton shakes his head, then says, "What is wrong? You should be proud. It usually takes four birth years to be ready for the Awakening."

"That's just it: It is too soon. I don't even think the high warrior believes his own words. I am not sure how to feel."

Trenton taps Aitan's shoulder. "Do not fret over such thoughts. Rejoice. It is a great honor that you are rewarded for your quick wit. Come now, your family waits ... as does mine."

Aitan follows Trenton to an inn—the White Moon—where their families will reside for their visit. Trenton guides Aitan through the crowd of patrons to the rooms. They stop at a door, where Trenton nudges Aitan to go in.

After Aitan opens the door, Kaede greets him first.

Squealing, she runs to him and hugs him around his waist. She exclaims, "Aitan, I've missed you!"

Aitan picks up his younger sister and twirls her around. She laughs and squeals even more. When he puts her down, he notices his baby sister, Nadie, walking toward him. She seems interested in playing too, but appears shy. Aitan bends down so he won't intimidate her and then reaches for her. She stops, and for a moment, Aitan can feel his eyes water at the thought his sister does not recognize him.

Aitan beckons her, "Come, little Nadie. It is me, Aitan. I've come to bring you sweets."

At the familiar sound of his voice, she explodes into a stumbling run and into his arms. He envelops her and squeezes just enough not to hurt her but to where she feels his love. As he showers her with kisses and Nadie giggles, she manages to turn and say, "Mum Mum."

Aitan stops and sets Nadie on her feet, where she promptly pouts. Aitan straightens and looks in the direction Nadie turned. He sees his mother, and his eyes begin to fill with tears. He watches her stand from the bed. She looks much smaller than he remembers.

Her smile makes him feel like a child again. Her face hasn't aged a bit, and just now, he notices the scent of one of her oils—lavender. Fitting, for her persona matches well with its characteristics: relaxed and soothing. Tears fall as she opens her arms and smiles. His mother is a quiet woman, but her love is thunderous.

Aitan runs to her and wraps his arms around his mother. He wants to guard her from any harm and ensure her peaceful existence. Not until this very moment did it ever mean so much to Aitan to become a warrior.

He almost crumples to the floor when he hears her voice: "Easy, Child, I am only flesh and bones."

He laughs at his mother's gentle humor and responds, "Much more than that, Mother, much more."

She reaches up and wipes each stream of his tears away with her thumbs. He feels the small calluses and how they contrast deeply with the silkiness of her unmarred skin. He remembers each one and recognizes their perfection.

"I've missed you much, Child. My, have you grown. It almost broke my heart that I did not know you right off. We must make our visits more frequent. Now sit. Malan tells me some unexpected events have occurred."

Wide-eyed, Aitan looks around the room. He has not seen his younger brother for many moons.

"Over here."

Aitan whips toward the voice; his brother has come through the door carrying a tray of various sliced meats, warm bread, spiced vegetables, and water. He sets the tray on a table, and their sisters run to it. Ahni gets there a moment later, delegating the distribution.

"I saw you come in with Trenton," Malan says. "Why are you looking at me like that?"

Aitan openly stares at Malan. He never realized how much Malan resembles their father. Malan has their father's bulk. He's shed the majority of his child's chubbiness, and he has grown in height. Still not topping Aitan, but definitely close. Malan's face makes Aitan feel as if he is looking at their father.

Aitan feels a twinge of jealousy, but he tamps it down and says, "Nothing, I haven't seen you in a long time is all."

Malan smiles a smile, reminding Aitan that his brother still admires him.

"Well, what's this Mother tells me?" Aitan asks. "Do you have something to share?"

Malan looks down first and then at their mother.

"Tell him, Malan. He is your brother. He won't be upset." Ahni looks at Aitan, ensuring what she said remains true.

"Come on, Malan. What is it?"

Malan looks back at Aitan and says in a low voice, "My troop is to perform the Awakening in one moon."

Out of the blue, Aitan laughs and shoves Malan. "Well, so is ours, little brother."

Malan and Aitan laugh while Ahni sits in bewilderment. After the brothers enjoy their accomplishments, they notice their mother's lack of rejoicing with them.

"Is there something wrong with the food, Mother?" Malan asks.

She shakes her head absently, thinking.

"Mother, what troubles you?" Aitan asks.

Ahni waves off their concern. "Oh, I just forgot to tell your father something."

Aitan and Malan soon forget their mother's strange behavior at the mention of their father.

"Father! Where is he?" Malan exclaims.

Ahni chuckles. "He is speaking with Gaylen. He will return soon."

The boys' disappointment lasts for only a moment as they indulge themselves in their familial surroundings.

Branson sits with Gaylen in his parlor. He has conflicting emotions. Being gardien of the Chozien comes with its share of responsibilities and secrets, but it does not seem honorable for him to hide such dangers from his wife. However, as gardien, his duty is to the Chozien, and as huntsman, his service is to the order. He does not know where husband fits in.

"As the Chozien grows older each year, we move closer to war," Gaylen states.

Branson nods. "Yes. But it is a risk you take to continue to keep quiet about the times ahead."

Gaylen shakes his head solemnly. "It burdens me every night to lie by my wife and to know what's in the future and not tell her. I cannot think with emotion; I cannot protect my order and my family with only my love. If I were to disclose all our fears, it would spread panic and distrust. If we are to fight this evil and win, we can only do it by our unity."

Branson sighs. "Yes, Dewan."

Gaylen stands and turns his back to Branson. He stares at a tapestry of a hawk flying, with the sun in its background. He asks, "Would you sacrifice your *ame* for mine?"

Branson's back straightens in offense. His voice is hard with pride: "Yes."

Gaylen halfway turns to him. "Why?"

Branson opens his mouth and then stops. He thinks a moment more before answering, "You are my dewan. I serve you and the Jade."

Gaylen turns fully. "Are you sure? You would be willing to leave behind your wife and children to save me?"

Branson hesitates, and his chest tightens before he again answers, "Yes."

Gaylen smiles slyly. "I see you hesitate. I cannot have someone stand with me who is uncertain."

Branson shakes his head. "No, Dewan. I am certain. I would give my living breath for yours. I would not pause."

"Why? Why should I trust your answer?"

"It would shame me, and what I have now would be nothing. I would be nothing. I could not put my family through that."

Gaylen raises his eyebrows. "Then act as such. It is unbecoming of a Bonne Ame to doubt his dewan."

Branson inhales deeply and bows his head in embarrassment and correction. "Yes. Forgive me."

Gaylen waves off the apology. "I don't want to have to keep reminding you of your position. Remember who and what you are."

Branson nods.

"You are aware that your son will be performing the Awakening?"

Branson nods again. "Yes, they both are."

"I was speaking of only Malan."

Branson answers, tight-lipped, "Yes, I am."

It exasperates Branson that when others speak formally, they do not recognize Aitan as his son. To him, Aitan is as much of his blood as his other children.

"Do you believe every novice troop is ready for the Awakening?" Branson asks.

"I have every confidence in our general and his high warriors. They are ready. Aitan must be named warrior before his thirteenth birth year. He will train with the warriors fully then. Aitan must be exposed to all the hardened nature of war. Doing so at a young age, it will grow and mature with him. He is a symbol of our strength."

Branson asks, "What of the other novices? Are we doing them a disservice by testing them too soon?"

Gaylen furrows his brow with an indignant sniff. "Of course not. Those novices have endured more than a four-year novice in two years. It would be a disservice to them if we did not promote their positions. Our next generation of warriors must be less forgiving."

Branson straightens proudly. "Aitan is ready; you have my word."

Gaylen nods and smiles absently. "I know."

Branson knows well what troubles Gaylen. In each of their meetings since Branson became gardien, he has seen worry in Gaylen. However, he never makes his awareness known. With each passing year, Gaylen's apprehension has grown, as it becomes increasingly apparent a war will soon be upon them. Negotiations have begun with ally orders, and once Aitan reaches an age of reason, he will accompany the sires to other orders. Soon it will be futile to remain silent about the war to the people.

Branson longs to get back to the inn, for his sons should be there by now and it has been a long time since he has seen them. "If that is all...?"

Gaylen relieves him, and Branson waits until he is outside of the dewan's home to hurry his steps to the White Moon Inn. Standing just on the other side of the door, he can hear his family's happiness. He furrows his brow. Even still, at this time of joy, he worries for their future. He knows there will come a time when he will have to tell Aitan that he has another brother, though not of Branson's or Ahni's bloodline. But that time is not now. Branson closes his eyes and inhales deeply. He turns the doorknob, and before opening the door, he puts on a warm smile.

CHAPTER
TWENTY

Later on outside, Branson shields his eyes from the high sun as he watches Aitan wrestling with Malan. Aitan laughs as he consistently pins his brother. Aitan glances at his father and his stern look.

He helps Malan up and begins to instruct him: "Look, Malan, when I come at you here ..." He demonstrates charging at his midsection. "... you should sidestep and hook your arm under mine, like so." Aitan moves him to the side and positions Malan's arm under his. "Now I have no defense. Depending on how fast I am moving, this will either trip me onto my back or leave my entire body open for a strike."

At Malan's nod, they reenact the move. This time, Malan moves too slow and only manages to sidestep before Aitan tackles him.

Aitan sees his brother's frustration and decides to take a different approach: "You must be quick about it. When your opponent charges at you that way, they are desperate, and a desperate enemy is dangerous. Because you are a warrior by service, you are trained for the kill. So I will teach you something different, but you must not use it unless your *ame* is in danger. Yes?"

Malan's eyes brighten, and his chest rises with the mention of his service. He seals the pact with his brother, saying, "Yes."

"So come at me like before."

Aitan beckons with his hands. Malan charges, and as he gets close to Aitan—so close he thinks he will tackle him—Malan feels a sharp pain in the soft area under and just behind his chin, right above his throat. Malan recoils instantly, more from shock, and Aitan seemingly materializes behind him with his arms around his neck. Malan coughs, and Aitan releases his hold.

Malan rubs the soft area behind his chin. "What did you do?"

Aitan holds up his hand with his fingers spread. "It is something I learned while training to be a huntsman. A fist is but five fingers clutched. They have the same power held straight and firm, like this." He straightens his fingers and holds them tightly together. "When you charged, your throat was left vulnerable. At the last moment, before you could react, I struck." He demonstrates. "My aim was the soft flesh here, right below the chin. It stings like the bite of a scorpion and stuns for just long enough to overtake your opponent."

Malan nods and asks, "Teach it to me?"

Aitan nods but warns, "You must be careful—a little lower and harder and I could have killed you. It was by instinct that I went behind you in preparation to break your neck."

Eyes wide and eager, Malan says, "I'll be careful."

Branson smiles as he watches Aitan teach Malan some of the huntsman techniques. He tilts his head to the side and bites into a ripe apple, sipping the sweet explosion of its sugary juice. He knows his eldest enjoys mocking his younger sibling; however, the Awakening nears and it is best they prepare each other. He makes a mental note to speak with Aitan about his elder responsibilities.

Gazing up at the clouds, he feels the wind shift slightly, light on his left with no slant in direction. He inhales and smiles inwardly, then takes another bite of the apple—faint ginger.

"You should be with your wife and children," Branson says without turning his head.

Trenton laughs and comes to stand on his left. "You've gotten much better, Sire."

Branson lifts an eyebrow. "Did you expect me not to?"

Trenton replies humbly, "Of course not, Sire. Achievements should be acknowledged. It shows in Aitan as well. He can beat most of the novices unarmed."

Branson grunts approvingly. "He has told me that he does not like his sword. He misses the twin blades."

Trenton smiles. "I understand this. I still have mine."

Branson chuckles a little. "Some habits will always remain." Then, turning his head slightly, he asks, "When do you plan on sending Simi to train?"

Trenton shrugs. "His mother is trying to keep him as long as possible. I don't mind it because I welcome the warm bed. Though, for Simi's sake, I have marked the day. He will start his warrior training next year."

"And what of little Zahn?"

Trenton shakes his head, laughing. "That one is a mystery. He enjoys vexing Kaede and Nadie."

Unable to contain his laughter, Branson exclaims, "I know! Do you know what it is like to come home to two screaming little girls and a little boy chasing them with some creature he's found?"

They laugh harder at the scene Branson describes. They share more laughs at stories of their children's adventures.

Finally regaining composure, Branson reiterates an offer he made previously: "You know, Trenton, you can spend more time with your family. I will be with Aitan while I'm here."

Trenton shakes his head. "No, Sire. I have pledged myself to the Chozien and to you. My family knows this. It is a great honor to be the protector of the Chozien. Despite your worry, I see much of them. My sons know their father, and my wife knows her husband."

Branson concedes, admiring Trenton's steadfast loyalty while noting this flaw in his own character. "Very well, then. By the way, how is the reunion with your wife?"

Trenton smiles. "She has missed me … and shows it well."

Branson and Trenton laugh again at the debauchery underlining the hint.

As the day grows late, Branson dismisses Trenton. Then, intending to educate his eldest son on the gravity of the Awakening, Branson calls, "Aitan! Aitan!"

Aitan looks toward his father. Branson motions for him to come. He trots to his father with obvious exasperation.

Branson laughs and shakes his head. "Why the long face?"

"Ah, Da, I wanted more time with my brother and sisters. I do not see them much anymore."

Feigning hurt, Branson says, "I know I am just an old man … but I do not see you much either. Is it too much I steal you away for a little while?"

Thinking his words struck more than his intent, Aitan stammers, "No, no, Da … I just meant … you know. I did not mean—"

Aitan stops as his father struggles to conceal his amusement and jabs him in his arm. Branson grabs Aitan around his head, and they wrestle. After a brief period of playful grappling, Branson allows Aitan to trap his arm behind him. Branson dramatically falls to his knees, rapidly tapping his free hand on the pinned shoulder. Aitan laughs at his father's theatrics and releases his wrist, letting his father stand.

Dusting off after their gleeful roughhousing, Branson acknowledges Aitan's improvement: "I must personally thank Chief Huntsman Len. Your skills have improved. It won't be long until you test for the name of huntsman."

Aitan remarks, "Chief Huntsman Len cannot take all the credit in my progress."

Branson must remember to thank the general for accommodating Aitan's continued huntsman training. With Aitan's early training and advanced experience, it was not such a difficult accommodation to coordinate with the chief huntsman for short returns by Aitan to the huntsmen's training yard. Though the chief understands the severity of the training interruption, he still must hold the Chozien to the standard of a Jade huntsman.

Branson cocks an eyebrow at his eldest. "Oh?"

Aitan grins shrewdly. "It seems the other novices do not believe me deserving of the title Chozien. So I must show them."

Branson laughs and ruffles his son's hair.

Aitan shies away. "It's not as if I won them all."

"Ah, but you are standing, are you not?"

Puzzled, Aitan looks up at his father.

"You see, Son, it is not who comes out as the victor on this day. But that you stand to fight tomorrow and the next. Your opposition will always look for weaker opponents, not resilient ones. Do not judge the war by the battle. Never forget that."

Branson sobers, remembering his original purpose of calling his son to him. Aitan sees his father's expression change; he settles himself for what is about to be said.

Branson smiles and exhales with added seriousness. "I am proud of you. I say this not as your gardien but as your father."

Aitan straightens and returns his father's smile.

Branson continues, "I have heard rumors of the Awakening. It is one that is most terrifying and glorious. You must rely on your training. Do not be distracted by childish rivalries. You won't have time for them. Your lives will depend on each other. It is easy to rely on our huntsmen's natural instinct to isolate and conceal ourselves. But this is not about you alone. Trenton tells me that a warrior does not fight for himself; he must fight for the best advantage of survival for *all* in his troop. Do you understand my meaning?"

Aitan has a thoughtful look. His answer isn't immediate but slow and decisive. He doesn't want his father to worry. He can't ignore the tug at his stomach, the increased pace of his pulse. He can see his chest thumping at each beat of his heart. He is anxious for the Awakening and feels he is ready; no, he is sure of it. He knows that out of all the novices, he will stand through any test because of his huntsman training. But the consideration of others ... this is the first time that he truly feels the strain of the Chozien. This will be a great test—more of compassion than stamina, more of selflessness than praise.

"Yes, Father."

CHAPTER
TWENTY-ONE

Aitan doesn't remember much of how he arrived to … wherever he is. He was awakened, blindfolded, hands bound behind him, and roughly thrown into what he figured to be a wagon by the feel and sound of it. Others joined him, and soon it was crammed so tightly that he sat up with his knees squeezed firmly to his chest. The travel was rushed and bumpy, making his return to sleep impossible. After some time—what he felt was about three sun sky shadows—they were shuffled out of the wagon and stood next to each other.

Now, still bound and blindfolded, Aitan flexes his hands and stamps his feet to loosen the stiffness, feeling the many prickly sensations promising the resurrection of feeling. Aitan jumps at the sound of a high warrior's voice and whips around to face the direction of its source.

He recognizes the voice as High Warrior Conrad: "Listen up! At this moment, you begin the Awakening. In war, battles are fought either where we know the land or where we must learn the land. You will have only a limited amount of food and supplies for shelter."

Aitan hears thuds on the ground around him.

"Make your way back to the spirit hold within five days."

He hears shuffling and branches cracking all around him … more than the average traveler would make even without training. And then the sound of retreat, both from horse hooves and boots. Immediately, everyone tries to remove their restraints. Low murmurs turn into audible frustration. Aitan lies on the ground and slips his hands underneath the back of his knees and then under his feet to bring his hands in front of him. He removes his blindfold and sees the throng of novices. Some have used the same technique to reposition their hands, while others still struggle. He goes to the closest person still blindfolded and slips their blindfold off and unties his hands. He is rewarded with the release of his own hands.

Someone whom he isn't familiar with yells out instructions: "Quickly, those of you who have your hands, free the others."

Everyone follows, and soon all are freed and looking through the sacks left behind or looking around them, hoping for some recognition. Aitan scans the novices, and he recognizes some but not all the faces. His eyes widen as he sees Romin. They haven't spoken since their initial reunion on the first day of warrior training, which resulted in a brawl and their seeming dissolution of friendship. The two strained friends stubbornly keep their distance.

The novice who spoke up earlier hurries to inspect the contents of bags. He spills everything out of each bag. The novices gather around to see what is laid out on the ground: various foodstuffs prepared for travel, shelter assembly items such as blankets and hides, and a few blades that they recognize for chopping and slicing.

The novice takes the lead by saying, "We need to divide the food between all of us. I need five people to help divide this twenty-eight ways. Who will help?"

Voices rise up to volunteer to help, and the novice selects the five and a few more by the sound of it. Aitan steps back from the crowd and goes to the edge of the clearing. He inspects the ground and the broken branches. He shakes his head, smiling at their thoroughness in covering their tracks. He looks off into the distance, noting that he would need to walk farther into the surrounding forest to isolate the direction whence they came.

He folds his arms and feels his forearm brush against his medallion. He looks down and tilts the medallion toward him. He reflects on the last two birth years. It has not been easy—training to be a warrior and establishing himself as a pillar of leadership. He remembers the mental turmoil he went through and does not want to repeat that during this critical trial. He slips the medallion behind his shirt to hide it.

Aitan rejoins the group, just in time to grab his portion of rations. He looks through them and notices that they are light compared to the journey timeline; they will need to find additional supplements to replace the energy they expend each day. He wraps his rations in the blindfold and secures it to his pants. Other novices see this and follow his lead.

"Who is everyone? I don't recognize some of you. I am Jaron."

Everyone states their name and the troop that they come from. When Aitan mentions his name, the novice named Jaron widens his eyes slightly, signaling recognition of the Chozien.

After everyone has announced their name, Jaron says, "We need to get going. We want to cover as much ground today before the sun starts to sleep. I remember hearing the high warrior's voice coming from here, so we should—"

Multiple objections interrupt Jaron:

"The wagon was here," one novice calls out.

"No, we were facing this way," objects another.

"We should follow this trail," states another.

Aitan loses track of the suggestions flying around. He realizes that everyone's perspective originates from the position they were standing and facing when they arrived. While he forms his own hypothesis, he hears raised voices and notices that the objections have turned into heated exchanges. He and a few others try to calm the novices, but insults start to fly and shoving follows.

Jaron yells, "Hey, hey, hey! We need to get back, and I am not going to waste time arguing about it. Someone pick up the supplies and let's go. This way!"

A few novices gather the shelter supplies in the bags and hoist them over their shoulders. Aitan hears grumbles as the troop files out. He takes one last look at the clearing, and before he leaves, he ties the strip of cloth used to bind his hands in a thick bush.

The novices walk for majority of the day until they find a pocket off the trail where they can camp for the night. They empty out the shelter materials, and everyone chooses a single covering. Aitan volunteers to cut kindling for several fires, as they will be spread out, given the limited space. He grabs one of the hatchets and strolls out a short distance. As he cuts, he hears someone approaching and turns to look, surprised to see Romin.

Romin offers a greeting: "Hey, Aitan."

Aitan's response is cool, still stinging from the two birth year old incident. "Hey."

Romin shrugs off the dry response and begins chopping at a young tree. "I figured I could pull my weight a little and cut a few stints for the shelters."

Aitan grunts.

Romin persists, "Look, I know things have been ... rough. But what are the odds that the two of us end up on the Awakening in the same troop? The Great Spirit has put us in each other's paths. I don't think that is something we should ignore."

Aitan laughs.

Taken aback, Romin asks, "What?"

Aitan collects himself and says between chuckles, "You sound just like your da. I'm sure he would be proud to hear you say that."

The friends laugh over the common joke of Romin and his father's constant talk of all things spiritual. They laugh at a few more memories just to seal their reunion.

Sobering up and getting back to their task at gathering necessities for the camp, Romin inquires, "What do you think of Jaron?"

Aitan shrugs and answers, "Meh. He seems to have the will of a leader."

Romin scoffs. "Really? Come on! He's selfish. He won't listen to anyone and orders us around. Who elevated him over us? Anyway, where do you think we are going?"

Aitan cocks his head to the side, recalling all the information he'd collected since the beginning of the day. "Well, we only have enough food for two days, three at the most. So we'll need to trap for food. We traveled for some time in the wagons, so we are definitely days from the spirit hold at this pace." He smirks before he continues, "The devenirs and high warrior definitely covered their entrance and exit. Had us all bound and blinded, then positioned us facing different directions so we can't know which way we came in." He walks to the trail they'd just left and points down. "This ground shows little evidence of recent human activity, and it looks heavily traveled by animals—good for hunting, which means we are moving farther from the spirit hold. We should probably search for a …Why are you looking at me like that?"

Romin stands there, wide-eyed and open-mouthed. He motions toward the camp. "Why haven't you said anything? We're wandering around in the wrong direction and you know it?"

Aitan raises his hands in defense. "Calm down, Romin. I put every-thing together just now. And I don't want anyone bringing up the Chozien thing."

Romin stacks the pieces of wood he collected and hurries Aitan back to camp. When they arrive, Romin, the more outspoken of the two, calls to the others to come get their kindling and stints for their shelters. He then rushes Aitan over to where Jaron sits, chewing on some of the dried meat from his portion of the rations and chatting with a few novices. He looks up at the duo as they approach.

Romin points at Aitan and says, "Aitan here has an eye for tracking. He found some things on the trail that we need to talk about."

Jaron stands up, and he motions them to the side, out of earshot of the other novices. A safe distance away, Aitan starts to repeat his find-ings, but Jaron stops him.

"Listen, do you think you're the first person to come up to me about this? I don't have time to *think* about everyone's worries. We need to keep moving; the path will come."

Aitan narrows his eyes at the lack of concern. "No, that is not how the woods live. Not this far away. If we stray too long—" Aitan halts his words when a finger jabs his chest, directly on his medallion hidden beneath his shirt.

Jaron hisses, "I know your name and who you are, *Chozien*. I don't need your huntsman ideas riling up the others. Keep your mouth shut."

Aitan inhales sharply.

Romin snatches Jaron's hand away and steps in front of Aitan. Romin's voice is low, almost threatening: "Don't touch him."

Jaron smiles mockingly. "You two run along. I'll get you back safe and sound."

He taps Romin on the shoulder, feigning kindness. In a louder voice, for the others to hear, he adds, "Thanks for the hand. Rest up. We start early tomorrow."

Jaron turns to leave, and Romin starts to go after him, but Aitan stops him by grabbing his arm. "Let him go. He's made up his mind."

Romin huffs.

Aitan thanks the Great Spirit for the patience the huntsman service has provided him and for the humility gained from all the penances High Warrior Randol placed on him. Without them, he's sure it would have been Romin holding him back from the obvious slight.

"Thanks, Romin, for defending me," Aitan says.

A stark contrast to their previous interaction with insults. This gives Aitan even more confidence in their renewed friendship, which, at this moment, he realizes he sorely missed.

Romin clicks his tongue and waves off the appreciation. "We'll die out here if we don't change our route."

They all set up their shelters and settle in around one of the fires.

Seeing that Romin's frustration still has a hold on him, Aitan opens up the conversation to at least plan for the inevitable realization: "He speaks truth, you know."

At Romin's aghast reaction, Aitan explains, "I mean, we can't be divided. Even if I'm right, all of us must make it back to be named."

Romin sighs agreement but throws up his hands in surrender. "What can we do?"

Aitan looks around and lowers his voice: "We will have our chance. Our rations won't last but two more days at best. Panic will spread, and he will struggle to contain it."

"How can you be so sure?"

"You have never been far from food. When you do not have access to the means of sustaining life, it is easy to become hopeless. Once you lose hope, it can easily be replaced with fear and desperation. I know this well."

"Your huntsman training?"

Aitan nods. "Yes. It is not 'til now that I see its meaning."

He sighs, noting the sun's slumber reminds him of his own. He encourages Romin not to worry, and they both retire for the night.

Morning comes quickly. Jaron and his companions make sure everyone wakes up quite early, using loud urgings, hand-clapping, knocking down shelters, snatching away blankets ... nothing the novices aren't used to already. Aitan and Romin share irritated scowls, toss their blankets in the pile in annoyance, and grab a quick bite ... remembering Aitan's warning on the impending food shortage. Before the novices begin their misguided trek, Aitan takes a moment to check all the campfires to ensure they have been tamped out. Again, his huntsman habits make an appearance.

The march seems to drag on. Aitan busies himself by searching the trail for signs of recent human travel, finding none—a bittersweet confirmation of his earlier claims with regard to the group's misdirection. Every step takes them farther from their reward and closer to their demise. By midday, Aitan starts to feel his anxiety rise. He recalls his father's advice: *"This is not about you alone."*

As if reading his mind, Romin breaks Aitan's thoughts: "What do you think? Have we drifted farther? What does the forest tell you?"

Noticing the inquiring gazes from the novices ahead of them, he shushes Romin. "Keep your voice down. We still drift away from the spirit hold. The trail won't hold much longer."

Yet again, Aitan's omen materializes as the group stops abruptly. The pair share confused looks and peer around the other novices in front of them. Soon low mumbles grow into frustrated outbursts. As the group begins to scatter, Aitan rushes to the front, leaving Romin to catch up. Once Aitan gets to Jaron, he stops in disbelief. Romin dodges by Aitan to avoid bumping into him, only to also be shocked. There, before them, stands the end of the trail. The trees and bushes in all of its glorious abundance cover the path proudly ahead of them.

When Aitan starts to walk toward the end of the trail, Jaron grabs his arm to hold him back, which Aitan promptly snatches away. A quick stare-down ensues before Aitan resumes his course. He reaches the end of the trail where the forest begins and looks for signs of people. He can feel the eyes of the troop on his back. After a moment, he returns to stand next to Romin.

"What did you see?" Romin asks.

Aitan takes a moment to find his words, which apparently is too long for Jaron, who probes, "Well? What is it? We're wasting time standing around."

Aitan folds his arms and looks to Romin. "It's as I said: We are far from the spirit hold."

Jaron rolls his eyes. "Speak plainly. We don't have time to translate huntsmen words."

Aitan looks at Romin when he answers, "There is no sign of any human travel ... for some time. We need to go back to where the first sign of people presents itself. Then send scouts out. After that, we'll know where to move next."

Jaron's eyes widen as he raises his voice in near panic: "That will cost a day. We don't have time to go back. What about food?"

Romin interjects, "Hey! He told you as much last night. You wouldn't listen."

Jaron throws up his hands and walks away. The rest of the troop seem aghast that the person they have been following would abandon them so quickly. Aitan scans the group and takes in the sight of the horrified looks and building anxiety.

Ideally, four-year novices performing the Awakening would have had the time to truly seed their survival instinct. As it is, having only completing their second year, the gaps in those two precious years of training are showing and, without a doubt, will spread.

Aitan sees the opportunity and seizes the moment to take command. "Everyone, calm down! We will make our way back, but we need to act now. Yes?"

He pauses, hopeful for the acceptance he needs, not from doubt in his ability to lead, but for his personal affirmation as his worthiness to be called Chozien. The compliance comes quick and `en masse, perhaps from desperation, but all the same, he hears no opposition, which makes the acceptance unanimous.

The invested trust of their lives in his hands ignites a flame of determination within Aitan, fueled by confidence. He jumps into action, calling for volunteer scouts. He soon dispatches them, armed with the knowledge of what to look for. With them being so far from the spirit hold, he needs to find the best active trail to march toward, which will in turn lead to the best route back. The spirit hold is a haven in every order. The Jade hold's population houses over eight thousand kinsmen, and with that kind of number comes a great trade market. Aitan knows that many routes lead to and from there, meaning there is no need to stumble along in the forest.

He relays a message to conserve their rations. This causes another fuss, but he promises to find them additional provisions. As an avid hunter, he knows he cannot guarantee this, as he will have to rely on traps since they have no weapons necessary for hunting. As well, traps require food to lure animals—food they are short of—and even the best trap will not always provide sustenance. He'll have to deliver, though, if he plans to keep the group together.

Aitan makes a mental note to take Romin's advice: Do not delay his doubts when it risks the survival of the group. To calm his anxiety, Aitan retreats again to the comfort of the forest. He busies himself with collecting and shaping branches as triggers for multiple deadfall traps. This time, Aitan doesn't hear Romin's approach, so engulfed in his task at hand is he. He jumps at Romin's voice.

Chuckling, Romin inquires, "What are you thinking? Why do you look so worried?"

"What? Do you even have to ask?" Aitan sighs. "I just promised everyone I would feed them—not an easy thing to do, Romin."

Still reeling from the victory over Jaron, Romin waves off Aitan's concern. "Cheer up! We will make it back in time to be named warrior."

Aitan shakes his head at his friend's ignorance of the dire situation. "We are running out of food. If we don't come up with something, we won't make it back even if we find the right trail."

"Listen, all you need to do is tell us what to do. A big part of leading is having to shoulder the risks and emotions of your people. The decisions you make will ultimately save them or condemn them. You must do so with courage and truth."

Aitan again goes speechless, this time out of admiration. "Did you just come up with that?"

Romin claps his friend on his back. "Of course not. High Warrior Victor told us it in training some time ago."

The two share a laugh at the random sincerity and continue to prepare the branches.

Afterward, with renewed confidence, Aitan assesses the reports from each scout to determine their next travel route. One report comes in which has very few trees cleared, while having plenty of brush, broken small twigs, and animal droppings in variety.

The second scout is a bit clumsy in his account. After some probing questions, Aitan deduces that there seemed to be a cut trail filled with many tracks; the scout, though, couldn't distinguish between animals or boots. The scout explains that he continued farther down the trail to see if he could make sense of his earlier observations. He reports seeing a clear split in the trail, and there he saw wagon tracks. He dared not go farther, fearing he would not find his way back.

Another report, the last to come, reveals more areas of cleared trees and, much farther into the woods, a small campsite. The site appeared dated based on the discoloration of the fallen leaves and now stiffened pine rushes. The logs seemed to be in their early stages of decay, and the presence of growth on the stones was a sign of no recent human activity.

Aitan takes in all of the details from the observations and makes a decision. He has everyone gather to announce the next steps: "Our scouts are back. The Great Spirit has blessed us. We have found a trail that will lead us back to the spirit hold." He points in the direction where the second scout came from, just behind them and to the left. "We will head through there until we come to an open path."

Then he looks up and notices that the day has passed its peak. He points again, this time to the sky. "Gather yourselves quickly. We don't have much sun left, and we need to cover ground. Remember to save your rations. I'll need help with setting traps once we make camp. Let's go!"

Interested in reading the land, Aitan leads the way through the trees next to Romin, along with the three scouts. Sure enough, they reach the established path the scout described. It certainly does look like a frequently traveled route. They continue along it until they reach the fork. Aitan checks each path for travel frequency and the direction of the footprints prior to making a definitive choice and going onward.

After a few more sun sky shadows, Aitan calls a stop for the day. While everyone busies themselves for camp, Aitan pulls aside the four novices who volunteered for trapping and takes them deep into the woods, far enough away where the noise of the camp won't drive away potential prey. He finds a heavy stone and takes one of the stakes he prepared earlier and balances the rock to lean on the stake. He takes a small piece of dried meat from his ration and places it on the inside of the stake so the animal will most likely trigger the trap and crush itself. He explains this construction and sends them out in varying directions to set up similar traps. With their unfamiliarity, he waits for them to muster back at the first location, and then they all return to camp together.

Romin meets him with updates on the troop's activities: "All camps have been set up with their fires. But, Aitan, there are whispers about the food."

This adds to Aitan's apprehension and the urgency of the set traps being successful. He presses his lips together and rubs his hands.

Romin sees Aitan's furrowed brow and warns, "I know you have much on your mind, but you cannot let your worry show. It infects and spreads."

Aitan nods in agreement and sobers up enough to appear calm. Sleep does not come easy for him that night. He tosses and turns, never really seeking sleep. His dreams are filled with curses of desperation and dissent. Failure and disappointment consume his emotions, threatening to distract his decisions.

He continuously runs through likely scenarios: What are the other options for nourishment if they find the traps empty come morning? How sure is he that this trail will not run out? What should he say to inspire and calm the troop if discord rises? What if they lose trust in him? He replays these scenes, rehearsing his actions and comments. He does find some humor, likening his repetition to what it must be like for the traveling storytellers anticipating an upcoming performance. Such is how the night passes in the throes of fear and promise.

CHAPTER
TWENTY-TWO

Romin shakes Aitan awake. He stands groggily and wipes away the sleep from his eyes.

Before Aitan can finish chastising himself for his late hours, Romin reminds him of the same subject that kept him up all night: "Your trappers are waiting. The camp is just starting to wake. Be quick about the traps; I'll take care of your pallet."

Aitan snaps his head up and back into the moment. He thanks his friend and runs to meet the greenhorn trappers. They check each of the five traps together. The first is triggered and empty. The next two traps are untouched. On the way to the last two, the morale seems low, even for Aitan, who knows the chances for success are slim. As they approach the fourth trap, they see that it has been triggered. This does not evoke any optimism, as the results thus far have been disappointing. But this time Aitan smiles: He sees a small twinkle with his hunter's eye. He quickens his pace. The others hasten to keep up with his stride until they all halt.

The novice trappers are wide-eyed and open-mouthed, expressing their shock. The twinkle Aitan had seen was the sun's reflection from the trapped animal's eye. He lifts the heavy rock up and sees that they've captured a squirrel. The others' joy is short-lived, though, as Aitan states the squirrel will only feed three of them. They can see that the last trap—the largest—has also been triggered, this one snaring an even larger animal: a possum. It will double the meat of the squirrel … though still not enough to feed everyone.

Back at the camp, the trappers raise their prizes up for all to see and are rewarded with cheers and relieved expressions.

Aitan calms everyone since he has to deliver the reality of what the meat will yield. "All right! All right!" He holds his hands up and waits for the crowd to calm down before speaking: "This won't feed everyone. I ask again for everyone to make this meat stretch as far as we can to feed anyone who has no more rations left."

With that, Aitan goes to work gutting and skinning the animals. He's quick about it. Fortunately, one of the blades provided to them is a knife. He sets each prepared animal over two fires to roast. The smell of roasting meat fills the senses, and glands begin salivating. It will be difficult for anyone to skip a bite of freshly cooked meat. While the meat cooks, Aitan, Romin, and a few other novices huddle together.

Speaking first is a lean, though athletic novice lass with gray eyes and skin the color of ground cocoa beans: "We are doing fine on water. Tomorrow we will start to run low. We should start to cut back now."

Romin asks, "Shouldn't we quicken our pace, then? We have only three more days left."

Another novice says, "Jaron is stirring up some of the troops. I do not know how many, but I am sure he means to riot."

Before the next novice starts to speak, Aitan squeezes his eyes tight, pinching the bridge of his nose as if struggling with a headache. His small inner circle exchanges looks of concern and curiosity.

After a moment of silence, Aitan collects his words and says, "We must *feed* everyone first. Without food, they will not be able to travel the distance. Without food, they can't increase their pace. And without food, we will have to worry about more than Jaron's tantrums. So we feed our troop now, and then we push the speed until our weakest stops us. We will make camp and set more traps to provide breakfast tomorrow—our last morning."

A novice gasps. "*Last?*"

Aitan nods. "Yes, we will be in the spirit hold by tomorrow's nightfall."

A small smile playing at his lips, Romin eyes Aitan and asks, "How can you be so sure?"

Aitan explains, "Where they first left us blinded and bound, I tied a piece of the bindings to a bush. If we were going in the wrong direction, I would have seen it."

The isolated group exchanges surprised and excited glances.

Before the group starts to express their joy even more, Aitan calms them and says, "We will only make it if we keep ourselves fed and moving."

The group talks strategy until the meat finishes cooking. Aitan portions it so that everyone gets some. Simply tearing strips of meat and handing them out to the line of novices proves to be orderly and quiet. Each novice thanks him with a salivating smile.

But then it is Jaron's turn to receive his portion. He snatches the strip of meat from Aitan's generous fingers and glares at him, snarling. Aitan ignores the insult and finishes serving. Aitan hears some audible groans when he halts the service and packs up the rest of the scraps of meat and bones, intending to redistribute to the most needful at midday and save some for the traps that evening.

The troop continues in the same direction on the trail from

yesterday. Aitan increases the pace to jogging at some points. He grows more confident that they are headed in the right direction as they press on. Farther along, he starts to recognize signs of hunting and even see some debris from travelers.

Sometime later, as planned, they make a stop for a quick recess, and Aitan hands out the rest of the meat to a select few. After just enough time for the recipients to swallow their mockery of a meal and the rest to relieve themselves, they get back on the trail.

Aitan pushes the troop to exhaustion. He knows this will drain them, and without food to replace that lost energy, he will have to depend on tonight's slumber and the hoped-for morning's catch. He takes the same novice trappers out, and this time they set twice as many traps over a larger area, with the expectation of yielding a filling breakfast.

Aitan falls asleep without remembering to close his eyes. Even with his body and mind fatigued, he finds his motivation up when he awakes, as he determined this would be the day of their return home. He and the other trappers go out to check the traps, returning with four animals: two rabbits and two squirrels. While more in number than the previous morning, the accelerated pace has made the troop ravenous. Aitan takes to skinning and gutting, a bit deflated but nonetheless thankful for the sacrifice these animals have provided. He positions the skinned animals over the fires and looks on in thought as it cooks.

Romin elbows Aitan and inquires, "What is it now?"

Aitan sighs. "I was hoping for more. I pushed us hard yesterday, and it would be better that we had more to fill our bellies."

Romin tosses his hands up in theatrical disapproval. "You mean this is all we have to eat? I mean, you could have done nothing, and we could be searching for berries and mushrooms."

Aitan rolls his eyes at the sarcasm. "Well, most of us haven't eaten since the last sun's awakening. We need good spirits for today's journey."

Romin punches his friend in the arm, then winks at him. "You worry too much. Look around you. There is absolutely no one—"

When Romin cuts his statement short, Aitan looks at him, then follows Romin's eyes until they land on Jaron. Along with a few others, Jaron is walking in their direction. He doesn't look to be in a particularly good mood.

He stops in front of Aitan and, in a loud voice, taunts, "Is this all we have to eat? I don't think this will feed all of us."

His clique heckles louder, drawing attention to the confrontation while Aitan raises his eyebrow at Romin with a telling look about his present concern.

Jaron continues, "How long do you expect us to keep moving like this? I bet you don't even know where we are going."

The troop starts to gather around the commotion. Aitan grits his teeth, annoyed that his own concern is being broadcast by a bitter, attention-seeking loudmouth. The novice trappers take offense at the belittling of their efforts and the sacrifice of their own food in order to lure animals to the traps, and they make this known to all. Jaron's comrades yell rebuttals. While chaos erupts around them, Jaron raises an eyebrow, folds his arms, and sneers at Aitan.

Aitan feels his face heat up. He also feels himself fill with rage, like the evolution of emotions that a slow swallow of water brings to one quenching their thirst. At first it feels refreshing as the cool liquid flows down the throat. It enters the body, and every muscle brightens with rejuvenated strength. But when the cup is drained, only the emptiness remains ... beckoning for more. The energy of the anger ignites him, all while in a revitalized state of mind.

Aitan's voice seeps with venom as he says, "Do you dare threaten our chance at survival?"

Romin snaps his head around to look at Aitan and hurries to say, "Hey, lads, let's calm it down a bit, yeah?"

He tries to get between the two, but Aitan puts his hand on Romin's chest and shoves him back without moving his eyes from Jaron. Romin stumbles but catches himself before falling, amazed at the amount of force Aitan generated.

Jaron lowers his arms and throws a menacing smile back at Aitan. He recognizes Aitan's demeanor and switches into a boxing stance, but hardly has he finished preparing himself when his head snaps back, stunning him for a moment. Aitan struck with a straight jab, hitting his intended target: Jaron's mouth just above his chin. While Jaron spits out blood from a split lip and moves out of reach, Aitan raises his own hands, palms out with one leg slightly forward. To the onlookers, this position looks to be more defensive and passive. But for huntsmen, this is the foundation of their combat technique and can be deceptive and dangerous.

The fighters circle each other, to the rousing of the onlookers. Aitan's eyes are cold steel; his movements, controlled and calculated. His opponent's, a direct contrast, exude confidence and stamina. Aitan begins to close the space between them. Jaron uses his reach advantage and sends two practiced jabs and then a cross. Aitan dodges all three and continues to press forward. Jaron begins to switch directions while swinging out with a right hook to force Aitan back. Aitan, though, waits for Jaron to set his back foot, and when Jaron's hook is barely halfway through its arc, Aitan connects with a thrust kick to his gut. Jaron grunts hard and retreats.

But Aitan keeps up the pressure and leaps forward off his front leg to deliver a flying jab. Jaron blocks and pushes Aitan back. Aitan immediately closes the distance again. Jaron doesn't wait and begins raining down punches. Aitan blocks all the strikes directed at his head; however, Jaron connects with a few body shots. Aitan winces and steps back, baiting Jaron. Seeing Aitan's retreat, Jaron charges at him.

Finally! Aitan absorbs the charge in order to position himself for a common submission tactic. He wraps his forearms around Jaron's exposed neck in what the huntsmen refer to as a guillotine hold. He squeezes until the untrained Jaron tilts his head back, hoping for relief but instead exposing his throat fully, which Aitan takes full advantage of. He slips his forearms fully underneath Jaron's chin and squeezes. Jaron immediately pulls at Aitan's arms, gasping for air. He tries punching wildly at Aitan's legs, but it proves futile. Aitan then drops to the ground, sitting and holding tight until Jaron falls limp. He releases him and rolls him onto his back.

Romin helps Aitan up. He claps him on the back in wide-eyed astonishment. Soon after, the rest of the troop offer their congratulations. Jaron's friends rouse him and stand him up too.

Aitan doesn't want to make this victory into a lifelong vendetta, nor does it help to have the troop split. He needs to repair what has been damaged. "This is not to be spoken of beyond this moment," Aitan says to everyone. "We will finish the Awakening today, and we will do it together. This should be a reminder of how much stronger we are together than divided. This is the lesson that we are meant to learn. It's not about finding our way home but *how* we make that journey. We listen to each other. We learn from each other. We sacrifice for each other. This is not about being friends or enemies."

He walks to Jaron, pride bruised from the humiliating defeat. Aitan offers his hand.

Jaron looks at it and then back at Aitan. He nods and, with a half smile, clutches his hand.

Aitan finishes, "We are family."

The troop cheers, perhaps for the gaiety or for the unity. Aitan doesn't care which. He knows that it will take time to fully gain any reasonable amity with Jaron, but at least this puts a stitch in the wound.

Shortly afterward, the troop makes two passes through the line to eat. They pack up their gear and set off. They travel the entire day. As the sun begins to descend behind the trees, they see the lights of the spirit hold appear in the distance. Aitan and Romin urge the troop to pick up the pace into a firm jog, with the promise of being named warrior awaiting them. They make it to the gate of the spirit hold under the cover of the moonlight. Guards usher them in and direct them to the barracks, where they are promptly fed. They gorge themselves and then fall fast asleep.

The next morning—closer to afternoon since the general allowed them to sleep in—the novices from Aitan's troop mill about the training yard. Aitan and Romin find each other and seek out novices from other troops who have made it back. Aitan is relieved to see that his friend, Kel, has returned. He also learns that Malan hasn't returned and that their troop is the last remaining one. This worries Aitan since today is the deadline for them to make it back, and he knows food has to be one of their challenges.

After some time spent socializing, they decide to go see their families at the White Moon Inn. Upon their entrance, the dining room erupts in jovial cheers from Aitan and Romin's family, as well as the other patrons staying at the inn. Both mothers are a ball of emotions, tears streaming while trying to remain joyful. The boys are bombarded with questions about their experience and challenges during the Awakening. Their fathers rescue them from all the curious questions and requests for storytelling by rushing them outside the inn.

Given his extroverted nature, Uric starts, "I'm glad you two have worked out your differences."

Branson places his arms on both of the boys' shoulders. "Yes, it is good to see you lads are friends again."

Uric can't help himself, seeing the awkward seesaw of Branson's arms from the obvious height differences in the boys: "I'd think you would get light-headed standing there so unbalanced." He chuckles.

They all share a laugh and continue chatting. Branson stands back to admire not only his son but his closest friend's youngest son. It is a great blessing to have the children share in the same friendship as their fathers. What a difference two years makes.

Romin is of similar height as Branson. His head, unshaven for the past four days, reveals dark-brown roots along with patches of facial hair. He's just as lean as his father but with more muscle, undoubtedly from the strenuous training.

Branson looks to Aitan. He has let his hair grow in thick curls—so thick that he uses a strip of cloth to hold his hair back. Ideal for huntsmen, but absolutely discouraged for warriors in the Jade Order. Branson makes a note to ask Reba to tame the dark mane with flat braids. Aitan sports a light mustache, beckoning for it to fill in. He hasn't quite reached his father's height, coming up to his chin. However, Aitan's bulk is quite impressive. His trapezius, chest, and bicep muscles have increased in mass. Aitan has a pretty good feeling that this is due to all those penances he's been serving over the past two years.

Just as the reunion begins, Trenton cuts it short by materializing next to his sire. He informs Branson that Malan has arrived at the gate —without many of his troop—and the seekers have been called. Branson wastes no time and races to the front gate. He gets there just as a handful of the remaining troop file in, all aided by other kinsmen. Branson counts only seven of them in total.

Branson and Aitan rush to Malan's aid, with Trenton shadowing them. They each wrap an arm around their shoulders and escort him to the spirit house. By the time they arrive, the best seekers skilled in healing have already prepared beds, and they gently lay Malan on one. The seekers start to usher everyone out so they can tend to the novices' injuries.

Malan grips Branson's hand before he leaves and smiles haggardly. "I made it, Da."

Branson's eyes water, and he smiles, at which Malan closes his eyes and collapses from exhaustion.

"I know, Son, I know," Branson whispers.

CHAPTER
TWENTY-THREE

Aitan does all he can to comfort his mother. Ahni, though, remains inconsolable. Not knowing whether her child will survive brings her to the brink of breaking. Branson holds Ahni, speaking words of encouragement against his own fear of losing a son. Once Ahni has wept herself to exhaustion, Branson lays her down and covers her.

Branson turns his attention to his eldest. "What happened out there? I warned him that we were pushing you too hard."

Aitan says nothing, standing there confused, as he has no way of knowing what another troop's experienced in the Awakening, nor does he understand what his father means by "pushing you too hard." His nature would usually dismiss it as simply the wild ramblings of a worried father, but something about his da's statement sticks in his mind. *Him?* he thinks. Who is this person that his father passes fault to?

Aitan decides to ease into discovering an answer to that question: "Calm down, Da. Malan will recover. The dewan has his best seekers tending to him and the rest of the troop."

At the mention of Gaylen, Branson spins around, and his glare is so piercing that Aitan takes a step back and raises his hands. He watches as his father struggles between loyalty, diplomacy, and fatherhood. Branson rakes his hands through his hair and murmurs unintelligibly until he plops down in a chair. He lays his head back and exhales deeply. Aitan can see the strain of politics and secrecy, how it tugs at his father's heart.

He tries to offer some reassurance: "Da, we will work through this. I don't understand. You warned us about how dangerous the Awakening is."

Branson presses his lips together and slams his fist on the arm of the chair. "No, Son, you do not understand. Listen, you cannot rush training. For you with all your previous training, this is now seven birth years, but for the others, it has just been two. And to put so many at risk at the expense of the Chozien is ... reckless."

His father's words start to sound far away once Aitan hears himself referred to in the third person at such a tender moment. He's always known that he's the Chozien, although his father has never referred to him in such an offhand manner.

Aitan feels his chest tighten and a knot develop in his throat. He clears his throat as an attempt to loosen his voice and starts to walk out the room. "I will go check on Malan and then attend to my duties as *Chozien.*"

Branson pauses his internal tirade and looks toward Aitan, bewildered. He follows him with his eyes as Aitan walks past him toward the door.

He grabs his son's arm to stop his exit. "What has you in a fit?"

Aitan turns to his father, more so for Branson to release his hold, and exaggerates, "What, you do not approve of the *Chozien* continuing his training?"

Branson eyes him. "Of course, but is it not too soon …"

When his father's words trail off, Aitan exhales and releases the latch on the door. "As gardien, you have a duty to the Chozien, and as a father, a responsibility to Malan. I will ease that burden as best I can."

He leaves with his father's whispers trailing behind him. He rushes through the halls and out the dining room to the open air of the spirit hold. He inhales and exhales, catching his breath from the emotions that he holds within and the tears he strains to keep at bay. He collects himself and heads to the spirit house to check on Malan. The seekers allow him in with the promise to keep quiet, as all seven novices are resting. He walks to where Malan lies.

He smiles briefly as he recalls a memory of waking in the middle of the night to a ball pressed close to him, only to discover Malan had sneaked into his bed. This continued to occur for two birth years until Malan grew into his own security.

The sentimental recollection passes as Aitan sees the bandages and bruises on Malan. His head is wrapped, with a light appearance of blood on the right side. His cheeks, chin, and jaws are bruised. He notices that Malan's shirt has been removed and a light sheet covers him. He slowly pulls the sheet back to reveal Malan's completely bandaged mid-torso, with more bruising showing around the bandages.

A seeker rushes over and replaces the sheet over Malan. "Perhaps it is best that the Chozien takes his rest. The Awakening is taxing, not only on the participants but the family as well."

Her tone does not convince him that she is making a suggestion, much like his mother.

"But these wounds look like he's been—"

She cuts him off as she eyes him: "You are not yet named seeker. Best to leave the healing to those who are, yes?"

He nods, understanding the command. Aitan leaves and heads to the huntsmen training yard, where he reunites with his fellow novices there. They are eager to know about the Awakening. Aitan deflects the conversation to avoid answering, and the novices proceed to help bridge the gap of two birth years' worth of training he's mostly been absent from, aside from his brief visits as allowed by General Haru. They spar for most of the day. The reunion has accomplished its task to distract from the vision of Malan and misplaced slight from his father.

As the day begins to wane and the novices retire to their accommodations, some movement across the yard draws Aitan's attention. He inhales sharply as he sees Branson, his father—or *gardien*, as Branson may have it.

After Aitan said he would check on Malan and then proceeded to storm out, Branson's thoughts remain muddled from the shifting events and emotions. He decides to give up for the time being and goes to lie beside Ahni. He wakes to shuffling around the room, mixed with female voices.

Hearing Branson stir, Ahni pauses her conversation and goes to pour him some water. "Enjoy your nap, dear?" Ahni hands him the water.

Branson sits up, raising an eyebrow at his wife's complete reversal of demeanor.

He asks, "Have I … missed something?"

Ahni and Reba laugh at Branson's wariness.

Branson rolls his eyes in exasperation and climbs out of bed. He shakes his head and throws his hands up in obvious frustration. "Between my worries about Malan, and Aitan leaving earlier fuming mad, and now your calm composure, I will lose my mind before my age takes it."

Ahni and Reba share puzzled looks. Apparently, they missed something themselves.

"What do you mean Aitan left upset? What did you say to him?" Ahni presses Branson.

Branson shrugs his shoulders. "That's just it: I don't know!"

Ahni crosses her arms and narrows her eyes. "What did you talk about?"

Branson recalls the conversation. "I had just laid you down. I was confused and feeling overwhelmed with Malan's state and the risk that we are all taking for the Chozien. All the secrets—What?"

Branson stops his storytelling as he notices Reba staring at him wide-eyed and Ahni cocking her head to one side, her mouth agape.

Ahni closes her eyes for a moment, asking the Great Spirit for patience before she asks, "Did you actually say that about the Chozien to Aitan?"

Clueless, Branson nods. "Yes. I'm pretty sure."

Amazed at her husband's insensitivity, Ahni replies, "Branson! It is enough that you carry the responsibility of being Bonne Ame, gardien, father, husband, and sire. These are all titles you have earned and *chose* to live by. Aitan is just a boy—your *son*. His burden is far greater than yours, and he has yet to learn what it will mean to the world. He cannot walk away from his fate. I, too, hurt for Malan, but it is not to lay that weight on another son. You dismissed him as nothing more than a … chore."

She finishes her chastising with a slap to his shoulder. He shies away as if more are coming.

"You need to go find him and make it right." She points to the door for emphasis.

"All right, all right."

Just before he opens the door, she reminds him that Uric awaits him in the dining room.

As Branson closes the door, he hears the beginning of the women's next topic of conversation: "Can you believe ..."

Branson finds Uric not in the dining room, but standing out front of the inn, looking unhappy, as expected, but Branson also notes concern.

Uric greets Branson and says, "Malan is resting from his injuries. The seekers have assured me that he will recover and be ready to train in one moon's time."

"One moon? The Awakening isn't *that* strenuous for those who return to need so much recovery time. Why so long?"

"Malan's injuries weren't from ... the Awakening," Uric answers. "It seems he was in some kind of brawl, but the wounds are too skilled to have been done by another novice, or just one for that matter. By the looks of the seven, they all took quite a beating."

Branson's breath catches.

Uric attempts to cool burning embers, offering additional information: "Gaylen has sent riders to find the rest of the novices in Malan's troop. Once any of them are able to speak, we will find out what has happened."

"I need to speak with Gaylen now."

Branson starts to stalk off toward the dewan's home, but Uric stops him.

Uric's voice flows calm and consoling: "Go see Malan first. It would be good for him to see you. We will speak with Gaylen with cooler heads."

Branson just grunts in agreement and changes direction to the spirit house, with Uric following. They enter and a seeker directs them to the healing quarters where the novices are being cared for. They find Malan, who happens to be lying awake.

Branson kneels next to him. "Hey. How are you feeling? These seekers taking care of you?"

Malan chuckles, then groans, covering his left side tenderly.

Branson furrows his brow and pulls back the sheet. His eyes widen, and he looks back at Uric, who responds with an expectant nod.

Not to alarm Malan, Branson replaces the sheet. "Can you tell me what happened?" he asks, hoping to ease his son into the recollection.

Malan nods, wincing a bit.

Branson presses on, "Could you walk us through the Awakening?"

Malan closes his eyes, remembering. He tells them that the first couple days seemed ordinary enough. Along the way of the second day, they noticed that they were being followed; they assumed them to be Jade warriors observing them. On the fourth day, though, the troop became suspicious. When Uric asks what brought it on, Malan explains that the "observers" had become careless. The novices could hear them and even see them among the trees. No warrior would be that obvious, even to kinsmen of their own order.

Then Malan shares how they made a plan to split into two groups and outrun the stalkers to the spirit hold, but before they could execute the plan, they found themselves under assault. They stayed with the plan to split into groups, which divided the aggressors. Still, some of the attackers caught up to Malan's group, and they were outnumbered ten to seven. The attackers surrounded them and closed in. He and the other novices went on the offensive, striking first, trying to fight their way free. It was futile, as they were quickly overtaken. After the attackers had beaten his group into submission, a few novices fell unconscious, and then the invaders began to argue.

"They kept pointing at me," Malan says, "but I could only make out a few words. I am almost positive one of them said 'Chozien.' Then I must have passed out, because the next thing I remember was being helped up by another novice, and then our group used the last of our strength to make it to the spirit hold."

Branson asks, "Can you describe what they looked like?"

Malan frowns, then shakes his head.

Branson doesn't prod further, but lets his son know that he did well and that the Jade will be happy to gain a warrior like him.

After telling Malan to rest, Branson and Uric walk out of earshot to mull over the story.

Uric states the obvious: "This was an outright attack targeting the Chozien."

Branson shakes his head in disbelief. "It was the perfect ambush. Had the Chozien been in that troop, he would have been alone and unguarded. Though, we are still missing why this happened and who these attackers were."

"Excuse me, Sires?" comes a voice from behind.

Branson and Uric turn to see a woman who has her eyes lowered and her callused hands clasped. Her sleeves are rolled up to just above the elbow, revealing lean, muscled forearms. Her clothing includes simple, loose-fitting trousers, and her shirt has smudges of dirt and stubborn stray straws. Branson makes an assumption she is a farrier.

Uric addresses the woman: "Go on."

She waves a hand toward a novice in one of the beds and states that her son was in Malan's group during the ambush. She adds that they just overheard Malan relating the events of the attack. She goes on to say that her son feigned unconsciousness during the ambush for fear that they would continue beating all of them.

Finally, she says, "He can tell you what they said and describe to you how they look."

Branson's eyes widen. "Quick, woman, take us to your son!"

She startles at Branson's sudden demand, then guides them to her son, just two beds away from Malan. She introduces him as Preston.

"Go on, dear. Tell them what you told me," his mother says.

The boy nods. "It is true what Malan said. But he took most of the beatings. I am not sure how he survived."

"Yes yes, what next?" Branson asks, his voice tight, impatient.

"Through barely open eyelids, I could see one of their men—a stocky one—walking near each of us where we lay, and when he returned to the others, they spoke low, though I could sense the stocky man was upset. He said that the Chozien wasn't there. The others pointed to Malan, but the stocky man shook his head. He said, 'That is the Bonne Ame's son, yes, but not the one named Chozien.' They argued more, and some even came to blows. They seemed afraid."

Uric remarks, "They feared death to return without their prize."

At Branson's nod, Preston continues, "One suggested that they release our *ames*—"

He halts as his mother gasps. Tears flow from her eyes as Preston goes on, "But the stocky one—perhaps their leader, I'm not sure—he said that it must look like we turned on each other. They argued some more on deciding to kill us, and then a rustling in the forest drew them away. It must have been one of the beasts of the forest. I waited awhile before I moved … I was scared they were watching. Finally, I rose and began to wake the others. We had to carry Malan the rest of the way."

"Were they warriors?" Branson asks.

Preston shakes his head. "No, they were still young, but older than us. Very new to combat, it seemed—like us. If not for the numbers, we would have stood a chance."

When he stops, Branson asks, "Is that all you remember?"

He nods, at which Branson thanks him for his service and bids him a quick recovery. The two men turn to leave, but Preston reaches out and grabs Branson's wrist.

"Sire! I almost forgot. When I was fighting one of them, I remember being knocked off balance, and I grabbed at their shirt. I saw the shirt underneath…. It was of the purest blue. They were of the Azurite Order; I'm sure of it."

Branson and Uric look at each other, speechless. It is a moment before they catch themselves. They thank the boy again and motion to speak outside of the spirit house. Branson lets Uric go ahead of him so that he can stop and bid farewell to his son, promising he will return.

In that moment, he takes in the changes in Malan. He is still his mother's height and much stockier than his older brother. Malan carries his muscle in his legs. Branson can only imagine the distance he can run at a high speed. His dark-brown, curly hair is cut short, with a baby-clean face free of any facial hair. He has his mother's skin tone, but his eyes belong to Branson—honey brown with a calm intensity and hidden vulnerability.

Outside, Branson finds Uric waiting for him.

"The Azurite are well known for siding with the Onyx," Uric says. "They would need to cross through Azurite clan territory on their borders. There was much risk to attempt this … assassination."

Branson offers, "What you say is all true. But something is still not right. The Azurite cannot make it through the Jade borders and into the spirit hold boundaries during the Awakening without raising alarm. They were not alone in this."

Uric makes a guess: "You think they had help from within the Jade Order? Your Foresight, perhaps?"

Branson shrugs. "Let us wait until the riders return and Gaylen summons us."

Uric says, "But—"

Branson holds up a hand to cut him off. "There is nothing we can do now. Save your thoughts for the dewan. Go to your family; we do not know the next time we will return home."

Before Uric leaves, Branson asks where Aitan has run off to, and Uric replies that he stopped at the spirit house nearly two sky shadows earlier and is now training with the young huntsmen now.

Branson thanks Uric and musters up his fatherly empathy, then heads out to see Aitan. His thoughts dwell on both the new details surrounding the attack on Malan's group and how he will regain his trust from his eldest son.

Soon Branson breaks from his contemplation as a fellow huntsman passes by and says, "Namaste, Bonne Ame."

Over the years, Branson has gotten accustomed to being addressed with his new title. He struggles more with the politics of it. Ahni, on the other hand, comprehends fully the need for diplomacy and the half truths. She's advised him many times on the responsibilities and traditions his new title has brought him.

He strolls to the sparring courtyard and leans on a small fence, watching Aitan train with the other novice huntsmen. He's impressed by the amount of development Aitan shows in his offensive skills, as well as the practiced focus he maintains with his defensive guard. It is a proud feeling for him that Aitan finds solace in the huntsman service. He waits for the novices to finish their training before he waves and catches Aitan's attention. Aitan finally notices his waving arms and makes his way to him.

Branson can see the annoyance in Aitan's stride but greets his son warmly nonetheless. "Well, we can say today's been eventful," Branson says into the silence.

Aitan nods absently and dusts off his hands.

Branson smiles. "Good to see you are keeping up with your huntsmen training. Commit more to your grapples. When you hesitate, you give your opponent the advantage."

Aitan shrugs. "I'll keep that in mind." Attempting to change the subject, Aitan asks, "Have you checked on Malan?"

Branson exhales and runs his hands over his face before he answers, "Yes, he's awake now. The healers say he will be back to training in a moon's time."

Aitan exclaims, "That's ... That's a long recovery for exhaustion and some bruises!"

Branson gives a calm nod. "Indeed, it is. But let the seekers provide their service. You will see your brother soon enough."

Aitan starts to rebut, but Branson stops him: "He is fine, Aitan."

Aitan senses that his father desires to guide him away from asking after Malan's well-being. He straightens, then makes the wrong assumption of Branson's comment and replies, "Of course. The Chozien shouldn't worry about such matters."

Branson laughs and shakes his son by the shoulders.

Aitan draws back, clearly confused.

Catching his breath, Branson says, "All right, enough of this. I have a way with words that conflicts with my sentiment. Your mother and the dewan have been struggling to rid me of this flaw." With his composure regained, he grips Aitan's shoulders and says with as much sensitivity a huntsman can muster, "You are my son just as much as Malan. At times, I struggle with myself over the demands my various titles give me. But it is not because I regret choosing you for my son. There are decisions one must make and commands we must obey. This can be in conflict with the character you strive to keep. But you are always who you are."

Aitan nods. He has experienced this same internal battle, mostly in his warrior training. He sees now that this will only increase as time goes on, and from the sound of it, his father will be there to guide him through it.

"Have I ever told you the story of how I became gardien?"

Aitan shakes his head. "I don't think so."

"Ah, well, let me tell you about one of my first lessons in obedience."

TWENTY-FOUR

The forest is in an uproar from erratic fleeing. The invaders are in a mad footrace to create as much distance between them and the Jade spirit hold as they can. They follow the same route south outside of the spirit hold borders, though dangerously close to the Rhyne Clan's borders.

One of them calls for a halt.

Another says, "Jasper, we do not have time for this. We need to keep moving until the darkness covers us."

"Then you go on! My chest burns with every breath I take ... and those are many."

The neophyte warrior plops to the ground. The others follow his lead, some lying on their backs with their chests heaving up and down. The one who protested paces back and forth. He wrings his hands together, stops to catch a thought, but shakes his head and continues pacing.

He does this for quite some time before another member huffs and says: "Will you stop walking around? They won't find us. No one travels in the deep night."

The restless one hisses back, "That is the least of our concerns! We attacked the wrong troop. Our mission was to rid the Jade Order of their Chozien. Do you know what our dewan will do to us once he finds this out? We are better off banishing ourselves."

Yet another young warrior addresses the problem: "Chedan assured us that it was the right troop."

Chedan jumps in, "I said what was told to me exactly. The man said when and where the Awakening would happen. He described the Chozien exactly as I said to you."

The anxious lad blurts out, "How did we get the time right but not the troop?"

Branches creaking from the trees off the trail alert the invaders. They leap to their feet and all stand, facing the rustling. A figure steps out from the cover of the trees, though he remains engulfed in shadow. They make out the figure to be wearing the Jade colors, with a hood pulled forward to cover nearly all of his face. They see a sword at his waist, but he stands leisurely, which helps reduce the possibility of a threat.

The hooded figure speaks, his voice deep: "Well, you all seem to have scuffed up this mission."

The apprehensive lad asks, "Where is your scout?"

By the sound of the man's voice, he's smiling as he answers, "He is watching for others. That is what scouts do, no?"

The young warriors relax a little.

The hooded man folds his arms and tilts his head. "Well now, we must get you all across the border before my dewan's riders find you." The hidden man turns to lead them, but then stops and asks, "Oh, a question: Why do the Azurite seek the death of the Chozien?"

A relieved raider answers, "As a testament to the Azurite alliance, the Onyx called for the death of the Chozien."

The man continues, "Why not just capture him for their own? The Chozien would then be of the Onyx. It would be a waste to kill him. That is not the way of the Onyx. Better to add him to their numbers, no?"

The same youth responds, "To shift the balance of power to the Onyx, of course. With the Onyx possessing the only Chozien, it would allow them to secure more alliances with the other orders. Remove the obstacle that influences the decision, then the choice is easy. You are right: This is the way of the Onyx. One in exchange for the many."

The man says more to himself than of the raiders, "Ah, so there really are two of them."

The young warrior starts to talk again, but the tense one hushes him and says, "We must be on our way now. Our dewan needs to hear of this."

"Ah, yes. Let us end our arrangement then."

At the man's statement, other shadowed figures materialize from the woods surrounding the invaders, the shadows descending on them.

Through the terrified screams that follow, another man appears beside the hooded figure and says, "Bury them deep—deep enough that the very roots of the tallest trees will feed off the warmth of their bodies. Best they have some use after all."

The riders return with the missing ten from Malan's troop. They report that they were bound and beaten as well. Soon a message circulates that the troop ran across a mother bear and her cubs. The troop sustained defensive injuries, but with their number, they managed to draw away the beast. In addition to undue distress affecting their judgment, they lost their way. The ten novices that missed the Awakening's five-day deadline will be granted leniency due to the unlikely circumstances.

Branson, Uric, and Trenton said their farewells to their families two days before the rest of Malan's troop returned. Branson and Uric once again reside as guests in Gaylen's house, while Trenton continues his duty as donateur. Each day, Branson and Uric eat breakfast together, though choosing to have their dinner alone; the constant politics, training, and worry through the day are too much for them to share with the closest of friends.

During the day, they train with their service. Uric has begun honing his Reach. He possesses a rare skill to alter the course of nature, and to do so under intense duress increases his ability to go unmatched in combat.

As a named huntsman, Branson continues to perform and perfect his service as he passes his days hunting and skinning, catching glimpses of Aitan's training. Seeing this inspires him to continue with his training in hand-to-hand combat and weaponry. Aitan has been called back to warrior training until he is named warrior, after which Branson feels almost certain that Aitan will return to huntsmen training—at least until he is called forth to train as seeker.

Spirit Keeper Keno joins Branson one evening on his way back from a hunt. Branson is a bit taken aback, but considering Aitan's upcoming commencement to enter spirit seeker training, he does not think much of it.

"Good eve, Keno. Treating my friend Uric well?"

Keno gives a quick, small laugh. "He's progressing quite well. He could do well with a few moons of training here."

Branson smirks. "You would do well to convince him of that."

Keno clears his throat and clasps his hands behind him. "I understand that the Bonne Ame has been blessed with Sight?"

Branson's only sign of hesitancy is a raised eyebrow. "This is true."

Smiling at the lack of curiosity from the huntsman, Keno continues, "Ah, you huntsmen are a predictable lot."

Branson simply grunts, so Keno goes on, "Yes yes, your Sight. Why don't you come by the spirit house tomorrow? I think it is past time we hone this ability of yours."

Branson considers the spare time he has until Gaylen summons them, then agrees to Keno's request. Back at the house, he notices that four sires have arrived: Clayton, Connor, Harwen, and Remy. They exchange greetings and seem to be not only famished but also weary from their travel. They retire with little conversation and pensive countenances. With the arrival of the sires from the closest clans, Branson deduces that Gaylen has called for a council of sires. By their composure, the events from the Awakening have already been communicated and they've rushed to the spirit hold, hence their haggard appearance. And just like that, Branson's interest to meet with Keno tomorrow increases. He could use the distraction.

The next morning, Branson arrives at the spirit house just as dawn breaks. He raps on the door and waits; no answer. He knocks again, harder and louder; again no answer. This time, he goes to bang on the door again, but a low, cracking voice calls out for him to return once the sun stands above the tree line. Branson leaves without acknowledgement, though with a mischievous smile. Spirit seekers waken the latest of all of the services. He does find joy in his purposeful annoyance.

He returns later at the suggested hour, and the energy at the spirit house is a stark contrast to the previous bolstering quiet. Roaming or otherwise engaged seekers welcome Branson; he is still not accustomed to their gregarious nature. He follows the directions to find Keno, who is apparently eagerly awaiting his audience.

As Branson walks through the halls of the spirit house, he smells a soothing scent. He recognizes the fragrance as eucalyptus and smiles at the thought of his wife, thus finding comfort in the maze of halls. The walls are smooth and seem to make their own pattern, bulging in some places, bending in others. He runs his eyes up the walls to the ceiling and notices that the stone finish carries on throughout the house.

He pauses and listens intently. He hears … *Water?* Slow moving, in all directions, soothing. He smiles inwardly as he knows he could fall asleep to the sound of the current and drips. He looks again at the wall, reaches out, touches it, and then looks at his fingers. Damp. He smells the substance on his fingertips and is awestruck.… It's water. He looks at the walls again, this time with an expectant eye, and notices that a slow flow of water streams down the walls. He is amazed at the majestic atmosphere.

"The 'Ones Before Us' called them Flowstones—a natural stone that grows in caves where water gathers."

Branson turns toward the voice and sees Keno smiling at his amazement. Keno stands next to Branson, who continues to admire the stunning cavescape that is the spirit house.

"You must be wondering where we acquired such stone. It was some time ago … two generations or three, I would say. The Jade Order made a pilgrimage of sorts to the Rhodonite Order. As a symbol of their alliance, their dewan revealed one of the many caverns the Great Spirit blessed them with for the upkeep of their beauty. The spirit keeper at the time, awed by its splendor, made plans to capture a piece of this land's fissure and construct our spirit house made of this stone. He was drawn by its link to the Great Spirit's *ame*."

He grips Branson's wrist to stop him from touching the wall again and smiles kindly. "Truly, I do understand its lure. But the oils from our skin detract from the flow of water.… It must be cleansed to keep the flow steady."

Branson looks again at the place where he previously touched, and he blinks in wonderment. The water has changed its flow to circumvent the tainted area.

Keno snaps his fingers, and a novice seeker comes to clean the area. Keno beckons Branson on through the halls.

Branson asks, "How is it that water flows inside without the rain?"

Keno explains, "Over time, the *ame* of the life-giving land merged with the stone and the spirit house. The *ames* of every living element, not just people, can be seen here. The smallest ant, the sprout of a seedling, and even the softest wind."

Branson grunts indifferently.

Keno laughs. "Ah, let us hasten before you lose your patience … even as a huntsman."

They travel through the spirit house, only to exit outside. A short distance ahead, Branson sees an opening into a cluster of trees. He would have thought he'd already seen every forest, tree, and trail the spirit hold has, but he would have remembered this one. The opening is adorned by tree trunks and branches that have been gnarled and twisted unnaturally into an oval pattern. He cannot see into the ingress of the unnatural void.

Keno stops short, and Branson looks at him expectantly, eyebrows raised.

"We are about to enter a sacred place—the Hearthtree," Keno says. "Here, you will experience the essence of the spirit hold's *ame*."

Branson furrows his brow. "The spirit hold has an *ame*? I don't understand."

"All things have *ames*. Some of us can see the *ames* of nonhuman beings and the elements themselves. Like Bonne Ame Uric. Each place … a community where the collective *ames* of its people are gathered—no

... united. Yes, united. This is not naturally done but must be driven together as a conduit to the sacred point. Ours is here." Keno points inside the black hollowness. "Only the spirit holds—"

With a raised hand, Branson stops the seeker from any further elaboration. "I'm sure your novices find this all very interesting. If we could move on...?"

Keno chuckles. "I didn't think it was possible to rattle the patience of a huntsman. Very well, let us begin."

Branson follows Keno into the unknown hollow and chides himself for allowing his current mood to interfere with his mental fortitude. On entering, the darkness engulfs them so much that he cannot make out the outlines of the expected foliage. He is not alarmed, as he can sense the familiarity of the forest elements around him. The solid ground compacts and shifts beneath his boots. The dull scent of the wildlife and timberland existing in its natural habitat hints to an artificial "cleanliness" of the space. Branson would be lost if not for Keno's voice leading them. He does wonder how Keno navigates through the dark.

"We have been gifted with Foresight ever since Creation. It has gone by many names over the generations. Even those who carry this talent have been referred to by various monikers according to the reception of their gift. I only know of seer, psychic, and ... ah, yes, mystic. I have also heard heretic and witch. You must have heard of these?"

At Keno's extended pause, Branson answers simply, "No."

Branson hears the smile in Keno's voice as he continues, "Ah well. You might take notice now. Yes yes, this should be far enough."

As Keno stretches out an arm with palm facing up, Branson cannot see anything. Then he narrows his eyes, and a light slowly blooms in the dark. At that, Branson widens his eyes, and he flinches slightly at the unexpected appearance of the spherical illumination. Next, he notes a small glimmer and peers deeper into the darkness behind the glowing orb, taken aback as he recognizes the source of the glimmer: the pupils of Keno's eyes. He likens the sight to the reflective glow in the eyes of animals in the dark, though not covering the entire pupil.

Keno looks past Branson, unmoving as he speaks, almost in a trance: "Our first memories are created by our senses. Sight and touch stand the strongest among them. We are all born with some capacity to See. To See what is, what is to come, or what has been. Those whose *ame* has heightened these sensations are able to manifest cognitions to talents we come to know as Sight, Foresight, or Hindsight.

"The purveyors of such talents come in many varieties: the addle-minded child, the rambling roamer, the harmless blind woman, the warmhearted baker, or the ordinary kinsman. They remain as reminders of what neglect and ignorance of one with such abilities can do. With such a gift, a purpose has been placed upon you. You must find this mission and carry it out without fail."

Keno closes his eyes for a moment, while his body visibly relaxes. He opens his eyes again without the glimmer and smiles. "Well, it seems you have been set on a path. Let's head back to the spirit house." He walks past Branson, this time keeping the light lit.

Branson stands there, dumbfounded. He pivots around and follows Keno, although still bewildered. Finally, he asks, "Well? Aren't you going to tell me what this 'path' is?"

Keno responds, "Oh, that is something you must find through your visions. I cannot foretell everyone's destinies, even the gifted." He chuckles at the thought. "We'll begin your training tomorrow. Not so early this time, hm? I will never understand the rush to …"

Branson stops listening, distracted by anxious curiosity. His questions seem endless: What is this "purpose" Keno speaks of? Is Branson already on the path now? How will he know what he is to achieve? Does this concern Aitan? Will Branson have to choose between his family and his gift? He certainly has much to think on.

He sleeps well that night, drained from the constant queries and scenarios. His dreams are blissful; heroic, even.

TWENTY-FIVE

Branson wakes eager to begin his training with the spirit keeper. By habit, he wakes just before dawn. Gaylen's cooks have prepared small portions of varying fares, akin to a huntsmen's breakfast. This time, instead of grabbing handfuls of nuts, dried meats, fruits, and stuffing them into his satchel, he sits down and fills a plate. He eats slowly while the servants clear the dawn meal and replace it with the traditional breakfast dishes. Just as the sires begin to enter, Branson speaks a quick greeting before he exits the dining hall.

Branson stops by the infirmary, an isolated area in the spirit house, where he spends time with Malan before he heads to the main courtyard. His son is mending well. The healers noted to Branson that his appetite has increased and he is moving around with less strain—all positive signs of a good recovery. As the sun sits high in its brilliance, Branson figures he has given Keno ample time to gather himself and makes his way to the entrance for his training.

This time when Branson knocks, a very amiable novice answers the door with a cheerful "Namaste, Bonne Ame!"

Branson nods. "Namaste."

The novice—a small, black-haired girl of about fourteen birth years—chuckles absently and steps out of the house, closing the door softly. Branson quirks an eyebrow, as he wonders if he is the one responsible for the small amusement. He shakes his head, not understanding the humor of the service, nor wanting to.

"I am Ewa. If you would follow me, please, Spirit Keeper Keno is awaiting you at the Hearthtree."

The novice stretches an arm to her left and guides him to the courtyard. They maneuver through the throng of novices and seekers. He doesn't see much of what he would consider "training." The assembly resembles a gathering of socialites who haven't seen each other in quite some time, or else kinsmen engaging in leisurely conversations as a reprieve from the day's service. He cannot imagine having so much spare time. He shakes his head in bewilderment, wishing for Ewa's escort to accelerate, as he can feel his chest tightening with this reckless abandon of wastefulness.

They finally reach the Hearthtree without Branson losing his enthusiasm, fortunately.

Smiling, Keno waves at the pair. "Namaste, Sire Branson. How is the day thus far?"

Branson nods and remarks simply, "Well. Malan is recovering."

"Ah, good. The young lad has his father's strength."

At Branson's nod, Keno dismisses the novice and turns to head into the Hearthtree, waving for Branson to follow. "Come along. Let us get started, then."

Branson follows Keno into the Hearthtree. This time, strategically spaced lanterns light the interior. This gives Branson the opportunity to appease his curiosity. He looks to the ground, and as he imagined, it has been cleared of most of the natural forestry debris. The grass has been sheared clean, with loads of gravel spread throughout the entire space to fill any holes, followed by several layers of dirt packed solidly and smoothed out. Clearly, the upkeep is a daily chore.

He turns his attention to the walls. The gnarled trunks and branches wind so tightly around each other that they blot out the light. They are shaped where the base tilts outward and then slowly curve inward as they meet at the top. He cannot see the ceiling since the lanterns give off just enough light to navigate, though he knows the height is steep, as the space feels airy and he can hear the faint echoes from their footsteps.

Just as he finishes his examination, Keno begins to speak, without missing a step. His tone sounds firmer and less casual, with his words deliberate and direct: "It is good that you have agreed to train your gift. There can be negative effects of the Sight if left untrained. It has been known to drive one mad or even cause blindness."

Branson gasps. "Blindness! Damn it, man, you might have mentioned this sooner!"

Keno shrugs his shoulders and, without breaking stride, remarks, "You fared well when you first made known your gift. Also, the Sight must be strong for such ill effects to happen. You are moderate, at best."

Branson scoffs at the matter-of-fact way the spirit keeper has judged his skill.

Shortly after their brief exchange, Keno stops and turns to face Branson. "This will do. We'll begin now. Please sit."

Keno does not wait for Branson to descend; he settles himself down in a cross-legged position. Branson hurries to join him.

While facing each other, Keno says, "In the beginning when time did not exist, there was no difference between day or night. There was no sound or smell. But even in the emptiness, we could see. Not in the sense with the physical eyes, but in the mind. This was when the Great Spirit envisioned the Creation of our world, including the beasts and beings to live within it. This was the origin of the ability. And as such, the Spirit thought fit to bestow this gift on a select few of the creations, though not without sacrifice and obligation to this world.

"So as the baker kneads the dough, it becomes tacky. The baker takes a handful of flour and gently sprinkles it over the dough." He imitates the sprinkle with his hand. "Too much and the dough becomes rigid, consumed with the structure-enhancing agent, increasing the demand on the host, distracting the focus on their calling. Too little and the dough struggles to grasp at fragments to complete a balanced binding. But just enough and the dough becomes malleable, rich with the elasticity of properly balanced structure and enough give to be controlled. This is how the Great Spirit has touched us all with varying degrees of empathy, vanity, ambition, sympathy, amiability, and so on. In this are extremes of the spectrum."

He stretches his arms out to either side of him. He wiggles the fingers of his left hand and states, "Those who are extremely social, adventurous, and enthusiastic, and then there are those ..." He wiggles the fingers of his right hand. "... who are extremely quiet, independent, and overly critical. These are the ones where the Sight will manifest most often. And you, Bonne Ame, are here." He finishes by waving his right hand and smiling.

Branson ignores the jest, remains stoic, and tilts his head. "This I know. How does this help me?"

Keno puts his hands on his hips and shakes his head. "I see you came eager to learn." He claps his hands. "Well, yes. Part of training is understanding the beginning and intent. Isn't that how you huntsmen train to hunt? The biology of the animal, what frightens it, and what attracts it, yes?"

Branson accepts Keno's comparison of training methods between the two services and respectfully nods.

Keno inhales deeply before he continues, "Now, because of your strong self-reliance, you receive your visions in solitude. This is why the Sight took hold of you during your meditation. But you didn't just *see*, did you?"

Branson shakes his head.

Keno presses Branson to communicate in ways other than body movements: "Like how?"

Branson answers, "I could smell and feel. It was as if I was there … with them. I *was* them. I was the wife cradling the head of my slain husband. I was the warrior rushing into the throng of battle. I could feel my blade pierce bodies, releasing several *ames* before I myself was killed from a … blade behind me." He hesitates and blinks his eyes, trying to gain focus. "I smelled the blood; it filled me. I was a novice rushing my kinsmen to safety. We were fleeing into the woods. I was so tired; my chest burned. I was so scared; my heart was racing. I was everywhere and everyone." Branson struggles to keep his composure, visibly shaken from the recollection.

Keno notices the strain and still pushes on: "You must embrace the sensitivity you have with your Sight. This is difficult for those who prefer isolation over socialization. You will learn to vocalize your emotions. You will run to them."

Understanding, Branson nods, and at Keno's arched eyebrow, he gives an audible response: "Yes, I understand."

Keno nods. "Good. Let us begin."

For the majority of that day and the five days thereafter, Branson rehearses improving his concentration during mediation and manipulating the personal perspectives while within the vision. By his fifth day of training, Branson manages to call forth the Foresight. He notices that he can no longer see the scene with the two hawks flying, with one being captured by the net. Keno tells him this is a limiting factor of his gift of Foresight: Once a vision comes to pass, he can no longer see it; he can only see forward, not backward. Keno further emphasizes the significance of Branson focusing on the details.

Branson is also able to see from the perspective of someone in the vision. He first goes for what is familiar and settles on the impression of being the Jade warrior who gets slain. The moment that the warrior dies, Branson releases from him. He then moves to the more … *sinister*, embodying the impression of an attacker.

Immediately, the scent of salt and rust rush at him. He feels an insatiable appetite and elation at the sight of the bright red liquid spurting out of the puncture he has just made in the Jade warrior. Just as he sets his sight on his next target, his *ame* is taken. The sudden withdrawal from the ravenous bloodthirst shocks him out of his vision, gasping.

Keno inquires, "What did you see?"

Clutching his chest, breathing heavily, he replays the vision: "I was a Jade warrior and rushing into battle. I cut down many of the attackers. It was chaos. Their numbers were too many, and I knew I needed to give my clan enough time to escape. The moment I fell, I immediately transitioned into the attacker who had claimed his *ame*." Branson pauses and puts his hand on his brow, digesting what he is about to say next: "I felt … fulfilled. As if this one life—the spill of his blood on the ground—would mean my immediate ascension to glory. But even then, it was not enough. I wanted more. The taste of the metallic odor of the blood still tastes fresh on my tongue." He spits and covers his mouth in shock at the aftereffects.

Keno sits back at the realization of what Branson's vision reveals. Only one order has a reputation for what they call "survival." All orders hold that the essence of life is in the blood and that the pouring of it onto the land glorifies the Great Spirit. With one particular order, though, this passion has been warped over the generations to a maniacal obsession with the life-giving fluid. He knows who the attackers will be: the Bloodstone.

Fortunately for Branson, Keno releases him from the intensive training that day. Branson, though, has no chance for a respite, as the remaining five sires have arrived, and thus, Gaylen calls for the council of the Jade Order to assemble, with the focus being the ambush during the Awakening.

The sires, Bonne Ames, general, spirit keeper, and chief huntsman file into Gaylen's private parlor. This is quite an extraordinary event. For all the members of the highest positions in an order to meet at the same time and same place is truly a risk. For one, it leaves the other clans vulnerable to an attack with their clan leader absent and accompanied by a large portion of their militia. And for another, a composed invasion on the meeting location could wipe out the order's leadership, crippling its existence. The latter is unlikely, considering that spirit holds are the most heavily guarded fortresses, but indeed, it makes this a grave reunion.

The conglomerate assembles and stands quietly. Branson passes by Clayton and is reminded of the gravity of the situation, as he does not smell the usual funk of libation and Clayton's expression defies his amiable temperament. He examines everyone as they settle in. All faces are of steel, and their posture holds a tense anxiety and alertness. It makes him uneasy for the sanctity and safety of the spirit hold ... as well it should.

Gaylen breaks the tense silence: "You have all received notice of the recent strike on our warrior novices during the Awakening. We must keep this news from our people and allies, as their support is needed more than ever. My initial concern is that this could have been a betrayal from within, though I have received knowledge to rule that option out."

Branson hears audible exhales and see the easing of posture from a few.

Gaylen continues, "One of the novices overheard the attackers talking. Branson? Uric? What did the young novice say?"

Branson and Uric look at each other, visibly shocked. They both stumble over each other, unprepared and still processing how Gaylen knew of the novice's comments without their report. Gaylen holds his hand up, and the Bonne Ames stop. The dewan points to Uric.

Uric retells the novice's account, during which comes a mix of exasperation and bitter grumbles at Uric's revelation that the novice identified their ambushers as being from the Azurite Order.

Once Uric finishes, the sires erupt with various outbursts:

Marquis is enraged at the audacity. "I have said this before: We are at war. We should gather our allies before the peace breaks. If we had done so sooner, we could have gained alliances with the Crystal and Amber Orders at our borders."

Clayton looks shocked, and while helping himself to a glass of Gaylen's fine brown whiskey, he volunteers to be the official convoy to garner the alliances.

Graham exaggerates his disappointment and seems more interested in slighting Gaylen's leadership: "We should have doubled our fortification and scouts at our borders. This would have been wise."

Remy counters with, "We would still not have suspected an attack on the spirit hold; no one would risk that."

As expected, Harwen agrees with Remy: "Yes, there's no doubt that if we had increased our numbers on the scout and the watch without letting our allies know, it would have caused suspicion. Just as we are watching, so are the other orders."

Tuan and Sim speak aloud though it's almost more to each other than to the rest of the council:

"To get so close to the spirit hold, they had to have help from within, yes?" Sim rubs his chin.

Tuan follows with, "Indeed, the timing of the Awakening was precise, but there's something missing. It is no secret who the Chozien is. They would have known which troop to target."

The room goes silent. Tuan's query resonates with everyone ... except Gaylen. Gaylen's expression does not seem to suggest any quandary within his own mind. Branson lifts an eyebrow and folds his arms, showing his irritation. He nudges Uric, who is deep in thought. Branson prods his chin at Gaylen. Uric swivels his eyes in that direction while not turning his head to avoid any attention. He shrugs his shoulders to show his ignorance of Branson's suspicion.

Branson rolls his eyes and leans in and whispers, "He is not as concerned as the rest of us. He already knows."

Uric mouths his realization. He takes another quick scan, then comments, "Neither does his personal council," referring to Haru, Keno, and Chief Huntsman Len.

Branson quirks one side of his mouth and whispers in an annoyed tone, "No doubt he's known about this before even the novice mentioned it to us."

Uric counters with a reasonable alternative: "Easy, Branson. They could be searching for tells within our order's leaders. These are extraordinary times; it is easy to fall astray."

Just then, Clayton blurts out, "The June Clan sits high on the border to the Azurite. Our scouts have not reported any unusual activity. I would have known."

Tuan looks at Clayton. "No one here is insinuating that you or your clan had anything to do with the plot," and then, seemingly rescinding his appeasement, adds, "although the border clans would be a likely candidate to provide aid."

Clayton's eyes widen at the suggestion. He exclaims as much, and the room erupts with emotions all around. Gaylen allows for this to continue for a few moments until he feels he's not seen any signs of guilt or skepticism in any of his sires. He holds up his hand for silence. However, the men are well into their discourse; they do not notice the command.

The general takes this gesture as insolence, and he expresses his displeasure through a roaring order to be quiet.

Gaylen waits for the silence to settle before he asks Connor to step forward, and he does so humbly, but with hints of pride.

Gaylen asks, "Your clan lies near the Azurite border as well?"

"It does."

"Were your scouts approached by anyone from the Azurite Order?"

Connor nods. "Yes."

Everyone gasps, not only in shock, but at Connor's calm.

Branson tries his best to mimic Connor's placid demeanor. He's apparently not succeeding, as Uric clears his throat while narrowing his eyes at Branson.

Where Branson struggles to maintain a smooth disposition, Gaylen succeeds: "Please enlighten us?"

Connor seems to have eyes only for Gaylen as he explains, "About six birth years after the Chozien was named, my scouts sent a report that Azurites had begun to roam closer to our border. Not many; only a small clutch. They appeared to be farmers and gatherers, not of a service, though still very unusual. So I had a scout approach them to see what they were about. They said as much, but I was not convinced. I ordered my scout to continue engaging with the band. Over the course of four birth years, the scout invented a relationship with one of the women and gave her the illusion he wanted to leave the Jade Order and join the Azurite so that the two of them could unite their *ames*. The Azurite woman approached her sire to gain consent. There could be only two outcomes: The sire would be ambitious and attempt to gain influence with his dewan, or it would reveal the original plot behind the straying Azurite kinsmen. Of course, there was the chance they could have made their way to the border unknowingly."

Marquis scoffs. "You would have to be a child to wander that close."

Grunts around the room show the unanimous agreement.

Connor continues, "The Azurite woman met back with my scout and stated that he had to prove his loyalty to the Azurite Order prior to her sire giving consent. This had to be quite a show, considering the circumstances and our history as rivals. My scout and I came up with a convincing enough demonstration." He pauses and shifts his feet a bit.

Remy bursts out, "Well, what was it, man?"

Connor says, "We decided to exchange details about the Chozien and reveal when he would be most vulnerable."

Save Gaylen and Connor, gasps and wide-eyed, open-mouthed faces adorn the room. Branson is the first to move. He lunges at Connor while yelling threats and questioning his intentions. Uric and Harwen react in time to grab at him, which delays him long enough for the others to jump in and assist in holding him back.

"That was reckless!" Branson shouts. "The novices could have been killed! Are you crazy? Those details about the Chozien are now with the entire Azurite Order. How do you expect us to protect him?"

"Hold a minute! Let him speak, Bonne Ame!" one of the sires exclaims.

They give Branson the time he needs to ease up. This is an understatement, as Branson begins pacing furiously behind a line of sires, all of them doing their best to keep an ear on Connor's presentation as well as an eye on their unpredictable kinsmen.

Connor continues calmly, though raises his voice to be heard over Branson's vocal fuming: "It was necessary. We had to make them believe that my scout had every intention of betraying the Jade. We do not hold the secrets to molding objects out of pure glass, as do the Rhodonite. We don't hold the mysteries of healing, as do the Amethyst, nor the location of the rarest stones from the Gold Order. We cannot even barter our own genes, like the mighty Tiger Eye."

Branson argues, "We have our herbs. No one can produce our kassmint."

He refers to one of the order's rarest herbs, which has the shape of a long pepper and the taste of spicy, lemony mint—just one of the many popular herbs and spices the Jade Order is known for, so much so that the Amethyst travel far to trade for its superior medicinal properties.

Surprisingly, Isaac responds, "That would cripple the Jade Order's economy. He is right, Bonne Ame: We have little of value, especially when we hold the Chozien."

Connor gives Isaac a cautionary look out of the corner of his eye at the subtle slight to Gaylen before moving on: "As you can see, this was my only choice. Of course, I gave only a few valid facts, but I twisted them with false details. It was just enough to validate the truth of what we said and to root out any possible betrayers in the clan who would have them question our reliability.

"Over the years, we shared development details about the Chozien.

It wasn't until the Chozien began his warrior training that the Azurite demanded we plot a mission to … remove him."

Raising his voice before the shocked grumbles sway the topic, Connor goes on, "My scout told them that the Chozien would be isolated during the Awakening and that we could not be the ones to act; however, we *could* get a small troop of Azurite warriors into the spirit hold and near the Chozien's troop without raising alarm. They agreed.

"Again, over the next two years, my scout remained in contact with the woman. As the time neared to the Awakening, my scout was set to meet with the Azurite troop, but this time I accompanied him with my face and identity concealed. We made the plan that we would escort them through the Jade land. I was identified as a person of influence so we would not be singled out as suspicious and would gain easy entry.

"Prior to this, I met with High Warrior Randol to disclose the upcoming raid. He shared the route with me that the troop would be on, and we mapped out the exact day and place of the attack."

Sim stops Connor, scratching his head. He says, "Hold on. How were you able to convince the Azurite that you could be trusted? That would have been the first time they spoke to anyone else but your scout."

Connor smirks. "I told them that I had ambition to unseat our dewan and this would be enough to turn the entire order against him."

Sim smiles, accepting his answer, but he is not yet finished with his interrogation: "And High Warrior Randol? I can't believe he would have accepted sabotaging the Awakening so easily."

Connor grips his chin, pausing for a moment before he speaks: "Yes, this, too, had me concerned. He was skeptical since we were so close to the Awakening. He was not happy that we had Azurites so close to the spirit hold either. He demanded to speak with my scout. He did. Next, he wanted to be at the encounter with the Azurites. This was impossible, as it could have caused doubt. He would not give his aid, though, unless he could hear and see the Azurites. So we hid him in some thick brush a fair distance away, although still in earshot. This was enough to convince him to assist, if only mildly." Connor looks to Sim for his nod to continue. "With High Warrior Randol, I knew exactly which troop to lead the Azurites to. As a pre—"

His huntsman's patience forgotten, Branson cuts in again, "They could have been killed! What could you have possibly said that a high warrior would willingly go along with such a risk?"

Connor finally turns to look at Branson, speaking directly to him: "You may have some age, huntsman, but you are just a wee thing when it comes to plotting and conspiracy."

Branson opens his mouth for a rebuttal, but Connor holds his head up, snapping Branson's mouth shut.

"I needed to know which troop the Chozien would be in and for High Warrior Randol to purposely form a troop that had the most stamina and top fighters. Your son, Malan, happened to fall into this troop. My scout reported characteristics of the Chozien, but he also mentioned those of your son. As you heard from the novice Preston, they couldn't find the Chozien among the troop ... because he was not there. The Chozien was never in any danger."

Mouth agape, Branson shakes his head. "But the troop that you led the Azurites to was! What if they decided to kill the troop anyway?"

Connor answers, "The plan was High Warrior Randol's, and as a precaution, he had a group of trusted devenirs trail the Azurite during the Awakening. This is why the invaders retreated before they could release any of the novices' *ames*. Unfortunately, the troop needed to take the beating to keep the scheme going."

Harwen jumps in with, "Well, I hope this elaborate sabotage yielded *something*."

Connor replies simply, "Aye." At Gaylen's nod, he reports, "The origin is indeed the Onyx. They move to make alliances now. It has most likely reached the shores that there are two Chozien: one with the Onyx and the other with the Jade. They want to eliminate any influence our Chozien has on the other orders to reduce the opposition. They prepare for war."

Marquis slams his fist on the table, "If that is so, we are birth years behind in preparation."

Harwen puffs his chest. "The Huin Clan stands ready."

Branson, sitting again, and Uric roll their eyes at Harwen's eagerness to gain Gaylen's favor.

Clayton has one last question and has to shout over the clamor: "Hey ... hey! What of the Azurite warriors? Did we just let them go?"

Connor smiles sinisterly. "We have taken their *ames*. They'll never be found. High Warrior Randol made sure of that."

The council nods.

But Tuan looks skeptical about Connor's explanation and says, "It is not the way of the Onyx to kill unless absolutely necessary. The Onyx are surely involved, but the death of the Chozien is not what they seek."

Marquis dismisses the uncertainty: "It is enough they dared come on the Jade lands, seeking to harm not only the Chozien but our kinsmen."

The sires in the room continue to discuss their next steps in fortifications and strategy, as well as in beginning to forge alliances. During the active conversations, Connor makes his way to Branson. Uric motions to Branson, bringing his attention to the sire.

"I meant no harm to your son. In these times, we do what we must to protect the order and those we love—most of the time, in that sequence."

Branson shrugs his shoulders, the sting of the risk being justified by the invaluable report still settling in.

Uric speaks to break the awkward silence: "What of your scout and the woman?"

Connor chuckles. "Ever the seeker…. The scout, of course, accompanied the Azurites into Jade territory, and he is safe. The woman had his son. Three birth years now. With no word from the assassins, she and the child will most likely suffer punishment for their failure."

Uric's eyes widen with astonishment. "Surely you can get to the child before the matter is settled?"

Connor shakes his head. "Their fate is sealed. As the days grew closer to the Awakening, he saw less of her. It was enough that they were sent by her sire, and her loyalty lies with the Azurite. He has his own family in my clan, and he'll be rewarded for his bravery and sacrifice."

Uric cannot believe this. The depths people will go to find love is the same to achieve praise or prove loyalty. Indeed, these are different times he is just now seeing with new eyes.

Connor taps Uric's shoulder in an attempt to comfort, but his words are cool: "The enemy will use anything and anyone to cloud your thoughts, judgments, and actions. Anyone can be the eyes and ears. Anyone can be the assassin or target. Children and women are no exception to this."

Turning away from Uric, Connor joins the others to engage in brainstorming for the upcoming war. Branson and Uric share a final look, and their eyes confirm that they both gleaned the same conclusion from Connor's cryptic message: The enemy is not the only one willing to use anyone in their machinations for the sake of their order.

CHAPTER
TWENTY-SIX

And so, the novices are named and now carry the title of warrior. This comes with its fair share of responsibilities. With their service well in hand, most, though not all, return to their clans and are stationed at various posts, such as the scouts to patrol the perimeter and the lires for carrying formal and sensitive messages within the order, as well as other posts—guards to maintain order and settle disputes, and engineers for building war machines. The post for strategists, though, is reserved for more seasoned and elevated warriors. None of these posts relieve any warriors from their training. Each post consists of deployments with intervals ranging from three to six moons, with the scouts being the longest. While they await their next deployment, it is back to the training yard for them.

With Malan recovered and finding his fit in the scouts, Aitan immediately begins his seeker training, which starts just before the sun is at its highest. So Aitan uses the early mornings to continue his huntsman training. He is about three birth years from getting his twin blades and gaining his huntsman title.

Aitan is greeted at the spirit house on his first day by Ewa, who escorts him to the courtyard. Aitan's first reaction to the place is shock, much like his father's, but rather from the sheer awe and wonder.

Ewa giggles. "Well, you definitely are having a different reaction to our slice of community than your gardien."

Aitan looks at her. "Oh?"

She laughs again and taps her lips. Aitan realizes she is bringing attention to the smile on his face. He laughs at his own oblivion. He instinctively tries to cover his mouth.

Ewa touches his forearm with a bit of pressure, stopping him. "Do not hide your joy. It is nice."

Aitan blushes from the compliment and rubs the back of his neck. "Yeah … haven't had much time to smile lately."

"I have a feeling you will smile more from your training as a seeker."

"And what of you? What brings you to train?" Aitan inquires, now finding himself wanting to know everything about this Ewa.

She smiles thoughtfully. "Ah, you know, I thought about the kind of person I am and which service would give me the opportunity to provide for the order the best. I enjoy meeting and helping people. I feel … whole when I can bring a smile to a sad face or relieve pain." And then with a playful elbow jab, she adds, "Plus, I don't think I could shoot an arrow with any bit of accuracy to hunt."

Aitan laughs. "It is not so hard. I can show you."

Ewa nods and holds out her hand. "It's a promise."

They shake hands, sealing their pact.

Noticing the gathering of curious faces around them, Ewa introduces Aitan: "Namaste! We have another novice to train in the spirit seeker service. We welcome Sire Aitan!"

Cheers are raised, and immediately novices and seekers surround

Aitan, all of them receiving him warmly and offering well wishes as he is introduced by his newly acquired title due to his naming as a warrior and, of course, being Chozien.

Ewa has to pull him out of the throng to make sure he makes it to his first lesson on time. They hurry their way to the far end of the grounds, where he sees several youths also milling around in what Aitan would describe as a garden—not the kind that produces food, but one that is beautiful and serene. Aitan's first thought is of its wastefulness. As they make it to the garden, Aitan sees two seekers talking to each other over a table with what looks like various flowers lying about.

Ewa announces Aitan to the two seekers: "Namaste, Teachers. We have another student. This is Sire Aitan."

And with that, she leaves while Aitan stares after her.

"Hey, you're …"

Not catching all the words of a novice speaking to him, Aitan blinks and turns to face the novice. Others quickly join them.

The novice presses for an answer, "Well?"

Aitan looks confused and asks for him to repeat his question.

The novice laughs. "I asked if you are the Chozien, Sire?"

Aitan nods sheepishly, hoping this lot isn't as judgmental as his experience with the warrior novices.

Another says excitedly, "You are already named warrior! And you are in training for huntsman service!"

Then another, a girl, states, "Not many will be able to say they trained with the Chozien. Eek!"

"All right, all right! Settle down! Let's begin. Everyone take your seats," the taller of the two teachers says to the novices.

The novices move to pick their stools, an assortment of varying craftsmanship but still better than the cold, hard ground or standing, which Aitan has grown used to in the warrior and huntsman services. He follows the other novices and grabs the first stool he sees. The novices, though, usher Aitan to the front and center, no matter how much he tries to excuse himself.

With everyone seated, the teachers begin their lesson and Aitan finds that the spirit seeker training had already started for the other novices, which sets him back quite a bit. He tries to catch up as best he can. He discerns that the flowers lying out on the table are actually specific plants used for both medicinal and corrosive applications. The teachers ask each novice to go through the garden surrounding them and locate the plants and identify their use. As expected, Aitan struggles, though not from the lack of aid graciously given from the other novices. The lesson moves on, with the novices learning how to make different medicines by either grinding or pummeling the plants and combining them with the appropriate portions to produce various healing ointments and tonics.

Aitan's first day of spirit seeker training ends in frustration mixed with excitement. He chooses to spend the night with his fellow huntsmen novices. To Aitan's surprise, they are very curious about the seeker training. He spends a good portion of his evening deflecting questions, simply because he doesn't have much of an impression after one day. If he is honest with himself, his thoughts are filled with the kind-hearted hostess, Ewa. Of course, he keeps this to himself; he doesn't feel in the mood to endure any more ribbing from his friends beyond his training as a seeker.

He is eager to arrive at the spirit house to see the vibrant Ewa on his second day of his seeker training. This time, he is interrupted on his way to the entrance of the spirit house by Trenton, his donateur. Aitan's disappointment shows, and Trenton seems more concerned than shocked.

Trenton immediately begins to console him: "Oh, come now. The seeker service is not going as expected? You have to give it time."

Aitan rolls his eyes at Trenton's misinterpretation.

"What?" Trenton says. "No? Then what is it? It cannot be me? I have stayed back to not hover."

Aitan holds up his hands to stop Trenton's assertions. "I was just headed to training, and I thought I might bid good morning to someone."

"Oh?" Trenton smiles and gives a sly look.

"Ugh." Aitan rolls his eyes again and runs his hand through his hair in embarrassment. "It is not like that. I just wanted to be nice. Never mind. You have me now. Was there something you needed to tell me?"

Trenton chuckles at what he assumes to be his charge's first attraction and then says, "Well, Sire, you are directed to report to the creek south of the well. There you will meet with your teacher."

Aitan gives his donateur an annoyed look at being addressed as sire, though he understands his donateur's proclivity to the formality. He nods and heads in that direction. He waves off Trenton's offer to accompany him. He makes a wide circle around the large social conglomerate to avoid as many interactions as possible, more so because the dark-haired novice occupies his thoughts, a feeling both new and foreign to him.

He makes it to the creek and finds Keno waiting patiently. Aitan immediately becomes anxious. It's not often that a dewan's elected official participates in training novices. He walks timidly to the spirit keeper, trying his best to exude confidence. Aitan finally stands in front of Keno in awkward silence that seems to last for several moments. Finally, Aitan notices Keno's shoulders shaking before the spirit keeper bursts out in laughter. Aitan feels extremely confused and a little irritated.

Keno gathers himself and holds up his hands. In between snorts, he explains, "You are so unsettled." Another snort. "There is no need to worry or be upset."

Aitan tries to feign confidence by simply declaring, "I'm not."

Keno sobers up a bit without losing his smile and sets his hand on the novice's shoulder. "Your spirit says different, young sire."

Aitan scrunches his brow. "What does that mean?"

Keno inquires, "Bonne Ame Uric has not spoken to you of his service?"

Aitan shakes his head. "Not in great detail. He's never really serious."

"Oh, Sire, that is where you are wrong. We are always sincere. Our expressions may not reflect that." He shrugs. "I can understand your point of view. To the untrained we can appear to be giddy jokesters or pious clerics." He pauses, reconsidering, and then recants with another smile. "Well, I suppose we are in the basic sense."

Feeling even more confused, Aitan says, "I'm not sure I'm following."

Keno exhales and invites Aitan to walk with him. "I'm sure you have noticed that seeker training has already begun. In fact, we started about a moon before the Awakening."

At Aitan's gasp, Keno states, "Our training does not wait, not even for the Chozien. But not to worry. I will assist in catching you up with the others. We'll begin ... at the end of the Old Age and the beginning of ours. The world was much different. We took comfort in the convenience of our basic needs: food, shelter, clothing, medicine. But this was not enough; we wanted more. So we continued to build and create new wonders. Some for good and some for destruction.

"This increased fear of every kind: fear to lose power, fear to be without, fear to be less than, fear to be avenged. The major world powers started to struggle. This tension built up over time, and it was not long before the Great Wars broke out and crippled many nations. When the survivors of those nations sought refuge with others, they were treated cruelly.

This caused them to form a network of the fallen. They are known as the Betrayers of the Peace. It was they who instigated the fragile treaties that resulted in the war which broke the world—what we call the Breaking."

Keno glances at Aitan and notices a bored look, but he continues nonetheless, "After the Breaking, chaos followed for many, many birth years. People became lost and wicked, and committed vile acts against each other. After some time, we took refuge with each other and formed societies that we now call orders, each one centering their society around their spiritual belief. This is known as our ducall.

"Because of the destructive capacity of the weapons from the Old Age, it is forbidden to create them. Eventually, the land began to reclaim itself. It took many generations for the erosion of unnatural materials created by our hands to rot and finally disappear. Even though you do not see the structures of the Old Age, their waste remains."

Keno stops and stares at the creek, then instructs, "Come and look here."

Aitan goes to the edge and peers into the water. He sees branches, twigs, stones, and other life from the forest. The water appears deep enough for fish, with a steady flow, and nothing seems out of place. Unsure of what he is looking for, he asks, "What is there?"

Keno replies with his own question, "What do you see?"

Aitan shrugs. "Water."

Keno shakes his head. "Although the water seems clear, it has an orange tint and must be cleansed. Our bodies have gained a small immunity to the iron that plagues our water sources. As spirit seekers, we remove such impurities."

Keno sits by the edge and pats the ground next to him. Aitan sits. He watches as Keno crosses his legs and clasps his hands in his lap. Suddenly, Aitan hears the water quicken. When he turns away from

Keno, he sees the water swirling in a circular pattern. Then he notices a brownish object begin to form in the center as the water swirls. The object continues to grow into what looks like a jagged rock. His eyes widen with surprise, and he looks back at Keno, who is smiling at him.

Keno explains, "What makes us spirit seekers is our ability to communicate with the *ames*, our spiritual energy. Think of a dream and being able to reach into it and control it. Now perhaps you are able to alter the subjects and their actions, or you feel the emotion of them. The Reach is the same. I see the water's *ame* and I grab hold, and in that strand, I can see the taint and massage it away from the water's *ame*. Until you have a Sighting, you will be able to do the same with your eyes shut. The stronger the Reach, the more *ames* you can manipulate."

At Aitan's frightened look, Keno assures him, "Don't worry, you cannot distort an *ame* or use the Reach to release one. Even with all the *ames* the dewan can summon, he cannot do this."

The whirlpool recedes, and they hear a plop, accompanied by a splash in the creek.

Keno relaxes the arch in his back and asks, "Why don't you grab that for me? My old bones will take a chill if I were to get wet."

Aitan immediately stands and steps into the creek. He stands there, gazing into the water, feeling the cool rush of the stream around his calves. His eyes widen, and he states, "It is … clearer." He reaches in and pulls out the lump of rock made of iron ore. He looks back at Keno in astonishment.

Keno stands, swatting at blades of grass and dusting the dry dirt from his pants. He chuckles. "That expression is always a pleasure. You will make a great seeker, Sire." After a long stretch, he sighs. "Let's head back so you can take that to the blacksmiths. I'm sure they can find some use for it."

TWENTY-SEVEN

Aitan continues his spirit seeker training over the next six moons, learning the discipline of healing, practicing self-reflection to promote Sightings, and engaging in positive social interaction. The last of the three proves the hardest for him. His struggle with social engagement makes it difficult to discern the genuineness of those he's conversing with. Even though Aitan's fellow huntsmen novices have always taken note of his congeniality, he finds it difficult to truly connect with any of the seeker novices. But even with his concerns, he daily finds some appreciation for the gregarious nature of the seeker service.

As one day's lessons and exercises come to a close, Aitan walks through the open courtyard with a couple of friends. He has a feeling of being watched. Of course, he knows his donateur is ever present—a presence that he and any within his circle have had to develop a familiarity with. But there is a fondness and curiosity to this observance. He looks around and finds the eyes of an almost forgotten attraction. Both he and she are engaged in conversation with others, but they stop mid-sentence, captivated in each other's gaze, smiling softly at the memory of a promised tutorial. Aitan's companions notice the distraction and follow his eyes, which land on the novice, Ewa.

Of course, there is no better way to forge a friendship than by taking every opportunity for a bit of ribbing. Ali and Sicily, Aitan's companions, exchange mischievous looks and give a wink.

Ali is first to remark, "Ah, you have taken notice of Ewa."

Aitan breaks their gaze and asks, "You know her?"

Sicily answers, "Of course. She stays in the novice quarters with the rest of us girls. Come, I'll introduce you."

Aitan freezes. In a mildly panicked tone, he stumbles, "What? You can't just—What if—No, we've met already."

Ali laughs. "Calm down, man! It's not like you fancy her…. Oh, you do!"

Aitan narrows his eyes at the banter and lowers his voice: "Keep it down. I don't even know her."

Sicily seems so tickled she has a hard time getting her next words out: "You can't be serious! She can't hear us this far."

Trying desperately to calm their amusement, Aitan says, "Stop laughing! She's looking over here. I'm serious!"

While Sicily attempts to catch her breath, Ali says, "You are still more huntsman than seeker. Let's put our training to the test, shall we?"

"No, please don't do—" Aitan clamps his mouth shut as Ali waves Ewa over.

"I'm going to beat you blue, Ali," Aitan says under his breath.

The trio meet Ewa halfway and greet each other.

"What has you lot so entertained?" Ewa asks with a bit of a chuckle.

Apparently, the jesting has become contagious.

Sicily gathers herself to answer. Before she does, Aitan nudges her with his elbow. She looks at him, winks, then clears her throat before she speaks: "Oh, we were just sharing a little jest on Aitan's behalf. How was training today?"

Ewa exhales in disappointment. "Today has not been the best. Well, this past moon, actually. But let's not bring down the mood with my struggles. It seems your day fares well?"

She focuses more on Aitan than the group. Ali and Sicily press their lips tightly, holding their laughter at bay while looking back and forth between Aitan and Ewa.

Aitan responds, "Oh. Uh, yes. It was good. I mean the day."

Ali and Sicily struggle to keep their bursting humor in with little squeaks.

Aitan rolls his eyes, blushing.

Ewa smiles. "Well, I do hope that lesson is still open?"

Aitan smiles and nods.

Ali smirks and says, "Oh?"

Also amused, Sicily inquires, "What lesson?"

Ewa finally addresses the comical duo: "All right, you two. You know it's not fun when only half of the party is in on the fun. I think we'll take our leave. Aitan?"

Ali and Sicily exaggerate their disappointment in their departure.

"Ah, Sicily, we aren't invited," Ali jokes.

Sicily responds in kind, "Don't worry, Ali, I'll stay with you. We have much to talk about over dinner anyway."

Ignoring his friends, Aitan leads Ewa to the huntsmen training barracks to pick up a couple bows and a quiver of arrows. He endures similar ribbing from his fellow huntsmen novices at the presence of his companion. Afterward, they go to a secluded part of the woods Aitan frequents when he trains with the other huntsmen novices. He and Ewa speak about their experiences and opinions on their seeker training along the way.

"Here," Aitan says. "We have made it. Wait a moment while I check the targets."

Aitan runs to the closest tree, where a thick, ragged patch of fur is nailed. He ensures that it is secured and isn't too full of holes. Satisfied, he returns to Ewa, who tries unsuccessfully to string her bow. He stands by, smiling at her doomed effort.

She looks up at him from her concentration and laughs while handing him the bow. "I must look like a child through your eyes."

Aitan shrugs and admits, "A bit. But it is expected, as I must seem the same to you in, oh, let's say, performing a Sighting."

She watches as Aitan slips the loop of one end of the string over the top half of the bow and then fits the loop of the other end of the string into a notch on the bottom half, locking it in place. He then holds the bow upright on the ground with the string closest to him and steps his left leg through the bow and string while using his right foot as an anchor on the bottom arm. Leaning the bow against his body for leverage, he slowly pushes the top half of the bow toward the string and moves the loop in place. He tests the tension before handing the bow to Ewa.

"Wow," Ewa says, "you made that look easy. Very easy!"

He smiles. "I have had nine birth years to learn. My da would turn me away if I could not string a bow in six counts or less."

Aitan smiles at her and winks. She laughs, surprised at his unexpected sarcasm. Aitan strings up his own bow and begins the archery lesson. He positions her in front of the target a fair distance away, typical for a novice—about the length of nine huntsmen. He turns her to face him and puts the bow in her hands.

"Hold the bow here." He takes her left hand and places it in the center of the bow. "Use only your three fingers to pull at the bowstring."

He takes her right hand and points to the three fingers, excluding the little finger and thumb, and curls them around the bowstring while nocking an arrow with her. Continuing with the posture instruction, he says, "Look at me."

She looks up at him, and they both share a laugh. The intent of his direction was to bring her head level, but their difference in height nullifies that. Realizing his error, he lowers himself. Her eyes follow his to where he tips her chin downward, bringing her head parallel to the ground.

He nods, satisfied. "There. Your head should be level with where you stand, hm?"

"Yes."

"Now hold the bow up and draw."

She does so, a bit confused.

Aitan aids her and then walks around her to inspect her form. He touches her shoulder holding the bow. "Relax here."

He waits until he feels the shoulder loosen and ease. He raises her elbow, holding the bowstring taut so that it is level with her back shoulder. He presses the center of her back until it straightens.

Seeing her shaking from the tension, he commands, "Release!"

She lets the bowstring go with an exhale. The arrow falls far short of the tree and glides on the grass.

He smiles and applauds. "Good, very good."

Ewa rubs her back shoulder and smirks. "How did I really do?"

Aitan folds his arms. "It takes many moons to develop this skill, and then many birth years to master. You don't expect to be the best archer after only one lesson?"

She giggles. "I suppose not. Again?"

He nods.

Aitan then watches her go through several simulations of drawing and releasing while holding the empty bow without actually pulling the string, breaking in at some moments to demonstrate something to her. Finally, he picks up another arrow and nocks it in place. This time, he steps behind her and places his hands over hers, helping her draw.

In the brief moment of closeness, it feels as if time slows so he can linger and enjoy admiring her. Her skin feels soft, almost unnaturally smooth. Her hair is dark brown, perhaps black, tied back into a braid, with loose wisps blowing in her face from his exhale. Her thin, almond-shaped eyes are a soft brown. At this proximity, he notices the tiny freckles across the honey-colored skin of her nose and nearest cheek—blemishes he finds alluring. Her head comes to just below his chin with her petite frame, making encircling her easy and comfortable.

Aitan whispers, "Find your hold position and anchor there. Fix your eyes on the target. Do ... not ... stray. Steady yourself.... Inhale."

He inhales with her and recognizes the soothing scent of lavender. He releases his hands from hers and steps back. He sees her wavering in her aim before she lets go of the bowstring. The arrow falls well short of the target again and sticks in the ground. Her shoulders slump in disappointment.

He reassures her, "Don't worry, you will get stronger each time. I'll show you."

Aitan picks up his bow, nocks an arrow, and draws back. His body relaxes while his focus remains intense. His back hand anchors under his chin, and his front shoulder is extended, set in place. He has the target. Just as he is about to loose his arrow, he feels a hand on his back forearm. He turns his head to look at her.

She has a somber expression while she appeals to him, "Don't. You'll hit the tree."

Aitan shrugs. "Yes, of course … so the arrow stops."

She shakes her head patiently. "Haven't you had a Sighting?"

He lowers the bow, annoyed, but considers her concern. "No, I have not. The teacher says that I am looking without seeing."

She smiles. "Ah. You are very much the huntsman. Although our service calls for seeking, it is not as if we are searching for anything."

Aitan feels even more confused.

She holds up her hand before he can say anything. "Just as you stand here before me, I do not need to *find* you. I see you along with your spirit—your *ame*. That is because it is of you."

She then points to the tree. "The tree has a spirit too. I can see its fear. I am but fifteen birth years, but I am also a four-year novice, and I am sure of what I see."

He nods, understanding her concern and her plea, but he still scratches his head, unsure of his ability to truly attain such a skill and perspective. At a recollection, he asks, "Why did you not see the *ame* when you took aim?"

She shrugs and smiles. "Not all seekers have Sightings. For those who do, there are different intensities. Some can see spirits from a great distance. Some can feel as well as see. While it is rare, there are those who can call the Sighting; yet for others, it calls to them." A brief pause and then a giggle ensues as she concludes, "Besides, I don't believe there was any threat from me hitting the target or even coming close."

They both share a hearty laugh and agree. The sun is soon to sleep, so they decide to end the lesson and make their way back to the huntsmen barracks, where Aitan returns the bows and quiver, then escorts her back to the spirit house. She thanks him for the lesson and bids him good-eve.

Before they part, she places her hand on his chest. "I know being Chozien is not the easiest of lives. As a huntsman and warrior, you anticipate and attempt to manipulate your opponent, but as seekers, we have no opponent. It is only you. Your struggle is with yourself. Remember what I say: Once you are at peace, the Great Spirit will come to you, and you will See. I hope you find your peace."

He smiles absently, speechless by the intellectual prowess of her words. She leaves while his hand covers the place her hand just vacated, feeling the evaporating warmth. She is not the only one who has learned something today.

TWENTY-EIGHT

Over the next few birth years, Aitan and Ewa develop a close friendship. Their frequent acknowledgements, playful banter, and routine updates on their progression through their seeker journey strengthen their bond.

She achieves her spirit seeker title in her seventeenth birth year. She finds her post as an apothecary. They begin to see less of each other as her service demands more of her time and as his training intensifies on honing his ability to gather *ames* around him to accomplish cleansings of varying degrees.

He continues to struggle with his inner reflection and surrender, which holds his Sighting at bay. This same year, Aitan receives his huntsman twin blades, completing his training.

Branson is a proud father as he sees his son's accomplishments, as well as those of his daughters. Kaede and Nadie have also chosen to follow in their father's service. Even the mischievous Zahn has joined the girls in huntsmen training, no doubt to continue his vexing.

Two birth years later Aitan is named spirit seeker. Aitan must balance his time hunting, building fortifications, and cleansing the streams around the spirit hold. It is his fortune that he is able to spend time at his gardien's hold, even if his visits are few and far between.

There has been an increase in Branson's household since Aitan and Malan were promoted. Branson now has his own scouts, which include Malan. Another huntsman has also joined the hold, taking to blacksmithing with his own smithy and a few apprentices. As well, the hold has also welcomed an assortment of household servants working as clothiers, masons, craftsmen, and gardeners. To Trenton's delight, the tannery has been operating for more than ten birth years.

A team of huntsmen take care of the hunting, skinning, and tanning. This has contributed to other necessities, such as soap made from the tallow. The servants' quarters have increased in size, with Reba organizing the day-to-day tasks for all, save Branson's household. That household remains under the watchful eye of Branson's loyal manservant, Gerald, while his wife, Breanne, continues to manage the kitchen.

Branson's manor now has more than a hundred kinsmen. He doesn't have his own guards, though he increased his security in other ways. Malan returned with ten warriors. They split their service between serving as guards and scouts. In order to accommodate his growing estate, Branson has had to clear more trees to make room for homes that servants wish to build as they join *ames* and move out of the servant quarters.

Since his manor is located at least a day's journey from the spirit hold, he has been building a curtain wall to surround him and those within. Since the Awakening, the sires have all been increasing their fortifications, as well as the number of patrols and scouts. And Gaylen has called for council with his sires more frequently as Aitan comes of age.

On this day at his gardien's hold, Aitan guides a large draft horse pulling a wagon of large stones. He is accompanied by his best friend, Romin, and five others also pulling loaded wagons. They are coming from a nearby limestone quarry, a two-day ride, with more stone to continue the expansion of his gardien's manor, as well as the fortifications.

Aitan and his party stop at the edge of the wall, where masons are hard at work stacking and sealing stones. He calls to Malan, who has just finished hauling some stones to the top of the wall on a sturdy ladder. Malan climbs down. At two birth years junior of Aitan's twenty, Malan's bulk has certainly increased in his chest and arms, maintaining his stocky build in comparison to Aitan's lean muscles on a taller frame. In addition, Malan has a scruffy beard and curly hair, cut short typical of a Jade warrior as opposed to Aitan's clean shave and thick, shoulder-length hair pulled back into a bun—a cross between a seeker and a huntsman's typical appearance. Not to mention Malan is covered in dirt and sweat.

"What took you so long?" Malan says. "We almost ran out of stones."

Aitan holds up his hands, feigning offense. "What do you expect? It is a four-day round trip to get them. We'll need to head back in a few days at this pace."

Malan smiles and greets his brother by clasping hands. They both stand back and look at the current work.

"It's looking good, little brother."

Malan sighs. "Yes, but there is still much to go until we are done."

Aitan laughs. "Well, you cannot finish before you start."

They move to the dwindling stone pile and start unloading the wagons.

Romin, standing the tallest of them all, asks, "I thought you would be out scouting?"

Malan responds tiredly, "Father ordered that I stay here and help with the construction. He wants me to start becoming more familiar with the daily duties of the manor."

Romin offers him some consolation: "That is good and as it should be. You are his heir, and your father trusts you with his safety, as do your kinsmen."

Malan shrugs and rubs the back of his neck. "I'm not sure about them. Some may think I am too young for such a position."

Aitan stops, breathing heavily, and says through deep breaths, "There … will always … be … opposers." He pauses to catch his breath. "It's the push and pull of nature. You will have to overcome—" Aitan stops and looks puzzled at the grinning faces looking back at him. "What?"

Romin folds his arms and shakes his head as he jests, "One wonders why you have yet to have a … um, what is it?"

With a chuckle, Malan answers, "Sighting."

Aitan rolls his eyes at the jab and does some quick playful shadowboxing with his friend and brother before they turn back to finish unloading the wagons.

A familiar voice interrupts Aitan's chore: "It is about time you returned. Malan was just about to run out of those stones."

At Malan's "I told you so" smirk and Romin's laugh, Aitan smiles fondly as Guilia walks up to them.

She has chestnut-colored hair with light-brown eyes to match. Her hair is thick, with loose curls just above her shoulders. Her skin is a soft bronze. One would think she spends her days in the sun, if not for her duties. Her days are filled under the watchful eye of Breanne, baking bread and pastries in the kitchen.

Guilia came into Branson's service five birth years ago with her mother and father and is five birth years Aitan's senior. She and her parents were free travelers, peddling their trade. Her mother is a clothier, while her father serves as a huntsman. They make the most magnificent shirts and trousers, rivaling the dewan's grandiosity. They are a great addition to the gardien's hold.

"It's good to know we were missed," Malan says, "however dutiful it is."

Aitan rolls his eyes at Malan.

"There are those who missed you simply at the sight of you," Guilia says.

Aitan clears his throat at the flirtatious tone of her comment. Changing the subject, he asks, "I see you were also duty bound, no doubt for Breanne." He nods at the small basket she carries, filled with fresh blackberries.

"Indeed. At one of the scouts' reports of your return, there is to be quite a feast prepared. This is for the dessert. Care to try one?"

She picks a single blackberry and holds it up to Aitan. At his nod, she reaches out and places the fruit in his open mouth. He closes on it, his lips grazing her fingertips as she pulls her hand away. They hold each other's gaze as he chews slowly. She smiles as she licks her own fingers seductively.

Smiling, Romin interrupts, "Well? Are they ripe? You know how particular Breanne can be with her ingredients."

Guilia giggles as Aitan casts an incredulous look at him.

"Yes, you are quite right," Guilia says. "I better hurry back. Looks like you will all have quite the appetite." Addressing Aitan, she adds, "It is good to see you back and well, Sire."

Aitan lingers for a moment as she departs, then he turns his attention back to the task of unloading the heavy stones, racing the sun's descent.

Branson, Uric, and Trenton walk the gardien's hold, inspecting the construction and discussing improvements. With Uric returning to the Huin Clan after the Beni, he does not have the additional responsibility of maintaining a manor and providing for kinsmen, so he is able to leave more frequently, which he takes liberty of doing to visit Branson and assist him with his upkeep and, more importantly, to reconnect their families.

Trenton stops at a particular location of the wall and looks around the grounds, peering at the opposite wall. He closes one eye while using his outstretched arm to align across the distance. Branson and Uric are both curious as to what Trenton peers at and proceed to mimic his one-eyed expression.

Trenton slaps the wall and states, "We should build the watchtower here and another at the far end there. That way, you will have a view of the rear *and* your front left guard. Also, the reverse on the other side."

Branson's eyes widen with disbelief, and he exclaims, "Holy shit, man! Have you lost your mind? I do not even have enough masons and servants to dedicate to the construction of the wall. I am barely keeping up as it is."

Trenton looks at him. "But, Sire, without the towers, the defense of the wall can be compromised."

Branson argues, "It is not so critical that I *must* have the towers for the wall to hold."

Before things begin to heat up, Uric clears his throat to interrupt: "Both of you have great perspectives. Let's see ... Trenton desires to ensure the safety of not only his sire, but also his family. And Branson must decide what is in the best interest of his people, as the defenses require many hands for many moons. Perhaps we can come to a compromise?"

Branson nods. "I am not saying no to the towers. After the wall has been completed, we can build something sturdy from the wood. This will give us the range without pressing my masons so hard."

Trenton opens his mouth to object, but Branson continues, "We will reinforce the towers once the masons have had their rest and tended to their service."

Trenton acquiesces, nodding.

Uric breaks the ensuing silence: "It seems the hunt is good. Your yield of leather, clothing, and meat is impressive. Trade must be good?"

Branson smiles. "Yes. I came across a huntsman and his family nearly five years ago at a border post's trading village on one of our peace campaigns with the Gold Order. They tend to frequent the northern borders near the Gold Order, as the trade there is more abundant. But I was able to convince them to come serve for the gardien of the current Chozien. The title does have its advantages. His wife is a clothier and happened to learn some of their high-quality methods in clothing-making. Look at the stitching here ... and feel the cotton on my shirt."

Uric pokes about the material and offers his compliments, even asking for fittings for himself and his family. Branson assures him that his clothier will see to them.

After an exhale more out of uncertainty than exhaustion, Uric asks, "No word from Gaylen on any unusual activities? It's been eight birth years since the Awakening."

Branson shakes his head. "I have not heard of anything outside of the council."

Uric asks, "Well, what about here? Is there nothing strange?"

Branson thinks for a moment, going over the past eight years for anything that would cause alarm. "Nothing out of the usual. All new kinsmen are questioned and watched for a long time before we let our guard down … a little."

"Anything more from your Foresight?" Uric adds.

Branson scratches his beard and shakes his head, frustrated. "I see the same thing. There is something about the glove on the hand that I keep seeing, but I can't pinpoint it. I have been trying to impress others in the vision to see if they will lead me to some conclusion. I don't know why only I see this one battle. It becomes more intense each time. Oh!"

Trenton jumps at Branson's exclamation.

"My visions tend to be very routine. But now there is a new one amid all of the chaos. A couple. Very loving and happy. I don't know what to make of it."

Uric asks, "Can you make out the faces?"

Branson shakes his head. "I have not gotten an impression on them. I just feel their passion for one another."

All three men have a silent moment, pondering various scenarios. Branson, musing about this for the first time, considers himself and Ahni first, but puts the thought away as it would be too obvious. Perhaps Gaylen and Zahrine? He isn't close enough in Gaylen's confidence to discern the feelings between the pair.

It is a mystery indeed. With no true conclusions or considerations, they retire for the evening. The men are greeted by their wives, who shoo them to the lavatories before Gerald catches their workday odor. After they freshen up, the three couples gather in Branson's great hall to enjoy a host of appetizers freshly prepared by Breanne and her kitchen. Spiced apples and pears, fresh cheeses, an assortment of breads and crackers, and a nice cider for the chill outside all fit the season and the occasion well. As this is Uric and his family's last evening at the manor, Breanne thought it fitting to send the sire off in good fashion.

Servants are clearing off the appetizers as their sons walk in, laughing and horseplaying. They rush to grab at the platters piled high with meats being carried out. In addition to Aitan, Romin, and Malan, there is also Uric's eldest son, Davin, with his wife, Aarti, who is six moons pregnant with their first child, and then Uric's only daughter, Kari. Trenton and Reba's sons are both at the spirit hold. Simi chose to serve there to be closer to his father, in admiration of his donateur's title, while Zahn trains as a huntsman's novice.

The younger generation greets each other with playful familiarity and fondness. They have just a few moments before Breanne reappears.

"My sires and siras, donateur, kinsmen, and ladies, please be seated, as your dinner is ready to be served," Breanne announces, her voice brimming with pride.

Everyone moves to their seats. Branson takes the head of table, with Ahni seated to his left and Uric to his right, followed by Uric's wife, Leesha. Reba seats herself next to Ahni, with Trenton by her side. Their children are seated sporadically.

Aitan turns to Davin and says, "Congrats, Davin! Last time I saw you it was at your wedding, and now you are expecting a babe. I wonder what it will be the next time we meet."

The friends laugh.

Davin rubs his wife's belly and responds, "It is sure to be good news!" He kisses his wife and then asks Aitan, "How is your service?"

Aitan opens his mouth to answer, but Romin beats him to it: "Ah, well, the *sire* here does not spend much of his days with us warriors. He enjoys the hunt and the ramblings of the spirit seekers. Between the two, I cannot see how he has time to even sleep."

"Hey," Davin responds to the slight directed at his service.

Aitan elbows Romin. "You would do well with some of the teachings. You wouldn't be so hot-headed and stubborn."

Romin rejects the notion. "I take that back.... You probably sleep more than the rest of us."

Again, laughter erupts.

Catching his breath, Aitan attempts to answer Davin again: "It is true, I spend my early mornings hunting. Some days, I return with a kill. And yes ... I continue to serve as seeker, cleansing our waters. I follow the creek farther each day, closing in on its source. I am able to cleanse large areas of water now. I think I could restore a lake, given the chance."

Davin seems impressed with Aitan's dedication. "Ah, it is good to see you so committed to your service. You have had a Sighting now?"

Aitan slumps his shoulders. "Unfortunately, no. I am hoping that as my strength grows with the focus needed to perform a cleansing, it will come to me."

Davin seems confused. "Have you spoken of this to any other seekers?"

Aitan swivels his eyes to Uric. He sees that Uric is well engaged with his father and donateur, so he shakes his head mildly.

Everyone notices the implied secrecy and smartens up a bit.

Kari touches Aitan's arm and asks softly, "What has you so ... distant? They are your family by service. They will understand."

Davin explains, "It is not so simple, Sister. Seeing spirits has little to do with strength. Our service is driven by our mental capacity and control over such. It is to be here ..." He taps the table to emphasize the physical presence in his explanation, then points to his head. "... while being at complete peace in that moment."

Aitan, Kari, and Romin—the latter two, even with being raised by a spirit seeker—all stare bemusedly back at Davin.

Romin snorts. "What does that even mean? We are all at *peace* now. I don't see any spirits." He looks up and down the table with great exaggeration.

Davin narrows his eyes at his younger sibling's ignorance. "That is because you are not trained, Romin. I agree with Sire Aitan: You could use some seeker training to focus that *energy* you have."

Romin brushes off the suggestion and asks Aitan, "Well, Sire, do you happen to see anyone's spirit? You are at peace now, aren't you?"

Aitan laughs while Davin interjects, "Being happy is not the same as being at peace, little brother."

Before Romin can counter, they are silenced by Breanne's loud claps.

Standing to the left of Branson, she announces the menu as servants file in with more platters of food: "Herb-roasted lamb basted in its juices; sweet carrots with ginger; peppery greens scented with oil and vinegar; a blend of crisp, seasoned beets, turnips, and squash; and warm honey bread baked with sunflower seeds. Please enjoy."

The diners wait and watch as servants place empty plates in front of them before laying out the platters of the listed food items down the center of the table. Finally, servants set empty glasses at the front left of each plate and then pour from decanters to fill each one with a bold, fruity deep-red wine.

While the diners serve themselves helpings, Breanne walks around the table, eyeing every detail of placement. Satisfied, she nods to a few remaining servants, who position themselves along the wall, waiting to attend to any request or need, and then Breanne exits the dining hall.

Family and friends dine on the carefully planned meal and remark on its expert preparation. Small talk continues in between bites and swallows.

Branson asks for a refill of wine as he reaches for another helping of the lamb.

Ahni looks to her husband, examining his state of being. She suggests with a smile, "Slow down, dear. We want you able-minded for the rest of the night. And we also don't want to empty the wine stock too soon. Best to avoid Gerald's wrath."

Branson smiles at his wife and jokes, "Ah, yes, we want to keep him happy."

Recognizing her husband's habits, Ahni inquires softly, "Is all well, Husband?"

Branson smiles questioningly at her and replies with a question of his own: "Yes..... Why do you ask?"

She taps his now filled glass with her fork. "You are heavy on the drink tonight. You only do that when you worry."

Branson gives a slightly awkward chuckle and tries to deflect, "Oh! No no, dear, I am just so happy—"

He pauses at Ahni's knowing look across her glass as she sips wine.

Branson smirks and relaxes his shoulders. "You know me well."

Placing her glass down, she asks, "What is it? We are family here."

Branson runs a hand through his hair and exhales. "Well, we were out walking the wall, and I was reminded of a vision. It is much unlike the fear and rage that I usually experience. This is one of love. I don't understand how this fits."

Leesha gushes over the vision. "Love! Well, that is a change. I wonder if it is a young couple? Maybe a wedding in the future of someone close? Romin certainly needs a companion to tame him."

Uric responds, "Sweetie, I don't think that is what the vision is saying."

Leesha huffs at her husband. "How do you know? This could be big news."

Reba chimes in, "Oh, this is so exciting! Can you describe them? No, don't tell us. I want to be surprised!"

Trenton is wide-eyed, stunned at their excitement on the idea of preordained nuptials. He tries to help temper the ladies' excitement: "I-I think that isn't what the visions foretell. It's more like images around a decisive moment in time. See …"

Trenton's voice fades out as Ahni and Branson share a silent look, both chuckling at the conversation. She caresses his hand, and he grasps hold of hers in return. She winks at him, noting that they will talk privately more before they both join the lively discourse.

At the sight of the food items, Aitan's stomach growls, beckoning him to satisfy his hunger. Once his wine is filled, he says a silent prayer to the Great Spirit and takes a ravenous approach to filling his belly. It seems Malan and Romin have the same tactic in mind.

Kari makes an observation: "I suppose the journey and the work on the wall has taken its toll."

Malan grins and covers his mouth as he says, "It certainly beats cold leftovers. We usually work until the last light and even still until the torches burn our eyes. Breanne leaves me enough, but I am too tired to eat my fill. You should visit more often, if Father will let me stop early for the day." He winks at her.

She smiles, rolls her eyes, and turns her attention back to her meal.

Romin agrees heartily, "Ah, yes! This is far better than the hard tack and jerky on the road. What do you say, Sire?" He elbows Aitan.

Aitan just nods his head, not wanting to interrupt his task at hand, which consists of biting at chunks of meat and eating mouthfuls of vegetables.

At some point, the eating slows and servants clear the table of plates, only to reset with smaller plates. Breanne enters again and reveals the dessert: apple tarte tatin with whipped cream. The servants slice into the dessert and set each triangle in the center of the smaller plates with a nice dollop of a creamy whipped topping.

Branson stops Breanne before she exits and stands to give his gratitude. "Before you go, Breanne, I'd like to give you and the kitchen my ... no, *our* compliments for the excellent meal you prepared for us. This has been a delight, and we applaud you for your efforts today and every day."

Branson begins clapping, and the others hurry out of their chairs to join him in giving the servants a standing ovation.

Breanne nods and curtsies. She bashfully accepts and, blushing, rushes the rest of the servants away so the family can complete their meal.

Husbands finish off their wives' portions, while Malan receives a second helping and Aitan and Romin fight over Kari's remaining bites. The couples take their leave, yawning their good-nights. Malan heads off to the warrior bunkhouses, choosing to sleep with his fellow warriors instead of his own room, leaving Romin and Aitan lounging by the stables not far from the servants' quarters.

Leaning over the empty hitching post, Aitan remarks, "It must be good to see your family again."

Romin takes a long stretch and joins Aitan at the post, resting his hands there rather than his elbows because of his height. He answers, smiling, "Yes. I didn't really know how much I missed them until I saw them. I do love vexing Davin. Certainly, putting his seeker demeanor to the test. I wonder if Kari has any suitors in mind or rather her eye on someone."

Aitan laughs. "Well, I think Malan is taken with your sister. I can't tell if she feels the same, though."

Romin hunches his shoulders. "I can't figure out women. First, they catch you with their eyes, and then they flirt with you … and others they fancy. Ah, well, I can't blame them too much. I find it difficult to settle on one myself."

The friends burst out in laughter. Their amusement subsiding some, Romin stoops over and picks up a piece of straw and puts it in the side of his mouth. He poses a similar question to Aitan: "What say you? I've seen you with Guilia. A lot of smiles shared between the two of you."

Aitan chuckles. "Yes, we share what time I have when I am here. She asks more of me. I look for ways to give her these things."

Romin waves a hand at the infatuation. "Yeah, yeah, but what about Ewa? You two are close. I thought for sure she would be at your side. She's skilled in medicines and tonics of the like."

Aitan is caught off guard. "Ewa? No, that was a long time ago. And she is soon to join *ames* with some warrior. Perhaps they are the couple my father spoke about in his visions."

At Romin's confused look, Aitan clarifies, "I overheard them speaking about it at dinner."

Just then, Romin jumps up and slaps Aitan in the arm.

Aitan starts, "What was that?"

He stops at Romin's smile and follows his gaze to the servants' quarters, where a maid is out hanging linens. A bit late in the night, though not uncommon. She is constantly glancing their way and smiling coyly while lingering over the laundry.

Romin straightens to his full height and claps Aitan on the shoulder. "Well, my friend, it is time I said good night. I'll see you in the morning, yes?"

Without waiting for a reply, Romin sets a fast pace toward the inviting lily.

Aitan stretches and, with a smile, says, "You can come out now."

He hears rustling in the straw behind him. Soon a hand reaches up and touches his left shoulder softly, though with pressure to ease him around. It is Guilia. He wraps his arms around her in tight squeeze, holding her there while she lays her head against his chest with her arms about his waist. He lays his cheek on the crown of her head, breathing in deeply the scent of frankincense and orange.

She looks up at him with a playful smirk. "It seems I have to compete for your interest."

Aitan rolls his eyes. "Romin has a big head. Because he can't settle his *ame*, he believes all others must be the same. I only have eyes for you."

She giggles and then, more fondly, says, "It is good to see you again. I am selfish to want to see you more and more."

"And I you." He kisses her softly.

"Will you be staying long? You only just returned."

He shakes his head. "I leave tomorrow with the others."

She pushes herself out of his embrace and folds her arms, pouting. "How long will it be before you return this time?"

Aitan tries to reach for her, but she dodges. He exhales and explains, "I have a duty to the Jade Order. As the Chozien, it is best that I serve at the spirit hold."

"But Malan has come home, and your father travels to the spirit hold sometimes and returns to his wife no more than five nights later. Why can you not do this?"

"Malan is not Chozien. My father's duties are to his manor; he is not needed daily at the spirit hold. He must now protect all of you. It is different. You know this, Guilia."

She relents and looks up in the night sky. "Our time is counted by the dark with the twinkling of the stars to keep our secret. I wonder how long I will have you before the stars look over you with another. Someone with … a title, maybe?"

Aitan scoffs.

Guilia stares at him. "I'm serious, Aitan. Us … what we are doing … it doesn't speak of longevity. Just wistful moments for a hopeless future."

Aitan takes her in his arms again to console her. "All my thoughts are of you. Of us. Everything I do here and at the spirit hold is to be a worthy life partner to you. I will speak with my mother. It is not said I cannot have a wife without a title. I will tell her the truth … that I love you."

At the last statement, she stiffens. He closes his eyes, cringing, thinking he may have made a fool of himself. Perhaps he'd gone too far.

He attempts to somehow recant his profession without being obvious. "I mean … Well …"

She steps back and looks up into his eyes. She smiles and then turns, leading him by the hand to the semi-bustling servants' quarters. She runs in and grabs a few blankets and a lantern. When she returns, they stop briefly at the laundry lines, then run off a short ways. Aitan takes one of the blankets from her and lays it on the ground while Guilia lights the lantern so that it is but a smoldering ember. He lies down on the blanket on his side, perched up on his elbow. She joins him and covers them with the blanket.

Just as she settles, he reaches out to caress her cheek and leans in for a kiss. She does not resist and welcomes his lips. Their kiss turns passionate as he wraps his arms around her waist, securing her while he lies her on her back. She clutches the back of his head, bringing him closer to her. He places kisses along her cheek, then her chin and down the side of the tender flesh of her neck. She raises his shirt, which he finishes by removing it over his head. She traces her fingers down his chest, stopping just at his waistband near his belly button, feeling his arousal.

He in turn runs his hand down the length of her body, stopping to caress her breasts, dragging his hand lightly down the middle of her belly. He raises her skirt above her hips and begins to caress her intimately with his fingers. He smiles as she arches into him from the sensation and presses her lips to his in a deep kiss, their tongues dancing with each other. Their bodies move sensually, simulating the love act.

As he feels her excitement grow through her moans and judging by the wetness covering his fingers, he assumes she is ready. He loosens the ties of his pants and pushes them low enough. She opens for him, and he settles in between her legs naturally.

In this moment, they stop and gaze at each other, anticipating the promise of euphoria. She takes him in her hand and guides him to enter her. He lifts up, braces himself, and slowly eases into her. He groans at the warmth and tightness. He moves his hips slowly at first and then picks up speed as the pleasure from each stroke intensifies. He feels her meeting him at each one in a carefully orchestrated symphony. She quickens her pace and receives him with wild aggression. She clutches his shoulders and arches into him as she exhales her release, accompanied by gratifying moans.

This only excites him more, and he continues his pursuit, plunging himself deeper until he stiffens even more, releasing all but his *ame* into her. He collapses on top of her, his head nestled between her breasts, both of them panting with pleasant exhaustion.

She tenderly rubs the hair out of his face and whispers, "Peace be with you, my love."

TWENTY-NINE

The following day, Uric and Leesha, along with Davin and his wife, and Kari, say their goodbyes and prepare to make their way back to their clan—not before Uric and Leesha are fitted by Branson's clothier for their new garments, of course. Malan takes the reins from one of the grooms holding Kari's horse while she lifts herself up. Romin wishes his parents well and clasps hands with his brother.

Branson promises to visit once their fortifications are nearly complete, with Uric and Leesha excitedly accepting. Branson sends four warriors, which include Malan, to escort them a portion of their journey, outside of his scouts' range and just before entering the Huin Clan territory.

Uric accepts out of respect, though reminding his fellow Bonne Ame that his skill with calling the natural elements has improved significantly due to his training with Keno during his very infrequent visits to the spirit hold. As well, his son, Davin, and daughter, Kari, have gone through combat training, albeit from the Huin Clan.

Malan leads the party out with a chipper smile. As the gate closes behind them, Branson kisses Ahni and heads to the pasture to check on the farmhands and animals. Aitan and Romin start back to the house to pack their things to be on their way back to the spirit hold.

"Aitan! I need your help sorting a few dried herbs," Ahni calls out to her son.

Aitan stops and shrugs. "Sure, Ma," he says, then to Romin, "I'll catch up with you at the stables."

On Aitan and Ahni's walk to the sira's coveted drying room that his father built for her in their first year of marriage, she smiles softly and looks up at him.

Aitan knows his mother well. She is quiet and patient. She can be fun, but she can also be stern. Over his birth years, he has come to know her many looks, and this one is as if she is peering into his conscience. He does not yet know how she is able to do that and still maintain a kind smile.

"You've been spending your spare time well?" she asks.

He coughs at the allusion to his relationship with Guilia.

He answers, "Yes, I find time to enjoy life as Chozien."

She responds with sarcasm, "Yes ... I am sure you are in no doubt of fair company."

They find a tree commonly used for shade. They sit on a well-crafted bench, though worn over the years.

She smiles slyly. "I see you have taken a liking to our bread-maker."

Aitan laughs out loud. "Nothing gets by you here. Who told you? I bet it was Gerald. He has his nose in everything."

She nudges him with her shoulder. "I'm your mother; I have eyes. And ... yes, Gerald did mention it to me."

Aitan smiles. "What do you think of her?"

Ahni shrugs and answers, "She is quiet. I have not spoken with her much. Her parents bring a great trade to our home. Word has spread about their clothing skills."

Aitan presses her: "But what of Guilia?"

His mother busies herself with brushing nonexistent dust from her lap while she gathers her thoughts. "I am not sure. The family is a mystery. I mean, they have been here for five birth years. Breanne tells me she does well in the kitchen and doesn't cause trouble. Reba says she gets along with the other servants and asks to contribute more than her share."

Aitan smiles. "This is good, then. Why do you hesitate? Please, I might be a spirit seeker, but I still need help unraveling women's thoughts."

His mother looks away, and as she goes on, her voice hints at unease: "It just seems I am the only one of us who is interested in knowing her. I ask around about her, but I do not hear the same inquiries from her of me."

Aitan laughs and pulls his mother in and squeezes her shoulders. "Oh, come now. You are a sira. I can imagine the anxiety she must feel to approach you or even the suspicion that would arise of someone asking too many questions. But I will mention this to her so she is more at ease in your presence."

She squeezes her son's cheek and asks, "She makes you happy?"

He replies confidently and softly, "Yes. Very."

Satisfied, she stands. "Good, then. Come now, let's get you packed and off to the spirit hold. I don't want you and Romin traveling too late."

"Why is it that you come to me now, at this hour? You risk much meeting me here," hisses a man crouching low and covered in the shadow

of the night, accompanied with the odor of several moons' worth of uncleanliness.

The concealed figure uses her cloak to cover her nose and sneers back, "There is little risk. No one would come this close to the stench. Besides, I am known to venture outside the wall at this time. The scout over here does not come this far. But if you keep up your grumbling, it may very well become a risk."

The hermit waves away the concern. "What is it, woman?"

She reports, "It is time. He is vulnerable now. Well smitten with the baking girl."

The hermit clicks his tongue. "This is nothing new."

The woman pleads in a high whisper, "What more do you need? You have the timing of the scouts, the routine of the servants, and now a distraction to lure him out. Even more, the Bonne Ame is having visions of the entangled pair. Set the play in motion."

"Ah, that is something. You might have led with that! I will pass along the message. You will know the time."

The woman walks away, smiling. Soon she will be free of this wretched order with all their incessant words of peace. How naïve the notion. There will never be peace; only the riches of the world will drive the trade. Whoever controls the trade controls the orders. Thinking of her reward, she reaches up to pull her hood down over her face, revealing finely stitched black gloves with golden thread.

Some moons later, Branson sits outside his home, looking over his manor. It is still yet to dawn. He's become accustomed to starting his days later now that he has his own huntsmen, though rising in the early morning is a habit not yet broken. Even so, it is not his routine that has him up so early; his spirit is unsettled. He reflects on a conversation he and Ahni had the last night Uric and his family visited:

"Well, are you going to tell me?" Ahni asked, placing her hands on her hips.

Branson feigned fatigue and unconcern. "Oh, it's nothing. I've just had a tiresome day."

She furrowed her brow. "Are you forgetting that you mentioned the vision at the dinner table? What is going on? Since when can you not share your troubles with me?"

He rolled his eyes and exhaled. "Really, I do not want to trouble you. I will figure it out; I just need to think about it."

Ahni pressed him: "I did not go into this marriage lightly. I knew what would be asked of you … and of me as your life partner. You have your private counsel with the sires and Gaylen. I can understand that. But this? These are *your* thoughts?"

Branson shook his head and sat down on their bed to explain. "Love, these are not *my* thoughts. They are … someone else's. They have meaning to them. I can't say if I am to save them or to seek them or to wait for them. There is always a message in the vision, but … seeing it is difficult."

Ahni joined him on the bed and grasped his hand, interlocking their fingers. "Look at me, Mari."

He turned to look at her and smiled at her affectionate reference to him.

"We are bound. Allow me to help. Women can see many more things than men."

He chuckled and relented. He told her about the warrior dying, the Bloodstone assailant, the grieving wife, and the people fleeing.

She sat back, contemplating. Finally, a thought came. She asked, "Can you tell where they are from?"

He nodded. "Certainly. They are of the Jade Order."

She shook her head. "No, which *clan*?"

He cocked his head to the side, thinking on this for the first time. "It would be the Rain Clan. Yes. They have the distinctive gold in their clothing." Before he could celebrate, he wondered aloud, "Why so far north?"

Ahni shrugged. "Perhaps the warrior died saving them?"

Branson shook his head, recalling the vision and using his wife's suggestion to identify the clan. "No, he is from the Zin Clan.... How is it that the Bloodstone make it so far into our borders?"

Ahni smiled, stood up tiredly, and kissed him softly on the cheek. "Now, Mari, that is for you to know."

While she undressed, he offered up another quandary: "There is a new vision—one with a couple."

Ahni immediately stopped and glanced over her shoulder. "Yes? What of them?"

He shrugged his shoulders in unabashed bewilderment. "I've not a clue."

Ahni faced him. "You have not seen them?"

He sighed. "I do not purposely impress everyone in every vision. It clouds my emotions. I like to keep myself separate from them."

Ahni nodded slowly, wondering, and then, more encouraging, said, "Well, I'm sure there is plenty to think on. Let's leave this for tomorrow and promise me that only I will be in your thoughts tonight."

He smiled slyly. "On one condition."

She squealed as he chased her around the room, tickling her before they turned in.

And now, as he sits outside, Branson sees his wife come through a side door in the wall, with her dark-green cloak drawn tight against the crisp air. He's noticed that she's been on early-morning walks lately. He meets her and takes her by the elbow, joining her on the way back to the house.

"Well, my love, what are you up to?" He smiles fondly.

She pulls back her cloak and reveals a bundle of eucalyptus leaves.

He takes them from her. "You can just send one of the servants out for these."

She laughs. "I'm well aware. With the kids all grown up and a husband who does not sleep past dawn, I've had to find use for my time. Besides, I do love the solitude. I can see the appeal of the early mornings for you huntsmen."

He snorts. "Well, it certainly isn't for leisure. I can assure you there is more effort involved."

She looks at him, exaggerating offense. "Hey! Gathering these herbs is not a trivial task. Our seekers have been kind enough to show me the art of healing."

Branson laughs at their play. He escorts her to their house, where he parts, noting that he plans to check with the clothier on how the new clothes for Uric and Leesha are coming along. He waits until the day gets going with all the bustle of routine before he makes his way to a small cottage near the tannery. He knocks on the door and waits for an answer before he steps in.

The interior of the cottage is tight, with raw hides and fabrics in an array of colors, partially finished apparel, and various spools of thread strewn about. A fire warms the inside. The mistress of the home looks to be readying for a journey; he notices her travel attire as she stacks wrapped parcels in crates.

"Be quick, now," she says without turning to see who has come in. "I must be off before midday."

Branson clears his throat at her brisk manner and preoccupied attention.

She looks over her shoulder and does a double take. Blushing, the clothier faces Branson and lowers her eyes. "Oh, namaste, Sire. I had no idea it was ... How can I help you?"

Branson walks deeper into the cottage and closes the door behind him. He smiles unemotionally. "I have come by to check on how the clothing for Sire Uric and his family fares."

She jumps, remembering. "Oh! Yes, I have it here!" She rushes from pile to pile, searching for the promised garments.

Branson shifts and presses his lips together, annoyed with the clutter and disorganization of the place, especially of items meant for a sire and his family. To calm his rising irritation, he turns to wandering about the cottage, picking up scraps of rough hide to more refined and softer material. He passes over several boots that are either in the process of being mended or waiting their turn. He sees the same for various clothing such as dresses, cloaks, slippers, belts, and pants. He is amazed at the amount of work a clothier generates.

His curious eyes bring him to the articles his clothier was packing as he arrived. He sees the typical travel items: loaves of bread and jerky wrapped in a cloth, skins of water, and what looks to be several finished pieces of clothing. He looks over them, admiring the fine needlework and then stops cold. His hand visibly shakes as he slides the mass of clothes aside. He blinks several times to ensure his eyes do not betray him. Yes, the color is spot on, black as the moonless night. He picks up the objects that has captured his attention and holds them close. The stitching is done with gold thread. He examines them more and notices that they are meant for a woman. He turns them over and over in his hand as the feeling of familiarity grows.

These are the gloves that have plagued his visions over the years.

"Ah, yes! Here they are. I have the pattern complete, though I am yet to select the fabric. It should be soft yet warm, no? I have thought of sheep's wool but that could be … Sire? Is there something wrong?"

At his clothier's voice, Branson turns to face her, his eyes narrowed in a deathly glare. Once she pauses her incessant ramblings, he raises the gloves for her to see.

The clothier responds, confused. "Yes?"

He walks to her. "Why do you have these?"

She steps back, bumping into the table behind her, "S-S-Sire, I am not sure what you are asking?"

He stands over her. "It is a simple question. The answer is just as simple."

A man's voice behind him calls out: "They belong to Sira Ahni. She brought them here to be mended."

Branson whips around to see the woman's husband and shouts, "You lie! I know my wife. She does not own anything black!"

A frightened voice from behind beseeches him: "It is true, Sire! I have not seen such of any kind. She brought them to me and ordered that I return them to her once I had completed them."

He swivels his eyes to the clothier and says, "If you are lying, I will personally return and cut out your tongue."

The threat lingers after he storms out of the cottage with the gloves in hand.

CHAPTER
THIRTY

Ahni stands in the kitchen, grounding up her freshly plucked eucalyptus leaves to prepare a soothing salve that is popular in the cold season. She hears the front door open and close sharply. She calls out, "Is that you, dear?"

Ahni hears no immediate reply, only footsteps—slow and deliberate. When they come to a stop in the kitchen, she wipes her hands on her apron and turns to discover her husband's glare. She smirks and says, "It seems the clothes for Uric and his family weren't to your liking."

Branson responds in a cold, emotionless tone, "You mistake my expression for disappointment."

She crooks an eyebrow. "Oh? Then what is it I am looking at?"

Branson inhales sharply at the woman's ease in keeping up the charade. He closes his eyes, asking the Great Spirit to contain his patience a moment longer, then snarls, "How long were you planning on continuing this ... deception? You had my children, woman."

Ahni shakes her head, completely lost. "Are you well, love?"

Even the prayers to the Great Spirit can no longer contain Branson's patience. "Love? Is this what you call love?" Branson throws the gloves on the table with a loud smack.

Jumping at his outburst, she picks up the gloves.

"Do you recognize them?"

She looks at him, blinking in awe. "They are the gloves from your vision. Where did you find them?"

"Oh, please! They are yours! It has been your hand in my vision. I've been blinded to recognize them as my own wife's!"

Finally, gaining understanding of his peculiar behavior and the accusation, she shouts, "What? You cannot be serious! I have not seen these until now. How dare you accuse me of this?" She slaps the gloves back on the table.

They stare at each other silently for a moment before Branson shakes his head in disbelief. "You leave me no choice. Guards!"

Two men enter the house, one with a rope in his hands. Branson steps to the side to allow them access to his wife. Ahni does not struggle but stares in wide-eyed incredulity at her husband's turned head.

"Take her to the stables in an empty stall. Keep a guard on her at all times."

Ahni does not resist as the guards bind her hands. While being led away, she says, "Branson, I have been at your side for over twenty birth years. I am the mother of our children and the sira of our land. When could I find the time to betray not only the Jade but *you*. Look at me!"

Branson turns his back to her and barks, "Gag her if she continues with her lies!"

Once she has been removed from the house, there is silence, save the nervous shuffling of the servants receding into other parts of the home, free from their sire's fury.

The actions and comprehension of the new discovery fills Branson's years of honed patience to capacity. He feels his breath catch in his throat and his chest tighten. He clutches his shirt as his eyes well with tears and his breathing turns into uncontrollable gasps. Realizing his composure is slipping, he grips the edge of the table and turns it over. The sound of the items on it shattering against the floor and wall reflects the feeling of his heart.

His screams of anger and hurt echo throughout the house. His outburst continues as he beats at the walls, feeling the sting of the wood as it returns his blows with equal power, taunting his bones to break. He rips away the hanging herbs she was using to make her soothing salve. How ironic: Her delicate hands with their healing touch could also carry the poison of a viper slowly injecting its venom into their prey. He runs his hands through his hair over and over, replaying countless moments with his wife. Was their entire time together a lie? How could he have been so gullible?

Soon his rage and rants cripple him as he slumps to the floor, a ball of pain, rejection, and sorrow. His body weakens such that he only has the strength to pour out tears from reddened eyes. He feels familiar hands wrap around him. He folds into the embrace, welcoming the warmth. Breanne slowly rocks Branson and rubs his head as he sobs into her lap until exhaustion forces his eyes closed into a miserable slumber.

Aitan stands in the spirit hold's butchery, breaking down a freshly skinned moose. He is just starting to separate the beast into its primals when he hears a commotion in the market. He wipes his bloodstained hands on his apron and rushes toward the noise. He finds a mass of people gathering outside of every vendor, inn, and home, crowding the streets. He looks ahead and sees a few men and women racing toward Gaylen's house. He overhears a few conversations.

One young woman with frightened eyes speaks to another: "It can't be true! Why don't they leave us in peace?"

An elder tradesman, guarding his goods from potential thieves, says confidently, "We are in the spirit hold; they will not make it this far."

Another man responds to him, seemingly a retired warrior: "You were not at the battles the last time the Onyx and Bloodstone attacked. We lost many and would have lost more without our allies. Best I prepare my sword again."

A hand touches Aitan's shoulder from behind, and then he feels himself pulled back and away from the crowd. He is jerked around and sees his donateur, Trenton.

Shouting to be heard over the bustling around him, Aitan asks, "What is it?"

Trenton nods in the direction of the riders. "Those are lires from the other clans. It could be that one of the rival orders has been sighted."

Aitan pulls his apron over his head and asks, "Where? Which clan? Why haven't we been given orders yet?"

Trenton places his hands on Aitan's shoulders to calm him. "Calm down, Sire. I'm sure we will know something soon."

Aitan starts to rebut, but before he can say anything, Trenton continues, "Remember your seeker exercises. Go back to your huntsman service. I will come fetch you if needed."

Aitan reluctantly gives in and returns to his butchering, frowning. He finishes processing the beast, with some cut into strips for jerky and cubes for stews, or chopped coarsely to be packed for sausages and smoked, while the tender muscles become steaks and rib racks. Aitan delivers the various prepared cuts of meat to the spirit house and warrior bunkhouses, as provided by the dewan for their service. He then delivers them to the innkeepers, who came by earlier for trade. His final delivery of the day goes to Gaylen's house. He heads around back to the kitchen, but before he turns the corner of the house, he hears some servants discussing the day's events and stops to listen.

"Have we sent for our allies yet?" a male servant asks.

"I should hope so. We will need the Amethyst and Rhodonite Orders by our side," answers another male voice.

"It is true, then! The Onyx move with the Gold, Azurite, and Bloodstone Orders against us!" squeals a young female servant.

Just then, Aitan feels a jab in the back of his shoulder. He jumps and spins around. Trenton puts a finger to his lips, signaling for Aitan to not make a sound. Aitan rolls his eyes, annoyed that he was so enthralled in the gossip that he didn't hear his donateur approach. Trenton's expression shows earnest alarm.

Aitan silently mouths, *"What?"*

"Deliver your meat quickly. We leave now to your father's manor. Quickly, Sire," Trenton urges in a heightened whisper.

Aitan nods and rushes forward to drop the goods off. When he turns the corner, the servants that he was eavesdropping on quickly hush each other.

As he passes, they greet him in unison, "Good eve, Sire."

When Aitan returns from the kitchen empty-handed, the servants are out of sight. Trenton tosses Aitan his travel satchel, and they rush to the stables, where the groom has their horses waiting. With dusk fast approaching, they set a hasty pace. They ride hard until the horizon streaks a deep purple and orange.

Trenton calls for a stop. He guides them just off the road to a small spot known to him. He instructs Aitan to clear the area and tend the horses while he collects bark and dried twigs. Soon Trenton starts a fire using his flint rock and knife. He adds more wood until the fire burns bright.

Aitan welcomes the warmth, as the nights have become colder; the White Rain season is upon them. He wraps his thick and heavy cloak around himself, finding comfort in its warmth. He can tell that Trenton is tense by his brisk behavior.

Aitan asks, "Should the fire be so big? We're out in the open."

Trenton nods. "We are still within the vision of the dewan's scouts. They know we are here. Just the beasts that roam will keep us company."

Aitan finally asks about the sudden departure: "What has happened?"

Trenton shrugs his shoulders. "I do not know. Shortly after you left to finish your deliveries, I received a message from your father. 'Bring the sun before it sleeps.'"

At Aitan's confused look, Trenton explains, "It is our code to return to the manor quickly. You are the sun. What comes after that tells me the meaning. This message is meant for a threat to the Chozien's life."

Aitan inhales sharply and looks around. "*Ames* be merciful! Might we have come with an escort man?"

Trenton responds firmly and slowly, "Lower ... your ... voice, Sire." Then he swivels his eyes to either side of him before he reaffirms, "I told you that we are within the boundary of the dewan's scouts."

Aitan nods his head, understanding the hint. He declines the jerky and soft bread that Trenton offers, having lost his appetite. He lies down on his bedroll and stares into the fire. He remembers feeling helpless and annoyed at the constant shielding. How will he ever shift the balance bespoken of the Chozien when others always coddle him? Exhaustion begins to set in as he settles down. It is not long before his eyes grow heavy and he falls asleep.

Late in the evening, his self-control once more intact, Branson makes his way to the stables. After awakening on the kitchen floor mid-morning, he sent his lire to the spirit hold with all speed to deliver a coded message to the donateur. Branson expects Trenton and Aitan to ride hard and arrive sometime the next morning.

Inside the stable, Branson nods at the guard, who greets his sire and takes his leave a short distance away, just out of earshot. Branson carries with him a lush fur blanket. He stops just on the other side of the wall separating the last two stalls.

"I know you are there, Branson."

He closes his eyes and grits his teeth as his heart welcomes the sound of Ahni's voice and the pride he feels at her ability to recognize his approach. He shakes away the sentimental feelings and hardens his face as he turns the corner. He sees her huddled in the far right corner of the stall, likely to avoid the wind draft. She has been given a light blanket, now wrapped tightly around her. She also gathered the straw around her to further insulate her body heat. Despite her efforts, she still shivers. Her hands and ankles have been tied to a longer rope that is knotted to one of the stall posts to allow her some movement.

He enters the stall silently and checks her restraints. He notes they are loose enough to provide some level of comfort, though secured with a bowline knot. He grunts at the contradiction of the intended compassion.

Ahni takes his reaction as disappointment at his guards' relief in her confinement. She scoffs and rolls her eyes. "There is some sense of disbelief in my guilt. No matter, the restraints are not necessary; I am not running. This is my home."

He curls his lip up in a half smile and tosses the blanket at her as he stands there. She catches it and quickly covers herself with it, exhaling at its warmth. She thanks him and again he grunts in reply.

Amazed at his continued skepticism, she looks away and laughs. "For a huntsman, I would have expected you to need more convincing."

He folds his arms and responds in kind, "For a captive spy so close to the Chozien, I would have thought you would be more careful."

Ahni throws off the heavier blanket and exclaims, "Yes! On that we agree!" And then, already noticing the absent warmth, she gathers back the blanket. She exhales and rests her head back against the barn wall. "When do I leave for the spirit hold?"

"You would be well on your way as we speak … if I had sent word."

She eyes him. "What? Why haven't you—" She stops mid-sentence, and her eyes widen with understanding. "You question my guilt."

Branson squats down close to his wife, his mouth set in a tight line before he says, "I'll admit my first reaction was quite … dramatic."

She clicks her tongue at his understatement.

He clears his throat, then continues, "I sat alone in our bedroom, sulking and berating myself to no end. I had already called for my fastest rider to send word to Gaylen. While I waited, I could not understand why something felt … amiss. I thought perhaps my feelings for you caused me doubt. But, no, it was the gloves. They were so *striking*. Beautifully made. So I went through your clothes … all of them. You do not have anything in your possession that resembles the same quality, save the one dress I gifted you. Then I thought back to the beautiful glass trinket Trenton gave you all those birth years ago."

He laughs in recollection. "You are so clumsy, always dropping it or forgetting where it is. I'm surprised it hasn't shattered into pieces by now. Tell me, do you know where it is now?"

She scrunches her brow and searches her memory until she finally shrugs. "I have no idea."

He smiles and touches her leg through the blanket. He whispers, "Exactly! It is of no matter to you. Even with an experienced clothier here, you still do not care for refined garments. But that is not all. This revelation led me to another: The thread in the gloves is of the purest gold. Even our brethren of the Rain Clan do not have gold threading so pure. The Gold Order saves this for their own. The betrayer is of the Gold Order."

Ahni sighs her relief. "Well, if the gloves do not belong to me, whose are they?"

At Branson's silence, she says, "Branson, *where* did you find them?"

He opens his mouth in shocked silence and falls back to sit on the straw, blinking his eyes.

"Branson? Mari? What is it?"

Snapping back, he moves to embrace her tightly and then kisses her soundly. "Forgive me, my love. I will have you released, but I need you to stay here for a moment longer."

Ahni calls after him as he rushes out of the barn.

He gives the order to his guard that no one is to leave the manor.

Malan joins him, still stinging from the imprisonment of his mother. Branson explains to his son what has happened and for him to remain vigilant, as the spy still lurks among them. Just as they begin planning how to capture the spy, a warrior from the wall announces a rider. Branson and Malan race to the front gate to meet the rider. Malan grabs hold of the horse's reins to steady it.

Branson asks, "What is it? What has you traveling in the dark of night?"

The rider, a lire from the Zin Clan, recites, "The Gold and Bloodstone Orders move on the Jade from the west, and the Azurite from the east. Make ready for war."

Father and son look at each other with stunned alarm. Branson offers the rider hospitality for the night, but she declines as she must continue on to the spirit hold. He nods, gives her a fresh horse, and sends her off with some additional food, as he knows she must make camp before she reaches the spirit hold, if only briefly. The dark has a way of bringing out the fatigue in everyone.

As such, with Branson's order that no one is to leave and that his wife remain guarded, he tells his son to retire for the night. Malan argues that his mother be released from her confinement. His father advises him that they must keep up pretenses so as to not alarm the betrayer. He further assures his son that the spy will pay for this transgression by suffering his mother's ire.

"Sire? Sire? It is time to return to your father," Trenton says, shaking Aitan awake.

Aitan rubs his eyes and stretches with a yawn. He flutters his eyes open to the early dawn, with the sun just peeking over the horizon and a slight amber glow in the sky. Trenton sets day-old bread with jerky next to Aitan on his bedroll while he gets the horses ready. Aitan gulps down his coarse breakfast and has his bedding rolled up by the time Trenton returns to stamp out the dwindling fire.

They set a steady but hurried pace. The sun has broken the tree line as they enter through the gates of the manor. Servants rush to take their horses as they dismount and make their way to the Bonne Ame's house. They rush through the door to see Branson, Malan, and a few other warriors standing around the table in the dining hall.

Branson turns at the barrage and calls them over.

Aitan says, "Da! Have you heard? The Bloodstone, Gold, Azurite, and Onyx move on us."

Branson says, "A lire came to the spirit hold and word spread." Then he quirks an eyebrow. "But the lire said nothing of the Onyx. They move as well?"

Trenton shrugs. "This is what was being spoken among the people and servants. I did not hear from the lires."

Malan and the other warriors begin to all speak at once with bold declarations of war plans.

Branson silences them with, "Be still!" Once all have quieted, he states, "This is meant to distract and split our defenses. They will attack, but it will be after our reaction to this ploy. Our allies have undoubtedly been informed and will send aid. We have something more at hand this moment."

Aitan exclaims, "What could be more pressing than war with four orders?"

Malan comes to stand before his brother and, with a hand on his shoulder, says calmly, "Mother has been imprisoned."

"What?" Aitan shouts, then shoves his brother away and turns to his father. "What does he mean?"

Branson raises his hands to calm him, and before he explains things to Aitan, he cuts his eyes at his younger son for his callous manner in approaching a delicate topic. "Not to worry, Aitan. She plays an important role to keep a spy unaware. We have found the gloves from my visions—the betrayer."

With a mock smile, Trenton says, "Oh now, this is a light in the bleak ... cold ... dark."

Branson rolls his eyes at Trenton's ill-timed humor. He continues, "I have given the order that no one is to leave. No one knows about the spy save us here."

Aitan's breath catches, and he asks, "Father, what of Guilia? Is she about?"

Knowing the sensitivity of the maze of lies and intrigue, Branson exhales and answers, "Before I gave the order for all to stay at the site, she had left with others to the Rhyne Clan for trade."

Aitan's eyes grow wide and frenzied as he turns to leave. "Are you mad? She is heading straight into the Azurite attack!"

Trenton holds Aitan at bay without too much trouble.

Choosing not to reveal much of his discovery of the spy, Branson addresses his son: "Aitan! Come now, you are Chozien. You cannot be so reckless. You think you can just leave and chase after one person?"

"What?" Aitan shakes his head at his father's disregard of Guilia's well-being. "Is this what it means to be a sire—to leave his own people to the slaughter?"

Branson slams his hand on the table. The room grows quiet again.

Branson moves slowly to stand in front of Aitan. His voice is steady and cautious: "*Boy!* You had better watch your words to me. The Rhyne scouts will find them and turn them away. Do you think a sire would allow more kinsmen into their hold with a war hanging in the balance? ... Hmmm, I'll have to let High Warrior Randol know the Chozien needs lessons in the state of war. Enough playing seeker for you, my boy."

Trenton clears his throat and interrupts, "Sire, we've just arrived and the dust is yet to settle from travel. Allow us some time to recover?"

Branson nods, his eyes not leaving Aitan as Trenton ushers the young man out of the house.

They walk out into the chill of the early dawn. Trenton throws his arm around his charge's shoulders, offering a bit of comfort. He guides him to the manor's well.

Trenton leans his hip against the base of the well while Aitan raises up a bucket. He observes as Aitan pulls the bucket out of the shaft, reaches in, and splashes water over his face. He uses his shirt to dry his face, only to leave streaks of wet dust. Trenton chuckles.

Aitan notices his donateur's amusement and makes a flippant remark: "I'm sure this is all funny to you. Your wife and children are safe under the care of my father and the spirit hold."

Trenton sucks air through his teeth before he replies cheekily, "Ouch! You wound me with your words. It is not I who has bound you here." He stands upright, grabs hold of the bucket, and scoops a face full of water, then pulls out a clean rag from his satchel to wipe away the grime. "A smart kinsman in his sire's service knows when to speak and when to listen."

Aitan starts to object, but Trenton continues, "This is the time to listen."

He waits for Aitan to relent, which he does by folding his arms and frowning.

"Your birth was foreseen by the Great Spirit, and for that, you have been blessed to alter the lives around you. Your father has been promoted to a rank that rivals the other clan leaders. This puts him as a direct threat in contention to make a claim as the next dewan. It does not matter whether he desires this or not; it is just so.

"With his rise in rank comes certain gains. He was gifted this land, and many flocked to be in the service of a Bonne Ame. Yet again, the pressure stacks as a sire with land, and people must provide opportunities for trade in order to flourish and maintain ... well, life."

He pauses to gauge Aitan's reaction, who seems unmoved. Trenton shakes his head. "You are spoiled. You are blind to the people around you, and your title affords you the comfort of what many will only dream of in their lifetime—*if*, after their day's service or trade is complete, there is even time to dream. You have a fresh meal each night, even at the spirit hold. You can choose to not bring a kill in or sleep during your watch or even be lazy during your trainings and you will still eat the same and sleep well.

"A baker cannot scorch a fresh batch of bread or sweets, a smith cannot forge a blade with cracks, nor can a warrior lose his wits while on duty. Each of those faults can cost a day's worth of time, the value of their goods, or an *ame*. You have not known battle. You have not made decisions that can lead to the deaths of many. Perhaps the Bonne Ame is right: You would do well to spend more time studying the strategies of battle and the economy. I'll make sure to pass along the order to each of your services."

Aitan slumps his shoulders and rubs his chin as he heaves a sigh. "It is not that I do not *appreciate* the benefits of the Chozien. I cannot focus with Guilia out there. I don't understand why we can't send our riders to ensure their safety."

Trenton makes a fist and gently, but with intention, strikes Aitan on the left side of his chest. "You have a good heart. But you are still just a child. I remember the days of my youth before I married. There are many women. Many arguments. Much love. But your duty is to the Jade Order first. If she is truly for you, she will understand."

Aitan leans back and rests on the base of the well. Finally giving in, he waves off his donateur. "Please, Trenton, I have kept you away from your wife long enough. There is no reason to watch over me within my father's manor. I can sulk without an audience."

Trenton grunts and squeezes the Chozien's shoulder before heading off to see his wife. His excitement grows as each step brings him closer to her.

THIRTY-ONE

Back at the house, Branson is keen on his entrapment plan. His objective: to lure the suspect into the same space with Ahni, then press them with questions of their past, disguised by interrogating Ahni.

Armed with the details, Branson, Malan, and two additional warriors head out to execute the ambush. Branson sends Malan to prepare his mother and then orders one of the warriors to fetch the suspect, while he and the second warrior wait outside the stable. With the air quite brisk, Branson paces back and forth while waiting for the warrior to return with the suspect so that he can release his wife and welcome her to his warmth again.

Finally, the warrior approaches with the suspect. They come to stand before the Bonne Ame.

"Good eve, Sire," comes the greeting from the hooded woman, her cloak closed against the night air and secured with a golden clasp.

Branson nods his acknowledgement and replies with a warm smile, "Good eve to you, my lady. How fares your husband?"

The woman pulls back her hood to reveal gray hair with warm brown streaks throughout. The face of the meticulous tailor looks back at him. She rubs her hands together to generate some warmth.

She answers, "He is well, Sire."

Branson looks to her escort, who shakes his head.

Branson exhales heavily and orders, "Well, now, let's get on with it."

He turns to lead them deeper into the stable. They enter the last stall to see Malan standing next to his seated, unfettered mother, his face stern and hand resting on the hilt of his sword.

Pulling the gloves from a pocket, Branson starts, "The sira here denies that she owns these gloves we found in your home. Can you recall the occasion when Sira Ahni brought the gloves to you?"

The clothier nods. "Oh yes, Sire." She stares at Ahni, seemingly in dazed smugness, as she retells the interaction: "Sira Ahni came to me in a rush. She demanded that I put all other items off immediately and set to mending her gloves."

Ahni opens her mouth to protest, but Malan puts a hand firmly on her shoulder to silence her, his face unmoved, an absolute mirror of his father's.

Branson then asks, "How would you say her mood was?"

The clothier wrings her hands as she looks into the distance. "Frenzied and irritable. I assumed the gloves held some treasured history, by her mood."

Once more shocked by the clothier's account, Ahni begins to object. She doesn't get much out before Branson orders she be gagged. Malan stuffs a cloth in his mother's mouth. She narrows her eyes at her son, at which he cringes inwardly, turning away before he spoils the ruse.

Next, Branson asks, "I'm sure in your birth years of tailoring, you have mended quite a few tears and holes. What kind of damage did this look like?"

She pauses and, again seemingly in thought, answers, "A rip from a thorn, right on the stitch. The threading gave way and separated the leather patterns." She shakes her head and smacks her lips before she adds, "That kind of repair would need all the stitching replaced."

Branson furrows his brow in confusion and inquires, "And?"

Still in thought, she presses her lips together in obvious frustration, then explains, "The thread is of the purest gold. There is none of its kind to be found around here. 'Tis a shame."

Branson makes a visible reaction at the revelation. Then he nods and asks his last question: "Oh, and finally, when did you say the sira brought these gloves to you?"

The clothier looks at Branson, a bit surprised, but does not answer.

He shrugs his shoulders and expounds, "Well, this must have been some time ago, no? These gloves are already mended ... with the gold thread, yes?"

She nods her head slowly, her eyes calculating.

Branson tilts his head, then looks to Malan, who removes the gag from his mother's mouth.

Ahni glares daggers at her husband and son. She stretches her mouth in exaggeration, and with a hint of annoyance, she says, "I think that was a bit much."

Branson shakes his head. "Well, dear, I had to be sure."

She snaps back, "That was clear after the second question."

Malan jumps in: "Ah, Mother, there is the matter of timing and also if there are others. She could have been forced."

Branson beams at his son's ability to discern the discoveries that came out of the questions. He smiles as he exclaims, "That's my son! You see, this is why I need you by my side."

"Excuse me," the old woman says. "What is going on?"

They all look at the clothier, whose bewildered expression turns to an unsettling calm as a wave of recognition washes over her. At this, there is no point in keeping up the pretense. Ahni stands, aided by Malan, and then dusts away the straw that has begun to mold itself to her arms, hair, and robes.

The clothier's lips curl into a cruel smile as she asks, "How did you know?"

Branson speaks first: "A huntsman always knows what is in order and what stands out. We are trained to see what does not fit." And then, with a mocking shrug, he adds, "Then, too, it helps to know your wife well."

The clothier furrows her brow in response to his comment. Branson breaks down the details, beginning with the gloves as an obvious clue. Perhaps accusing anyone other than his wife or family for that matter, it would have been plausible. He explains that where the prickly thorn brush grows is too far away from the manor, and his wife would never stray so far. He adds that he has a dedicated scout who trails his wife whenever she leaves the hold, at which Ahni widens her eyes in shock.

Branson holds up the gloves and says, "These fine adornments and detail are not something we of the Jade care for. I'm sure you have noticed as much over your time here. Most of your efforts are spent repairing old garments and boots rather than making new ones."

She snorts at the comment.

He closes his explanation: "Your greed for abundance and the obses-sion of lofty possessions go beyond one who cherishes her craft. This is a ... reverence. One known to the Gold Order."

The clothier laughs and flicks her hand at them. "Hearing this is more ... exciting than I thought. It has been a lofty penance that I live among you for so long. My price is high, and I will be rewarded wonderfully."

Branson's face becomes serious just as the warrior who escorted the clothier wraps his arm around her throat.

"Who's to say you will enjoy this wealth?" Branson asks.

She barely manages to let out a chuckle, then strains to mock, "You have no idea of the Gold Order. Even if it is not I who will savor my glory, my family will, and the Great Spirit will bless my *ame* for it."

Branson slams his fist against the wall of the stall, causing Ahni to jump. "Enough!" he says. "You will tell me what you have done or I will let my dewan have you. Even with the promise of wealth to appease the Great Spirit, your tongue will loosen. I offer a peaceful release to your *ame* and—"

His words halt when the warrior holding the clothier jerks suddenly, his eyes surprised while his face expresses great pain. He releases her and struggles to reach behind him. He is wrenched upward before falling to the floor. Where the Jade warrior once stood, the clothier's husband now stands. Malan and the second warrior react and unsheathe their swords. The man grabs for his wife and holds a knife to her throat.

She shrieks and exclaims, "What are you doing, Sharad?"

The man hisses, "Hush!"

Branson steps toward them, but Sharad snaps, "Don't move!"

Holding up his hands, Branson stops and says, "Look, Sharad, what is your plan, eh? Come now, you won't harm your own wife?"

The man sneers, then laughs. "You are right. I would not harm my wife. Though my first loyalty is to the Gold Order. She will live in comfort and wealth at my sacrifice."

Branson folds his arms with a curious expression. "Oh? How is that?"

Sharad shakes his head while clicking his tongue at Branson's false conclusion. "I would have thought the Bonne Ame of the Jade Order would know something of the power wealth affords one."

Branson waves offhandedly with his response: "I have seen your cottage. Barely room to fit all your … 'work,' is it? There's not enough demand to produce that amount of labor. No, you hoard the memories of others, experiences from their services, tales of their travels, their joy in celebrations or sadness in their loss. I see little of how much wealth you can accumulate from this."

Sharad's eyes gleam with pride and pleasure at the Bonne Ame's summarization of his property. He smiles behind the head of his captive. "Yes! Very perceptive! I seem to have misjudged you before. Of course, there are tangible goods that hold a certain price: precious stones, jewelry, land, homes, and titles. But you see, not all riches are visible to the ungolden eye. Wealth is not determined by how much *I* value my goods but the price you place on them. It is fascinating what one will give in exchange for those memories you speak of."

He then turns his attention to the woman he holds. He rubs his head against his hostage's cheek. She recoils slightly.

Sharad speaks unemotionally: "Mena, you spoke too much. Not that it matters now. What has been done is done. Your *ame* will grant you the prize you were promised. You have done well."

The woman smiles.

Branson realizes what is happening and lunges forward just as the man slides his blade across the loose, tender flesh, slicing deep into her throat. She gurgles, and blood spurts and spills out of the opening. She drops to her knees, covering her throat as she falls forward to the ground.

Sharad dodges Branson's clumsy reach and stands ready. "Ah, but you should know what I have of value to you, yes?"

Malan and the second warrior slowly walk to their left, attempting to encircle the Gold operative.

Branson eases up his attack, concerned, and demands, "What is it?"

"As expected, after the donateur went off to his house, I saw your dear Chozien sneaking to the stable, so I knew you'd told him Guilia was on her way to the Rhyne Clan to trade, just as I'd told you. But I managed to speak with him before he left, telling him I had received word that our daughter was captured and being taken toward the Zin Clan where the Bloodstone gather. So now the Chozien races to your western clan, where he thinks he will save his woman. Love will do that, eh? Cause you to betray your sire and father. Even ride bravely into the savage Bloodstone."

Branson takes a sharp intake of breath as Sharad laughs and holds up his hand to stop the trio from descending on him.

Through his enthusiasm, Sharad's manages to continue his derision, "You do not truly possess the Chozien anyway. He's always belonged to the Onyx Order. And that is not all. No, I harbor more than just your eldest son."

Through gritted teeth, Branson forces, "What?"

The Gold kinsman sobers, stands taut, and casually answers, "Your wife."

As quickly as Sharad's answer comes, a flash of steel leaves his hand and crosses the stall, followed by a loud thud against the wall. The three Jade kinsmen spin in that direction. Ahni lies slumped against the stall wall, the wooden handle of a blade protruding from the right side of her abdomen.

Malan drops his sword and runs to his mother as he screams, "Maaaaa!"

He tries to lift her, but she yelps in pain, at which he recoils.

Branson says, "Leave her, Malan! You will make it worse." Then to Sharad, he yells, "Bastard! You have guaranteed your death."

Sharad shrugs comically and then states the obvious, "Meh. You wouldn't have let me keep my *ame* anyway."

Drawing his own dagger, Branson replies, "I will carve out your heart and display it over my hearth to be handed down my bloodline through the generations."

Sharad exhales. "Yes, now you've got it. Wealth! Exciting, isn't it?"

He doesn't wait for an answer as he turns to sprint down the breeze-way of the stable. But he stumbles when his trailing leg gets caught by something. He looks back and sees that the warrior he attacked now holds his pant leg. Sharad delivers a solid kick to the warrior's face, which is enough to gain his release. The delay, though, has given Malan enough time to react faster than either his father or the second warrior, being that Malan is closest to where Sharad now clambers to his feet. Malan picks up his sword and, with an underhand grip on the hilt, plunges it into the spy's back. Judging by the placement of the blade, the spinal cord is severed, and its owner dies instantly.

The second warrior rushes to his fallen comrade and checks for a pulse. He shakes his head at Malan and then moves on to the slain enemy. Meanwhile, Branson rushes to his wife and looks at her wound. Ahni groans with every movement.

Branson motions to Malan. "Help me carry her home. I'll send for our healer."

Malan nods and does as his father says. The second warrior returns to aid in lifting the sira, but Branson waves him off and barks, "Bring me the donateur!"

It doesn't take long for the seeker and his apprentice to arrive at their sire's house. He instructs them to carry Ahni into the master quarters and then shoos them out.

When Trenton bursts through the door with Reba a few moments later, they find the house in an uproar. A servant tells them about what has happened to Ahni, and Reba cries out upon hearing of her friend's condition. Just as Trenton begins to console her, Breanne comes to relieve him of his wife's melancholy so that he may attend the sire.

Branson waits for him in the hall, surrounded by his best kinsmen from each service. Branson looks to Trenton and waves him over.

Trenton reaches Branson and says, "Sire, we are bonded by more than my service. Your breath is my breath, so your pain is mine also."

Branson nods. "Thank you, my friend. I will surely share your kind words once she recovers. You are here for something else. I've had it confirmed that Aitan has left the manor."

Trenton jerks back, his face a mix of horror and anger. He curses as he turns to leave, but Branson stops him by saying, "You will have time to redeem this error. I need your mind here for now."

"But, Sire," Trenton says, "I can catch up to him if I leave now."

Branson simply looks at him, stone-faced.

Trenton bows his head. "Yes, Sire, I am here."

Branson nods again and briefs Trenton on all the recent events. Trenton doesn't have time to react or digest his emotions of anger and dread. His anxiety increases after hearing of the discovery of the spies, along with concern over what snare they have led Aitan into.

The conglomerate offers various suggestions and ideas, but Trenton cannot shake a feeling and asks, "Why send him to the west?"

Branson recalls what Sharad said and offers, "There is the assertion that the Bloodstone will overtake the Zin."

"That is not possible," Trenton says. "Our clans hold them off on many fronts."

Branson thinks aloud, "Why the Zin Clan specifically? Aitan, as Chozien, could pass through to any clan."

He then remembers how he and Ahni discussed one of his visions: the refugees of the Rain Clan fleeing while the Bloodstone slay a warrior from the Zin Clan.

What happened to the aid from the other clans?

Branson curses. "Those evil bastards."

One of the warriors asks, "Sire?"

Branson elaborates, "I have had two visions of the battles: one with the Rain Clan and the other with the Zin. I couldn't understand how they were able to overpower us. It is as if they—"

Malan cuts in to finish the conclusion, almost in awe: "Split our defenses."

Branson looks at his fastest rider. "Ari, ride ahead of me to the spirit hold. Speak with Keno first. Leave the Glen Clan to aid the Zin and pull the Crystal allies to the west. Explain my vision."

Ari nods. "Yes, Sire." He leaves to carry out his mission.

Branson moves on to his best ranger: "Farah, ride to the east. Retrieve Guilia. Be mindful of the impending battle. Your mission is to bring the girl back, not provide relief to the eastern clans." And to his tracker, Liam, he instructs, "A warrior like Farah can also use a huntsman's eyes. Follow the trade route unless there is a change."

They both nod without hesitation and set out for their journey.

To another of his seekers, Branson says, "Prepare the vessels with the blue powder. Make sure Farah and Liam carry two each."

"Yes, Sire," the seeker says, and then he is off.

When the world began to reclaim itself, the seekers discovered the weapons of the Old World. During the Breaking, anyone who possessed and used such a weapon could release many *ames* and wreak havoc. Soon these weapons became few until they no longer existed or the effects of their contents diminished so much that they no longer were of use.

The seekers examined the machines to understand the construct. After taking them apart, they found a white, powdery substance.

The chemistry behind the substance's elements was beyond the comprehension of anyone without the education; however, they eventually succeeded in unraveling its composition. The power that could be harnessed by the creation and deployment of these weapons was immeasurable.

To quell the compulsion to possess these weapons of massive annihilation, it was a unanimous decision by all spirit seekers across the orders to ban its manufacture. Though the recipe is known by all, they joined again to create a blue powder that creates the loud roar of an explosion with a bright, blinding flash to disorient those within the range of impact.

There were those who pushed the boundaries of the restricted edict, but they were dealt with by those within their own order before the others would rise against them. Truly, this order from Branson has been made with the utmost urgency.

He is left with Trenton and Malan. He finally releases Trenton, who stops to speak with his wife briefly before he disappears into the cold night.

"Father?"

Branson turns to his son and tiredly runs his hand over his face. His eyes stay closed, long enough for Malan to inquire again: "Father, what is it I should do?"

Branson opens his eyes and sets his hands on his son's shoulders. He forces a small smile. "You will stay here and act in my name. I will wait as long as I can to be the first face your mother sees. But I must leave for the spirit hold. As gardien, I have lost the Chozien. And as a Bonne Ame who has Foresight, it is crucial I be at the war council.

I need you to protect our home and keep our people safe. They trust you and respect you as my heir. I have made sure of that since you have come home to us."

Malan reaches up and places his hand over his father's on his right shoulder. "Yes, I will. Call for me if Mother awakens."

Branson squeezes his son's shoulders with a little push to set him on his way. If there are two things he is certain of, they are Malan's ability to lead and his military prowess. Peace might be the divine duty commissioned to the Jade by the Great Spirit, but anyone else who crosses these walls will meet a death ten times over.

CHAPTER
THIRTY-TWO

The healer emerges from Branson and Ahni's quarters, wiping blood from his hands. His apprentice follows behind him, then hurries away to clean his surgical tools. The seeker exhales, exhausted by the late hour and the arduous suturing for such a deep injury.

Branson starts to rise from the chair he is slumped in, struggling to keep himself awake. The healer waves him back down. Branson, emotionally and physically drained, accepts the gesture and collapses back in the chair.

"The wound is deep, Sire. Her blood loss is enough to be praised by the Bloodstone. Sira Ahni bore the pain until she fainted from the exertion. I got the bleeding to stop, and the wound stitched and bandaged. But, Sire ..." His expression turns worried, until at Branson's urging, he finishes his statement, "I have seen many wounds in my time. This is one that you thank the Great Spirit to cherish the last moments."

Branson nods his understanding and thanks the seeker.

As the seeker leaves, he advises, "She is sleeping now. Do not wake her. Her rest is vital to her recovery ... the Great Spirit be so merciful."

Branson tiptoes to the room that he and his wife built and slept in each other's arms for many birth years. Pushing away the sentimental emotions, he straightens and puts on a smile for good measure before entering.

There are a couple lamps lit, casting a soft amber glow across the room. The room smells of rosemary and blood. The red stains on the floor legitimize the veracity of the healer's concern about her wound. He kneels at his wife's side, where he sees the care his servants took to lay her on fresh sheets and clear the room of any evidence of the healer's efforts.

He touches her once vibrant brown skin, now pale and dry to the touch. He goes to her collection of salves, balms, and creams to return with one that reminds him of her. He scoops a bit of the thick, scented salve with his finger and smears it gently on her hand. He lays his hand over hers, allowing his warmth to soften the mixture, just as he has seen her do. Feeling the salve melt, he massages her hand until he is satisfied with the softness. He smiles as the lavender scent wafts in his nostrils, stirring memories of her touch, her smile, the annoyed expressions, her laughter, his comforting during her wistful moments while their children were away from home, and their playful interactions.

But his heart craves her voice. If he could hear her now, it would make seeing her condition so much more bearable. The streams of wetness on his face come without warning, without resistance. He touches her cheek.

In his grief, between sniffs, he whispers, "You are so brave and innocent. You trusted me to protect you. I have failed you. Be sure to remind me of this for many birth years from now." He leans in closer, his lips just grazing her forehead as he speaks, careful not to disturb the bed: "I need you to be strong. I know there is much I have asked of you in our marriage. Just one more … come back to me."

He kisses her lightly on the lips, savoring the feeling and the promise of reciprocation. He adjusts the blanket over her and stands. Then, with one final look, he leaves the room.

Breanne waits outside for him, her eyes reddened and puffy from the constant flow of tears. She wipes her nose with a cloth as she sniffles. Gerald comes forward to console his wife.

Branson gathers himself, as he will need his wits about him in the upcoming days. "I will be leaving just as the moon begins its slumber. Malan will lead the manor. Ensure this is made clear and obeyed."

Gerald nods and responds, "Not to worry, Sire. I will have Sira Ahni tended to. I have also packed your satchels for your stay at the spirit hold. Breanne has taken the liberty to prepare your favorite dishes to remind you of home even if it is just a day's ride."

The manservant notices Branson's exhaustion in his half smile and ushers him back to his room. "I will have blankets brought to you. You must get some rest if you are to be of any use to the dewan. I will awaken you at the specified time."

Branson complies and promptly collapses on the floor under his wife's uneven breathing.

True to his word, Gerald wakes his sire with enough time to eat a prepared breakfast, much more substantial than his typical hunter's spread. Branson kisses Ahni once again before he sets off to the spirit hold. The warrior and huntsman chosen to accompany wait for Branson to ready himself. As Branson finally rides out of his manor, any seeker with Sighting would have visibly been able to see his dull spirit.

The journey to the spirit hold is filled with an array of emotions, self-doubt, regret, anxiety, and confidence, so much that by the time Branson arrives, he feels spent. Even still, rest remains far from him. With Branson's arrival being anticipated, a stable girl comes to take the reins of his horse while he dismounts right after he enters the spirit hold. She informs him that his things will be taken to the dewan's house and waiting in his room. He nods and offers her the packed meal in one of his satchels, as he has no appetite.

She smiles and thanks him.

With Branson's usual escorts out on missions, he took care to instruct his newly charged escorts during their trek about the expected decorum for their time at the spirit hold. Normally, they would go with him to Gaylen's house and wait outside with the escorts of the other sires. But due to the urgent nature of this visit, they will meet him there.

The residents make no effort to hide their stares and whispers. Their worried glances are a sign of the impending threat, though based mostly on conjecture and gossip. Branson continues on his path, acknowledging greetings and ignoring calls for specific details or shouts of protest.

He makes it to Gaylen's home, where a servant ushers him to the dewan's parlor. Branson finds Gaylen, Keno, Haru, and Len already there. Their expressions couldn't be more divergent from each other. Len has a calm demeanor with a calculating overtone. Haru appears edgy—and annoyed with Branson's late arrival. Keno's mood is the most noticeable, as his face mimics the same concern as the others, though with a hint of a smile.

Gaylen acknowledges Branson first: "Namaste, Bonne Ame. We received your message. My prayers for a swift recovery to Sira Ahni."

Branson nods. "Thank you."

Gaylen turns to the topic, referring to Branson's message: "Well, we have four orders moving on our borders. You suggest, though, that we not send aid to our northwestern clans. Why?"

"The Jade Order has a great military offense on the western border," Branson says. "If we reduce that might from any of the fronts there, we risk opening a weak point close to the spirit hold."

Gaylen turns his eyes toward the ceiling and thinks a moment before he replies, "Yes ... but if a concentration of their warriors is marching there, should we not send aid to our clans?"

General Haru folds his arms and peers at Branson, awaiting his response.

Branson clears his throat. "It is a ploy, Sire. The spy I found in my manor sent the Chozien to the Zin Clan. They anticipate the guard will be less."

Gaylen and his three councilmen look at one another with raised eyebrows and interested shrugs or nods.

This time, Keno continues the questioning: "If I can be more direct, your lire spoke of your Foresight. What do your visions show you?"

Branson looks at each person, gauging their expressions for genuine consideration or mocking ignorance for relying on his gift as a credible military source.

He breathes deeply and conjures his confidence, then says, "Yes, Spirit Keeper. My visions support my advice. The warrior I see being slain by the Bloodstone is of the Zin Clan. We would need to pull our defenses from them for it to be possible for the Bloodstone warriors to make it so far inside our borders."

Keno goes on, "But what of the other clan fleeing in your vision? Should we not bring them aid?"

Branson nods. "We only need to ask the Crystal Order to send warriors."

Gaylen folds his arms and shakes his head. "No, Sire Clayton has already heard from them. They will not send aid."

Branson furrows his brow. "They mean to join the Onyx, then?"

Gaylen shakes his head. "No, they mean to not take a side."

Branson goes silent while he searches his memory to recall the scene.

Eyeing Branson, Keno inquires, "What is it, Bonne Ame?"

Branson runs his hand through his hair, puzzled.

Keno shifts his voice to a soothing tone: "Tell us what you see."

Branson recites the scene again as he has seen it multiple times before. "I do not know where they are fleeing to."

Haru lights up. "Ah! If the Crystal Order will not provide their warriors, they may still provide asylum to our kinsmen. If our people are to flee, then we shall give them a place to go."

At the puzzled looks, the general elaborates, "Branson speaks true: Our enemies intend to split our defenses, but our scouts number them as having only enough for one large battle, not a siege. If battle should occur, we should have a refuge for our people to retreat to. It is better for our warriors to defend our order without the distraction of the people."

The council plans out the details to protect their people and recover the Chozien. Afterward, as they disperse, each councilmember makes a stop with Branson before they exit. Haru comes to stand before Branson and puts a hand on his shoulder, giving a squeeze of appreciation and respect before he leaves to carry out the military stratagem. Len follows and reaches out his hand. Branson grasps forearms with him. He leaves, as not only are warriors present in the battles, but the huntsmen stand alongside them as their archers. Len must also send orders for securing the sanctuary for the Hawk and Rain clans.

Next comes Keno. His smile is wide as he stands with his back straight and his chest puffed, a teacher proud of his student. "You did well, seeing the details in your Sight to conclude the vision."

Branson nods, though with little enthusiasm. "My wife holds the wisdom; without her, I would not have seen through the maze of symbols."

Keno puts a hand on Branson's arm as he says, "May the Great Spirit keep you and see you through this trying time. Your pain is not lost to me."

Keno exits the parlor, leaving only Branson and Gaylen. The dewan walks to a small table nearby, where sits a finely made glass container filled with a dark-brown liquid. He uncorks the container, takes two fist-sized glasses, and fills each a quarter of the way. He then offers a glass to Branson, who accepts it with a nod.

He watches as Gaylen swirls the liquid in the glass and sniffs it. Satisfied, he takes a short gulp. Branson follows the same routine. When he inhales, his eyes involuntarily close as remembrances of home arise unbidden—the smell of wheat berries being ground into flour while his wife speaks with Breanne in the kitchen, discussing the various bread recipes to try next for dinner. Next comes the strong scent of oak, prompting a memory from the woods: He leans casually against a tall, fat tree, watching as Aitan takes aim with his bow. Aitan looks at him for approval and smiles as he turns back to his target.

Though comforting, the recollections are a sullen reminder that the two people who began his family with him are either lost or suffering. He cannot help but feel guilty. To avoid becoming overwhelmed with despair, he drains his glass, getting a surprise at how smooth the liquor slides down his throat, with just a slight burn. Equally so, he feels a sense of numbness, allowing him to set aside his emotional distractions. He reaches his glass back out to Gaylen, who refills it.

"The Crystal Order may lack in courage but certainly makes up for it in their whiskey distillation," Gaylen remarks with a troubling smirk.

"Yes. That they do."

Gaylen offers a gentle smile as he says, "There are many things I can say as a dewan to his Bonne Ame to acknowledge your dedication to the order while your wife lies with a serious injury. But as a friend, my spirit is in as much agony as yours. My thoughts conflict with my emotions, and I struggle to remain vigilant and brave for my family, clans, and the order. I share this burden with you. You are not alone. As it is, we are stronger together."

Branson smiles at the reassuring words and speaks his gratitude. He drains his glass again and leaves. An emotionless line of sorrow on his lips replaces his smile. Even with all the other *ames* of the Jade Order, there is no escaping the Great Spirit's call on his life.

THIRTY-THREE

Trenton starts his third day on his swift journey to catch up with Aitan. He has been constantly rehearsing the scolding he plans to give him. Yet, this day has his huntsman's intuition ringing with uncertainty and his warrior instincts in disarray. Since he has been on the trail, he hasn't recognized any tracks that belong to a single hurried rider—mostly wagons, pack horses, and footsteps in large groups. He has come across small groups heading toward the safety of the spirit hold, of which none recall having seen a lone rider. He continues on, tense inside and out.

He sees a pair approaching on horses in the distance and rides up to meet them. Trenton recognizes one man as being a warrior from the Zin Clan, but he cannot make out the identity of his companion because of the hood hiding her face. The Zin clansman holds a rope that extends back to the second horse. His companion, however, is not restrained, but hides behind the warrior and under her hooded cloak.

Trenton addresses the warrior: "Namaste."

The warrior replies in kind.

Trenton continues, "I am in search of the Chozien; he would be traveling alone."

The warrior shakes his head. "No, I would have known. This area covers my scout post."

Trenton drops his shoulders and moves to continue on, but his curiosity forces him to ask, "Where are you headed? Isn't your clan preparing to defend against an attack?"

The Zin warrior nods and replies with some annoyance, "Yes. Indeed, we are awaiting word from the spirit hold. We are on the way there now. I scouted this woman traveling alone and escorted her to Sire Remy. After hearing the tale of her travels during a time of battle, my sire has deemed that she repeat this to the dewan before she is allowed to pass through the Zin land."

"What?" Trenton says. "Pass *through*?"

The warrior nods. "This is what sparked caution. Who travels alone for trade and heading toward a battle? It is ... odd. You would think one would seek protection, not to continue toward the danger."

Trenton moves his horse more to the left to have a clearer look at the woman, though still unable to see her through the hood of her cloak. He demands, "Pull back your hood, woman."

The mysterious traveler doesn't move.

The Zin warrior, exasperated by the insolence and the delay in their journey, reaches up and jerks the hood back.

Trenton's eyes widen with a sharp intake of breath. Such is his shock that his horse steps back, shakes its head, and snorts from the stiffening of Trenton's forearms pulling at the reins. Trenton relaxes to calm the horse.

His reaction is not lost on the Zin scout. "You know this woman?"

Trenton nods slowly, his eyes showing his fury. "She calls the manor of Bonne Ame Branson home. She was to be off with a trade caravan to the Rhyne Clan." And to the unhooded woman, he says, "You are far from the eastern border, Guilia."

The Zin scout exclaims, "Guilia? She claimed her name to be Birdie."

Trenton ignores the scout's anger. "We will go to Sire Branson's hold."

The scout tries to protest, but Trenton calls out, "I am donateur to the Chozien. Your sire will not remember a lone woman; he is too busy with battle preparations."

The scout agrees, though not without concern.

Trenton, the scout, and Guilia enter the Bonne Ame's manor two days later. The donateur tells the gate warden to send word to the sire that he has returned but to omit that he does not have the Chozien with him. After leaving the horses at the stable to be tended to, Trenton leads Guilia and the Zin scout to the main house, where Branson awaits them. Trenton notices that his sire has a bit of a stressed appearance and red eyes, as if he hasn't slept in some time.

Still, for appearance's sake, Trenton greets Branson with, "Namaste, Sire. I have—"

Branson abruptly pulls Trenton in for a hug, catching the donateur off guard with such a public display of emotion while officially presenting visitors, one of whom is a captive. But Trenton embraces his sire and then pulls away to finish his announcement.

"Sire, as I tracked Sire Aitan, I met up with a Zin scout escorting Guilia to the spirit hold. I interrupted their destination to bring them to you, as we understood that she was to go east. Sire?"

Branson stares at the Zin scout as if he recognizes him but doesn't believe his eyes. He walks slowly toward the Zin warrior. He eyes him, then taps his head, chest, and shoulders, ensuring that the man who stands before him is indeed real.

The Zin scout looks at everyone uncomfortably before he decides to break the awkward silence. He clears his throat before he says, "Ah, I am called Jaafar. I saw this woman on the trail during my scout rotation. I brought her to my sire. He ordered me to take her to the dewan."

Branson looks at him. "Why is it you are scouting the inner Jade territory?"

"Sire Remy received orders to hold our warriors in place," Jaafar replies. "If we were to send aid to the north, all eastern scouts would remain within the clan walls for added defense against a Bloodstone invasion. But since we have not drawn ourselves out, they have moved away from the borders. This is why I remained at my post."

Branson nods with astonishment, and then, waving a hand at Guilia, he inquires, "And what of her? Why is she being sent to the spirit hold?"

Trenton speaks up: "Sire, she claims she was passing through the Zin Clan for trade. While it is uncommon for trade to continue across clans and orders during a possible invasion, it is even more rare to see a lone traveler. This did not sit well with Sire Remy, and he has ordered her to be handed to the dewan."

Branson quirks his eyebrow and scowls at Guilia. "You and your order have created enough turmoil in my house. It is time you pay in full, not only the value of your worth to the Gold but the value that is mine."

His encounter with the Gold spies has prepared him for the order's greed, as well as how to manipulate this to his advantage. She further confirms this notion, as once he speaks his words, she reacts with a gasp and eyes that look glassed over with fear, no doubt aware of the high interest that she must repay for the treachery and the Bonne

Ame's embarrassment to his dewan. She knows it will be a high price—one that will keep her in his debt for most of her life, if not the whole of it.

Her reaction does give Branson pause, which he plans to exploit for his gain. He looks at Guilia and then Jaafar, saying, "Go and cleanse yourself of your journey and return to me. Be quick."

At the Bonne Ame's release, Jaafar and Guilia follow a servant to the servants' quarters to make themselves presentable and have a more inviting meal than the hard travel tack, assuming their appetite is still present.

Trenton waits until they are out of earshot before he asks, "Sire, how is Sira Ahni doing?"

Branson feigns relief and forces a smile. "There is comfort when I am surrounded by the loyalty and support of my people. She rests now."

Trenton nods, accepting his sire's response, not wishing to push for more detail. Instead, he asks, "Is there something amiss about Jaafar? You stared at him as if his *ame* appeared from the spirit world."

Branson's face lights up with awe and relief. His voice has a tone of hesitant amazement as he explains, "His face is one that I have seen much over the birth years, but not in person. It is as if he has stepped out of my visions into the physical realm. Do you recall the warrior who ran boldly into battle with the Bloodstone, cutting down as many as he could before his *ame* was released from behind? That is he. When I used my Sight and impressed on him, I felt his fierce loyalty and fearlessness as he rushed into the thick of fighting. He fought bravely.

"If what he says is true, Gaylen has stayed true to his word to maintain the Zin as the western stronghold to the inner Jade boundaries. The Bloodstone must have retreated once they saw that the Zin Clan remained vigilant. There was no need to pull warriors from their inner boundary scouting posts. This allowed us to halt the escape of the Gold Order spies."

Trenton echoes the same amazement. Even still, he remains unsure why Branson is granting hospitality to Guilia and asks as much.

Branson's answer is confident: "There is something she treasures at her home, and she wants to return safely back to it. The other Gold spies died willingly and forced our hand into releasing their *ames*. This one seeks life … and is willing to betray her order to do so."

Trenton raises his eyebrows and nods, impressed at his sire's insight.

Branson releases Trenton to reunite with Reba before duty claims him in the next sun shadow change. Meanwhile, Branson revels in admiration of the return on his investment in his divine gift. Deciphering his Foresight has essentially changed a strand of the future—not only saving this scout's life but the lives of many of his kinsmen. Furthermore, it has created an advantage and opportunity to plant eyes and ears within the Gold Order—a welcomed victory in the face of the demoralizing turmoil that has visited his house over the last few days.

As he enjoys a moment of accomplishment, Trenton returns and asks, "Pardon, Sire. Where is the Chozien? With my detour adding more days to my journey, I assume he's returned with Farah and Liam. I'd like a word with him on the distress that he has caused by abandoning his duty and … to reclaim some pride from him abusing our trust."

Branson's mood changes to one of defeat. He motions to the house as he replies, "Ah, I was hoping to wait until you had a chance to rejoin your wife. Come, much has happened over the last few days. We'll need a strong drink."

Farah and Liam ride at a comfortable trot, much to Farah's chagrin. Farah wants to hurry to recover Guilia because she considers such a mission beneath her usefulness, but she is forced to endure the company and measured tempo of the huntsman. According to Liam's tracking and their initial aggressive pace, they should catch the trading caravan soon. Liam suddenly pulls back on the reins of his horse, causing it to rear up on its hind legs and sidestep before it settles. Farah slows and turns around. Liam has already dismounted by the time she rejoins him. He squats down as he studies the ground.

Still mounted, Farah rolls her eyes and asks, "Now what, huntsman?"

Completely unaffected by her irritation, Liam replies, "Another cluster of tracks here."

The ranger's response drips with sarcasm: "Yes ... that is common with a caravan."

Liam shakes his head and points toward the tracks. "These do not belong to a caravan. I count eight mounted riders encircling another single rider."

Farah furrows her brow. "Speak plainly, huntsman. I'm not clear what you mean."

Liam stands and looks up at the ranger. "A trading caravan has come this way, though we have not been on *their* trail."

Farah's eyes widen in exasperation, and she parts her lips to express her disdain over the intentional deception, but snaps her mouth shut as the huntsman puts up a hand.

"Be still," Liam says.

At her silence and the raise of an eyebrow, he explains, "There have been signs that a single rider has been on the same trail as the caravan. Even though we have passed large camps no doubt from the caravan, there have also been camps deeper in the woods of a lone traveler. On further inspection of the camp, it became clear who it belonged to."

When he pauses, the ranger looks from side to side in exaggeration and inquires, "Well, who?"

Liam states, "Sire Aitan, the Chozien."

At that, the warrior snorts and chuckles. "Those camps could belong to anyone. How could you know that it is the Chozien?"

Liam goes to his horse and pulls something from the saddle. He opens his fist and lets fall what looks to be a mix of debris such as hay and grass.

Farah shrugs. "It looks like horse feed. What of it?"

"That is true: It is horse feed. But if you look closer, you will notice the blend of supplements that our sire's hold adds to our horses' diet. Our breed is known for their temperament because of this. There are traces of valerian. Only our sire risks trading with the Gold and Bloodstone Orders for this plant."

Farah dismounts, interested. She squats down and scrapes up a handful of the contents that Liam spilled. She sniffs and immediately recoils from the recognizable valerian odor of unclean feet.

"So?" she says. "It could belong to any of our kinsmen in the caravan."

Liam walks back to his horse. "No, that blend is reserved for our high-bred trading horses. Our own horses do not follow the same diet. Only one unfamiliar in commerce and the commodity would bring *this* feed, if any at all."

Farah exhales in exasperation. "Damn it! Why is he here? He should be going west."

Liam shakes his head again and says, "These tracks lead off the main trail and into the woods, more east than north, away from the Rhyne Clan."

Farah takes a moment to consider their journey thus far. Everything has seemed as it should be. The roads have been lightly traveled—as expected with battles brewing. Patrols have diminished greatly since they passed the spirit hold's eastern boundary a day ago. With a day's ride away from the Rhyne Clan, they have not yet entered its boundary. It would be uncommon for a scout to be so far out, let alone eight.

With the new information, they abandon their mission to retrieve the Gold Order's spy and set off to rescue the Chozien, and thus, their path leads off the open road and into the forest. They ride for half the day before Liam pauses to camp while he scouts ahead. He follows the freshly cut trail while Farah stays back with the horses.

Just as the daylight begins to wane, Liam hears faint voices and movement in the distance. He veers off the trail and into the thick of the trees. He employs the huntsman's "Walk in Humility" technique, removing his traveling boots. With his wrapped feet, he cuts his movements to about half the normal speed, and feeling each object with every step, he shifts his weight to avoid the sound of any loud snaps from twigs or the crunch of dried leaves. Keeping his eyes in front of him, trusting his extremities and senses, he guides himself through the branches until he draws close enough to clearly see the people and hear the voices.

It's a camp of seven figures, all hooded in the usual Jade green, with six huddled around a small fire barely large enough to warm a single person and then another one sitting alone off to the side. Liam doesn't see or smell meat roasting, only the occasional movements of bringing hands to mouths. He searches for the Chozien and soon sees that Aitan bound with a rope to the trunk of a nearby tree, with a gag set on his mouth. Liam looks away, calculating the inputs. Why would Jade scouts bind the Chozien and move in the opposite direction of the spirit hold? Why are they taking so much effort to avoid detection? As the hooded group begins to converse, Liam turns his attention back to camp.

One of the figures remarks, "What reward will our dewan give us once we return with our charge, you think?"

His companion seated next to him snickers. "Seti, you always look for more than gratitude."

Seti responds dryly, "That does not fill empty bellies."

One pacing and wrapping a cloak about themself says, "It would have been better that we traveled with warmer gear. Who would have thought the Middlelands would be so cold?"

They continue to exchange gripes while taking bites of what Liam assumes to be hardened trail bars and jerky. The one sitting off to the side, isolated from the others, rises and walks toward the throng of criticisms. When the loner comes to stand across the fire in front of the others, they all stop talking.

The voice that speaks sounds feminine: "Your shortsightedness is an annoyance I shall not bear any longer. You speak of reward, Seti, yet upon your return with the Chozien in our chain, our kinsmen will shower you with gifts of favor. What do you expect? Land? A title?"

The others around him chuckle. Liam sees the one called Seti lower his head in shame.

Then, to the one complaining of the cold, the female says, "Saxon, what of the cold? It has been nearly two moons since we have left our spirit hold in the Upperlands. It seems you have been jaded by the feigned comfort the stroke of heat brings. I'll do well to remember this and give you another turn in the ice pond to numb your senses."

Saxon mumbles, "Yes, High Warrior."

The high warrior reaches up and removes her hood, and the firelight allows Liam to see a caramel-toned, dark-haired woman. Her hair is a multitude of twists twined together in a single braid behind her head. Her face bears a scar across the right cheek, somewhat fresh, though well on the mend. This does not distract from her strong cheekbones, almond-shaped eyes, and curved lips thinning in ire.

What catches Liam's attention is not her features but the adornments around her neck and ears. While it is rare to see, Jade kinsmen will sometimes wear the colors of another order, such as the Tiger Eye brown favored by the huntsmen service to blend in with the woods for hunting, the Rhodonite rose favored by many dewan's attendants, or even the Hematite gray used by many who serve in the kitchen or garden, as it is the cheapest. But where there is leniency within attire, embellishments are not tolerated. Rings, necklaces, and medallions must sport the beholder's stone of their order, with the exception of an otherwise decorative metal or bone.

Even at this distance under the cover of the light of the moon, the glint from the meager fire reveals a stone of the purest, deepest black, unmistakably identified with the Onyx.

Liam turns from the cluster while he muses over the realization that a troop of Onyx warriors now lies within Jade borders and have captured the Chozien. Liam stops cold as he feels the sharp tip of steel pressed to the back of his neck. He holds his hands up in surrender. He feels the blade tap his shoulder twice, communicating for him to turn and face its owner.

He turns to see a hooded Onyx kinsman hovering over him. Liam can barely make out the features hidden within the shadow of the hood. He opens his mouth to speak, but his captor holds a finger up, which halts his speech. Once Liam nods, the figure reaches up and slowly pulls back the hood. Her face looks calm, carrying an emotionless expression, but her eyes have a steely glint about them. Liam can feel the gloating from her gaze. He figures for certain this is the raiding party's huntswoman, but the ominous glee can only be recognized as that of the Onyx Order.

Her voice comes light and soft, a stark contrast to her boastful disposition, as she whispers, "How many?"

He responds in the same indifferent manner: "Only myself and the beasts of the woods."

The Onyx huntswoman stays silent a moment, considering his answer, before she purses her lips. "No. There are no clans nearby."

Liam's response is quick: "I don't live under a sire. My land is about two sun sky shadows' ride east of here."

His interrogator shakes her head. "No, your clothes are of a ranked kinsman to his sire. How many non-réclamés?"

Liam recognizes the term the Onyx use to refer to any kinsman not of their order, as if their *ames* are lost and must be reclaimed and inducted back into their ranks. He stares back at the Onyx hunter, silent and unmoved.

Then, materializing out of the darkness, a shadow speeds through the crisp night, slicing the air in two and ending its course in the Onyx woman.

She jumps, shock replacing the arrogant gleam in her eyes. Her mouth moves as if trying to speak, but she struggles because the iron tip of an arrow piercing her throat now chokes the life from her. As her grip on the sword loosens, Liam's reflexes prove quick enough to catch it by the hilt, promptly laying the sword soundlessly on the ground. Immediately after, her knees begin to buckle. He darts in and props the huntswoman up while still on his knees, then cradles her as he lowers her to rest upon the raw, cold, forest floor.

Liam searches the darkness in the direction of the arrow's source. He stares for a few moments while his eyes adjust until he sees the outline of another person. He makes out the exaggerated waves beckoning him to abandon his stakeout. He looks down at the dying Onyx hunter and realizes her *ame* has been released to the Great Spirit. He closes her eyes before he makes his way out of the dense woods and back to the open trail, where he joins his rescuer.

THIRTY-FOUR

After Liam sets off to scout ahead, Farah takes to preparing the camp. She tends to the horses first. She ties the reins around a tree trunk. Next, she removes the tack and checks them for any sore patches. She lifts each leg and checks their hooves for stones, clearing them as she goes. She empties one of the large waterskins onto the grass near them. She ends with a quick brushing.

Satisfied, Farah clears away debris for a small fire pit. Since it is just the two of them and only for the night, there is no need to dig a hole; simply clearing all grass, leaves, and twigs down to the topsoil and then building a ring of rocks will suffice. She collects various sizes of sticks and fallen branches and organizes them into a cone shape, with kindling at its center. Using her flint, she creates a spark and, with controlled breaths, soon gets a fire going.

Farah then attempts to busy herself with routine tasks around the campsite, checking the horses, stoking the fire, and walking the area. The repetitions, though, become too mundane and redundant, resulting in increasing her anxiety. She looks in the direction Liam went and mutters a curse before she goes to her pack and grabs her short bow and quiver, then follows in the huntsman's steps.

As Farah makes her way on the trail, she chides herself for straying from her service's principles. Warriors pride themselves on their kinship, which serves as the conceptual basis of dividing warriors into troops—the single most intimate group of warriors. The practice integrates a diversified selection of warriors through extremely arduous training, tactical battlefield scenarios, executing tasks, and serving penances, forming a bond stronger than any blood relation. Each troop shares in all triumphs and sorrows, which results in a high-functioning military unit. And for Farah, leaving a kinsman to pursue an unknown enemy alone equates to a grave dishonor—to herself, to her service, and to Liam.

Noticing that the daylight has started to fade, she pauses to check the sun's position. She mentally notes it just peeking above the crown of the trees. Even at an accelerated pace, she doesn't know if she can catch up to him or, worse, be able to find his body. Determined, she keeps moving. She may not be able to track as well as a huntsman, but given Liam's fresh tracks, his lead direction, and the size of the cut trail, she feels confident that she treads the right path. Her elite training has equipped her with many talents beyond the typical warrior service. She makes use of one now: her ability to move in enemy territory ... even if it is within her own order's borders.

Fortunately, as the night begins to take over, she finds Liam's boots propped against a tree. She easily recognizes how his trail changes to a different direction. She lifts her eyebrow at the boots and shakes her head, wondering why anyone would separate themselves from their footwear, risking injury to a significant part of the body. The new trail looks noticeably narrower than the main one she has been on, letting her know that the party either split off or altered their travel formation. Either option increases the lethal risk, which prompts her to switch her draw on the bowstring from three fingers under the arrow to moving her index finger above it. She steps lightly, carefully shifting her weight with each plant of her boot as she marches to support her kinsman and closer to the enemy.

Farah constantly scans all around her. She can only hope that she doesn't run into the line of sight of their scout. She comes to a sudden stop, frozen in place as her eyes lock on a small, flickering light far into the distance. She creeps forward one slow, careful step at a time, ready to discern any sign of threat. She soon can distinguish the outlines of people clustered around a small campfire, their number uncertain. A movement out to the far left grabs her attention. She watches as a shadow moves with purpose and stealth among the trees until it stops. For a clearer look, she moves in closer and to the left until she manages to string together the scene from the glimpses of the flares the campfire produces.

She feels her heart thumping in her chest as it increases the rate of blood circulation throughout her body. She has to make a decision, and it is made in less time one can blink an eye as she raises her bow. She uses the adrenaline from the sudden blood rush to slow her breathing as she waits for the perfect flash of light to set her target. As she releases her draw, she hopes that the huntsman's reflexes are as good as his service boasts. She is already nocking another arrow as she sees the dark shadow go stiff; she knows she made good on her target.

Time seems to drag on as she watches the shadow ease down. She waves until Liam begins to make his way to her. She retreats back to the wider trail and waits for him to emerge. As she waits, she reflects on the recent events. Any training can prepare one for only so much.

It has been over twenty birth years since the previous war. She was only a three-year novice at the time. Even after she had been named warrior, she did not see battle, though she begged for the chance to protect her order. But the Great Spirit laid out another path for her. High Warrior Randol ordered that she and another thirty newly named warriors be isolated to undertake special training. They endured two birth years of grueling exercises, sleep deprivation, and advanced instruction, woven in a tightly spun pattern designed to challenge their very sanity. They came out on the other side with something elegant, something wiser, something lethal, something sinister ... something more. And even still, her hands grip her bow so hard that she can feel her pulse through her fingertips as she holds steady, waiting for the trees to shake and reveal friend or foe.

As expected, the thin tree limbs do shiver slightly, though not from the same location Farah exited. This activity comes nearly an arm span to her right. In a single motion, she turns while drawing back on her bow. She hears Liam call out before she relaxes.

She lets out her frustration and relief in a high whisper, "Damn it, man!"

Liam comes out from the cover and wipes away the leaves. He calmly walks to his boots as if he was not just within a splinter's width of being captured and nearly having his *ame* released.

As he shakes his boots before slipping them back on, he remarks, "It is the Onyx, and they have Sire Aitan."

In a mix of shock and outrage, Farah sputters, "What? Where? Here?"

Liam looks up from lacing his boots and replies, "Yes."

Farah rolls her eyes in exasperation. "Look, this is no longer a simple retrieval order. It is an invasion and a declaration of war. We need to rescue the Chozien and eliminate these ... outlanders. And that is not to be done alone."

The huntsman stands up and nods.

Farah was expecting an argument and not quiet acquiescence. At his waiting look, she mumbles that they should get back to camp.

As they walk, she asks, "How many are there?"

Liam answers, "There were eight. You killed their huntswoman, so now one high warrior commands six."

She nods, considering. "Good. They will be at a disadvantage without their navigator."

"Navigator?"

Farah nods. "Yes. If a hunter is in a warrior troop, they do more than hunt for food. They steer the path and are able to learn new land quickly."

Farah can hear the awe in Liam's voice as he asks, "And if they are not able?"

She shrugs. "Then there is one among them trained with those skills beyond what is expected of a warrior."

Liam guesses, "Like you?"

Farah chuckles, shaking her head at the oversimplification of her extended training. "No, there is more to a ranger than navigating."

Liam nods. "Indeed. Your arrow hit its mark. I do not know a warrior who can do that through the trees without the sunlight. That is why I circled behind you on my return here. I was unsure who made that shot. I had to be certain."

She furrows her brow at the obscured compliment and offers one of her own: "I did not hear you come up behind me. Your steps are like mice whispers."

Liam shrugs as he says, "To put anything between you and the land creates a … dam. Remove the barrier and you will know the ground you walk on."

She chuckles, cautious of the Onyx presence. "Sounds intimate."

"Such is the result of passion," Liam remarks, confirming the ranger's interpretation.

By the time they reach their camp, Farah has gained enough information about the invading troop to piece together a rescue mission. She knows the risk is high, considering they are two against seven. They have two advantages, and she plans to exploit them to the fullest.

Farah walks Liam through the small-scale operation. She explains that they have the equivalent of four sun sky shadows before the Onyx realize their navigator's *ame* has been released. Thus, she deems it best that they strike before then. She states that she will send a barrage of aerial attacks to draw the Onyx warriors away from the camp. With the majority of the warriors gone, this will leave one, perhaps two guards with the Chozien. The huntsman will dispatch them, since close combat is to his advantage. Afterward, he will free the Chozien and lead him back to the horses, and then they will make their escape.

While Liam prepares the horses to be ready for a quick mount and brisk gallop, he considers the plan Farah has laid out. It is sound enough, and he feels confident he will have no trouble rescuing the Chozien, but he is still left unsettled. For Farah to convincingly disguise her charge as multiple attackers, she will need to unleash multiple arrows within seconds of each other, if not in parallel. She will also need to hit a target to make the threat believable, and in such a dense forest, it will be near impossible to accomplish such a feat while keeping enough distance to avoid capture or, worse, sacrifice.

Liam finishes with the horses and glances at Farah. He watches as she sharpens her sword. The rhythmic push-and-pull strokes are fluid and graceful—mesmerizing even, as she smooths away the blade's edge dullness, with the sword's sole purpose being the destruction of the perfection that is the human body. So intense is her focus that she appears to have fallen into a trance. Satisfied with the condition of her sword, she turns her attention to her throwing daggers.

She glances up in the direction they came from. She smiles absently as she looks over the Jade lands.

Even Liam, who avoids facial cognition of emotions, recognizes the melancholy intermingling with pride in her expression—the look of someone who knows what lies at the end of a chosen path ... a look of remembrance. Liam nods, surmising that the warrior does not expect to return with him and the Chozien.

After some time, Farah calls Liam to arm and ready himself so they can carry out their rescue and escape plan. He nods and checks the horses once more. He joins Farah as they set down the same trail from earlier that evening. At the same place the trail narrows, Liam hands Farah the satchel of explosives their seeker prepared, then he heads off to make a wide circle on the left.

Farah comes to a point where she has a visual on the enemy camp and yet enough cover to conceal her. She sees them in the process of breaking camp. With the smallest bit of sunlight on the horizon, she sets out the still-kindling charcoal Liam made. She carefully pulls out the containers with the blue powder and counts only three. She curses at the huntsman's negligence. She blows on the smoldering wood, adding a bit of dried twigs until a small flame takes. She lights the fuse of the first explosive and edges in closer to the camp. She takes a deep breath and says a quick prayer before she heaves the explosive. She doesn't wait until it lands, already nocking a single arrow and taking aim. The vessel hits one of the trees and erupts in a blast of smoke and fire, catching the Onyx warriors off guard. She fires the arrow, but with the forest so dense, she hits a tree nearby. She hurries to fire another, hitting another tree. She races back to light another vessel.

The Onyx warriors scramble into a defense formation. Two warriors stand in front of the Chozien while five others flank the camp in a half moon, swords drawn and shields up. The high warrior, meanwhile, orders they stand their ground. When another blast hits closer, the warriors turn to face the incoming direction, but the high warrior halts them, ordering them to watch their field.

A few arrows later, the high warrior orders two of the flanking warriors to advance on the source, while having the warrior—other than herself—guarding the Chozien fill in the gap. Farah is relieved to see that the warriors have started to separate from the troop but is disappointed that she couldn't draw more away. She retreats back into the trees to make her stand, drawing her sword.

When two Onyx warriors come within view of her, one advances more aggressively. He rushes at her, swinging down with his sword. She does a series of light, agile deflections and dodges. She uses his momentum and then makes her attack with several deep slashes across the inside of the attacker's sword forearm and outer bicep. The warrior grunts, as he can longer maintain hold of his blade. Farah does not wait for the sword to fall as she immobilizes him by adding another cut to the inside of his upper thigh, twisting the blade as she drags it across the front, just above the knee. This time, he yells with pain as he falls to the ground. She pounces on him and sinks her blade into the back of the neck, severing the spine. His body goes limp.

Farah rolls off and away to stand ready for the next assailant. Farah notes that the other warrior has stopped a short distance in front of her, dropping his sword and shield. He unravels his cloak, and as it falls away, she sees the iconic Onyx knee spikes. She curls her lip in disgust.

The Jade consider the use of this ancillary armory distasteful and cowardly. Nevertheless, the spikes are as lethal as they are dishonorable. She isn't surprised that her opponent discharged his order's prized primary weapon—the long sword—as she now watches him brandish a large kukri mêlée knife—as imposing as it is purposeful.

Without taking his eyes off Farah, he yells back over his shoulder, "It is only one!"

He crouches low, taking a more compact body positioning, no doubt after witnessing his kinsman's defeat. Then the battle begins. They circle each other, slow, cautious. Farah strikes first, making a series of feints designed to draw him out. She makes another strike closer. He easily moves to block it, but she only attacked to reduce the threat of the knee spikes. As her opponent finishes blocking her blow, she whips her left leg into a savage kick that lands on the side of his right knee. He recoils, shaking the wounded leg, now favoring the other.

Moving in with confidence, Farah lunges, aiming at his left shoulder. He counters, and she shifts direction while giving a forward slash. He blocks her again, but this time counters with a jerk of his right knee. She disengages at the weak attempt of a knee stab.

He smiles.

She presses her lips together, irritated that she misjudged the Onyx's pain tolerance.

They continue to exchange blows, though she notices he does not take advantage of opportunities to overpower her. He is delaying. Irritated with the display and the time being lost, she rushes in with an aggressive attack of smooth slashes targeting the torso, arms, and neck. He finally catches her sword in his kukri, forcing her blade down. She pulls her blade back to disengage, but he manages to wrench it out of her hand. Yet she still manages to strike out with her left hand, slashing his face. He touches his cheek and feels the warmth and sting. He looks at her clenched left hand and sees a small throwing dagger.

"Enough!" He rushes at her in a rage.

Farah knows she has reacted too slow to his quick change in demeanor, and she's knocked down onto her back, gasping for breath. As the warrior keeps himself from falling as well, he manages to lash out with a fist and knock the dagger from her left hand. Still on her back, Farah flails her arms, searching for either of her weapons as he comes upon her. Her right hand finds a branch, and she swings it wildly. One strike with his kukri knocks it away.

Just then, she hears an ear-stunning blast from behind them. They both stop, confused and uncertain. Next comes a piercing whistle that snaps them back into the present. Her mind again fixates on her precarious position, and she unleashes a series of targeted kicks to his ankles, shins, and then a final strike to the groin. The Onyx warrior howls and doubles over. Farah uses the time to do a backward roll out of harm's way, moving into a defensive crouch. The warrior, though, simply keeps an eye on her as he gathers up his weapons before trotting away toward the sound of the whistle, wincing as he glances back one last time.

Farah wrinkles her brow in bewilderment as she searches for her sword and dagger. Once she finds them, she takes off after the Onyx warrior. As she comes upon the commotion, she sees smoke dissipating from the blast, with a couple of the warriors still disoriented while the others have taken cover behind their shields. Suddenly, three arrows slice into their defense. One of them hits a disoriented warrior. He falls to the ground, writhing in pain. She looks in the direction of where the arrows came from and sees movement. A shadowed figure runs farther to the left away from her, and then another trio of arrows fly into the invading cluster, this time with no one hit.

She watches as the high warrior sends three warriors to confront the attack while she stays behind to guard the Chozien, along with the slightly injured warrior that Farah herself just fought. Farah's gaze follows the shadow figure as it runs deftly through the forest before it stops for a brief moment. In that instance, her eyes widen as she stares at Liam. He smiles and nods before he heads off into the woods, with the trio of Onyx warriors in close pursuit.

Noticing an odd scent of smoke that couldn't have come from the blast, Farah dismisses it and returns her attention to the pair guarding the Chozien. They both stand ready. While it is only two, Farah estimates that they are most likely the fiercest of the troop. She admits to herself that it is a battle she cannot win alone. Choosing to concede and report back to her sire, she sneaks back to their camp, taking note of some white smoke rising in the dim light a little ways from the enemy camp, but remaining focused on hurrying back to her sire's hold. She packs her travel bags and then unties Liam's horse so that it may freely roam the land.

It is a small gratitude she can offer the huntsman for his sacrifice.

THIRTY-FIVE

Farah sets a brisk pace, stopping at the spirit hold to give her report, and then at the earliest opportunity, she leaves to her sire's hold. She enters Branson's hold, defeated and bracing for his ire. A groom meets her and takes her horse. His look of surprise does not go unnoticed.

Before he leaves, she inquires, "Has the donateur returned?"

The stable hand shakes his head. "No."

When she says nothing in reply, he asks her, "Anything else?"

Farah shakes her head, and he leads her horse away.

With the donateur not yet returned, her thoughts immediately consider the worst scenarios. It could be the Bloodstone have encroached on the western border just as the Onyx have to the east. Or perhaps Trenton is still out searching, unaware their greatest rival now has the Chozien in their grasp. Before her mind goes too far, she requests an audience with her sire.

She doesn't have to wait long. Branson enters the room with the classic huntsman's stoic demeanor. Farah notes a shadow cast over him and a hardness not present when she left. It would be better that his mood were lighter, considering the ominous report she is about to deliver.

Farah says, "Namaste, Sire."

Branson replies unemotionally though weighted, "Namaste."

Farah does not waste time: "I can personally confirm that the Onyx are within our eastern borders and they have the Chozien."

His reaction comes with a rage-charged torrent of questions and commands: "What? No no no … he wasn't supposed to be there! Bring me my weapons, damn it! I will hunt them down myself, and the Old World will hear their screams before I release their *ames*. Where are my arms? Gerald, man!"

Farah attempts to calm the building storm: "Sire, they have crossed outside of the Jade borders by now. Best we plan—"

He whips around, targeting her with his fury. "Who are you to offer counsel to me? The Chozien was within your sight. How are you here and not him?"

A sharp female voice comes from behind: "That is enough!" Breanne stands with her hands on her hips in her worn brown apron with a maternal scowl. "What is this? We all serve you, Sire … by choice. This is not an ordinary warrior who stands before you; she is your best. We have lost enough." She mutters about keeping it down before she returns to the kitchen.

Branson clears his throat and lays a hand on the back of his neck. He looks at Farah and says, "Let's start again, shall we? Are you certain they were Onyx?"

She nods once. "Yes, Sire. I put down two myself and wounded another."

He frowns and looks downward, but then his head snaps back up and he looks at her. "Where is Liam?"

Farah's shoulders slump as she explains, "We were outnumbered. I made a plan so that it would divide them. Only two came for me. I killed one, but the other … was highly skilled. Then there was an explosion, and the Onyx warrior retreated back to his troop. I gave chase, but he had rejoined them by the time I caught up. I saw Liam. He had created enough of a diversion and more of a threat to cause them to change formation. Still, he was only able to draw three away, and the remaining warriors guarding the Chozien were too much for me to face alone. Liam led the others away so that I could report back to you."

Branson nods in silent memoriam at his loyal kinsman bonded in service. "What can you tell me of them?"

Farah recounts the huntsman's reconnaissance in avid detail, her battle with the two enemy warriors, her near-death encounter, and finally her reluctant escape. After she finishes, Branson just stands before her, arms folded.

She rotates her eyes from side to side and finally asks, "Yes … Sire?"

Branson asks, "Anything else?"

Farah searches her memory and, after a moment, shakes her head. "No, Sire."

Branson takes a step closer. "Anything at all? Something strange or doesn't fit maybe?"

She feels a bit of curiosity at the question, though she only shrugs as she describes, "There was … smoke. Lots of it, wafting into the sky."

Branson probes, "What color was the smoke?"

She answers, puzzled, "White."

"When did you notice?"

Farah pauses, replaying that day over. "I could smell it when I saw Liam draw the Onyx warriors away. Also, I saw it when I prepared to leave."

Branson nods. "Good."

Baffled by his encouraging response, she says, "I don't understand."

Branson explains, "It is an ancient form of communicating over a distance. Only a select few know this. White smoke comes from burning damp material … most likely grass. The steam gives it the white color. Liam used the smoke to alert the nearby clans of the enemy's presence. When you stopped at the spirit hold, did they seem surprised by your report?"

Farah crosses her arms in dumbfounded realization.

Branson goes on, "They appeared blindsided but rational. They commanded you to recite the details to our dewan's inner council but nothing more. Then they dismissed you to be on your way to me." And then more to himself, "They did not bother sending a rider to me, knowing my reaction would be … emotional."

"Yes. That is what happened."

Branson leans on the dining table and breathes deeply. Pressing his lips into a thin line, he resigns himself to resist his paternal instincts … a second time.

Turning to his ranger, he orders, "I will go to the spirit hold once the donateur returns, and you will accompany me there."

Farah nods. "Yes, Sire."

He releases her and turns away, but stops as Farah says, "Sire, it was my intention to die in that forest in the effort that it would bring back the Chozien—your son. My *ame* would have been at peace knowing you two were reunited."

His back still turned, he nods. "I know, Farah. I know."

She leaves, swallowing down the lump in her throat. She has only a moment to wallow in her hurt pride as she has to jump out of the way of a servant rushing by, finding herself thoroughly confused by the servant's announcement a moment later:

"Sire! The donateur has returned. He has Guilia with him."

Having given Jaafar and Guilia plenty of time to refresh themselves from their travels, Branson sends for them. He receives them in his great hall, where the hearth is in full blaze. The inviting warmth and comfort from the fire contrasts sharply with the crisp atmosphere created by the bitterness of the host and those with him. Trenton stands to the right of Branson, with Malan and Farah just behind him to his left—all wearing stern looks, though Trenton's appears more flushed than usual. Jaafar and Guilia stand before the group. No servants are present, save for an occasional appearance from Breanne, who pops in and scans each person's demeanor, looking for shifting feet or frequent swallows to determine discomfort or thirst.

Branson looks at Guilia and cuts straight to the point: "I can imagine you long to return to your order. Perhaps a reunion?"

Guilia purses her lips as she folds her arms over her chest and looks away from Branson's gaze.

Branson chuckles and concludes, "Yes, I recognize the look of longing. It is of no matter to me ... though it holds significant value to you." He takes in an exaggerated inhale, smiles, and continues, "The heart is like this—confuses the mind, influences actions, drives decisions, and perhaps changes loyalties, no?" He arches an eyebrow, ever watchful for a slip in her composure.

She rolls her eyes, then shakes her head. Just before she lifts one side of her cheek into a lopsided grin of defiance, she bites her bottom lip. Try as she may, there is no mistaking the surrender one has when they anticipate the release of their *ame*.

It is a grim feeling when one realizes they cannot outrun death. Yet, just before they begin to snap the link to the physical world and empty their psyche of the innate affections that define their existence, there is a brief moment of remembrance—a memoriam to their life and the lives of others connected to them, to the experiences and lasting imprints of memories that bubble up to the surface, where the most powerful of emotions expose themselves despite their owner's immense effort to keep them hidden. It will reveal itself in various forms: a small, gentle smile, a tensing brow, hands clutched or balled into fists, or a forlorn bite of the lower lip.

Seeing the proof and tiring of the banter, Branson folds his arms as well and offers, "I will give you a proposal that your Gold kinsmen never gave me. I will repay your debt to the Gold in exchange for one of my own."

Guilia responds with a sarcastic giggle. "Oh? How do you propose to do that? If I return without the others, it is likely they will suspect me of betrayal just as I stand before you now with the same uncertainty."

Trenton snorts. "You think your sire sent you here with the expectation you would return to him? What more information can you give? Your task is done. Whether you return or not, it does not matter. It never did. You were a sacrifice whether you knew it or not."

"What? No!" Eyes wide, Guilia shakes her head. "No ... no! I was assured upon my return ... that I will have someone waiting for me," she says, her voice fading toward the end.

Now Branson rolls his eyes and exhales audibly. "We all have someone waiting for us here and in the spirit world. We take solace on the day our *ames* are released and reunited with them."

Branson waves off the sentiment and returns to the topic. "As the donateur has stated, your *ame* is a sacrifice ... though it doesn't have to be."

Guilia stares at him for a moment, then gives a tiny nod and asks, "What do you want?"

Trenton answers, "You will return to your order. Report that the mental state of the gardien is crumbling. Unleash whispers that, prodding or left unchecked, can be used as currency, given your order's alliance with the Onyx. Convince your sire to send another spy, but you must vie to be the saisir—the intermediary. With you controlling the communication between the spy and the Gold, you will interpret the information as we intend."

"Fine," she says, adding a shrug. "What of the saisir my kinsmen spoke with?"

Trenton shakes his head. "That one was from the Onyx. He is not likely to return. We will make sure of that."

She nods slowly, cautiously satisfied, and then inquires, "How will I explain how I made it through the Jade lands?"

Malan huffs a clipped laugh. "You won't."

She eyes him. "I don't understand."

Malan says, "You will enter your borders from the Bloodstone lands."

"What? You cannot be serious?"

Malan states, "Shouldn't be too much for you. You are allies."

"No," she says, "the alliance lies with the Onyx. Once word spreads that they have the Chozien, new alliances must be made."

Malan waves a dismissive hand. "Your escape from the Jade won't come with many questions if you have risked traveling through the Bloodstone territory. The Onyx warriors are covering ground quickly. It's best that you do the same."

Branson steps in to interrupt the growing tension: "Your escorts will get you as close to your homeland as possible."

"Escorts?" Guilia asks with a raised eyebrow.

Farah steps forward. "I will be with you."

Guilia looks Farah up and down before she asks, "And?"

Farah points to Jaafar.

Guilia turns to look at him, just as he points at himself in surprise.

"Me?" Jaafar says. "But I'm just a scout."

Farah raises her hand. "Settle down. We all start as scouts. When you are called to a higher purpose, you accept; otherwise, you are just another body in the front line. This will make you worth three."

While this does not give comfort to the Zin scout, he nods.

Upon seeing Jaafar's acceptance, Branson begins laying out the details: The trio will travel on the western border using Jaafar as their guide. When approached by any Jade kinsman, they will claim to be emissaries from the gardien, traveling to the Hawk Clan. Since they will be without an official seal, they will have to rely on Jaafar and the gardien's reputation. Once across the border, if any Bloodstone confront them, they will put themselves forth as traveling traders with a hired guard. Jaafar will use the possessions from the house of Guilia's deceased kinsmen to support their act. Farah and Jaafar will mostly likely only be able to safely get as far as a day's ride inside the Bloodstone. So Guilia will need to travel alone into the southeastern border of the Gold Order and then on to the spirit hold. Within a full moon's time, she must go to the border post nearest to the Rain Clan to give her report.

The meeting ends, with the tension just as palpable as when it began.

THIRTY-SIX

It has been two days since the failed attack by the Jade Order. Judging by the meager performance, the Onyx high warrior surmises that it was a happenstance that the Jade kinsmen stumbled upon them, but they were far too skilled to be randomly traveling alone and that far off the open road, so she has pressed her troop harder than usual.

With their navigator dead, they turn south until they cross into the Amber Order lands and then head east, hugging the border. The Amber and Jade Orders are wartime allies, akin to the Onyx and Bloodstone Orders. In this case, there is no war yet, so while their presence is not ideal, it could appear threatening, given the history of the Onyx Order, and in the Amber, the past speaks volumes.

Fortunately, the trek proves mostly uneventful, with their only interaction coming from being trailed by a band of Amber warriors. The Onyx high warrior knows that they were undoubtedly scouted by the nearest clan, who in turn sent warriors to ensure they keep their distance. If news had somehow traveled to the Amber regarding their high-profile prisoner, they would have been stormed, killed, and the Chozien rescued.

With the Azurite border days away, and with the Amber warriors reducing in number along the way, the Onyx high warrior removes Aitan's gag, pausing to gesture for silence.

Aitan raises his hands up, hoping the offer might extend to his restraints. At the high warrior's counter to keep the gag in place, he drops his hands and shoulders in defeat. He thanks the Great Spirit for the relief given to him, however small.

Aitan, though, decides to take a shot at the high warrior: "The Onyx must be desperate to risk war by taking hostage the Chozien of another order."

She rebuffs with a click of her tongue. "Then you do not know us very well."

He scowls with embarrassment as the others chuckle.

"Tell us what life is like as Chozien in the Jade Order," the one called Saxon asks.

At Aitan's stubborn silence, Saxon cajoles, "Come on now. There is nothing that we do not already know."

Aitan puffs his chest and states, "As Chozien of the Jade Order, we are on a campaign to strengthen existing alliances and forge bonds where there are none."

"Some good that's done you," mocks another warrior who has tended to be silent.

The Onyx laugh at the comedic jab from an unlikely source.

Saxon remarks, "Alliance without allegiance is as brittle as the trunk of a dead tree. Once the base cracks, the branches will all crumble."

Aitan replies, "Without unity, no one will flourish. You cannot take power by force."

The high warrior speaks up with a biting tone: "What do you know about power? You Jade speak of peace as if you are exempt from every effort to achieve it. Peace does not come with talking, it does not come with kind hearts, and it certainly is not without cost. There is a dark corner in every clan, every order. Once known, it cannot be unknown. Once seen, it cannot be unseen."

Aitan stares at the high warrior a moment, then says, "The absence of fear dulls the emotions, hardens the heart, and bears fruit to dread, discord, and panic."

He looks away slightly, distracted by all the raucous laughter of the other warriors, but then he turns back to the high warrior and whispers, "Who is all this rage for?"

She widens her eyes at him and then shouts to her warriors, "Pipe down! I want to avoid contact, not attract it! Watch the Chozien, and if he speaks again, gag him."

Aitan goes silent but remains in thought. As each gait brings them closer to the Azurite border, he watches as the last of the Amber riders fade with the sun on the horizon. The group camps that night with a raging fire. Grateful for the heat and yet disheartened at the looming reality of his situation, Aitan wraps his cloak around him, rests against a tree, and closes his eyes. Just as he starts to drift off, he feels his boot being nudged. He blinks his eyes open to see the high warrior standing above him. She reaches out a bundle to him. He takes it and slowly unwraps it to reveal dried meat and fruit. He sets it to the side and returns to his resting position.

Aitan opens his eyes again as he feels a thump next to him. He rolls his eyes. "Doesn't your rank allow you to pass on your turn for guarding prisoners?"

She ignores his slight and states, "Our fare isn't as flavorful as the Jade's, but I'm sure your stomach will enjoy it nonetheless."

Aitan huffs a breathy laugh. "It's not the food, but the company."

She clears her throat and asks, "Is this ... well, I mean ... Is this something they teach in the Jade—telling someone's past in front of others?"

Hearing her hesitate—as well as from sheer muscle memory—he softens his tone while turning to the high warrior and offering an apology. He stops, narrows his eyes, and grits his teeth.

The high warrior shakes her head slowly with an incredulous expression. She finds her voice and explains her reaction: "The Jade did not teach you about deception?"

He defends his earlier query about her resentment from a past offense that obviously still plagues her: "Yes, but I also have a heart. It seems as though you do not."

The high warrior responds with a shrug. "Deception is done with a purpose. There is no greater love than for one to mislead another to save their kinsmen and beliefs. You will learn that in the Onyx for your own sake, and quickly."

Aitan rolls his eyes, hiding his worry of the warning. "Present."

"What?" the high warrior asks, looking at him.

"Earlier you said I was speaking about your past. I was referring to your present."

Looking away, the high warrior returns to her stern demeanor and retorts, "I see we can add decorum to that list of improvements."

Aitan snaps back, "You don't need to be trained to see when one bears animosity toward another, but you may need to be trained to give a damn. Perhaps a brother, no?"

The high warrior ignores the quip and changes the subject: "You should eat. We'll be meeting with the Azurite tomorrow. Perhaps they will have something more appropriate for a Chozien."

She drops a waterskin next to him and starts to leave, but she stops and turns her head to the side, with her back still to him as she says, "A leader who does not lead by example will always see the backs of their people."

The high warrior leaves. Aitan takes a bite of one of the strips of jerky, and he is quickly reminded of his appetite. While he eats, he watches the high warrior as she walks the camp. She is meticulous as she checks the rations and travel supplies. She walks to each warrior, inspects their weapons and takes inventory of their projectiles. She finally takes to the horses. Her face softens to a tender affection. The horses have already been tended, but she goes over each one. First, she checks the gums for discoloration and moisture. Next, she rubs the bridge of the nose as she places her other hand under its jaw. She waits a moment before moving on with her inspection. Completing her check, she runs her hand across the back and down its shoulder and hip, lifting each leg to examine the hooves. She takes out her hoof pick and removes any stones or buildup.

She lingers a bit more with one horse; Aitan concludes it to be hers. He takes note of its shiny chestnut-brown coat and braided tail—a beautiful mare indeed. She affectionately strokes her mount, and at times, he can see the high warrior's lips moving. As she leans her head against the horse's cheek, he can see her body relax. He feels envious of the solace the high warrior finds in the comfort of a familial presence. Conflicting his envy is his growing ire of the hypocritical nature within the Onyx.

Five days later, the high warrior sends one of the warriors to ride ahead and seek out the Azurite scouts to announce their presence. The warrior returns just after midday and announces that a group of Azurite envoys will be sent out to meet and escort them to the nearest clan. They ride the rest of the day, with the envoys showing up just as they finish setting up camp for the night.

To Aitan's relief, the envoy of four brings with them a freshly smoked deer shank and an assortment of vegetables. He watches as the high warrior and a pair of the Azurite kinsmen walk out of sight and hearing distance, while the two others set to making dinner. The male Azurite gets to work affixing a spit. He finds two Y-shaped sticks and then a third that is sharpened to make a skewer, then pierces the meat with the sharp end and slides it to the middle and positions it on the other two branches over the fire. While he warms the meat through, the female Azurite prepares the vegetables, slicing them into smaller pieces. Aitan catches a glimpse of onions, carrots, and potatoes. She fills a pot with water, bones, chopped produce, and some spices.

With his captors all occupied and the night chill creeping, Aitan wraps up in his cloak and drifts to sleep. Sometime later, he feels someone shaking him awake. He rubs his eyes open to see the female Azurite, smiling. He feels warmth and notices a second fire has been built closer to him. He quietly thanks the Great Spirit. He sits up and accepts the steaming bowl offered to him. He sniffs the stew and immediately begins spooning mouthfuls into his mouth. He raises his eyebrows as he bites into a hearty dumpling, expressing his satisfaction.

"How is the stew?" the Azurite kinswoman asks.

Aitan nods without stopping.

The woman chuckles and pours water into a cup. As she stretches the cup out to him, she remarks, "We built another fire closer to you. You are too far from the only one. I'd imagine the white rain will be here in a few days."

Aitan looks up and says around a chunk of deer meat, "Thank you. It's nice."

She leans in and whispers, "I added a bit of the Jade spices."

He looks up, surprised at the mention of his order.

The woman smiles warmly and taps his leg maternally, giving a squeeze at the end. She continues, "You know the Azurite and the Jade are most alike."

Aitan smirks. "I doubt it, Mistress."

"We may disagree on the approach, but the destination is the same."

Aitan recites a saying learned from his seeker training: "'What's gained by ill-gotten means spoils the bounty.'"

The woman shrugs. "When your path is made clear, you will achieve it by any means."

At Aitan's silence, she offers a warning: "You are in no shortage of devotion. Cling to that while with the Onyx."

Aitan furrows his brow and asks, "What does that mean?"

The woman shakes her head. "You do not know what it takes to be an Onyx kinsman?"

Aitan recoils with disgust. "Onyx kinsman! I'm a prisoner." He holds up his bound hands for emphasis.

The Azurite glances around and leans in to whisper, "You will be treated as rien. Nothing. Zero. The Azurite will—"

Aitan hears a rustling from behind him and footsteps, then a familiar voice: "I think the Chozien has eaten well. Thank you for the meal."

The Azurite smiles tightly and excuses herself, taking the empty bowl with her.

The Onyx high warrior sits next to Aitan again, exhaling heavily.

Aitan looks at her in exasperation.

She rolls her eyes and remarks, "Your offense is becoming ... unfitting."

And just like that, Aitan is convinced his opinion of the Onyx is valid.

"What do your Jade teachings tell you of the Azurite woman?" She nods in the direction of the woman.

It's Aitan's turn to roll his eyes.

The high warrior urges, "Give it a try."

Aitan blows a raspberry. "She's … thoughtful."

The high warrior agrees. "Sort of like a mother, maybe?"

Aitan grimaces. "I wouldn't go that far. I'm sure the Azurite covet the Chozien just as much as the Onyx."

The high warrior laughs and ruffles his hair. "You are a quick learner."

Aitan shies away from the sarcasm and looks at her sideways. "I'm far from a novice."

She nods with a taunting smirk. "Are you sure?"

Aitan responds, irritated, "Are you forgetting you kidnapped me? That I am your prisoner and restrained like some animal? You sit here like you know me; you do not. But you are everything I expect from an Onyx."

Aitan finds solace in the silence that follows.

The high warrior surprises herself with her awkwardness. She breaks the silence by speaking solemnly, capturing a memory: "When I was named warrior, I was so happy. I thought my father would be too. It was like my whole world depended on his approval." She pauses a moment before she continues, "I remember looking through the crowd for my family. It wasn't until the crowd dispersed that I knew they had not come. I returned to my clan, and when I entered my home, my family would not look at or speak to me. I lived like this for a few moons. Finally, Saxon disclosed to me that my parents felt dishonored."

Gaining interest, Aitan says, "What? … But why?"

"I have two brothers who were named warrior ahead of me. It takes six birth years to attain the title; I achieved mine in five."

Aitan exclaims, "Six birth years!"

She chuckles and confirms, "Yes, but we start training much earlier."

"That is a great accomplishment. Still, why would they feel dishonor?"

She explains in a matter-of-fact way, "My father adores his sons. He takes my success as an attempt to overshadow them. So I left to serve at the spirit hold. That was about thirteen years ago. I've never looked back."

In a soft voice, Aitan says, "But you do."

She eyes him. "What did you say?"

Aitan replies, "You do look back—and you are hurt." He watches as her eyes narrow and her jaw clenches.

Despite the signs of ire, she gives a tight smile and remarks, "Well, look who thinks they know someone." With that, the high warrior stands and states, "Get some sleep. We start before the sun rises." She stops at the small campfire and speaks over her shoulder, "You are right: You are my prisoner. I need not be concerned with your comfort." She stomps out the fire and extinguishes any hope of a relaxing slumber.

Aitan watches her leave and mumbles under his breath, "Well, I suppose she is angry."

The next day does indeed start early. Aitan notices that the high warrior has increased the pace more than any other. Still, midday has long passed when they finally enter into an Azurite clan hold through mechanically enhanced gates that their order is known for. The clan's sire and his council greet them upon their entrance.

"Namaste. I am Sire Kenson. Welcome to the Candor Clan. I think we can remove the restraints now," he says, looking at the Onyx warriors.

One of them makes a move toward the Chozien, but the Onyx high warrior holds up her hand, stopping him.

She says, "He is prisoner of the Onyx."

At the sire's nod, the high warrior unsheathes her dagger and grips the rope between Aitan's hands. She holds his gaze, a slight lift in her brow warning him she won't take any escape attempts lightly.

Aitan's face mirrors his father's stoicism. A single pull of the dagger releases his hands. He rubs his wrists and steps aside the high warrior, discounting her presence to address the sire: "Namaste. Would your hospitality extend to a warm bed and meal?"

Aitan notes the sire's head is balding, with a clutch of thin gray strands, a short-cropped beard, and brown eyes outlined in a dark color.

Sire Kenson puffs his chest out as he states, "You are free to go anywhere here." He turns to one of his council and says, "Please escort the Chozien to our best lodging establishment. See that he is fitted with the purifying surfactants and clean garments to freshen the mind. Knowledge is best obtained with an unburdened countenance."

Aitan smirks over his shoulder at the scowling high warrior before he is led away by the saluer—the ceremonial greeter or escort. Not many orders find this position purposeful, the Jade order being one of them.

The saluer takes Aitan to a spacious inn with high, vaulted ceilings in the lobby, and the man beams with pride at Aitan's wide-eyed expression.

"This was called a 'hotel' before the Breaking," the saluer says. "We did our best to have our artisans resurrect its glory in our time. And directly to our left is the restaurant. Dine to the serene sounds of the classic harp."

Aitan scans the room, seeing a scattering of diners in casual conversation. He nods, clearly impressed.

The saluer continues, "Our chef trains in the finest culinary arts highlighting local ingredients. I recommend the dry-aged, garlic-seared buffalo. Absolutely delicious."

Aitan steps out of the way of a group of entering Azurite kinsmen.

"Ah, let us continue on to your accommodations; the dinner rush is upon us."

He leads Aitan through the partition across the lobby.

As they walk down a hallway, Aitan points at a lamp whose light is not sourced from fire. "The Azurite are known for their advancements. How is it that you are able to produce light without fire?"

The saluer looks at Aitan with amazement at his interest. He launches into an explanation that Aitan loses interest in quickly, only remembering the phrases "wind turbines" and "kinetic energy," undoubtedly because he's never heard those words in combination before. Thankfully, they soon stop at his room.

"Ah, here you are." The saluer opens the door for the Chozien.

Aitan inhales the clean scent of frankincense. He walks to the bed and collapses on it.

The saluer chuckles and informs him, "I will send up fresh clothes and have your traveling attire washed and ready for you in the morning."

Before the Azurite leaves, Aitan stops him to ask, "I'm looking for something a little bit more ... lively than the restaurant. Anything like that around?"

The saluer smile widens. "I know just the place."

Standing on an elevated platform as he leans on the railing, Aitan takes a sip of his drink as he looks across the throng of patrons engaging blissfully in social interactions or dancing to the melodic tunes being played by the musicians. He smiles absently as memories surface from times past when he freely partook in similar activities with his own friends. He feels his chest tightening at the fond recollections and at how he has been stripped of making more of them. He fears what he does know and what is to be expected. He scolds himself for being arrogant and selfish.

His naïveté led him here. He fears for his mother's worry and his father's guilt as the price of his disobedience. He gulps down the rest of the liquid in his cup, hoping to remember but wanting to forget.

A raised voice close to him disturbs his wallowing. He turns to see a smiling woman dressed in alluring attire, quite appropriate for the place.

"What did you say?" he asks.

Standing next to him, she reaches out her hand, offering a clear glass filled with a brown liquor and a dried orange peel floating in it. "I said, you look distracted. We come here to forget our troubles."

Aitan forces a smile and takes the offered libation.

She ignores his sour mood by smiling and introducing herself, "I'm Camille."

He starts to return the pleasantry, but she jumps in, "I know who you are. Everyone does."

Aitan nods. "I suppose I should have expected that."

The woman called Camille points to the glass in his hand. "You'll enjoy that. It's called an Old Fashioned. Heard of it?"

Aitan shakes his head.

Camille laughs. "I'm sure you have seen and heard several new things since you arrived. We Azurite embrace many inventions from the Old World. Life can be so much more when you reduce the effort it takes to live it."

Aitan smiles tightly and counters, "Yes, at the cost of your *ame*. The further you distance yourself from the essence of life, the more you risk losing hold of the world around you. The Old World became over-zealous with their pursuit of innovation to the degree that they did more harm to the very people they sought to save. You cannot embrace the good of history without the bad if you intend to break the genera-tional curse."

Camille sits there, speechless. She looks at him with shock in her eyes before she finds her voice: "Impressive. I did not know the Jade are so well versed in the Old World."

"I was tutored by the Amber Order."

Camille raises her glass in front of her. "A toast: to knowing the past and protecting the future."

Aitan smiles for the first time and shrugs as he touches his glass to hers. She takes a sip of hers, and Aitan begins to follow suit but stops as he feels someone step in.

He does not need to see the face since he recognizes the voice and immediately rolls his eyes in apparent annoyance as the intruder looks at Camille and says, "I am sure the Chozien appreciates the hospitality."

Aitan notes that the Onyx high warrior manages to say it in an overly pleasant tone. Camille exchanges glances with the Onyx kinswoman and then the Chozien before she nods awkwardly and turns to leave. The high warrior stops her, though, and takes the glass from Aitan's hand, then gives it to her.

The high warrior smiles and states, "We don't need this. Would you take this with you? Oh, thank you."

When Camille turns away, the high warrior loses her smile and looks at Aitan in admonishment. He holds his hands up in confusion. She puts a finger to her lips for silence and waves him to follow her. She leads him to a table, which has two glasses sitting on it, with Saxon sitting in one of the chairs. The music is lower, so they do not need to strain to hear. The high warrior nods to Saxon, and he leaves as the two of them sit.

The high warrior points to the glass in front of Aitan and advises, "It is best when it is cold."

Aitan looks down in his glass. He sees a shimmering, clear,

amorphous-shaped object surrounded by light-pink liquid. Confused, he looks up at her.

She feigns as if he is questioning the color and clarifies, "Oh, it's flavored with cranberries. It's festive during this time."

Aitan narrows his eyes and tilts his head to the right. He heaves a sigh, then asks, "What are you doing?"

She shakes her head and says in a reproachful tone, "You are not among friends. Do not accept anything unless you know who it is coming from." She taps the rim of her glass.

Aitan furrows his brow in confusion and then blinks. In a low voice, he exclaims, "So now you offer me another drink from someone I do not know."

The high warrior shrugs and replies, "Oh, aren't you clever! I would think we are well acquainted by now." She picks up the glass in front of Aitan and takes a sip, then sets it back down, smacking her lips. "Your drink has been tested and has been found to be untouched, oh Great Chozien!" the high warrior says in a loud, formal voice.

Aitan snatches the glass up as the high warrior shakes her head, annoyed. They sit for a moment, taking various swallows of the flavorful cocktail.

It's the high warrior who breaks the silence: "I applaud you for your performance earlier today with the Azurite sire."

Aitan smirks. "The Azurite can be very reasonable with the right flattery."

The high warrior sniffs. "It sounds … unreliable."

Aitan counters, "It was necessary. Aren't you Onyx trained to adapt?"

The high warrior shifts the topic in a display of her own adaptability: "We took twin blades from you. You prefer the huntsman service over others?"

"It has its advantages."

"Seems dull most of the time."

Aitan clicks his tongue at the ignorance. She laughs arrogantly. He can feel his face heating with anger.

Tired of being the subject of conversation, he says, "You seem young for a high warrior."

She laughs again and takes a sip before she responds, "Yes, that I am—both young and a high warrior." At his expectant look, she elaborates, "Taking this mission is my promotion. All our high warriors are known. We need a new face, one that would not raise suspicion. I was selected, but I named my price: my promotion and being able to choose my troop."

Aitan nods. "Quite the ask."

She scoffs. "They could have refused; I couldn't."

Aitan offers a different perspective: "The Great Spirit challenges us every day. You were chosen by more than just your general. Don't waste it haunted by the intention."

Her expression becomes bemused, having not considered that point of view before.

Unaware of her contemplation, Aitan presses her with, "Let's see, you would be about twenty-five birth years, right?"

The high warrior nods.

Aitan smiles. "Congratulations! Keep it up and you'll be a general in no time."

The mood relaxes, with the rest of the conversation becoming light-hearted. Coming upon the late hour, Aitan does his best to conceal a yawn, though he's unsuccessful.

The high warrior chuckles. "Best you retire. You have a long journey ahead of you."

He admits to his tiredness and raises his glass for a final toast, which she accepts and nods gratefully to. He stumbles as he stands, partly from his inebriation.

Confident he's gotten his balance, he smiles and bids her a good evening. "I look forward to seeing what change you bring to the Onyx."

Aitan waves and trudges away, leaving the high warrior somber.

Saxon comes to stand behind her. "Why toy with him? He begins his descent tomorrow."

The high warrior shrugs. "What he says may be true. He will see my rise as a high warrior.... It just may be from the prison."

THIRTY-SEVEN

The trio of Farah, Jaafar, and Guilia makes quick time traveling along the Bloodstone-Jade border. As anticipated, Jaafar's identity and familiarity among the Jade scouts sees them through the Hawk Clan lands. Surprisingly, they encounter no Bloodstone, though this does not divert their initial plan to accompany Guilia for a day's ride within the Bloodstone territory. Soon enough, Farah and Jaafar part ways with Guilia, reminding her of the debt and the cost of default.

On her own, Guilia crosses the southeastern Gold border and makes contact with the nearest clan. Scouts from there transport her to the spirit hold, where she waits for her dewan. She does her best to slow her breathing and settle her nerves while avoiding the suspicious stares from his assembled council.

"Well, I must say, I am as pleased as I am shocked to see you have returned!" the dewan booms as he walks into the greeting hall.

Guilia hides her disdain as she curtsies to accept the welcome. "Thank you. I come bearing favorable news."

A hefty man with a plump belly and bald head, sporting a beard with a single braid, the dewan laughs with pompous glee. "Well, let us hear of it. What could be more compelling than the capture of the Chozien by the Onyx?"

She nods, and with all seriousness, she weaves the tale she was given: "The gardien has been given many great blows—foremost, his wife being gravely injured and the Chozien taken by the Onyx. Given the right persuasion, we can influence the actions and choices of a strong Jade leader. In my time among them, I learned that the gardien is a close confidant to their dewan. We will possess what the Onyx desires."

The dewan nods, impressed.

But his general eyes Guilia and asks, "Be that as it may, how are you here and not Mena and Sharad? They have known this way of life more than you."

Guilia inhales sharply, feigning offense. "Yet, I had more to claim upon my return."

At the general's waiting look, she continues on with the pretense, "We planned to join the trade caravan, but the gardien sealed the gates. They slipped me out of a small, concealed door by the wall before the guards claimed it. Once out, I was able to head north."

The general furrows his brow. "But once you were discovered missing, they would have sent kinsmen out to find and bring you before the gardien. You cannot evade a skilled huntsman or warrior."

Guilia clarifies, "Being part of the trading caravan was always my cover, as it was headed to the eastern Jade clans. The Chozien's infatuation with me would draw him out alone to save his woman from riding into a possible Onyx battle. This is where they sent their kinsmen."

Not yet assuaged, the general goes on, "With the threat of war between our borders, traders would be held until the threat has diminished or you were able to bypass the interrogation. Again, a skill you do not possess."

"I did not have to disguise myself; my reputation as a clothier still holds. I was held with other travelers until the Bloodstone had receded from the borders, then I quickly made my way into Gold territory alone."

The dewan holds up a hand toward his general. "That is enough, Itai. The girl must be weary from her flight and enduring several birth years among the Jade's delusional ducall of peace."

"Just one more question," Itai says. At the dewan's nod, Itai asks, "What happened to Sharad and Mena?"

She shrugs her shoulders. "Their fate is unknown to me. It was they who commanded I return here and not to wait."

Itai looks to his dewan and says, "They have surely been captured or put to death. Their deed is done and even so presents us with an unexpected asset that would be of considerable value. The Onyx may hold the Chozien, but we wield the influence."

The dewan nods. "Indeed. See to it that their families receive the agreed reward."

"It will be done," the general replies.

At the mention of reward, Guilia inquires, "Dewan ... if I may, I have also succeeded. My debt—"

His laugh cuts her off, and as an afterthought, he says, "Oh yes! When you entered the hold, we summoned your mate. I release Naomi to you."

At his last declaration, a woman comes out of one of the side rooms. She and Guilia lock eyes and race to each other, falling into the other's arms as they tearfully comfort one another. The women do not linger, but hurry from the hall, hand in hand, leaving the Gold council with much to discuss.

After they depart, the dewan asks his spirit keeper, "What does her spirit tell you?"

A small elderly woman shuffles into view, aided by the general. Her tattooed face holds many birth years of her service.

She responds, "Her *ame* showed a dull yellow with a purple hue and flickered when she spoke of her journey through the Jade and of her recount of the gardien. It is hard to say whether it be a lie or fear. If it were a lie, it would be brighter. She was certainly … cautious. Perhaps a mix of fact and fiction." She laughs. "Goodness, it changed to mighty red when she spoke with the general. I don't think she appreciated the slights you gave her."

Itai clicks his tongue. "The Jade may be arrogant, but they are not fools. She did not make that journey home alone."

At this, the dewan stands and commands the general, "Well, tell me who helped her, then."

The general answers, "It will be done."

The couple lies in bed, shuddering from the consummation of their reunion. They relish the silence and each other's presence. Guilia reclines across her wife's breast. She runs her fingers up and down Naomi's arm. She pushes herself up and rests on her left elbow as she gazes at her bonded *ame*. Guilia reaches up and caresses her love's chestnut cheek. She traces Naomi's thick eyebrows, full nose, and plump lips. She curls her finger around a tuft of the brown, curly locks. Overcome with joy, she kisses Naomi softly.

Wrapping her arms around Guilia, Naomi asks, "What was it like to live among the Jade?"

Guilia laughs. "It is like everywhere with people and those who seek dominion over others. It was odd to have seen so many who did not want for excess, Naomi. Of course, there are the poor and the clandestine activities of those whose ambitions are greater than they will ever be. But the gardien is kind ... as he is cunning."

Naomi senses a heaviness in her last words. "Why do you despair so?"

Guilia shrugs. "It was just all so new and strange. As traders, the wares we brought with us as we set off on this mission were undesirable. We misjudged what they value. But as I lie here with you, I now know."

Excited by a potential opportunity to increase their position, Naomi proclaims, "Good, now our debt is paid! We will use your knowledge from living among them to name our price. As long as we hold this between us, we can never be severed again, and our gains will mound on top of each other."

Guilia nods her head absently, as she no longer has the desire to covet more. She wants nothing more than to live the rest of her days with Naomi. The general is right: Guilia is not skilled in acts of deception. She wasn't chosen because of this, but rather for her youthful appearance to distract with lust. For her to accomplish this, she had to break her fidelity vows to gain the trust of the Chozien. She now realizes it is not easy to share many intimate moments with someone and not develop some kind of attachment. She knows this guilt will haunt her for some time. She will complete her bargain with the Jade gardien and free herself from the politics of greed. For now, she will bury her shame in Naomi's embrace. Guilia's kiss is filled with myriad emotions and desire, and Naomi returns it in equal fervor. One would describe their coupling as passion beyond boundaries, beyond lifetimes.

Aitan wakes up groggy, massaging his head. He sits on the edge of the bed and stretches. One look around reminds him of his present situation and the imminent threat looming over him. He stands, rolls his shoulders, and stretches out his arms. He goes to the washbasin and turns a lever that lets out a steady stream of water from the spigot. Fortunately, he was introduced to plumbing on one of the peace campaigns to the Azurite spirit hold. He scoffs at the thought, agreeing with the Onyx warrior: *Some good that effort did.*

Untrusting of the spiritual energy lacking in the Azurites and their ability to use the Reach, he closes his eyes and grasps at the strand he knows as the water's *ame*. He can feel a surge from its purity, such harmony and pleasantness. He looks over the bowl and opens his eyes. His eyes are glazed over with a silver hue as he manipulates the element. The water ripples as the expulsion from the cleansing clumps together. Satisfied, he knocks away the impurities with his hand and turns the lever the opposite direction to stop the flow of water.

He splashes the water over his face, using the soap to cleanse the sleep away. Once done, he pulls out the plug in the center of the basin to release the water. He watches the liquid collide in chaos as every drop clamors to its liberation. It does not last long, as the flow takes the shape of a circle. A swirl forms, disappearing and reappearing as the water becomes fierce and attempts to disrupt the protective berm, but the swirl never breaks. Salvation achieved, only the echo of the escape remains to fill the emptiness.

Aitan grabs a towel and dries his face. As promised, his traveling clothes have been cleaned, and he even notes a few mends. He welcomes the comfort as he dons the Jade attire. He stops in front of the door and straightens his back more. He takes a deep breath, opens the door, and walks through the threshold to captivity.

The saluer from the day before guides Aitan through the establishment and out the entrance. There, he finds ten or so heavily armored Onyx warriors waiting. Aitan lifts an eyebrow at the show unfolding in front of him. One of the warriors binds his hands again, though not as tight as before. After securing Aitan, a pair of warriors hold him by the arms and follows the entourage toward the front gate.

At the main gate Aitan sees the Azurite sire and his council and, surprisingly, another Onyx troop of seven. He searches for the high warrior or anyone from her troop, but is disappointed to see none of them. He does notice a wagon fitted with steel bars, resembling a cage more than a carriage. Six Onyx kinsmen surround the wagon, awaiting command. Putting the cage aside in his mind, Aitan returns his attention to the new faces.

Sire Kenson speaks in ceremonial volumes: "The Azurite Order has fulfilled its contract with the Onyx. You will provide the agreed yield of your berry harvest, and our arrangement will be complete."

The apparent leader of the new Onyx troop saunters forward—a muscular man with a full head of red hair and bearded in the same likeness. His ears are gauged with plugs the size of the length of his little finger and of the color of a moonless night. He wears traditional travel attire. His sword's hilt peeks out of his heavy cloak. The metalwork looks impressive, and the pommel holds yet another onyx stone to set the balance.

His voice comes forth low and deliberate: "The Azurite will receive their exchange once the Chozien has crossed the Onyx border."

Sire Kenson chuckles. "Oh .... ah, yes, of course. You will have safe passage through our lands."

The Onyx troop leader looks at Aitan and jerks his head toward the cage, ordering, "Get in."

Another Onyx warrior stands next to the door of the cage and opens it, smiling while chewing on a piece of straw.

Aitan puffs his chest and glowers at the Azurite sire. "You betray the Chozien for *berries*? I thought the Azurite would have demanded more, given your intelligence."

Sire Kenson just smiles. "It is more than just berries. We welcome inquisitive minds like yours. Perhaps you will attend one of our academies in the future."

Aitan clicks his tongue in defiance as he walks to his next transport. The Onyx kinsman holding the door bows and waves his arm deeply, as if welcoming an honored guest, clearly mocking him. Aitan ignores him and steps into the cage, stooping under the frame. The Onyx kinsman puts his boot in the middle of Aitan's back and shoves him the rest of the way in. The door closes, and Aitan hears it lock. While his new troop of captors gets on preparing for the long journey, he sits on the straw and leans against the metal bars.

Aitan finally sees the high warrior. He exhales, the condensation appearing in white puffs from his mouth. "Here I was thinking you had too much drink last night and would be sleeping through the midday."

The high warrior grins. "Oh, you haven't seen me drink in excess."

He chuckles. "I look forward to that day."

She smirks, then loses her smile and leans in closer to whisper, "You will be traveling with a very different troop now until you reach the Onyx spirit hold."

A smile playing at his lips, Aitan responds, "A shame indeed, as I was just getting used to yours."

The high warrior frowns. "Your charm will not aid you, but only fuel their disdain and perhaps encourage harm."

Shrugging, Aitan retorts, "I am elated at your concern. It is my purpose to spread peace. This is but an extension of the Jade's campaign."

The high warrior shakes her head. "You are bound to be a réclamé—a reclaimed *ame*. Your life as a Jade kinsman ends now, and your journey to become Onyx has begun. You will be put through torment as a testament of your will to show that your *ame* is worthy to be reclaimed."

The Onyx troop leader calls out, "Ah-lam! We are set to leave now."

The high warrior turns and nods at the man.

Aitan brightens, and as the company leaves, he says, "You are called Ah-lam. We are now known to each other. Peace be with you!"

She shakes her head at him for his pious ignorance. The Libérer will change him—the intense trials imposed on voluntary applicants vying to be of the Onyx Order because they were not born to it. The Libérer serves to liberate the *ame* so that a person may experience the full Glory of the Great Spirit and all the power that comes with it.

Ah-lam finds herself surprised that she hopes the Libérer will not result in Aitan's madness. Those with strong *ames* resist the most, though they are pushed the fiercest. If Aitan holds true to his teachings as he proclaims, he will not break so easily, condemning himself to much agony and misery.

EPILOGUE

Desire and duty are like two writhing and slithering serpents—both necessary and threatening to the life cycles of creatures, creeping into the jovial and blissful paradise between even father and son. The vile wickedness coils their scale-skinned bodies about their victim's most cherished securities: faith, freedom, and family being high among them. The intent is clear, so as the overzealous miser stingily hordes and clutches fanatically to his riches either earned or stolen, the elongated reptiles twist and constrict until paralysis remains but an inch away.

Consumption not being the immediate objective, the serpents purposefully plunge their deadly fangs into their prey's naïve defenses and let loose the venom. The victim feels the sting; the toxin seeps in, corrupting as it fills veins and follows along to the volatile but precious sanctuary of the infected. Here, the seed of suspicion and fear are planted, though not yet rooted. It will take time for this germ to mature and grow before its hold grows firm; however, this scene does not have to come to be.

To a trained body and mind, the insidious poison can find its usefulness. With preparation, the intended target would recognize the immediate threat and employ the leurre—a hypnotic maneuver mastered by the Rhodonite Order—to manipulate the target into revealing the poison's true intent. All is not lost, as what is lost, sacrificed, and suffered opens the path to wield the Gloire—a faith strong enough to destroy mountains or protect the Great Spirit's creations ... only bestowed as a blessing upon the selfless. The path is set; it is wise to tread lightly or be consumed by the alluring infection.

Such is this world, interrupting laughter and calm, holding hostage the very gifts the Great Spirit bequeaths. Where visions of a couple entangled in fiery devotion and the haunting cage disappear, new ones will emerge. Where the price of independence is treachery, the seeds will be sown and another price named. Where disgrace and despair loom, redemption is keen, but concealed. Unexpected appreciation creates new emotions that will test the mightiest of loyalties. Nigh the time lurks ever closer that these serpents let loose their machinations upon the unsuspecting mice. The Chozien must be ready and willing to embrace his darkness.

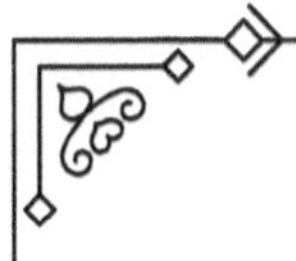

GLOSSARY OF TERMS

Ame': an individualized spirit of a living element

Attendant: A kinsmen/kinswomen in service to the Dewan/
Dewana to entertain high ranking guests. Each
Order has their own rules to the latitude which
an attendant may extend to the guest.

Attetnes: also known as 'desert walkers'. An evolved race
fit to live in the desert or mountainous regions.
Their blacksmithing craftsmanship is masterful
and they rarely make contact with humans.

Banni: The term referred to kinsmen/kinswomen who
have been banished from their Order

Bonne Ame': A revered title that is gifted to kinsmen/kins-
women who have performed a valiant deed.

Chozien: The child the Great Spirit chooses to instill with
an elevated ame'

Dewan/Dewana: The title the leader of an Order is known by and
their spouse

Ducall: guiding principle the people of each Order live by

Lire': The term referred to kinsmen/kinswomen who carry communication between clans and Orders.

Order: organized communities of people

Relican: the name the Attenae refer to the people of the Orders, it is a derogatory reference.

Saisir: The term referred to someone who is a contact or handler for a spy

Service: Kinsmen/kinswomen are allowed to study as a novice in a specially recognized skill. If they fulfill the requirements of the service, they are named and must chose a profession of which to contribute to society

Sire/Sira: The title the leaders of clans or strongholds within each Order and their spouse

SERVICES:

Warrior: the military force of the Orders: military, guards, scouts, etc.

Spirit Seeker: the health providers and educators of the Orders: healers, apothecaries, teachers, astronomers, biologists, etc. Secondary role in the military

Huntsman: the necessity and nourishment providers of the Orders: blacksmiths, hunters, gathers, butchers, clothiers, farriers, etc. Secondary role in the military

CHARACTERS

Gaylen: Dewan to the Jade Order

Zahrine: Dewana of the the Jade Order, wife to Gaylen

Harwen: Sire to the Jade Order's Huin Clan, known as a brownnoser and braggart

Remy: Sire to the Jade Order's Zin Clan, known as a brownnoser and braggart

Connor: Sire to the Jade Order's Rhyne Clan, known for his unyielding loyalty and humility

Clayton: Sire to the Jade Order's June Clan, known as a socialite and for his indulgence in libations

Marquis: Sire to the Jade Order's Glen Clan, known to jump at the first hint of a war

Graham: Sire to the Jade Order's Hawk Clan, known to be envious and secretive

Isaac: Sire to the Jade Order's Trace Clan, known as a strong strategist

Tuan: Sire to the Jade Order's Dun Clan, known as a strong strategist

Aitan: Jade Order Chozien

Branson: Huntsman in the Jade Order, Gardien of the Jade Chozien, and holds the rare title of Bonne Ame, belonged to the Zin Clan.

Uric: Spirit Seeker in the Jade Order, best friend to Branson, and holds the rare title of Bonne Ame, belongs to the Huin Clan

Trenton: Warrior of the Jade Order, Donateur to the Jade Chozien, not born of the Jade Order

Haru: General of the Jade Order

Keno: Spirit Keeper of the Jade Order

Len: Chief Huntsman of the Jade Order

Randol: High Warrior in the Jade military, serves at the spirit hold

Ahni: former Attendant of the Jade Dewan. Wife to Branson

Leesha: Wife to Uric

Reba: former Attendant of the Jade Dewan. Servant to Branson and Reba. Wife to Trenton.

Malan: Ahni and Branson's first-born son, in the Warrior service, and foster brother to Aitan

Romin: Uric and Leesha's youngest child, in the Warrior service, and best friend of Aitan

Breanne: Head of kitchen at Branson's manor

Gerald: Head of Household at Branson's manor

Kel: Warrior who trained with Aitan as novices and childhood friend of Aitan

Ewa:	Spirit seeker who trained as a novice with Aitan and childhood infatuation of Aitan
Ali:	Spirit seeker who trained as a novice with Aitan and childhood friend of Aitan
Sicily:	Spirit seeker who trained as a novice with Aitan and childhood friend of Aitan
Farah:	Ranger—an elite Warrior in service to Branson
Liam:	Huntsman, best tracker in service to Branson
Jafaar:	Warrior scout of the Zin clan
Giulia:	kitchen servant of Ahni and Branson. Love interest of Aitan
Mena:	clothier, fictional mother to Giulia
Sharad:	clothier, fictional father to Giulia
Dyconn:	Onyx Dewan
Makani:	Dyconn's eldest son and foster brother to Zeke
Zeke:	Onyx Chozien
Ah-Lam:	Onyx High Warrior sent to capture the Jade Chozien
Saxon:	skilled warrior in Ah-Lam's troop

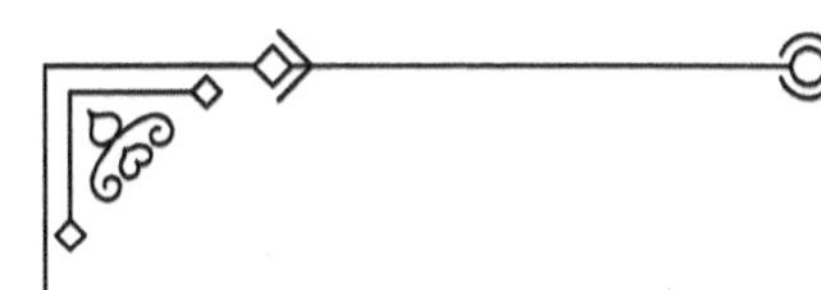 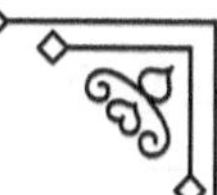

ORDERS

AMBER *(Yellow)*
◇ SEEKERS OF WISDOM

Tutors of history and spies of the present.

Owl for its wisdom and stealth

AMETHYST *(Purple)*
◇ SEEKERS OF HEALING

Highly trained doctors of many practices

Fox for its quick sense

AZURITE *(Blue)*
◇ SEEKERS OF WELL

Being: Innovative academics and engineers

Wolf for its social, intelligent, loyal, and self-control

BLOODSTONE *(Red)*
SEEKERS OF SURVIVAL

Healthcare scientists and expert surgeons

Ox for its strength, longevity, sacrifice, and well ground

CARNELIAN *(Orange)*
SEEKERS OF CREATION

Avid Fishery, Archeology, Botany, and Culinary

Snake for its transformation and never looking back

CRYSTAL *(White)*
SEEKERS OF TRUTH

Prominent Seekers and Distillers

Camel for its humility, willingness to aid, and stubbornness

GOLD *(Gold)*
SEEKERS OF WEALTH

Repute for its Loan Sharks

Tiger for its patience and planning

HEMATITE *(Gray)*
SEEKERS OF STABILITY

Staunch Pirates and Assassins

Rabbit for its protection and fear

JADE *(Green)*
SEEKERS OF PEACE

Politicians; main setting

Bear for its steadfastness and nourishment

ONYX *(Black)*
◇ SEEKERS OF POWER

Agrarian culture; control of supply chain

Lion for its authority and courage

RHODONITE *(Rose)*
◇ SEEKERS OF BEAUTY

Expert Artisans (Masons, painters, metallurgy, etc.) and Tacticians

Deer for its compassion

Peacock for its confidence

Giraffe for its awareness and vision

Scorpion for its strong sense of intuition

TIGEREYE *(Brown)*
◇ SEEKERS OF STRENGTH

Intelligent geneticists and biologists

Elephant for his power, strength, and honor

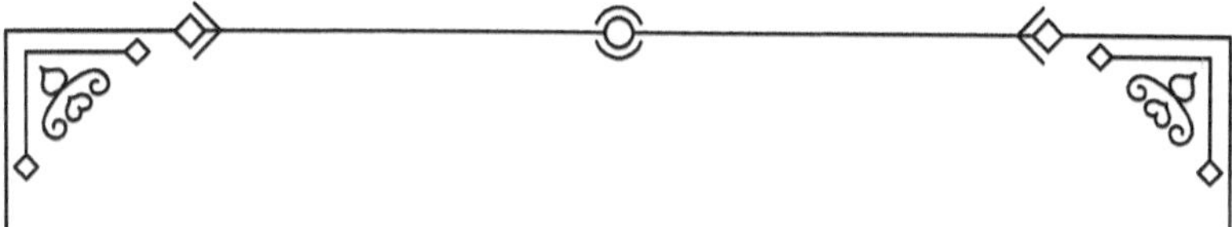

AUTHOR'S NOTE

Ever watch a movie and thought a bigger plot twist or more character development would have made it that much more impactful? I stopped critiquing movies because I realized this was someone else's work and a lot of passion went into its development. That's when I decided I'd write my own books and tell my own stories. I have my genre locked in as fantasy, but I love stories which have a past which was quite prominent but has since fallen—enter the dystopian genre. If that was not enough, I especially love series because it allows for additional character development, political intrigue, and carries over time without feeling the need to rush…because there's another book to carry on the story and introduce more characters and discovery of new land and people. That makes it a Dystopian Epic Fantasy genre, right? I have waited over 20 years to finish my first book—that ends now.

My inspiration for all my books is to showcase the many prejudices, unconscious biases, stereotypes, internal conflict, mental health, moral values, and finally how the belief in the "means justify the ends" using the indulgence of such negative influences is played out. It almost never does but what if this time it did. I interpret religion and how it influences the ways of life split across diverse peoples and communities. There is a cling to spirituality with the basis of what the "faith of a mustard seed' will do. This would bring about what we today would consider 'supernatural' abilities; however, in my fantasy world they are natural. I also wanted to bring to the forefront prejudices from a cultural standpoint and the ignorance of that. Once the characters begin to develop, their physical features become more descriptive. You'll notice that I tend to be vague in appearance characteristics as I want the reader to make their own assumptions of which in the later books I will reveal more to their ethnicity. This is to confront how we first perceive characters and then once the 'ethnicity' is revealed, challenge the reader to feel the same about the character even if they are different than originally thought as well as engage them subconsciously on why they inferred the character the way they did originally.

I showcase the societal challenges throughout my books in allegories. There is a bit of political intrigue but there is also internal turmoil in which I use syllogisms to draw conclusions based on premises that appear to be related. The most fun I had writing was implementing plot twists, to explore grief, betrayal, and self-doubt. In addition to creating the story, I utilize a Naïve Narrator point of view in the Introduction and the Epilogue to give insight into the society as well as summarize the events and leave anticipation for the next book. Most of the book is spoken from the first-person point of view of the current protagonist as they change during time lapses and characters. Through all of these, I am very keen to explain and explore the character's perspective articulated in emotions and the consequences of holding them in—enter mental health and therapy. I believe this makes my story more relatable and personal. I want to create a personal investment in my books, not just because the story is great but because it translates to real life events, emotions, decisions, and consequences.

The best investment I made for my book is the developmental editing. Even with me rereading my book many times over and catching little typos here, word usage, and embellishments there, I hadn't realized I had left out much of the world itself. There were many questions and reordering of certain blocks that really brought my world to life along with the plot. Of course, I had my mother as my beta reader and she kept me honest, but she knows how I think, so it wasn't as objective. It was still good to get validation from both strategies.

I most definitely grew as a creative writer. I've worked in corporate America for nearly two decades and I couldn't push the boundary of creativity in my writing. I had to do so through public speaking. But my passion was writing, and I made a promise to myself that I would not lose sight of that. I have learned to start with an outline first because ideas just fly out while you are brainstorming, and it can end up in a big clump of 'what's going on here'. Also, I learned to set goals for my targets. I have a very busy family life and there will be weeks without me touching my manuscript because my mind is too active. I tried to force that, and I would end up frustrated that I sat for hours and only wrote a paragraph or page. Life is life and it's worth living.

Follow along with me on my blog www.movingwithmeaning.com as I post about my everyday life to see if you can find the inspirations from my posts and how I incorporated them in the story. Connect with me and create a community of growth.

Thank you for your support,
Krystal B. Clark

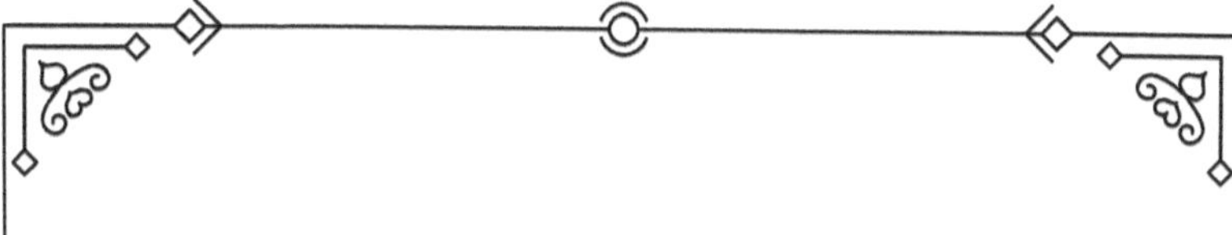

ABOUT THE AUTHOR

KRYSTAL B. CLARK is an author and life coach behind @movingwithmeaning82. She is an IT Professional, creative writer, public speaker, and life coach. Her work crosses multiple disciplines and boldly addresses the many contributors to mental health and how it manifests in the subconscious. As an IT Professional, Krystal has performed as a facilitator, practice leader, guest speaker, career coach, and much more in her technology companies. As a creative writer, she has a portfolio of literary works yet to be released but has decided to change career paths and share her life lessons in the form of creative expressions. Follow along with her on her blog, www.movingwithmeaing.com and engage with the community and peruse some of the other services she offers. In addition to her expertise in the IT Industry, she has continued to train and hone her skills through various recognized life coaches as she is most passionate at delivering excellent service and products.

* 9 7 9 8 9 8 8 9 1 0 2 0 6 *